SEARCHING

for

PILAR

PATRICIA HUNT HOLMES

RIVER GROVE
BOOKS

Published by River Grove Books
Austin, TX
www.rivergrovebooks.com

Distributed by River Grove Books

Design and composition by Greenleaf Book Group
Cover design by Greenleaf Book Group
Cover images: ©iStockphoto.com/Alexey_M; ©Shutterstock .com/Sandra_Violla; ©Shutterstock.com/Trong Nguyen; ©Shutterstock.com/aoforza

Publisher's Cataloging-in-Publication data is available.

Print ISBN: 978-1-63299-153-9

eBook ISBN: 978-1-63299-154-6

First Edition

For Julie

Chapter 1

PILAR

I t was not like Alejandro to be late from work. Pilar's husband always walked home at the same time, calling out for his "beautiful ladies." When she heard him, nineteen-year-old Pilar would scoop their baby, Concepción, out of her basket and run to meet him, ready with a kiss. But tonight she had been waiting over an hour past his usual arrival time, with still no sight of him.

Every ten minutes she stepped outside the fence that separated their small blue concrete house from the dust and noise of the street. She saw only a flock of chickens, pecking in the dirt for scraps to eat, and three mangy dogs following them. Two of the hens began vying for something in the dirt, wings flapping, feathers and dust flying. The dogs barked loudly at the squabbling chickens, and then the group hurried on down the street. She didn't see Alejandro.

It was late September 2007. As it had for centuries, life in San José ran like a slow-motion clock. Their church, Our Lady of Perpetual Help, presided over the central plaza, the tower bells ringing the Angelus at 6 a.m., 12 p.m., and 6 p.m. Men went about their business, women tended their kitchens and gardens, and children were born and grew up and had more children. The Holy Sacraments served as a cause for celebrating and mourning along life's way. Nothing much ever changed.

The town's men mostly worked in pottery manufacturing and ceramics, as they had since their city became a colony of Spain.

Generations often lived together or next door their entire lives, fathers handing down their trade to their sons. There were few secrets.

Pilar absently rocked her nine-month-old daughter while she waited. She fingered the delicate silver crucifix her parents had given her as a Confirmation gift. She wore it every day. The sun set in the west, filling the sky with a dusty pink.

Suddenly, she became aware of someone approaching her from behind, footsteps kicking up dust and heavy breathing. "Oh!" Pilar realized Alejandro was standing behind her, silent. She could smell that he had been drinking—probably more than one cerveza. His black hair, always neatly combed, was disheveled. His long black eyelashes almost covered his beautiful brown eyes. Perhaps most surprising, his broad shoulders, where she loved to lay her head at night after they finished sweetly making love, were stooped.

"What's wrong, mi vida?" she asked. She meant it when she said he was her "life." His pain troubled her, so she took his hand in hers. "You don't look well. Why are you so late? Did something happen?"

"Oh, Pilar," Alejandro mumbled.

"Tell me," Pilar urged him. "You scare me. What is it?"

"Señor Jimenez told us at the end of the day that he'd sold our factory. The new owners are moving our tools and designs to China." Alejandro raised his shoulders and dropped them. "I don't know how to do anything except paint pottery."

Pilar helped her husband into the house. The living room, small but tidy, was furnished with hand-me-downs from relatives. A handwoven rug covered most of the floor. Photographs of family members were grouped on a table around a ceramic statue of Mary holding baby Jesús.

Pilar was petite, and Alejandro, a head taller than her, was difficult for her to support. They stumbled into their bedroom. She put him to bed, removing only his shoes. She saw that, even in sleep, distress creased his handsome face. She closed the door quietly, tiptoeing back outside.

Concepción was making soft little cries. She was fair skinned like her mother and had the same full pink lips. Her hair and eyes were very dark brown. She wasn't walking yet but could sit up and amuse her parents enormously by trying to crawl. Pilar picked up the baby and held her close as she carried her inside. "Hush, little one. Everything is going to be all right. Your mami, papi, and guardian angel are watching over you. We will never let anything bad happen to you. I promise."

Pilar sang her the lullaby about Mother Mary, the one her mother had always sung to her, until she fell asleep. When Concepción closed her eyes and drifted off, Pilar sat down and tried to digest Alejandro's news. *He has lost his good job at the factory! What will that mean for our family?*

Nothing that had happened that day had prepared her for this unexpected turn of events. She thought back, trying to make sense of things.

The day had begun as usual with Pilar on her knees, saying her morning prayers. They always ended with "Thank you, God, for blessing me with so much—a loving family, sufficient food, good work, and bountiful blessings, amen." She'd finished with a quick sign of the cross.

"I smell something delicious," she sang to Alejandro. He stood beside their wooden kitchen table and chairs that he had decorated with turquoise and pink paint, eating the warm tortillas and beans Pilar's mother, Yolanda, had dropped off when she'd picked up Concepción for the day. Pilar reached up and ruffled his thick black hair.

"Here is your café con leche," Alejandro said as he set a mug down. He pulled her closer and kissed her slowly. "Good morning, my love."

"Mmmm, you taste as good as Mama's tortillas. Probably because you have eaten almost all of them!" Pilar replied.

Alejandro laughed. "I couldn't wait for you. They are best when warm. I am helping you keep that beautiful figure."

Pilar had to smile. Alejandro knew how to tease and compliment her at the same time. He could always make her laugh. She found it impossible to get mad at him.

"This is my favorite time of day, Alejandro—when it is just us."

"It has been just us since I saw you in line on the plaza in your First Holy Communion procession. You were seven, and your brother and I were nine. You were so pretty in your white dress and veil. I told Diego, 'Someday she will stand beside me wearing a wedding veil.'"

When they had eaten all the tortillas and beans, Pilar washed and dried the breakfast dishes. Then she made Alejandro's lunch for the day while he finished getting ready for work. Alejandro said, "Your mama asked me to remind you that your brother's club is playing in the league championship tomorrow. He will be disappointed if we are not there."

"Diego! Fútbol and girls are the only things in his head. I don't think Diego will ever settle down."

"Diego could do anything he set his mind to do. He's just not motivated. But he is your brother and my best friend. We must support him no matter what he does."

Alejandro gave her a quick kiss as he left for work.

Alone, Pilar washed herself. She liked to have everything clean and fresh. She pulled a simple white cotton dress over her head and slipped on a pair of sandals. She ran a comb through her long black hair and twisted it into a neat knot in the back with the silver barrette her parents had given her when Concepción was born. After fastening her crucifix, she took out her mirror and looked at herself. People had told her all of her life that she was beautiful. Her black hair was thick, as were her eyelashes, which framed her dark brown eyes. She had a light complexion, and her facial features were delicate. Her breasts were ample but pert and her waist small. All of the boys in school had tried to get her attention, but her heart had always belonged to Alejandro.

Pilar was secretary to Alberto Mendoza Gomez, the portly patriarch of the family who owned the Mendoza Pottery Factory. It was not large, and she was the only person in the office besides her boss. He liked to tell customers in front of her, "Pilar was born with a beautiful head for numbers," which always made him laugh and her blush. She managed the books and accounts and orders from buyers.

At 2 p.m., Pilar had walked to the house where she had grown up to have dinner with her parents and Concepción as usual. Then she'd returned to work for an uneventful afternoon. Nothing unusual had happened to give her warning of the misfortune to come.

· · ·

The Jimenez Pottery Factory had been the largest employer in San José. When it closed, all of the workers sought other employment. Although young, Alejandro had been considered the best pottery decorator at the factory. As a result, Pilar and Alejandro did not think he would be unemployed for long. He looked for work at the other pottery companies in San José. But everywhere he went, the owners told him the same thing: "I regret I have nothing for you. Cheap foreign competition is killing our business. I can barely keep my longtime employees busy. You are young; you should look for another line of work."

"But all I know how to do is paint," Alejandro would reply.

Then one day, Alejandro noticed a belt that Pilar was wearing. It was leather, with red roses embroidered on it. It gave him the idea that he could use his skills to decorate other leather goods. The next village, Santa Cruz, was known for its fine handcrafted leatherwork. Alejandro drew up some designs on paper that could be reproduced on saddles, boots, handbags, and other accessories. Pilar encouraged his idea, suggesting things that could be decorated with flowers or birds, which women might especially like. A cousin had a friend who owned one of the better leatherwork factories in the town and provided Alejandro with an introduction to the owner.

"Your work is beautiful, Alejandro," the proprietor told him. "In another time, I would have hired you immediately. But today buyers don't care about authenticity or beauty. They only want to buy the cheapest product, and they don't care if a Mexican serape is made in Mexico or India. It is a terrible time right now."

After several months, as rejection followed rejection, Pilar watched her husband gradually lose hope that he would find work and be able to support his family. Other craftsmen were digging ditches or doing nothing at all. Now, instead of their house being full of laughter, it was silent—except for when Alejandro lost his temper. Pilar was afraid to say anything to him that might begin an argument. She tried to keep Concepción from crying, because it irritated her father. He had started sleeping on the couch. She knew he was embarrassed and ashamed of his idleness, so she didn't complain when she picked up empty cerveza cans or tequila bottles each morning.

One night when Pilar was exhausted, however, Alejandro complained about having rice again for dinner. She snapped, "I am out working every day to put food on the table, and you are doing nothing!" Then she slammed the door and slowly walked to her mother's house. On the way, her mind kept telling her that she was justified in her frustration and anger. But her heart told her that she loved Alejandro and she needed to be more patient with him. She realized that forces beyond his control had dealt his pride a cruel blow. She decided it would be up to her to find a way out of their predicament.

When Pilar entered her parents' house through the kitchen door, Yolanda saw the state she was in and wrapped her arms around her. She told Pilar to go ahead and cry it out. Yolanda and her daughter had always been close. Pilar told her everything, and now she buried her head in her mother's breast and let the tears fall until there were no more.

Pilar resembled her mother physically, except that Yolanda was a great cook and loved to eat what she prepared. At fifty years old, she was stout, and her black hair was streaked with gray. Still, people would describe her as a handsome woman. She was good-natured and fun loving, but devoutly religious. She and José, Pilar's father, had been doting, if strict, parents to their two sons and Pilar, who came between the boys in age. José owned a store that had belonged to his father. He sold hardware and other supplies to small businesses and farmers. Their family was not wealthy but was relatively well-off compared to families where the men worked as craftsmen or laborers.

"I did not mean to say such an awful thing, Mama. I need to be more patient. He is not himself," Pilar said. "But I feel helpless!"

Yolanda took Pilar's hands in hers. "Yes, it is hard on a man when he can't put food on the table for his family. Alejandro is a proud man. He is talented and has always worked very hard. Until now, that hard work has been appreciated. But thank God you have a job, Pilar. I pray to the Virgin every day to intercede on behalf of you and Alejandro. You are a strong woman, and he is a good man. You will find a way."

Pilar sat down at the table and began to nibble on a tortilla. "Work is slow at my factory too, Mama. I am afraid I may not have a job for long. I see how much money is coming in and going out. Señor Mendoza won't admit it, but we are operating at a loss. I don't know how long that can continue. It is harder for a woman to find work than a man."

Yolanda poured her a cup of café con leche. Then she sat down opposite Pilar. "I can't believe how things are changing since people have stopped buying authentic Mexican pottery," Yolanda said. "The Suarez family moved to Mexico City to live with relatives while Luís looks for a job. Lupe and Anna Jimenez moved in with family in Monterrey."

"Do we have family anywhere else?" Pilar asked.

"No. I think Victor Chavez, one of Alejandro's uncles, lives in the United States, but no one knows where. He left home a long time ago when he was just a boy. He may be dead."

"I just want my family to be safe and happy again." Pilar sighed.

CHAPTER 2

THE STRANGER

The Mendoza Pottery Factory sat one block off San José's main square. Stacks of handmade plates, bowls, trays, and candleholders, as well as the business offices, took up the first floor. The craftsmen worked on the second floor. In November, two months after Alejandro lost his job, an unfamiliar man entered the office and approached Pilar.

"Good morning, señorita," he said to Pilar with a deferential nod of his head.

"Señora," Pilar corrected him, using the proper term for a married woman.

"Pardon me." He smiled. "You look very young. My name is Enrique Torres Hernandez. I represent a group of department stores in Mexico City. I would like to look at your pottery and perhaps make an order." He handed her his business card.

The man was attractive, clean-shaven, and tall, probably in his late thirties or early forties. He wore a white shirt and an expensive-looking dark blue sport coat. His skin was tanned, and his eyes and gelled hair were brownish black. Pilar detected a faint odor of cologne.

"Our stores are experiencing an increase in the number of tourists who wish to buy authentic Mexican kitchenware. I apologize for not making an appointment, but I was in the area and someone told me about the fine work you produce here."

Pilar was surprised to hear the man say there was a demand for the pottery produced in San José. It went against everything she had recently been hearing. Nevertheless, it was what she wanted to hear, so she was inclined to take the stranger at his word. After all, he was from Mexico City. Perhaps this meant the work would come back to San José and Alejandro would secure a job.

"Por favor, señor, if you would follow me, I will show you the workshop and our inventory," Pilar said to the man. "You can leave your briefcase here if you like."

It was Pilar's duty to show the product to buyers. Señor Mendoza knew that Pilar's beauty and friendly manner made for good marketing. Besides, he was old, overweight, and plagued with gout. He only left his comfortable upholstered chair in his office when it was absolutely necessary.

The stranger appeared genuinely interested as Pilar showed him the work being done by the craftsmen. He picked up and examined some of the pieces in progress. He asked questions of the craftsmen. At the end of the tour, she took him to Señor Mendoza's office.

"I am impressed, señor, and I will report favorably back to my managers," the man said. "You can probably expect a substantial order soon."

"This man could be an angel sent from God," Señor Mendoza whispered to Pilar.

Passing through Pilar's office, the man stopped. "You are obviously a talented young businesswoman," he said. "You should consider moving to Mexico City, where the companies value someone with your skills. You could make a lot more money."

Pilar was surprised that a man she had just met would speak to her so familiarly about such a personal matter. It made her feel a little uneasy. She didn't know how to respond, so she looked down and didn't reply.

The stranger put his briefcase on a chair, opened it, and took out a folded newspaper. "I have finished reading this. If you are ever interested, this paper is a good source to find out what jobs are available in the capital. My wife's cousin is looking for a job, and I noticed a good secretarial position. I was going to give this to her for her cousin, but you take it." Removing a silver pen from his jacket pocket, he casually circled a small ad, gave Pilar the paper, and started to walk to the door. Then he stopped and turned toward her.

"Oh, but please pardon me, señora, I forgot you are a married woman. I meant no impropriety, and of course you would not be interested. I will look forward to seeing you here again on my next visit." The man smiled.

Pilar examined his face. He seemed sincere. He had made an innocent mistake but corrected it. "Buenas tardes," Pilar said, bidding him goodbye.

"Hasta luego," the man replied, implying he would see her again.

For a second, Pilar thought it was odd he seemed so sure they'd meet again. But a new customer was certainly a good thing, and this probably meant he intended to become a customer. Absently, she placed the newspaper on top of her bookshelf.

• • •

Two weeks passed. Concepción needed a pair of shoes—her first—but there was no money to buy them. Pilar was a proud young woman and hated to ask her parents for money, but she didn't know what else to do. On the day she was about to ask, she was surprised to find Concepción in her mother's arms at the end of the workday, wearing new baby shoes.

"These shoes were so pretty, Pilar, I just had to buy them for our little princess. I hope you don't mind," Yolanda said.

Pilar and Alejandro ate beans and rice for every meal, except when they couldn't afford beans. Every evening Pilar watched Alejandro, unshaven, slumping on the couch in front of the television, numbly watching a fútbol game, a cerveza in hand. Before the factory closed, he'd been a hard worker who only drank at parties. Now, she hardly recognized her husband. His eyes were dull; the energy and creativity she so loved about him had disappeared.

Two weeks after the stranger visited the Mendoza Pottery Factory, Pilar arrived early for work. She picked up the newspaper she had set aside and read the ad the man had checked.

EXECUTIVE SECRETARIAL POSITION—Established company seeks executive secretary. Excellent salary, paid vacation, and other benefits. Call Señora Diaz at *xxxx* to schedule an interview.

Señor Mendoza said the man who gave me the paper could have been an angel sent by God. What if he was? Pilar asked herself. *Maybe this is God showing me the way. If the salary is enough, it could hold us over until Alejandro finds a job. Surely, there are many jobs in the city.* Pilar's mind raced. *Maybe Alejandro will snap out of the sad state he is in! I will light a candle at church and pray on applying for the Mexico City job.*

The idea of leaving San José, working for strangers, and living in a big city terrified Pilar. But she was more terrified about her family's future in San José and was desperate for a solution.

I know Alejandro will not want his wife becoming the breadwinner— although I already am. Maybe I should not tell him, she concluded. *After all, it is just an interview. If I do not get the job, he will never need to know.*

The next day she arrived early at the office. Her hands shook as she took the newspaper off the bookshelf and folded the page with the ad on it.

Since I was a child, I have always told Alejandro everything, even the silliest little things I was doing. Ay Diós, do not strike me dead for my pride in thinking I have the answer, she thought, twisting her crucifix.

She dialed the ad's telephone number. After one ring, a woman answered.

"Hola, Corazón Company, Alma Diaz speaking," she said.

Taking a deep breath, Pilar answered: "Hello, I am calling about the executive secretary position."

"Sí," the woman answered. "Can you tell me about yourself?"

"Well, my name is Pilar Carmen Chavez Gonzales. I am nineteen years old, and I have worked as the secretary to Señor Mendoza, the owner of the Mendoza Pottery Factory, for two years. I graduated from secondary school and studied business skills . . ."

When Pilar finished, she waited for the woman to say she was not qualified. Instead, she heard, "What is your availability? We need to fill the position quickly. The woman who had the job for ten years became ill and had to retire."

"Well," Pilar hesitated, "what exactly is the excellent salary?" Hearing the number, Pilar sucked in her breath. It was three times what she currently earned.

Pilar tried to take notes in her unintelligible style of shorthand on a piece of paper.

"Could you come in this week or next week for an interview? We are flexible on time," Alma added. "Why don't you give me a call back soon as to when we can expect you?"

"Muchas gracias, señora," Pilar said.

Pilar sank in her chair. *Should I go to Mexico City?*

CHAPTER 3

MEXICO CITY

Pilar had never been to Mexico City. She had heard Diego say it was at least a two-hour drive without traffic. *Even if I decide to go to Mexico City, how am I going to get there?* she thought, and then it hit her: *Diego!*

Her older brother drove into Mexico City every week to pick up supplies for their papa's store. Pilar knew that as soon as Diego finished, he drove to the Cruz Azul stadium, one of the places where the professional fútbol teams played.

Pilar set out to talk to Diego. She knew where to find him. When not at work in their father's store, her brother was either at practice in León, where he played for a feeder fútbol club, or hanging around the local fútbol pitch, where he was the center of attraction. He was taller and had longer legs than any of the other players and was extraordinarily fast. By the time he was fourteen, everyone who followed fútbol had known Diego was special. They thought he was the best player to ever come out of San José. It was general knowledge he was destined to be a star someday, maybe even play for the Mexico national team. At eighteen, he'd started playing in the semi-pro league, where coaches and agents had thought he would stay briefly before moving up to a major pro team.

Because everything had come easy for him, however, Diego hadn't wanted to work hard to advance to the next level of his game. His career had stalled. At twenty-one, he should have been playing in Mexico City, but he was still in León. His coaches were beginning to wonder if he had the necessary drive to play for a big-city professional team after all.

A local celebrity in San José and even León, Diego was somewhat arrogant about his natural abilities. All the young men wanted to be him and took every opportunity to play with him or drink with him in the local bars. All the young women wanted to be with him. They came to his games and made it plain they were available to him.

When Diego saw Pilar, he flashed the dazzling smile she loved.

"Diego, can I talk with you?"

"Sure, Pilar." Diego put his arm around her shoulders and led her to sit on the bottom step of the bleachers.

"Diego, do you go alone on Wednesdays to Mexico City?"

"Sure. Do you need me to pick up something for you?"

Pilar hesitated. She knew lying was a sin, and it was a struggle to tell the lie she had practiced, even though she told herself it was for a good purpose. "I was thinking about going with you next week. It will be Alejandro's birthday soon, and I want to buy him a new shirt or something as a surprise. It might cheer him up." Pilar realized she was fidgeting with her hands. She put them behind her back. She didn't want Diego to see how nervous she was.

"Sure," replied Diego, silently calculating how much less time that would leave him to hang out at the Cruz Azul Stadium.

"This is a secret. You won't tell anyone, right?"

"Right." Diego grinned, amused at his little sister's earnestness. "This is our secret mission. You know I love adventures."

Now that it was possible for her to get to Mexico City, Pilar concluded that she was meant to go. The next day, Pilar called Alma Diaz back. "I could come in for an interview midday next Wednesday. How long will the interview last?"

Alma seemed delighted to hear from her. "Let's make it 1:00 p.m.," she said. "That will give you plenty of time to get here. The interview is approximately one hour. Is your husband bringing you?" Alma asked.

At first, Pilar thought this question was odd. But then she realized how far she was traveling. She didn't want to tell a potential future employer she was doing something so important behind her husband's back.

"No," Pilar replied. "My brother has errands in Mexico City, and I am getting a ride with him. He will pick me up after he finishes."

"Perfect," said Alma. "Our building is in the Colonia Tabacalera, near the Monumento a la Revolución. Go one block west of the monument, turn left, and it is the second building on the right. Suite 435."

Pilar tried to jot down the address but was so nervous she wrote down only the suite number.

• • •

Making excuses at work and with her husband turned out to be easier than Pilar expected, although she realized she was committing the sin of lying again and felt guilty. Alejandro seemed preoccupied when she told him her cousin Elena was ill and she was going to visit her next Wednesday.

"I have an idea, Pilar," he said. "I could create and sell paintings of local life to tourists in San Miguel or Guanajuato. I can borrow money to buy canvases and paint."

Though he was excited and it was the first initiative he'd shown in months, he was still rooted to his place on the couch, empty tequila bottle nearby. *At least he has thought of something else he could do to make money*, Pilar thought hopefully. *My interview is next week. I will see if he acts on this idea, and maybe I won't have to go to Mexico City.*

But Alejandro had not taken any action to follow up on his idea as of the following Tuesday. So, on Wednesday morning, Pilar dressed in her best white blouse, black skirt, and a white jacket. She put on a small pair of silver earrings to match her crucifix and wore her Sunday black shoes. She fastened her hair with her silver barrette.

She held Concepción and kissed her repeatedly, telling her she would be back soon. The baby fussed, causing Pilar to have second thoughts. It was painful. Nevertheless, she told herself she was doing this for Concepción's welfare.

Not telling her mother what she planned to do was difficult. She had always told her everything. But she was afraid Yolanda would talk her out of what she planned, and she didn't want to embarrass Alejandro any more than she already had done by admitting he couldn't take care of his family.

• • •

Pilar was waiting for Diego when he pulled up on the dirt road behind the bleachers.

"Very nice, Pilar," he said admiringly when he saw her.

Pilar blushed and smiled, but the trip terrified her. She had never been more than fifty miles outside San José. She'd never been to a big city or gone anywhere alone.

"Listen to this song, Pilar," Diego said as the truck raced along the road. He banged his fist on the steering wheel during a particularly soaring lyric in a Marc Anthony song.

"Oh, Diego," Pilar said. "You are so adorable. But can you ever be serious?"

By ten thirty, they were traveling through the sprawling suburbs of Mexico City. Pilar felt awed by the vastness of the urban landscape. Pastel-painted houses on the outskirts of the city covered the hillsides. Many appeared unfinished, with metal bars sticking out of the concrete walls. Goats and dogs wandered along the side of the road.

As Diego drove farther into the center of the city, Pilar saw churches, schools, apartment buildings, and stores everywhere, seemingly one on top of another. Here and there she spotted Christmas decorations, but she did not feel in the mood for any kind of celebration. She choked on the dense industrial smog, an unpleasant change from the clean, dry, fragrant air in the country.

"How many people live in this city?" Pilar asked Diego. "It goes on forever! Do you ever get lost? It is overwhelming!"

"Almost twenty million. I had the same feeling when I came here the first time with Papa," Diego said. "I felt confused and scared. But I know my way around now."

Diego kept the windows of the truck open, which made the roar of the traffic deafening. Throngs of people filled the sidewalks. Pilar had never imagined there were so many people in the whole world. Pedestrians dodged cars as people tried to cross the congested streets. Taco stands competed with automobiles for parking spaces.

"I need to go to the Colonia Tabacalera, near the Monumento a la Revolución," she told Diego.

"I know where it is. It's on the western edge of downtown."

Diego parked opposite the monument. "Um, do you need me to go with you, Pilar?" he offered, glancing at his watch.

Pilar could see he was worried about having time to watch the professionals. She said, "I have directions. You can drop me off and pick me up here. At 4:00 p.m.?"

"Are you sure you don't mind?" Diego asked, his face brightening.

"I don't mind," Pilar said, although she was terrified of walking on the streets of Mexico City alone, and she hesitated before she got out of the truck.

"Bueno!" he said. "Nos vamos esta tarde. We will meet again this afternoon!"

Pilar stopped at a taco stand with a faded yellow umbrella for a quick bite to eat. The taco seller tried to start a conversation, but she just smiled. She kept checking her watch and fumbled for change to pay him.

Pilar surveyed the neighborhood. It was filled with centuries-old, once-elegant homes. Office and apartment buildings had replaced some of the houses, but everything looked run down. Salsa music blared from a cantina down the block where two women in very short skirts and high boots stood outside talking to a group of men. The people sitting at the other tables did not look like her mental picture of business people. A dark young man dressed in jeans, sunglasses, and a black leather jacket with tattoos on his neck and hands stared at her. It made her uneasy. She avoided making eye contact. She wished she had asked Diego to stay with her, but she had no way to contact him. She didn't want to stay where she was with the dark man staring at her.

Pilar saw a shabbily dressed woman about her own age standing nearby, staring at the people eating at the tables. She looked hungry. A thin little boy was crying, holding tightly to her hand. The pair made her remember why she had taken the desperate steps she was taking. She wished she had some pesos to give the woman, but her purse was empty after buying lunch.

At 12:55, Pilar found the building. It was a nondescript old concrete office building with several coats of red and black graffiti on the outside of the ground-level floor. She had never ridden in an elevator, so she took the stairway, although it had an unpleasant smell. Telling herself to be strong, she finger-combed her hair, said a quick Hail Mary, and straightened her crucifix. She entered suite 435.

The only thing in the room was a row of five metal folding chairs lined up against the wall. Pilar hesitated, then took a seat and waited for something to happen.

Shortly the door to the hallway opened again, and a petite, pretty young girl with curly brown hair and hazel eyes came into the room. The girl smiled nervously as she sat down. Pilar guessed she was probably thirteen years old. *I wonder why her mother is not with her?*

The door to the inner office opened and a tall, attractive woman with a stylish black suit, high heels, and auburn hair pulled back into an upsweep stepped into the reception area. She was the most sophisticated woman Pilar had ever seen, straight out of a telenovela. She wore a thick silver chain around her neck. Big silver rings covered her fingers.

"Señora Chavez?" she asked.

"Sí, señora," Pilar spoke up, standing quickly.

"Won't you come into my office? I am Alma Diaz. It is good to meet you." She motioned for Pilar to sit in a large overstuffed chair on the other side of her desk while she looked Pilar up and down, an approving smile on her face.

Looking around, Pilar observed two gray upholstered chairs, a small wooden side table, a bookcase, and a desk. Paper shades covered the windows. Picture frames sat on Alma's desk, but they were turned the other way so Pilar could not see what she assumed was Alma's family. The bookcase held few books. A framed map of Mexico City provided the only color on the wall. A small vase with red roses sat on the desk; their sweet smell helped calm her nerves.

"Perfect," Alma said, smiling. "We are glad you came to see us. Can I get you something to drink? Café? Cocoa?"

"No, thank you. I just ate something."

Alma's brow wrinkled slightly. "Perhaps later," she said. "Let's get to know one another, shall we?" Alma moved to the chair next to Pilar's. "That is a lovely crucifix."

"Thank you," Pilar replied.

"I can see you are a woman of faith. Do you have siblings?"

"Oh, sí, two brothers, Diego and Carlos. My older brother, Diego, drove me here today, and I am meeting him at the monument at four."

"How perfect," Alma said. "You have a big brother to watch out for you."

Pilar decided that she liked Alma. She felt comfortable with her.

Just then, a door to a side room opened and a large man in a tight-fitting suit came into the room. He did not smile at her.

"This is Señor Jesús Cruz Ayala," Alma explained. "He is the owner

of the company that is hiring an executive secretary. He will sit in on
the interview. Now tell us about what you have been doing at your cur-
rent place of employment."

Pilar recited the litany of her many responsibilities at the Mendoza
factory. As she spoke about that with which she was familiar, she relaxed.

Señor Cruz stood up. "A pleasure, Señora Chavez. I hope to see you
again soon," he said.

After he left, Alma smiled and said, "Well, that went very well. You
will be hearing from us before you know it."

Pilar was ecstatic. *God always provides the way*, she thought, getting up.

"Don't be in a hurry, Señora Chavez. You must have a little cup of
coffee with me to celebrate." Alma walked to the table and poured
two cups. The rings on Alma's fingers sparkled as she moved. They
were mesmerizing.

Pilar took a cup. "Thank you; it smells delicious."

"Perfect," Alma replied.

Alma sat back down behind her desk and leaned back, one long leg
crossed over the other, relaxed. When her skirt rose, Pilar noticed a
tattoo of some sort of animal on her upper thigh, which seemed out of
place on such an elegant woman.

"Now, tell me about yourself outside of work, dear. You have children?"

"Sí, señora, a nine-month-old girl." Pilar sipped her drink, which
tasted like cocoa. "This is delicious," she said. "Concepción is crawl-
ing now. It is so amusing to watch her trying to drawl, I mean crawl,
across the broom—room. Concepción tries to hold on to the table
and stand, but she falls over, and then she um, she . . . she falls. That's
it. She falls down . . ."

Alma seemed far away suddenly as Pilar squinted to focus on her
and tried to gather her thoughts. Her ideas seemed scrambled.

"Are you all right, dear?" She heard Alma's voice as if it were coming
from very far away.

Pilar tried to tell her she wasn't feeling well, was dizzy, but the words wouldn't come out. Then everything went black as her body slumped back in the chair.

CHAPTER 4

DIEGO

At 4:10 p.m., Diego arrived at the place where he had left Pilar earlier. He scanned the intersection. Not seeing Pilar, he pulled out a fútbol magazine and flipped through the pages. When he glanced at his watch, he realized it was 4:25 p.m., and Pilar was still nowhere in sight. *Perhaps she cannot see me,* he thought. *I will get out of the truck and walk around for a few minutes and look for her.*

"It's time to move on," a traffic police officer said as he slapped the side of Diego's truck. Diego walked slowly back to the vehicle, started the motor, and pulled out into the traffic. For an hour, he circled the monument again and again until he was almost out of gas.

What if Pilar is lost? The streets are confusing. Where did she say she was going? I do not think she told me. I was in such a hurry to get to the stadium that I did not notice which direction she walked. I should have stayed with her. I am so stupid!

Diego knew he would not be home before dark. He was less worried about his mother's scolding than he was about his sister. He could not go home without her. He pulled into a gas station and filled the truck's tank. He noticed a neighborhood police station in the next block. It was a typical nondescript concrete bunker of a building. Everyone had always told him that going to the police voluntarily could only lead to trouble, but he had to get help, and he didn't know anyone in the city.

Entering the station, Diego saw four police officers standing around the room smoking cigarettes. The air in the room was thick and harsh with smoke. There was a small television propped on one of the desks, and they were all watching a fútbol game. The announcer spoke fast in a loud voice. It took a few minutes to get their attention. He yelled, "Pardon, señores!"

"What do you want?" a short, burly officer with a cigarette hanging out of his mouth finally asked Diego while looking over his shoulder at the television. He sounded irritated at being interrupted. The other men cheered a goal. "I am Lieutenant Juan Carlos Ruiz Perez, in charge of this station," he said. Annoyed at having to look up at Diego, he straightened himself to his full height, though he still had to look up.

"Señor," Diego said, loud enough to be heard over the noise. "I need help. I drove my sister into the city today. She wanted to shop for a surprise for her husband while I did some business for my father and went by the Estadio Azul for a few minutes. She was supposed to meet me at four at the Monumento a la Revolución. But she never came. I need to find her and take her home."

"Hmmm, how old is your sister?"

"She is nineteen. She has a husband and baby in San José, and she wanted to be home before dark. They don't know she was coming into Mexico City."

"Why not?" the lieutenant asked.

"She said it was a secret."

"From whom?" The lieutenant's curiosity was piqued.

"From everyone."

The lieutenant turned his head to cough a deep cigarette cough. Then he said, "Did she tell you where she was going to shop?"

"No, señor."

"It seems strange she did not give you an address or ask you to stay with her. Mexico City is a dangerous place for young women alone."

"She said she didn't want to hold me up on my business." After hesitating, he added, "She knows I like to watch the professional fútbol clubs practice. She was being considerate."

"It doesn't seem like you were being considerate of your sister, leaving a young woman from a small town alone in this part of Mexico City," the lieutenant said sharply.

"I guess not, sir," Diego replied, realizing how thoughtless he had been.

"Do you see any clothing shops or markets in this neighborhood?" the lieutenant asked Diego, taking his cigarette out of his mouth and looking hard at him. He was not smiling. "If the surprise was for her husband, why did she ask you to keep it a secret from everyone else?"

Diego looked down and shuffled his feet. Nevertheless, he tried to answer in a strong voice, "I don't know, señor." In the context of the lieutenant's questions, he was starting to realize the oddness of Pilar's actions and that his own conduct had been careless at best.

"You don't know much, do you?" Lieutenant Ruiz stated as he walked into his small office and motioned for Diego to sit down in the chair across from his desk.

Sinking into the chair, Diego looked pleadingly at the officer. "Will you help me find her?"

"It's too early to consider her a missing person," Lieutenant Ruiz replied in his gruff voice, flicking the ashes and taking another drag on his cigarette. "That is, if she is lost. Perhaps this is just another case of a pretty young woman who got tired of living in the country and talked her brother, who doesn't have a brain in his head, into helping her make a getaway to the city. She is probably meeting her lover here, and you will never see her again. On the other hand, she may get homesick or the lover may beat her, and she will run back to her husband in a few days. We see situations like this every day."

"Pilar wouldn't do that, señor," Diego protested.

"Is her husband wealthy? A gang could be holding her for ransom."

"No, he does not have any money. He lost his job recently."

"Women have left their husbands for less," the lieutenant sneered.

Lieutenant Ruiz seemed to be mulling over something, but then he abruptly said, "In any case, it's late. Before you get into trouble yourself, go home and wait at least twenty-four hours. If she shows up, all is well. If she does not, come back, and I will fill out the paperwork for a missing person. Eventually the paperwork will get to headquarters, and maybe a search will begin. Now I need to get back to the game."

"But . . . ," Diego whimpered.

The lieutenant coughed again, and this time the cough was even deeper. "Be careful driving home. The roads are unsafe after dark. Don't pick up anyone. You hear me, boy?"

Diego felt like a fool. He could hardly make his legs walk out of the police station. He knew that Pilar had not run away with another man.

What else could have happened? She probably got lost. Surely some good person will help her, give her shelter, and bring her home. The police are not going to look for her.

It was dark when Diego left the police station. No one was on the street where he'd parked his father's truck except for a few skinny stray dogs searching for food and two men dressed in jeans and leather jackets, leaning against a streetlight, smoking and casually perusing the streets. Something about them made him walk faster. With his long legs, Diego stepped quickly over the dogs and hurried to the driver's side of the truck. He was anxious to get home. Inside the truck, he grasped the steering wheel hard and banged his head against it.

Why am I such a fuckup? What am I going to tell Alejandro? What will Mama and Papa say? They will be so angry with me! Diego's body was shaking all over now.

The drive home seemed endless. Diego did not turn on the radio, worried that he might miss a sound that indicated banditos were following him as the lieutenant had warned. He kept going over the events of the day. He remembered that he had been late arriving at the meeting point. *What if something happened to her in that ten minutes while she was waiting for me? Whatever happened, it is my fault!*

When he reached San José and pulled into his street, it was past 1 a.m. Light enveloped his parents' house. All the lights were on in Pilar and Alejandro's house, too. In fact, the lights were on in most of the houses on the block. Neighbors stood in groups, talking. The local police chief's car was outside the gate to his sister's house.

Diego stopped the truck at the end of the street. He considered turning it around and driving anywhere far away.

No, I need to face up to this, he told himself, spitting out the gum he had been absently chewing. *The important thing is to find Pilar. I deserve whatever punishment is coming to me.*

"There is Diego!" Señor Marco, the neighborhood busybody who lived next door to his parents, yelled. Hearing him, his parents ran outside.

"Diego, Diego!" José shouted, waving his arms and stepping in front of the truck. His face looked drawn but relieved.

His mother was not far behind. Her eyes were red and swollen.

Opening the door, making the sign of the cross—more out of unconscious habit than intent—and taking a deep breath, Diego stepped down from the truck. Before he could say anything, his mother grabbed him and threw her generous arms around him.

"Gracias, Diós, you are all right," she sobbed.

"Where have you been, Diego?" his father asked him, arms folded in front. "What excuse could justify you almost killing your mother with worry?"

Diego did not want his mother to let go. For the first time in nine hours, he felt safe.

"Oh, Diego," his mother sobbed, "Pilar is missing! She said she was going to visit cousin Elena, but she never came home tonight. Alejandro is practically out of his mind with worry. The police are looking everywhere for her. The baby is at our house. She will not stop crying."

Diego glanced at the front door of his home, where his brother stood in the doorway, holding Concepción, rocking her in his arms. They looked like limp, sad doll figurines. Guilt washed over him like a tidal wave. *Oh, Pilar, where are you?*

CHAPTER 5

SAN JOSÉ

Diego pulled away from his mother. He looked his father in the eyes.

"What?" José asked, seeing the pain etched on Diego's face.

"I know about Pilar, Papa."

"How could you? Haven't you been in Mexico City?"

"Sí. Pilar went with me. She asked if she could go with me today so she could buy a present for Alejandro's birthday. She wanted it to be a surprise and made me promise not to tell anyone."

"But where is Pilar now?" his mother asked.

Diego looked at the ground. "When we got to the city, I dropped her off by the Monumento a la Revolución in the Colonia Tabacalera as she asked. We were supposed to meet at the same place at four. When I arrived, she was not there. I waited and then kept circling again and again. But I never saw her, Papa."

Yolanda grabbed her husband's steadying arm.

"I went to the police and asked them to help me find her. But the lieutenant in charge said it was too early to consider Pilar a missing person. He told me to come back in twenty-four hours if she doesn't come home."

Señor Marco, hovering nearby, asked, "Did he say anything about what might have happened to her, Diego?"

Diego hesitated, but his father motioned for him to continue. In a low voice only his parents could hear, he whispered, "The lieutenant said she probably was meeting a lover in the city. That's why she didn't tell anyone where she was going."

"What?" Yolanda erupted. "Did you tell them Pilar is a virtuous woman with a loving husband and a child? She would never do such a thing! She doesn't even know any other men!"

"Yes, Mama, I told them. But he said they see such situations every day. I don't think they will search for her. She probably got lost. She doesn't know the city. But she is so smart. She may have gone to a church. Because we don't have a telephone in our house, the priest couldn't call us, but he will probably bring her home tomorrow."

"We had better tell Alejandro and Sergeant Montoya." José sighed. "They are looking for her north of here. She told Alejandro she was going to San Fernando to see Elena. But Elena was home all day, and she says Pilar has not been there."

"It is not like our daughter to be secretive." Yolanda sighed. "We talk every day. She has always told me everything."

"Come on, Diego," his father said, taking his arm. "You need to tell this to Alejandro and Sergeant Montoya. Alejandro is out of his mind with worry."

Alejandro didn't move for several minutes after Diego, finally breaking down in tears, finished the story about what had happened in Mexico City. Yolanda had never seen her confident son cry. She forgot for a moment how angry she was at him and pulled him to her.

"I am so sorry, Alejandro. I don't know what happened. We had a plan, but Pilar just didn't come back. I picked up Papa's order like I always do, and then I went to the Estadio Azul for a little while. Then I went back to where we'd agreed to meet," Diego said.

Diego consciously omitted the fact that he had been ten minutes late arriving at the meeting point, not that it would have made a difference. He was too ashamed to admit how careless he had been with his sister's safety.

"Why didn't you tell your father you were taking Pilar with you when you left the store?" Alejandro confronted him. "Why didn't you tell me? You should have known a naïve country girl should not be wandering around a big, dangerous city alone! I can't believe you went to watch fútbol and left your sister alone in the city! How could you be so irresponsible . . . so selfish, Diego?" He was shouting now.

"She told me she didn't need me to go with her when I offered. And she made me promise I would not tell anyone. She wanted to surprise you," Diego murmured, hanging his head.

"Did you go to the place she was shopping, Diego?" José asked.

"She didn't tell me exactly where she was going. She said it was close to the monument."

"Did you go to all the clothing shops and markets in the area?" José continued.

Remembering the lieutenant's words, he said, "The lieutenant I talked to said there aren't any in that neighborhood—only office buildings, apartments, convenience stores, and bars."

Sergeant Montoya, a short, rotund, balding older man, had been San José's police chief for thirty years and knew all of the parties well. He asked, "What district of the city was that, Diego?"

"It was the Colonia Tabacalera," Diego replied.

Sergeant Montoya grimaced. "That's a rough area."

Alejandro sank back on the couch and put his hands over his face. He shook his head as if to deny what he was hearing.

The room was deathly quiet. Yolanda was in shock. She hung on to José's arm as if that were the only thing steadying her. The neighbors gossiped outside. Finally, Sergeant Montoya, who had been running scenarios through his mind, cleared his throat. "I think we are all tired, and we can't do any more tonight. We will send a search party to Mexico City as soon as the sun comes up. None of us knows the capital well. It is enormous, and finding one woman will be extremely difficult. But we will do our best, Alejandro."

• • •

No one slept that night. José and Carlos tended to Concepción, who fussed, refusing to go to sleep. Diego and Yolanda sat at the kitchen table for a long time. "This table is where Pilar and I made tamales to celebrate the feast day of José's patron saint just last week." Yolanda sighed. "Where is my daughter now?"

Diego recounted the day's events over and over, trying to find a clue as to where Pilar could be. Fingering her rosary beads the whole time, Yolanda half listened to him. She was praying for her daughter's safe return and for help to forgive her son's irresponsibility.

At the first light of morning, Alejandro appeared at José and Yolanda's door, a grim look on his face.

"Yolanda, we are going to Mexico City. Sergeant Montoya thinks Diego should come with us to show us where he last saw Pilar."

Diego rose from where he had been sitting all night. "I want to help."

In Sergeant Montoya's car, Alejandro didn't look at his old friend and brother-in-law. He stared straight ahead the whole way, fists clenched. Diego guided them to the spot near the Monumento a la Revolución where Pilar had asked him to drop her off.

At Sergeant Montoya's suggestion, Alejandro and Diego had brought photographs of Pilar from her wedding day. The photos showed a beautiful, smiling young woman. Her long, silky black hair was crowned with flowers. She had a fair complexion and refined features, the most striking of which were her dark brown eyes and long black eyelashes. Her lips were full and naturally pink. She was glowing, as only a happy bride on her wedding day can glow. There was a soft blush of excitement on her cheeks. She stood beside a smiling Alejandro, her head at his chest, her hand holding his. A white lace dress accentuated her petite yet voluptuous body.

They walked the sidewalks and entered the lobbies of buildings. No one they approached remembered seeing the girl in the photograph, until they came to a taco stand with a yellow umbrella.

"I remember her," the vendor said. "I may be old, but I can still appreciate a pretty woman. She bought a taco and a jugo. She sat at that table and ate, but she kept checking her watch. After a few minutes, she left."

"What time was that?" Sergeant Montoya asked. "Did you see which way she went?"

"It was around quarter to one or so. She walked that way," he said, pointing west.

"If she was checking her watch, she could have had an appointment at one, close to here," the sergeant said. "Let's split up and see what is in that direction within a fifteen-minute walk. Search everything and meet me back here in three hours."

Despite what the lieutenant had told Diego about there being no shops in the area, Diego and Alejandro looked anyway for a store or market where Pilar might have shopped. Sergeant Montoya stepped into the bars in the area and looked around. Alejandro moved quickly from place to place, a look of desperation on his face and alcohol on his breath, which made some of the people he approached shy away from him. Diego took his time and stepped off the main street to look along the first block of the side streets perpendicular and on the block parallel to the street on which the taco stand stood. Without knowing it, he walked past the building where Pilar had interviewed with Alma the day before. He noticed the red and black graffiti on the side of its first floor. Otherwise it looked like many of the buildings on the street.

After the three hours passed, Diego, Sergeant Montoya, and Alejandro met back at the taco stand. "I'm afraid I have nothing to report," Sergeant Montoya said. "Did either of you find anyone who saw her yesterday?"

"No, señor," Diego said. "No one."

"No," said Alejandro. "But she couldn't have just vanished," he moaned. "This is not like Pilar. She must be here somewhere."

No one knew what to say, so they stood silent.

"Let's talk to the police again," Sergeant Montoya finally said. He watched Alejandro take a small bottle of tequila out of his jacket and take a drink. He frowned but didn't say anything. Alejandro had been sober when they'd left San José, but as the day progressed, he had been sneaking more and more drinks from that bottle.

Diego directed them to the police station he had visited the night before. It was a small, nondescript concrete building with only a small sign indicating its purpose. Sergeant Montoya straightened his hat, made sure his shirt was tucked into his belt, and shook as much of the city dust off his uniform as he could. Entering, he asked in an uncharacteristically officious voice to see the officer in charge.

A minute later, Lieutenant Ruiz came out of his office. "You are back, I see," he said to Diego. "Did your sister show up yet?"

"His sister is my wife!" Alejandro said in a loud, belligerent voice.

"May we speak with you in private, lieutenant?" Sergeant Montoya asked, gently moving Alejandro aside.

The lieutenant focused his gaze on Alejandro, who was younger and taller than him. "Come into my office, please," he said to the group in an official voice.

The lieutenant sat down on his chair behind a cluttered desk. He had elevated the legs of the chair so that he sat higher than his visitors. He motioned for his guests to take a seat on the mismatched wooden chairs across from him. Diego stood off to the side.

"Well, sergeant," Lieutenant Ruiz asked, "what is your assessment of this woman's disappearance? Where has your investigation led so far?"

"We have just begun," Sergeant Montoya explained. "When Señora Chavez did not return home last night, I sent my deputy to San Fernando to question the relative Señora Chavez said she was going to visit. The woman told us she had not expected a visit from Pilar yesterday and that Pilar had not been there."

"Has she ever made visits like this before? Maybe gone to visit a sick friend and not come home when she was supposed to?" the lieutenant asked, looking at Alejandro.

"No," Alejandro replied. "This is the first time."

The lieutenant coughed. "Continue, sergeant, please."

"Around midnight, when Diego returned from Mexico City, we learned that she had gone with her brother to Mexico City instead. We drove here early this morning in order to search for her in the area where Diego last saw her. A taco vendor remembered she'd bought a taco from him about 12:45 and then left, heading west. We spread out and searched the area for three hours. But no one else remembered seeing her, unfortunately." He handed the lieutenant one of the wedding photos of Pilar.

"She is very beautiful," said the lieutenant.

Diego looked at him and pleaded, "Now will you help us find her?"

"You said she had a job. Did you ask her employer if she told him where she was going?" the lieutenant asked. "Do you know if anything new or strange happened at work recently? Are you aware of her having a friendly relationship with any of the men at work?"

"No," said Alejandro, choosing to ignore the policeman's implication. "Pilar likes to work in an office. She is very intelligent and has a lot of energy. But she is an excellent wife and mother, too!"

"No disrespect meant," said the policeman with a blank face. "But could a beautiful, energetic young woman like her have become bored with life in the country and wanted to see more of the world? Every day dozens of women and girls come to the city looking for more adventure in their lives. Some come to meet someone. Unfortunately, some are too naïve, and bad people prey on them."

"What do you mean?" Alejandro asked. "What bad people?"

"I am afraid that this part of town is an activity center for kidnappings of women, girls, and even young men and boys. The drug cartels have expanded their activities into trafficking of people and human organs in order to make more money. Mostly they supply their products to the United States, where they are already well established. They entice women to Mexico City with promises of love, adventure, jobs, or other things. Once here, the women disappear. In most cases, they are never seen again."

Alejandro let out a low moan.

"But that is just one possibility," the policeman continued. "It is very common for women to come to the city to have a secret rendezvous and then go home again when the excitement wears off or the man leaves her. Sometimes this happens when there are problems at home," the lieutenant added, staring at Alejandro.

Alejandro's face had turned white and his arms hung limply at his sides.

"Or," the lieutenant said, "on a more optimistic note, she might have been lost temporarily and has found her way home." His voice softened. "She may be there waiting for you. You never know. Fill out this report, and I will file it with the federal authorities, just in case."

"Thank you for your time, lieutenant," Sergeant Montoya said, rising and taking Alejandro's arm. "Diego, wait for me outside with Alejandro."

"Lieutenant," Sergeant Montoya said, after Alejandro and Diego left the room, "I have known Pilar Chavez for all of her life. She is a good, smart, pious young woman. I would be surprised if she was involved in anything like an affair with another man. I have also known Alejandro since he was a baby. He is a good man who has fallen on hard times because the pottery industry has left San José, and many of the men like him who were talented, hardworking craftsmen are out of work with no prospects. Idleness breeds despair and drinking. The man you see before you is not what he seems. I will leave you with the picture of Pilar in case you learn anything . . . anything at all. Here is my telephone number."

Standing up, Lieutenant Ruiz coughed his tobacco cough again. "I understand, sergeant. But remember to check with her boss and ask if he knows or has seen anything suspicious. Women often share their thoughts and secrets with their coworkers more than their families."

The search party slowly walked back to where they had parked. "Those bastards are not going to do anything to help us find Pilar!" Alejandro punched the side of the police car.

"Since we are here, shouldn't we ask at the churches in the neighborhood if they have seen Pilar?" Diego asked.

Alejandro agreed. "Pilar has always been very religious. It makes sense she would go to a church for help."

Sergeant Montoya said, "I will find a pay phone and call my deputy to ask if Pilar has come home."

Diego and Alejandro set out together to look for Pilar at the churches and rectories in the neighborhood. There were relatively few. Within hours they had finished without any luck.

At that point, Sergeant Montoya concluded, "We might as well go home. Perhaps she will be there by the time we get there."

Diego grabbed Alejandro's shoulders. He looked more serious than Alejandro had ever seen him. "I will find her, Alejandro. I swear to you. No matter how long it takes; I won't fail Pilar again."

• • •

It was 9 p.m. when the search party reached San José. Nevertheless, Alejandro insisted they talk to Pilar's boss right away. Sergeant Montoya drove to Señor Mendoza's home.

"I apologize for interrupting your evening, Señor Mendoza," Sergeant Montoya said when he came to the door. "But we are searching for Pilar. She didn't come home last night."

"I was surprised when she didn't come to work today," Señor Mendoza said. "It's not like her. But I thought she must have found her cousin to be worse than expected and had to stay a little longer. I didn't mind. She is such a hard worker, and the factory is not very busy now."

"Where did Pilar tell you she was going, señor?" Sergeant Montoya asked.

"She told me she had a cousin in San Fernando who was ill and she was going to take the bus and visit her," he answered.

"Pilar didn't go to San Fernando. It seems she rode into Mexico City with Diego on his regular supply run. But she didn't meet him at the agreed time to come home," Sergeant Montoya said.

"Oh, Diego! It's not surprising that lazy boy would be involved," Señor Mendoza sighed. He had not seen Diego standing behind the others. Diego ducked his head and stuck his hands deep into the pockets of his jeans.

Sergeant Montoya asked quickly, "Has anything out of the ordinary occurred at the factory recently? Did Pilar say anything to you about being unhappy or discontent?"

Alejandro bit his lip and frowned.

"Not to me, although I can't help but notice she is worried about Alejandro not having work now and the financial strain on her family. I would like to pay her more, but we are barely making a profit these days."

"Did anyone new visit the factory recently?"

"Now that you mention it, yes. There was a buyer from a group of Mexico City department stores who came by a couple of weeks ago. Good-looking, nicely dressed man. I had never seen him before. Pilar showed him around the factory. He said the stores he represents would be sending us a big order soon. We need a big order. I have been waiting for it to come in."

"But it hasn't?"

"Not yet."

"Do you have his information, señor?"

"His card is at my office."

"Please, señor," Alejandro interrupted. "I am afraid to wait until morning. Could you take us there now? Maybe she said something to him or he knows something."

"I will do anything I can to help," Señor Mendoza said. "You know Pilar is like a daughter to me."

The search party followed Señor Mendoza to the factory. He led them to his office and found the stranger's card on his desk. "Here it is," he said.

Diego spoke up, eager to be helpful. "We could look up his company on the Internet."

"Do you have a computer here, señor?" Sergeant Montoya asked.

"No, unfortunately. We are a small company, and we do things the old-fashioned way, I am afraid. Pilar is a genius with numbers, and she does all the bookkeeping by hand. If we need more, she goes to the Internet café on the central plaza."

"They stay open late," Diego said. "It is mostly young people who use the Internet, and they go there after work. The connection is better than in any of the computers in houses or businesses in town."

Sergeant Montoya thought for a minute and then said, "Okay, Diego, let's give it a try."

"I will go with you," Señor Mendoza said.

When the search party and Señor Mendoza arrived at the Internet café, Diego set to work on one of the two new computers. A search bar appeared. He typed in the name of the company on the business card that Señor Mendoza had given them.

"NO RESULTS" appeared on the screen. Diego sat back.

"Maybe I typed it in wrong," Diego mumbled, attacking the keys more slowly this time.

"NO RESULTS."

Alejandro sighed. "Try his name."

Diego typed the name Enrique Pablo Torres Hernandez. "NO

RESULTS." He tried various shortened versions of the name, but the outcome was always the same.

Señor Mendoza asked, "How can he not exist? The man was here."

"What else do you remember about him?" Sergeant Montoya asked.

"He was very pleasant and polite. I had to go home for a nap, but he stayed and talked some more to Pilar. Not long, I don't think," he added.

"Can we search Pilar's desk?" Sergeant Montoya asked.

"Sí, sí, of course. Search the whole factory if it will help!"

"The desk will do," the sergeant said. The group walked back to the factory, and Señor Mendoza took them to Pilar's little office. Sergeant Montoya began by opening drawers and looking for anything out of the ordinary. "What's this?" he asked, pulling out the notepad where Pilar had jotted down some of the information Alma had given her.

Bending over to examine it, Señor Mendoza scratched his head. "I don't know. It is not an order; those are all on forms. It is a list of some sort, but the writing is faint and looks like Pilar's shorthand, which I have never been able to read. I don't think it is factory business."

"May I take it?" the sergeant asked.

"Of course, of course," Señor Mendoza answered. "I will do anything I can to help. I will ask my wife to say a rosary for her safe return home."

After taking Señor Mendoza back to his home and thanking him, the search party drove to the police station. They wanted to examine the notepad more closely. It was the only tangible potential clue they had uncovered.

The unknown identity of the stranger was troubling. Diego remembered the lieutenant's theory that Pilar had gone to the city to have a romantic meeting with a man; an impossible scenario if one knew Pilar. *Or was it?*

A few of the words on the notepad were legible. "Mexico City" was clear. A word that could be "corazón" was legible. There were some numbers. But they seemed random. The word "Wednesday," which was the day Pilar and Diego had gone to the city, could also be deciphered.

"I think she was going to some appointment or prearranged meeting in Mexico City on Wednesday," concluded the policeman. "But what all these numbers are is anyone's guess."

The sergeant looked at Alejandro. He looked pale, his eyes were glassy, and he was weaving. "I will take you home, Alejandro. You are exhausted, and you will need your strength to help us find Pilar."

"I don't know what is worse," Alejandro said, looking at the floor. "Was Pilar meeting another man? Was she kidnapped and taken away? Was she killed? If she were lost, she would have found a way to contact us by now."

His mind was racing. *Is this my fault? I know I have been difficult to live with since the factory closed. Did I drive her away?* Alejandro put his hands to his face and wept. "Oh, Pilar, where are you?"

CHAPTER 6

EDUARDO

Pilar opened her eyes and tried to focus. She was no longer in the big chair in Alma's office. Her head was pounding. *I am lying on the floor!* she realized. She tried to raise her arm to get up but could not.

My hands are tied behind my back! Struggling, she discovered her ankles were also tied together. *Santa Teresa, where am I?* She could hear people talking in the next room. *Where is Alma?* "Alma!" she called. She heard a groan coming from behind her. "Who's there?" Pilar asked, her voice shaking. The person behind her groaned again.

"Alma?" Pilar asked.

"Where am I?" the person behind her asked in a child's voice that was groggy and frightened.

"Who are you?" Pilar asked.

"Josefina. Who are you? Where are we?" the child responded.

"I'm Pilar," she said. "I'm tied up. Can you untie me?"

"I can't move. What's happening? I want my mama!" the girl replied, her voice full of panic.

Pilar slowly became aware of her surroundings. Shades covered the windows, and the room was almost completely dark. *It must be night,* she thought. *How long have I been here? Is it still Wednesday?*

The girl behind her was crying now; her sobs grew louder and louder. The conversation in the next room stopped, and someone opened a door. Alma stood in the light coming through the cracked door. Her weight was on one leg, her hands on her hips. She was frowning. Alma's stylish updo was gone; her auburn hair flowed loose and wild.

"Who is making all the noise in here?" Alma asked. She located the source of the crying and walked over to Josefina. Pilar recognized Josefina as the girl who had entered the waiting room after her. The man Alma had introduced as Señor Cruz, who had sat in on part of her interview with Alma, stood behind Alma. But he was not wearing a jacket or tie now. His shirt was unbuttoned. She could see that he had a menacing tattoo on his chest. He looked different, bigger, frightening.

"Make that one shut up, Jesús," Alma barked at him.

The big man stepped over Pilar as if she were a mound of dirt and loomed above Josefina. "You heard her, bitch. Shut up!" he yelled.

When Josefina didn't stop, he kicked her hard in the ribs.

The girl doubled over with pain. The loud crying stopped, but she whimpered softly. Her clothing was disheveled, and her short skirt was up almost to her waist, her shoes scattered on the floor.

"I don't want to hear another sound out of you three," Alma said, looking menacingly at Josefina.

"Why are you doing this to us?" Pilar cried.

Alma looked at Pilar, and then her lips formed into a thin smile. "Congratulations," she said. "You got the job. All of you. You three are coming to work for Eduardo and Rosa."

Pilar tried to gather her thoughts. *Who are Eduardo and Rosa? Did she say three?*

"Pull the fat one over here with the others," Alma ordered Jesús.

He walked to the back of the room and bent over. He was dragging something toward Pilar. She couldn't make out what it was at first. *It's a body!* she realized. *Ay Diós!*

"She's not dead, that one, if that's what you are thinking," Alma said. "She just hasn't woken up yet. I doubled her dose. Might as well be dead, though. I'm not sure what we will do with her. She's not very pretty. But I'm sure Eduardo will find some use for her. Get some cold water and splash it on her face."

"Sangre Negra's men will be here soon," Jesús grunted, looking at his watch.

"Perfect," Alma said. "Well, our time together is almost up, girls."

Pilar screamed at her. "I need to go home to my husband and daughter. My husband will be looking for me. My daughter is just a baby. She needs me!"

"You told me you didn't tell your husband about the job interview, Pilar," Alma said.

Ay Diós, she is right, Pilar thought. *How could I have been so stupid not to tell anyone where I was going?*

"Tsk, tsk. Didn't your mother teach you that you shouldn't keep secrets from your husband, Pilar?"

It was a sin not to tell Alejandro that I was going to Mexico City to interview for a job. He might have stopped me. He might have come with me. But he didn't seem capable of acting. I meant well. But it was still a sin, and now God is punishing me.

"I only asked if your husband was coming with you," continued Alma. "I didn't tell you to come alone."

She didn't, Pilar thought. *It was my own high opinion of myself that I thought I could save us on my own.*

"But then again, the job would have been taken before you got here if you had said he was coming with you."

Alma laughed as she closed the door behind her.

She's right about all of it, Pilar thought. *What was I thinking? What must Alejandro be thinking? Maybe Diego will come looking for me. But he doesn't know where I was going. I should have told him. I should have asked him to go with me like he offered. I have been such a fool!*

Josefina, still bent over in pain, asked, "What are they going to do with us? I want to go home. I want my mama. Carlos told me the producers he works with liked the photos he took of me. They

wanted me to do a screen test for a new telenovela. Alma was supposed to be my agent. When Carlos finds out what these people are
doing to me, he will be so angry! He will call the police. He said he
would meet me here after my interview. Where is he? Where is he?"
Her voice was frantic.

"I don't know," Pilar said. "Maybe he will find us and free us."

"Yes, he knows where I am. He will come soon, gracias a Diós."

"Yes, gracias a Diós," Pilar said. "You are young, but you were smarter
than me."

The third girl in the room was awake now. "Who is here?"

"Pilar and Josefina," Pilar said in the direction of the voice. It was
too dark to make out her face. "What's your name?"

"Teresa. My head hurts, and I can't move. I was interviewing for a
sales job in a department store. Rico said we could be together here in
the city if I got the job. I could leave that boring shithole of a town.
Alma said the interview went well. We were celebrating. But then
everything went black!"

"Does Rico know where you are?" Pilar asked.

"Yes, he drove me here, but he said I would look more mature if I
went on my own. He was waiting outside."

"That's good," Pilar said. "We have two chances of being rescued."

"I'm sure he will come looking for me when I don't return," Teresa
said.

"We just have to wait to be rescued. It will be okay." Pilar was trying
to steady her nerves and convince herself as much as the younger girls.

It was less than an hour later when the door to the dark room
opened again and Alma and Jesús reentered. Alma switched on an
overhead light, momentarily blinding the girls. They had been in the
dark for a long time.

Now Pilar could see the other girls' faces. She had seen Josefina in
the waiting room and thought the girl looked young. But now the lipstick was gone and the mascara smudged so that Josefina looked even

more like a child. She couldn't have been more than thirteen. Her hazel eyes were red from crying, and her curly hair was a wild mass. She was very small and fragile looking.

Teresa was a larger girl, tall and overweight. She looked hard, like she had had some bad experiences in her life but had steeled herself to dealing with them. She was not pretty like Josefina, but her face was not unattractive. She had long black hair that looked as if it hadn't been brushed recently and dark eyes with skin that looked as if it had seen a lot of sun. Pilar guessed she was about fourteen years old.

When their eyes adjusted, Teresa and Josefina both cried out their friends' names.

"Carlos!" Josefina exclaimed.

At the same time Teresa called out, "Rico!"

"Honestly, Eduardo, you have so many names I can't remember who you are half the time," Alma said in a coy voice to the man standing beside her.

"Eduardo?" Teresa asked.

"Ay Diós," Josefina moaned.

Pilar recognized the stranger who had come to the Mendoza factory a week earlier and given her the job advertisement. *I have been such a fool!* She blushed.

"What's the matter, Pilar? You have nothing to say? Aren't you glad to see me again?" The man winked at her. "I am glad to see all of you. We only have a short time together now, but we will be reunited soon. Then you will make me a lot of money."

Pilar was bewildered. "Who are you to treat us like this?"

"I am your owner, Eduardo Antonio Ayala Perez, from the long line of Ayalas of Monte Diablo. My father owned many women and taught my brothers and me to do the same. The men in my family have made their living off the backs of stupid girls like you for generations, right Alma?"

Alma smiled a thin smile at Eduardo and mumbled, "Sí."

"You have met my youngest brother, Jesús. Soon you will get to know Guillermo. He is not as gentle as Jesús." Eduardo laughed.

"You liar! Bastard!" Teresa roared at Eduardo. Jesús responded by kicking her hard in her stomach.

Josefina began crying again and only stopped when Jesús stuffed a filthy rag in her mouth. Then Eduardo motioned to Jesús to follow him to the other room.

"You are a woman," Pilar shouted at Alma. "How can you do this to us?"

"Because I've been where you are going," Alma said slowly in an icy, even voice. "It's better to be where I am now than to be where I have been—and where you are going."

"What do you mean?" Pilar asked, anxious to keep Alma talking. She had her hand on the light switch, the door half-closed, and was about to follow Eduardo. "You weren't drugged and tied up."

"Not at first. But like you girls, I was a fool and trapped myself."

"What do you mean?" Pilar asked.

Alma hesitated. "Believe it or not, I grew up in a wealthy family. When I was fourteen, I met Eduardo during a family vacation in Puerto Vallarta. He was handsome and said he was rich. He told me that I was beautiful and he was in love with me. He convinced me to go in his car to meet his family. His father had trained Eduardo to trap young girls. Once they had me, there was no way out."

"Have mercy. Help us escape," Pilar pleaded.

"Too late. There's no way out for you now. The best you can hope for is to survive as long as possible," Alma said, walking out of the room.

Eduardo and Jesús wrapped each girl in dirty blankets, tying ropes around the bundles to keep them from getting away. They carried the hidden girls one by one down the back stairway. At the ground floor, a concrete cavernous space, the building abutted a deserted, dark street.

Pilar saw a white, windowless, unmarked van parked in the street. An old man wearing a loose white shirt and pants with a brown serape sat leaning against a wall at the far end. She didn't think he saw them. He was slumped over with his head facing the ground. She cried out to him anyway, but Eduardo roughly clamped his hand over her mouth.

First Josefina and Pilar were dropped and rolled out of their blankets onto the steel floor of the van. When they finished loading Teresa, two large men dressed in black T-shirts and jeans with tattoos covering their arms got out of the van.

"Do you have the money for the ride?" one of them asked Eduardo. "The price has gone up ten percent."

Eduardo protested, "We had a deal."

"The market has changed. Sangre Negra is getting into the business ourselves. It will cost you little guys more for transportation from now on."

"I'll just take them across myself," Eduardo announced. "Open up the van."

"You don't want to do that, pretty boy. You know El Tigre. You wouldn't want to lose your handsome head over this, would you?"

Lying on her side, Pilar listened with horror. She heard Eduardo's angry voice say, "Fuck! Between Sangre Negra and Rosa Rodriguez, a businessman can hardly make a profit these days." Then she heard him walk away.

"Where are we going?" Josefina asked Pilar.

CHAPTER 7

CAPTIVES

Pilar, Teresa, and Josefina rolled around like logs in a slow-flowing river. The van was dark and smelled from gasoline. Pilar heard the brakes squeal and the motor roar as the driver stopped and started in city traffic. Through a crack in the back doors, she could see streetlights.

After what she guessed was at least an hour, the stopping and starting ceased. The light through the opening between the doors faded away.

"Pilar, do you know where we are?" Josefina asked.

"From the bumpiness, I think we are driving along a small road. But I have no idea where we are."

"I'm scared, Pilar."

"Don't worry, Josefina. We will get out of here somehow," Pilar said, trying not to reveal her terror. "You need to be strong. We will find a way to escape. They can't be watching us all the time."

Pilar kept thinking, *I must get back to Alejandro and Concepción. Alejandro will be so worried, and Concepción needs me.*

"Does either of you have a mobile phone?" Pilar asked, although she knew it was unlikely. Only wealthy people had that luxury, and they were all poor country girls.

"No," the other girls said.

The van made a sharp right turn, and she heard gravel scattering beneath its wheels. Something that sounded like branches was snapping against the sides of the van.

The van slowed to a stop and then backed up slowly. The motor stopped.

"End of the road, chicas," a tall, mustached man in jeans and a black T-shirt called to them as he opened the doors of the van. His arms were covered with tattoos. He pulled Pilar out first and untied the ropes binding her ankles. She leaned against the van, trying to steady herself after being immobilized and shaken for so long. She surveyed the garage. It was large. In it were two new-looking pickup trucks and a long, low red sports car. Several men dressed like the driver came out of the house, carrying large guns. The man with the mustache prodded her with his gun barrel to enter the house. "Let's go," he said. "El Tigre wants to see the goods before he leaves in the morning."

The house was large and appeared to be new. They walked through the kitchen, where a woman who was dressed in black and looked very old was cooking something in a large soup pot. A delicious aroma filled the room. Pilar thought of being in her mother's kitchen and felt her stomach ache. *It has been a long time since I ate that street taco. I am starving.* She gazed at the pot, but the woman kept her back to the girls, appearing not to notice them.

The man pushed Pilar into a large living room with a stone fireplace and many upholstered chairs scattered around. Handwoven rugs covered its tile floor. Large animal trophies and framed art hung on the walls. The bright flickering light from a roaring fire made everything seem otherworldly. A short, pudgy man with scars on his round face and small, quick eyes sat in the biggest chair. He wore his stringy black hair in a ponytail. Pilar thought he was the ugliest man she had ever seen. Later, she would learn he was known as "El Tigre," the regional head of Sangre Negra, one of Mexico's most vicious drug cartels. He motioned to bring her closer.

"Very beautiful," he said to the other men in the room. "Take her clothes off," he ordered.

In an instant, a guard ripped off her blouse and skirt. Pilar cried out in terror as her clothes fell to the floor.

"All of it, stupid," the man in the chair ordered. The leering guard quickly tore off her undergarments, making her stumble. Pilar stood naked and mortified in front of the men. They whistled and uttered dirty things to each other.

"Mother of God, protect me!" Pilar cried out, vainly trying to cover herself with her bound hands.

The men laughed. El Tigre said, "Sorry, she can't help you here. Only I can help you, and I don't help girls like you. Your job is to help us. You will make that pig, Eduardo, and the old bitch, Rosa, a lot of money with a face and body like that. I can only sell drugs once. But they can sell you over and over again."

Pilar felt the blood drain out of her head.

"They go with the next marijuana shipment to the United States," El Tigre told the mustached man. "Put her in my room tonight. After that, she goes in the building with the others."

He pushed himself up out of the deep chair. "You are in charge when I am gone, Jorge."

The mustached man grunted as he picked up Pilar as if she were a feather pillow. He carried her to a large bedroom lit only by a row of fat yellowish candles that briefly reminded Pilar of the candles people burn in church when they want to ask God for special indulgences. They were lined up on the fireplace hearth, underneath a crucifix hanging on the wall. Pilar silently begged God to take her away from this place and the ugly man who she knew would soon be coming.

Jorge dropped Pilar onto a big bed and left the room, closing the door hard behind him. Pilar clutched at the bedspread beneath her, trying to use it to cover herself, but her bound wrists made the task impossible. She lay naked and scared, trying not to cry.

After a long while, the short, ugly man entered the bedroom; he seemed not to notice her. He casually undressed without saying a word.

He went into an adjoining room for a few minutes. Pilar smelled the sweet, smoky scent of marijuana. When he returned, he was smoking a joint and carrying a black leather strap.

"You are a very lucky chica," he said. "You can tell the other girls you spent the first night of your new life in the bed of El Tigre. It will be a night you will remember forever."

The tiger! Pilar shuddered.

Pilar fixated on the leather strap with horror. She instinctively knew it would be used to torture her.

El Tigre roughly rolled Pilar over on her stomach. She screamed when the leather strap snapped against her buttocks. He whipped her again and again, enjoying Pilar's pain. Then he pulled her to the edge of the bed and fucked her from behind in her vagina and then in her anus. As El Tigre thrust into her again and again, her skin stretched and tore until she screamed even louder. She had never thought a man would enter her anywhere but her vagina. Shame welled up inside of her, but her screams only seemed to energize him as he pounded her again and again. The sheets became wet and warm with her blood.

Gradually, Pilar felt a darkness overcoming her brain. When she opened her eyes, she could not clearly focus on anything. The room she was in seemed far away, and her head became light.

Just when Pilar was about to lose consciousness, El Tigre stopped. He lit another joint and sat on the edge of the bed and smoked it. But he wasn't finished.

When Pilar felt cold water pressed hard against her face, she regained consciousness. El Tigre pushed her over on her back, ignoring her bleeding. He climbed on top of her chest and stomach, forcing his erect penis into her mouth. "Suck, bitch!" he ordered.

Pilar didn't know what to do. El Tigre was suffocating her, and she could hardly breathe. She did nothing to respond to his order, so he thrust harder and harder. When a sticky fluid filled her mouth and throat, she had no choice but to swallow.

Temporarily satisfied, he withdrew but continued to sit on top of her, causing her stomach to give up its scant contents onto her face and mouth. Her arms, still tied behind her, were aching under his weight. But he seemed not to notice or care about the bile she had vomited or her pain.

When his penis was erect again, he fucked her hard in the vagina. His fury was relentless. Pilar was too tired to scream or resist now. Her mind drifted. The picture of Alejandro, so gentle and intimate, making love to her in their little bed appeared in her mind. Their love had been so pure, so innocent. But as the picture faded away, she wondered if she would never know that kind of love again. This horrible, ugly man had stolen her purity. He had made her unworthy of a good man like Alejandro. One thought kept running through her brain: *Diós, por favor, let me die now and end this nightmare!*

Then she lost consciousness.

• • •

Pilar woke up hours later, bruised, bloody, and in excruciating pain. Her hands were no longer bound, but there were deep cuts where the ropes had been, and her arms, crushed by his weight on top of her, were sore and painful. She was still bleeding from where El Tigre had violated her. Her mouth was as dry as cotton, only with a disgusting taste. She realized that she was not in El Tigre's room anymore, and for that she was grateful. But the place she was in was dark and dank, the concrete floor rough.

"Pilar, are you all right? Can I do anything for you?" She heard the words floating above her but couldn't reply. *I want to die right now. I'll never be fit for Alejandro to touch as his wife again. I am ruined.*

"Please, Pilar, talk to me," Josefina pleaded. "What happened to you last night? Well, never mind. You don't have to tell me. I am so afraid. I need you, Pilar. You are stronger than me. I never should have left my mama and papa. They were so kind."

Pilar eventually deciphered Josefina's voice in the fog. The girl was young and terrified. Images of Concepción drifted through her tortured mind.

I must survive. Concepción needs me. These girls need me. I must find a way for us to escape and to get back to our families.

It was late morning when they heard the sports car roar out of the garage. Ten minutes later, someone unlocked the door to the room they were in. Jorge and two other men entered. When these same men had carried Pilar back from El Tigre's room, one of them had said to Teresa and Josefina, "We'll be back for you in the morning, chicas." And here they were. They looked serious as they unbuckled their belts and pulled off their dusty boots. They walked toward the girls.

"Don't touch me!" Josefina screamed. Her face was white, and her hands trembled. Thirteen-year-old Josefina, who had grown up in a loving home and had never even kissed a boy her own age, was terrified of what the men were planning to do to her. Teresa, who had suffered years of abuse growing up, attempted to comfort her by trying to convince the child that although the men would hurt her, she would survive.

She told Josefina that she had been raped many times by her stepfather and brothers but that she had survived by telling herself that one day a man would come to save her and he would take care of her. When Eduardo had seemed to be that man, she had followed him willingly.

"But look at me now!" She laughed dryly. "My prince turned out to be a frog!"

"The little one wants to go first," Jorge said, approaching Josefina. "Tie her up against that pillar."

"I'm a virgin!" Josefina screamed again.

"Better yet." Jorge smiled. "I'll have her first. Consider this job training, chica. Not every man will be as gentle as me, though." He sneered as Julio and Chico laughed.

"I want her next," Julio said. "I can say I was only the second man to fuck a pretty young virgin." The others laughed.

The men raped Josefina, one after the other. At first, she closed her eyes tight, but Jorge slapped her and barked at her to open them.

"Smile like you are having a good time," he ordered. "Now moan with pleasure so I know you want it."

Josefina opened her eyes, but there was only terror in them. Jorge rammed her again and again until she moaned with pain.

"That's not very convincing." Chico laughed. "I bet I can get a better moan out of her."

When Julio and Chico finished, Josefina looked like a rag doll, hanging limp from the pillar.

They took her down and tied Teresa to the same spot. Teresa's eyes were narrow and filled with hatred.

First Chico and then Julio raped her, but Teresa bit her lip and stayed silent. When it was Jorge's turn, she spit on him to show her contempt. Jorge punched her in the stomach in return.

"That will do for a start," he said. "Tomorrow we will be back. I know you can do better. There's no getting out of this now, so you may as well make the best of it."

"What about that one?" Chico asked, pointing at Pilar.

"She's barely conscious," Julio said. "El Tigre had her last night. It doesn't look like there's much left for us."

Jorge looked down at Pilar, curled up on the floor, bruised, swollen, and bloody.

"We're hungry, and you don't look like you would be much fun. We'll start working with you tomorrow," he said.

"The old woman is making a stew," Jorge said to Julio and Chico. "I've worked up an appetite this morning, and the kitchen smells good. Let's go. These bitches aren't going anywhere, at least not for a few days."

After that, the men left the basement, locking the door behind them. Teresa allowed herself to curl up in pain and told Josefina, "At least we are still alive, little one. That's really all you can expect in life."

"I'll never be all right again," Josefina answered. "Yesterday I was going to be a TV star, and now I am a whore. I will die if they come back."

"You won't die," Teresa said. "You'll just wish you were dead. We are more valuable to the pigs if we're alive."

"It won't be forever," Pilar whispered. The others turned to look at her. She had not spoken or moved while the men were in the room. "We will escape. I must get back to my baby." Pilar's voice faded out. Exhausted, she fell into a dark hole of sleep.

The men held Pilar, Josefina, and Teresa captive for three days and nights. They continually raped, beat, and verbally abused the girls, trying to break their spirit. They yelled degrading things at them:

"You are nothing."

"You aren't even human."

"You are female dogs, bitches, only good to be used by men."

Josefina stopped talking or eating.

"Please eat something," Pilar begged her. "You must keep up your strength if we are to get out of here." Pilar felt as if she had let her own daughter down. "Please eat. I promise I will take care of you until we are free."

But shock and despair consumed the young girl.

The woman that the girls had seen in the kitchen the first day brought them clean but used clothes and food from time to time. There were no windows in their room, so the girls had no way of telling time or what day it was. Everything that happened seemed random. Seeing the woman up close, Pilar realized she was not as old as she'd thought she was the first time Pilar had seen her. The woman just looked worn out. Her skin was sallow from not getting enough sunlight, and her shoulders slumped. She had a limp that Pilar guessed was due to an injury inflicted on her by one of the men who worked there. When she brought them food, the woman kept her gaze low, never looking directly at the girls.

On the morning of the third day, Pilar whispered to her, "Will you help us escape, señora? You probably are also a captive. We will take you with us. Just leave the door unlocked, and let us know when they are asleep. You can tell us where the nearest police are. We will help one another."

The woman stopped but didn't look up. She hesitated for a moment before she dropped the tray of food she was carrying on the floor. She fled, and Pilar heard her lock the door.

"There's no place to go," the woman whispered through the keyhole in a voice that belied many years of hopelessness.

• • •

While it was still dark on the morning of the fourth day of captivity, their captors awakened them.

"Get up!" Jorge barked. "It's time for you to move on. One of our trucks will be here soon to take you across the river."

Another move! I don't know if it is even possible to hope that someone is looking for me or for Josefina, but the farther we travel, the harder it will be for anyone to find us. Pilar looked around the place in which they had been incarcerated. The walls were constructed of stone, with mortar between the stones. In some places, the mortar had crumbled and there were cavities. Pilar removed her mother's barrette from her hair. She hated to part with it, but she reached as high as she could and pushed it far back into one of the crevices before she joined the others outside. *If anyone does look for us, perhaps this will tell them that I was here*, she thought.

While they waited, Jorge, Julio, and the girls stood in the darkness outside the hacienda. It was cool, and the thin cotton dresses the old woman had given them to wear on the first day of their confinement were not enough to keep them warm. Josefina shivered and was so weak that she could barely stand up. Pilar surveyed their surroundings.

This might be our only chance to escape, Pilar thought. *There are three of us and only two guards. If Teresa and I each run a different direction at the same time, one of the guards must stay with Josefina. Teresa or I might make it to safety and send help to rescue the others.*

Pilar moved closer to Teresa. When she thought the men were not looking, she whispered her plan to the girl.

"Sí," Teresa nodded.

But while Pilar was preparing to give the signal to start running, she heard Jorge say, "Don't even think about it, bitch," as if he could read her mind.

"There's no place to run. The local police work for us. No one will help you, and I will kill you for trying."

Pilar's heart sank.

"Where are we going?" she asked.

"Does it matter?" Jorge shrugged.

CHAPTER 8

THE ANSWER

"Diego?" Yolanda exclaimed upon entering her kitchen the morning after the search party had gone to Mexico City. "You are up so early!"

Diego usually never woke up until Yolanda roused him for work or a fútbol game or practice. But here he was, dressed and sitting at the table, earnestly writing something in the journal with the blue cover that she had given him for his tenth birthday. He had never used it.

"I've got to figure out where Pilar is, Mama. I've made a timeline of everything that happened on Wednesday."

Yolanda sat down across from Diego. "Son, I know you feel responsible for Pilar's disappearance, but it's not all your fault. Pilar acted very strangely. Ever since she was a little girl, she told me everything. But whatever she was doing in Mexico City, she kept it a secret from me—and her husband. That was wrong."

"You don't think she was meeting a man, Mama, do you?"

"People do crazy things, Diego. I have stopped being surprised by anything. But no, I don't think Pilar would do such a thing. She's been in love with Alejandro since she was seven years old. His drinking has put stress on their marriage, but that is temporary. He is a good man and a hard worker. He will find another job, and things will get better. Pilar loves him, and she loves Concepción more than anything."

Just then the baby woke up in the other room and started crying.

Everyone had agreed it was better that the baby stay with her maternal grandparents for now.

Yolanda stood up to tend to her, but she stopped and turned around. "I don't know what she was thinking or why she kept it a secret. It doesn't make sense. But I don't think Pilar would run off with another man. My fear is that she ran into bad people." A tear fell from Yolanda's eye. "But don't tell Alejandro I said that."

José entered the kitchen, carrying Concepción. Cradled in her grandfather's strong arms, she had stopped crying.

"Papa, I'm going back to search Pilar's office again. Maybe she left something behind that will tell us something."

"Yes, go, son. It was late last night, and everyone was tired."

• • •

Diego was waiting when Señor Mendoza arrived to open the doors of the factory, something Pilar had always done.

"Señor Mendoza, would it be possible for me to search Pilar's office again?" Diego asked.

The owner hesitated. "We should call Sergeant Montoya."

"Every minute may count, señor. Por favor! There might be a clue that will help us find Pilar before it's too late," Diego pleaded, shuffling his feet.

"Too late for what?" Señor Mendoza frowned.

"I don't know." He couldn't say what he was thinking. "Too late to find her. Mama doesn't think she would have run away with the stranger who came to the factory. But maybe he knows something about where she went. If I can find him, maybe that would help."

"We already looked for him and his company last night, and we couldn't find either."

"I was exhausted. I might have typed something in wrong."

"All right, Diego. I can see you won't go away until I let you in.

But call me right away if you find anything, and we will get Sergeant Montoya down here."

"Thank you, señor," Diego said over his shoulder as he hurried to Pilar's office.

Entering the office, Diego stopped to let the adrenaline settle down. *I need to do a thorough search of the room. I can't miss anything.*

A bank of gray file cabinets stood along one wall, opposite a table with a fax machine and an old copier on top. To brighten up her surroundings, Pilar had had the walls painted blue, her favorite color. A small side table held a coffee pot and some mugs made in the factory. A desk with a rolling chair and a wooden guest chair filled the center of the room. Framed pictures of Alejandro, Pilar, and Concepción were on the desk.

I should start with the desk and work outward, Diego decided. Pilar's desk was as tidy as her house. There was a pile of invoices and several papers in a file box but nothing unusual. He opened the middle drawer of the desk. Pens and paper clips were in orderly places. The top drawer contained brushes and personal items. The bottom drawer held files. He looked through them but found nothing out of the ordinary. There was nothing on the floor or in the small trash can next to her desk. He moved to the bank of file drawers.

Potted plants and more pictures of the family, including one of him and Pilar smiling and hugging each other the day of his school graduation, lined the top of the cabinets. *I'm sorry, Pilar,* he whispered. He didn't expect to find any clues in the file cabinets, so he put them aside for now.

Diego moved to the copier machine. The tray was empty. He lifted the lid. There was a newspaper page on the glass. *It must have been the last thing she copied on Tuesday,* he thought.

Diego picked up the paper. It was a Mexico City newspaper.

That's odd, he thought. *I've never seen a Mexico City newspaper in San José. Why would Pilar have one?*

Just then, Señor Mendoza poked his head in the door. Seeing him, Diego asked, "Señor, does anyone here read a Mexico City newspaper?"

"I have looked at it occasionally," he said, "but I don't subscribe. None of my workers would have any use for it. Why do you ask?"

"There's a page from one on the copier."

Señor Mendoza stroked his beard. "Now, why would Pilar have that? What section is it, Diego?"

"It's the 'Help Wanted' section."

"What? Was Pilar looking for a different job? In Mexico City? That makes no sense. Her family is here. I thought she was happy in this job. Everybody here loves her. She is so good at it."

Señor Mendoza paused to think and then said, "Perhaps Pilar was looking for a job for Alejandro. He hasn't had any luck here, and I know they need the money. She said she was on an errand to buy him a gift. Yes, that must be it."

"The page she copied has the ads for 'Clerical And Administrative.' I can't imagine Alejandro working in an office, Señor," Diego said. Then he noticed it. "Wait! There is a checkmark on one of the ads. It's an ad for a secretary. There's a telephone number to call!"

"Do you think we should call the phone number and see who answers, Diego? No, we should wait for Sergeant Montoya to ask him what to do," Señor Mendoza replied. "We need to be careful and not get ahead of the authorities. They know best how to handle these things."

"I'm not so sure of that," Diego said. "I don't think the Mexico City police have any interest in finding Pilar. We may have to find her ourselves. Let me finish my search of the office, then go to the police station."

"Yes, and we should call Alejandro. We should share any good news with him. I guess this is good news?" He looked questioningly at Diego.

An hour later, Señor Mendoza, Alejandro, Diego, Sergeant Montoya, and old Chuy, his deputy of twenty years, were gathered at the town jail.

It was an old stone building that performed many municipal functions, including serving as the police station. Sergeant Montoya placed the newspaper on his desk. The note they'd found the night before sat beside it. The sergeant picked up the receiver and dialed the number in the ad. The telephone rang once on the other end, and then a mechanical voice reported: "This number has been disconnected."

The sergeant let out an audible sigh. "The number is disconnected, I am afraid."

"Another dead end," Alejandro said as he shook his head and leaned against the wall.

"Try calling the number on the stranger's business card," Diego implored. "Maybe he will know something."

Sergeant Montoya dialed the number. Again, there was no ring on the other end, and the mechanical voice reported that it was not a working number. The sergeant just said, "Nothing."

No one spoke.

Diego picked up the notepad they'd found in Pilar's desk and tried once more to decipher the words and numbers.

"I think part of this is an address," he exclaimed after staring at it for a few minutes. "It's not a complete address. But I think 'suite 435' might be here. That could be an office or a hotel room."

At the word "hotel," Alejandro turned toward Diego and glowered.

"I didn't mean she was going to a hotel," Diego said. "It is most likely an office."

Diego crossed his arms in front of him. "Because this ad is for a job, we should look for an employment agency or company, perhaps with 'corazón' in the name, and an address containing the number 435 within a fifteen-minute walk from the taco stand that the old man said Pilar walked away from. We can look for places in the direction she went."

Sergeant Montoya was impressed. He didn't feel any closer to finding Pilar, but at least Diego had suggested a logical search plan.

"Can I use your computer, sergeant? I'll go online and search for employment agencies in that neighborhood with 435 in the address," Diego said. "I will let you know what I find."

Without waiting for an answer, Diego sat down and typed in some general words to get started.

Mexico City is an enormous city, and the computer in the police station was very slow. It took Diego the rest of the day to comb through the data. When Sergeant Montoya wanted to go home for the night, he asked Diego if he had found anything.

"No," Diego replied, laying his forehead on the keyboard of the computer. "And I looked at the address of every employment agency I could find."

"Well," Sergeant Montoya said, exhaling the smoke from his cigarette, "maybe it's not an employment agency. Why don't you see if there are any other companies in the area with 'corazón' in the name. And are there any hotels in the area? I am not suggesting anything. I just think we should be thorough. But let's keep this between us."

"I understand," Diego replied, "but I still don't think that Pilar would have run off with another man. I don't care what some of the neighbors are whispering."

"Neither do I," the sergeant said. "I have known both Pilar and Alejandro since they were children. Pilar is a smart, virtuous woman. But we need to try everything."

The next morning, Diego resumed his search, this time looking for other types of businesses with the word "corazón" in them, and hotels. There were a couple of companies and fifteen hotels.

"Tomorrow," he told Sergeant Montoya, "I will ask Papa to let me take his truck into Mexico City and check out these places."

"Take Alejandro with you, Diego," the sergeant said. "Let him search the company offices. You search the hotels and buildings. He needs something to do besides worry."

Or drink, Diego thought.

The next day Diego and Alejandro drove into the city. The ride in the truck was uncomfortable. "Here, Alejandro," Diego said when they were parked near the Monumento. "Take this list of companies that have 435 in their address or the word 'corazón' in their name."

Diego waited until Alejandro was about a hundred meters away and then set out to investigate the list of hotels. He visited all of them over the next four hours, but none of the desk clerks reported seeing a woman who looked like Pilar. Tired, he returned to meet Alejandro. He found him sitting at a table outside a bar. He had obviously had a few drinks. This irritated Diego. He wondered if Alejandro was capable of staying sober enough to help find his wife.

"I didn't learn anything, Diego," Alejandro said in a plaintive voice. "I know I have been selfish and thinking only about my own misfortune since the factory closed. But if I drove Pilar away, I will never forgive myself."

Diego watched as he filled his glass again from the cheap tequila bottle on the table.

Diego and Alejandro had been friends their whole lives. Although they were the same age, Diego had always looked up to Alejandro. He was a serious man and a talented craftsman, and he had been a good husband and father. Before the last few months, he hardly ever drank alcohol. Now Diego realized that he had been too preoccupied with his own inconsequential life to notice how low his old friend had fallen. Neither Pilar nor his mother had complained to him about Alejandro. Suddenly, he looked at his sister's husband with a feeling close to disgust.

Is this what Pilar has been dealing with? Diego wondered. *I know I am partly responsible for whatever happened to my sister, but maybe I am not the only man in her life who let her down.*

• • •

Diego returned alone to Mexico City the next day and the next. He double-checked the addresses on the list he had given Alejandro. He didn't trust that Alejandro had been thorough in his search. In one building off the main street, which had red and black graffiti on the outside of the first floor, he found an office that had a suite 435. He entered and found the suite. He looked through the window in the door and saw that it was unoccupied, with only some folding chairs and a desk in the room as far as he could see. He wrote it off his list.

On the fourth morning, his father met him in the kitchen before he could head out the door. José was holding the keys to the truck.

"Diego, you have looked everywhere," he said. "I need you at the store, and you haven't been to practice all week. Your mother and I are worried about you, and you look like you are getting sick between all this driving and not sleeping at night."

Diego reluctantly returned to fútbol practice and work at the family store. Except for when he was in León, he showed up early, worked hard, and stayed to lock up after hours. A regular customer told his father, "Diego seems to be more serious and helpful these days." But others, predisposed to think of Diego as a shallow playboy jock, openly blamed him for Pilar's disappearance.

Although Diego didn't talk about it, he hadn't given up looking for Pilar. He remembered his last conversation with Lieutenant Ruiz when the lieutenant told him that many girls in the area had been kidnapped and killed or forced into the sex trade. He initially had dismissed that possibility because it was too dreadful to contemplate. Now, he began to allow that Pilar may have indeed been kidnapped.

On his regular Wednesday trips to Mexico City to pick up store supplies, Diego skipped trips to the fútbol stadium to return to the Colonia Tabacalera.

One Wednesday afternoon, Diego went back to the Mexico City

police station. He strode with determination into Lieutenant Ruiz's office.

"I didn't expect to see you again, young man." The lieutenant frowned as he looked up from the newspaper on his desk. "Still looking for your sister?"

"Sí, señor. I want only a minute of your time. I need to ask you about something you said to us."

"What was that?"

Diego didn't want to know, but he felt like he had to follow up on all leads, no matter how distasteful. He kept looking down at the floor.

Lieutenant Ruiz didn't say anything.

Diego cleared his throat before he spoke. "You said gangs kidnap girls in this area. If that is what happened to Pilar, how do I find out where they might have taken her?"

"Stop right there," Lieutenant Ruiz said, getting up and closing the door to his office. "You don't want to go messing around in any of that business. That's how you end up with your head cut off and your body in a mass grave in the desert. Do you want no one to be able to find you either?"

Diego was taken aback. *Surely, that is not something that would happen to Pilar!* He felt the blood drain out of his face.

Diego cleared his throat again. "I know it could be dangerous, but I owe it to Pilar to do everything I can to find her." Diego lifted his head and, staring resolutely at the policeman, said, "You said there was a gang that controlled this area. I need to know who they are."

"Boy, I have a family too. I can't help you."

Diego was standing where he could see a cabinet on which there was a photo of a smiling younger version of Lieutenant Ruiz, along with a woman and two smiling little girls. It was a picture of a happy family. He realized the lieutenant had a lot to lose if he did anything to attract the attention of the cartels. He looked back at Lieutenant Ruiz.

Observing the pain and regret in Diego's eyes, Lieutenant Ruiz

hesitated and then said, "Each cartel marks their members with iden-
tifying tattoos. You can probably figure out who is a gang member of
which gang if you look at their tattoos—but you must do so discreetly.
If anyone asks you, I told you nothing. Not a thing!"

"Thank you very much, señor. Do you know where they take the
girls?"

The policeman hesitated again and then sighed. His daughters were
teenagers now, and he worried every day about their safety. He had
seen a lot over the years and was hardened to tragedy, but Alejandro's
evident grief and regret touched him. It made him think about how
devastated he and his wife would be if one of their beloved daughters
disappeared. He knew it would destroy his wife, and he would never
forgive himself for not protecting her from the criminals he knew so
well. Now this tall, muscular young man was standing before him,
shoulders slumped with remorse, begging for his help in finding his
sister—a sister who was probably dead or worse. She could have been
raped, beaten, and smuggled across the border and be living the life of
a slave in some bordello by now.

"If you insist. Word on the street is that they send them to the
United States in shipments of illegal drugs. After that, she could be in
Houston, El Paso, Las Vegas, or anywhere north. Who knows?"

Someone knocked on the door and started to open it.

Before the door was even halfway open, Lieutenant Ruiz stood up,
pounded his desk, and started yelling in a loud voice at Diego, "I'm not
telling you anything, boy. I don't know a thing about your sister. Now get
out of my office, and I don't want to see you here again. Understand?"

At the sound of his raised, agitated voice, several of the policemen
outside the office looked up. They glared at Diego. Then a policeman
walked over and grabbed him, pushing him down the hallway toward
the station's door to the street.

Outside, Diego assessed the information Lieutenant Ruiz had given
him. The alternatives the policeman had presented were horrifying.

Not that he hadn't considered them as possibilities himself. In any case, it did not deter his resolve to find out what had happened to Pilar and rescue her if she was still alive. The information only made his mission seem more urgent.

• • •

If he was going to find Pilar, Diego realized he needed to be in Mexico City. But he would have to support himself and still have time to search for Pilar. The only things he knew how to do were work in a general store and play fútbol. He didn't like working in the store, even though he knew his papa held out hope that his older son would grow tired of the sport and take over one day. His seventeen-year-old brother, Carlos, had a mind for business and liked working in the store. At his young age, Carlos was a much greater help to their papa than Diego. So Diego needed to convince their father that his younger son would make a better merchant than he ever would. He decided to enlist Carlos's help in this plan.

Besides, if he took a job in Mexico City in a store, he would be working for a boss who doubtless would not be as generous as his papa had been with time off for continuing his search. And he would hate his job.

That left fútbol. He admitted to himself that he had hurt his career by reveling in his success with a minor league team, working for his father, and spending time with girls. He wasn't sure if there was still time to redeem himself with the coaches and agents so that he could advance to a Mexico City professional club. That was what they had expected of him since he was fourteen years old, but he needed to renew their faith in him.

As soon as Diego arrived back in San José, he began to put his plan into action. He asked Carlos to go out with him that night. Carlos was as good looking as Diego but smaller and shy. Like Pilar, he was good at math and loved to read books. He worshipped his older brother and was flattered that Diego wanted to spend time with him.

Once alone, Diego confided, "Carlos, I am a better athlete than you, but you are a better businessman than me. It's true that because I am the oldest, Papa wants me to take over the store someday. But I can't be the fútbol player I want to be if have to tend a store. Besides, I hate being inside all day, and you don't seem to mind."

"I do like working in the store, Diego, but are you saying you would step aside for me to take over the family business?" Carlos asked, astonished that anyone would turn down such an opportunity.

"Gladly," Diego replied. In the back of his mind, Diego realized that if he didn't succeed in having a fútbol career, he could be giving away a reliable income. But finding their sister was more important. It was the best thing he could do for his family, and for himself. It was time to put Pilar first—something he had neglected to do the day she'd disappeared.

"But what about Papa? He expects you to succeed him as he succeeded his papa," Carlos said.

"I've thought about that," Diego said. "I will tell him I have to go to practice full time or the club will let me go, which is probably true. I won't be able to work in the store for a while. While I am gone, you take over my hours and find ways to be helpful and improve the business. Papa can be stubborn and set in his ways, but I suspect you have ideas about how things could work better. Make him rely on you so that he can't do without you."

"I can't believe you are doing this, Diego," Carlos said, excited. "But I know you have always wanted to be a professional fútbol player. And I know you can be. Maybe your plan will work out for the best for both of us." Carlos hugged his brother. "Thank you, Diego."

Diego started going to practices early and staying late. He didn't go out at night, and he got plenty of sleep. He did extra workouts and practiced scoring goals. It took a few months, but by the opening of the

2008 season, the consensus among the coaches was that Diego might finally live up to his potential.

During the 2008 season, Diego was the high scorer in every game, leading the León club to a championship. At the end of the season, he received several offers to move up to larger city clubs. He was only interested in getting to Mexico City, though, so when one of the best city teams made him an offer, Diego immediately accepted.

Carlos had done everything Diego had told him to do at the store. Their father was more pleased than ever with Carlos's work ethic and ingenuity. When Diego announced he was moving to Mexico City to play fútbol, José supported his decision. He was happy Diego had become more responsible and focused.

Yolanda was still quietly mourning the loss of her daughter. The thought of their older son leaving home added to her sadness. They had always been a noisy, happy family. Only Concepción made her laugh now. But she wanted what was best for Diego, so she sent him off with hugs and kisses. Diego didn't tell anyone he was leaving to continue his search for Pilar.

During the 2009 and 2010 fútbol seasons, Diego played for the Mexico City club with a ferocious energy that excited the thousands of fans in the stadium and energized his teammates. He was more successful than ever, scoring goal after goal. Besides his athletic prowess, Diego was a handsome man who had charisma. The Mexico City newspapers and fútbol fan magazines ran pictures of him scoring goals. Celebrities sought him out with invitations to parties. But he usually made excuses, saying he needed his sleep. He sometimes went out with women but was never in a serious or exclusive relationship. His reluctance to party with his teammates and his increasing popularity caused some of his teammates to resent him. But he was too caught up in his sport and his mission to notice.

Playing fútbol on the professional level was most challenging. In the beginning, standing on the pitch with thousands of people watching and cheering, the field lights glaring overhead and salsa music blasting from a corner of the stadium, he'd felt a little intimidated. But playing at the professional level also forced him to become disciplined and serious. By the end of the 2010 season, he was regarded as one of the best up-and-coming players of the day, not only in Mexico but internationally.

• • •

After he moved to Mexico City, Diego spent many nights—when he didn't have to play in a game or practice—searching for Pilar. He scouted the local cantinas and even brothels, hoping she was still in Mexico City. But he didn't find her anywhere. He remembered Lieutenant Ruiz telling him that the cartels often smuggled kidnapped girls across the border to the United States. Reluctantly, he came to believe that was what had happened to his sister. He refused to consider that she might be dead.

During the second part of the 2010 season, Diego returned to the Colonia Tabacalera. He knew a lot of time had passed and the trail would be cold, but he had run out of ideas. He thought he might have missed some clue and wanted to give the place where Pilar had last been seen one more look. He wore black and tried hard not to be noticed. He looked for the men he had seen the night of Pilar's disappearance. He thought they might know or have seen something. They might even have been involved.

One night he found two men who looked as if they might have been the two he had seen that night back in October 2007. They were standing under the same streetlight—only this time there were three men instead of two. Two wore black leather jackets, but the other was wearing a black T-shirt, and his arms were bare. Diego couldn't see the man's arms clearly in the streetlight, so he decided to use the camera on his cell phone. When he zoomed in, Diego saw that tattoos covered the man's arms, including a large tiger. The men didn't look at all friendly, and he wondered how to approach them to ask if they had seen anything that night.

"Hey, you! What are you doing?" Diego heard one of the men yell at him as the other two spun around, glaring.

Diego froze momentarily. But when the three men took off across the street, running toward him, one brandishing a large knife that glinted under the streetlights, Diego spun on his heels and ran. He turned at the next corner, hoping they wouldn't see him. No such luck. The only advantage he had was his phenomenal speed. He expected he could outrun them, but he didn't know the neighborhood. He felt disoriented in the maze of streets. In the middle of a block, he turned again quickly to see if they were still behind him, only to have a hand grab his arm. Terrified, he thought one of the men knew the streets better than he did and had cut him off somehow.

Shit! Diego thought. *I'm dead.*

"Psst! Come in here," the man who had grabbed Diego said. He was an old man dressed loosely in a white shirt and pants with a brown serape. He motioned for Diego to duck into the narrow, dark gap between the buildings behind him. Diego did, crouching down behind the old man as much as he could, and the old man sat down, his back blocking the gap where Diego hid. A minute later, the three men ran past them and kept going. They stopped at the next corner, looking in all directions. They must have thought they had lost Diego because they walked away, cursing.

When the three men were safely out of sight, the old man asked Diego in a hoarse voice, "What are you doing here, boy? I've been watching you these nights when you come around."

"Nothing, none of your business," Diego replied hastily. He was irritated that he hadn't gone unnoticed like he'd thought.

"Anything that goes on here is my business," the man whispered back. "I live here. Stalking those devils could get you killed. I wouldn't do it if I were you."

"You live here?" Diego asked.

"Around here." The man waved his right arm in a wide swath.

Diego looked intently at the old man. He was small and thin, not more than the size of a ten-year-old child. His hair was long and completely gray. *He seems harmless. Maybe he knows something.*

"I'm searching for my sister, señor. She disappeared in this neighborhood three years ago. Have you seen any suspicious activity?"

"Everything is suspicious around here." The old man chuckled. "I am very hungry, though. I think better on a full stomach."

"Sí, of course." Diego pulled some pesos out of his pocket.

The man took the money and motioned Diego to come closer. Then he whispered, "Sometimes, late at night, I used to see men bringing big bundles of blankets or sheets out of these buildings. The bundles seemed very heavy. It took two men to carry some of them. Sometimes the bundles moved, made human sounds, female sounds."

"And?"

"They rolled whatever was in the bundles into the back of a white van."

"And?"

"Money changed hands. Sometimes there was an argument, and other times the men in the truck and the men who carried the bundles laughed and slapped each other on the back. But the van always pulled away quickly and was gone. Poof!"

Diego was intent on the old man's every word. He felt himself grow cold as he pictured his gentle, beautiful sister smothered in a blanket and roughly dumped into a van like a sack of trash. He felt weak in the knees. After a few minutes he asked, "Where did you see these men and bundles?"

The man was expressionless as he stuck his hand out again. Obviously, he had become inured to the worst of human behavior, living on the street in the Colonia Tabacalera. Diego put more money in it, and the man smiled. "Behind the office building with the black and red graffiti on it over there," he said, pointing to a side street. "But I didn't tell you nothing, right?"

"Right," Diego said, distracted.

He realized that the building the old man had described was the one with the empty office suite 435 that he had looked at and dismissed three years ago.

Mierda! Diego thought. *I missed it.*

• • •

It was several days later when Diego was able to get away from practice early enough to visit the building with suite 435. The entire time he couldn't get away, he was anxious and annoyed. When he was finally able to return, he studied the graffiti on the outside of the first floor of the building. He tried to read it, but it didn't seem to be words, just scribbles.

Entering the building, he quickly ran up to the fourth floor. He peered in the window of suite 435 to see if anything had changed from when he'd been there before. The folding chairs and desk were still there, although they were in different positions. But this time the door to the inner office was open, and he could see a bookshelf with very few books on it. He tried opening the door to the suite, but it was locked.

Diego wanted desperately to get into suite 435 and search it for clues. He took off down the staircase two steps at a time until he reached the first floor again. A young woman wearing short black hair, a black mini skirt, red high heels, and long red fingernails sat at a desk in the leasing office, flipping through the pages of a movie magazine.

She quickly sized up Diego, put down her magazine, and gave him a coy smile.

"Buenos días, señor. Are you interested in leasing space?" she asked, twisting a strand of her hair.

"Sí, I am interested in one of your suites, suite 435. A friend visited it once and told me it might suit my purposes. Would it be possible for me to see it?"

Checking a book on her desk, she said, "Sorry, suite 435 is rented."

"I looked in at the window in the door, and it is empty."

"Some of our tenants come and go," she said with a shrug. "My boss says it's just like that. We don't pay much attention to what they do, so long as they pay their rent on time."

"That is disappointing," Diego said, moving closer to her. "My friend thought that suite would be perfect for my business, and I would be interested in a long-term arrangement. Could I just look at it? Your boss and the tenant wouldn't have to know."

He gave the girl a flirtatious smile and stood tall so she could see his muscled arms. The young woman smiled back and then rummaged in a drawer in her desk and dangled a set of master keys in front of him. "Well, I guess it would be all right if I went with you."

Once inside suite 435, Diego looked everywhere for a clue that might indicate Pilar had been there. The inner office was sparsely furnished. One of the overstuffed chairs had been ripped on the arm, and some of the stuffing was coming through. But there was no sign of what the office was used for. A thick layer of dust covered the furniture, and the light fixture was burned out, all indicating that no one had been there for a long time. Spotting the door on the side of the interior office, he asked, "Where does that lead?"

"It's a second office for storage or whatever. We can look at it together," the girl said with a smile as she took Diego's arm and gently pulled him inside.

"Ay Diós!" the girl exclaimed when she turned on the light. She stepped back.

Ropes and handcuffs lay in one corner of the room. The occupants had piled a few old blankets in another. There was what looked like dried blood stains on a blanket and in the middle of the carpet.

Damn! Diego thought, feeling sick but struggling to look composed.

"What happened here?" the girl whispered, stepping closer to Diego, scared now.

"Nothing good," Diego answered. He noticed another door across the room. "Where does that lead?"

"It's the back stairs leading to the service area at the base of the building. I don't think we should be here. Let's get out," the girl pleaded.

"Just a minute," Diego answered, pulling the draperies open and inspecting the windows. Someone had nailed them shut. The door to the back stairwell had a lock that required a key to open it. It was locked now.

"This room was used as a prison to keep whoever was in here from getting out," Diego said.

The girl was pulling Diego harder, trying to get him to leave the suite.

"All right," he said. "I've seen enough. We can go now."

Back downstairs in the office, the girl was so nervous she did not flirt with Diego anymore. "I don't think we should have done that. Please don't tell my boss I let you in there."

"No, of course not," he assured her. "But I am curious. Can you tell me who rents that space?"

She hesitated, so Diego leaned over the desk toward her and twirled her hair around his finger. "I won't tell anyone you told me," he said, leaning even closer.

The girl looked nervous, but she slowly got up and opened a file drawer. She pulled out a file labeled "Suite 435." She let Diego look over her shoulder to see the name of the lessee—Corazón Company.

The name "Corazón" was the same name Diego had seen in the ad in the Mexico City newspaper he'd found in Pilar's office over two years ago in 2007. He had a flashback to the Internet café in San José where he, Alejandro, and Sergeant Montoya had frantically searched for the company and concluded it didn't exist.

Diego now knew that Pilar had been kidnapped from this very building and that he had missed it entirely.

But where is she? he wondered. *Is she even alive? Could she be all the way across the border to the north, like Lieutenant Ruiz suggested? If so, how will I ever find her?*

CHAPTER 9

ACROSS THE RIO GRANDE

*P*ilar *was sitting on the bench in front of their house, holding Concepción in her arms and watching Alejandro sketch a picture of them, as he liked to do. Concepción giggled as she played with a wooden toy José had made for her. It was a beautiful, sunny spring day. Her mother walked toward her, carrying a basket of fresh, warm tortillas.*

Suddenly Pilar felt a jolt, and the dream shattered. She was awake. She tried to get oriented, but it was almost pitch black all around her. It felt like two other girls were curled up around her in a very tight space. *Why does it smell awful, like body odor and something else, something disgusting? Where am I?*

Then Pilar remembered being in a dank room with a concrete floor, stone walls, and pillars, with two other girls and three men who assaulted them over and over. She remembered her night with El Tigre, and it made her feel sick. Instinctively, she reached for her small silver crucifix. It was still there. It had always made her feel comforted, but now fear was more powerful.

Someone opened the door to the compartment. It was night, and she could only feel a man's rough arms pulling her out. She stumbled when he set her on her feet. Her legs had gone to sleep. Her head pounded from the drugs Jorge had forced her to swallow before he'd pushed her into the truck, and she was groggy.

The man led her from the truck to a long, low cinderblock building in the middle of a parking lot. Another man with an automatic rifle grunted for him to put her in a room at the end of a hallway. Stained sleeping bags covered the floor, and an awful smell came from a bucket in the corner. The man who had pulled her out of the truck pushed the other two girls, still half-asleep, into the room.

"Wait here," a man told her gruffly in bad Spanish. "Eat this."

Pilar looked at her captor. He was a muscular white man with light hair and a beard.

He tossed some cold corn tortillas to Pilar. The tortillas were stale, but she was starving, so she ate one of them, saving the rest for the other girls.

"I'm thirsty. Can I have some water?" Pilar asked.

"That will cost you, chica. What do you have to give me for it?" the man grunted.

"I have nothing," Pilar answered, sinking to the floor. "Please, we must have been in that truck a long time."

"You have something I want," he said, grabbing her arm, pulling her up, and pushing her against the wall. He unzipped his jeans. When he was done, he walked into another room, came back with a bottle of Topo Chico mineral water, and casually tossed it to her.

• • •

After two days, the light-haired man told the girls they would move on that evening. Pilar had heard a television somewhere in the building. Some of the language had been English, with which she had a basic familiarity. She'd learned a little in school and sometimes she'd had to deal with English-speaking customers in her work at the factory. But the voices on the TV had spoken quickly, so she'd been able to understand only a few words. Once, she thought she'd heard Christmas music. *They are taking me farther and farther away from Concepción and*

Alejandro, she thought. *I have to find a way back to them before I go any farther.* She swallowed her pride and approached the bearded man as he was taking her to a waiting van.

"Are you going to tell me you will miss me?" he asked, and then he added with a laugh, "I'll miss you."

"Maybe you could let me stay behind?" Pilar forced a smile. "We could go to your house, and I could cook for you. I'm a good cook. I would be there just for you."

Squinting, he hesitated for a minute. Then he said, "Yes, and run away when I am gone. Do you know what Sangre Negra's men would do to me when you didn't show up with the others?"

Pilar did not know, but she knew it was pointless to try to persuade him.

"You can kiss me goodbye," he laughed, grabbing for her.

Pilar backed away. *I can't let them defeat me, no matter what they do to me. I must get home to my child.*

• • •

Two men took the girls to a large, enclosed white-panel truck. A group of men speaking different dialects of Spanish, looking the worse for travel, were loaded in with them. *They must have been in the other rooms,* Pilar thought. There were no seats in the van, and the air was stifling, despite a few holes cut out of the roof of the truck.

Pilar guessed they were in the truck for about seven hours. Her legs were cramped from standing, although the girls took turns making space for one of them to sit down for a while. The driver stopped for gas several times, and she could hear conversations in Spanish, but increasingly in English, outside the truck. At one stop where there seemed to be a lot of people in the area, she cried, "Help us!" but another passenger quickly clamped his hand over her mouth.

"Don't make any noise," he whispered. "We are across the river. We will get good jobs in the United States and be able to send money back to our families. But if the police catch us, they will put us in prison or send us back."

"Por favor, señor, we are good girls. These devils kidnapped us. They brutalized us in ways I cannot say. We want to go home to our families. These two girls are just children. I have a husband and baby who need me."

"We men have families to support. We need the work in Los Estados Unidos so we can send money back to them."

"I am the main person supporting my family, señor. My husband is ill. It is just as important for me to go home as for you to go to a strange land where you don't speak the language and don't know you will get a job," Pilar heard herself argue.

"You are just women," the man retorted, growing angry. "You don't know what you are talking about."

Pilar turned away and screamed, "Help us!" louder than before.

The man, who was large and strong, clamped his hand over her mouth as hard as he could. Pilar stumbled and fell against Josefina. He kept his hand over her mouth until the van had pulled back out onto the highway.

The noise from the road grew louder and more consistent. Pilar guessed they had entered a city—but which city and which state? She tried to remember the geography of the United States. Was this Texas, New Mexico, or Arizona? California would be too far. It had been a long time since she'd studied geography in school.

The truck finally stopped, and the driver opened the back door. It was night. The outside air was muggy and warm, but it felt good compared to the stifling, rancid air inside the truck. The driver ordered everyone out. Pilar saw that they were in a neighborhood with similar houses all around. She could hear dogs barking. They walked, one by one, into a one-story house with a fence around it.

"Lie down," a guard ordered them once everyone was inside. "Don't think of trying to leave. There are armed guards all around the yard. We will shoot anyone leaving this house. Men, take off your trousers and put them in a pile over here."

Several of the male passengers protested this last order. "We can't go out or go to work without our pants," the man who had silenced Pilar objected. But when a guard leveled his gun at them, they obeyed.

Pilar looked for Josefina and Teresa. They had gotten separated. When she found them in one of the three small bedrooms, they all smiled for the first time since their ordeal began. They hugged Pilar as if they were schoolgirls separated over the summer, reuniting. "I am so relieved to see you, Pilar," Josefina said. "Do you know where we are? I am so scared. I want to go home."

Pilar wrapped her arms around Josefina to comfort her. She was surprised at how much she had worried about the two younger girls when she hadn't been able to find them—how she felt responsible for them, even though she barely knew them. *They are so young and scared*, she thought. The girls clung to her, sensing that she was stronger than they were.

The next day, after they slept, Pilar studied the house, looking for a way to escape. But escape seemed impossible. Someone had nailed the windows shut, and groups of armed men sat and talked or drank at the front and rear of the small house. There was one bathroom and always a line to use it. At one point it backed up, and no one came to fix it. It was fall, but it was still hot outside. It was unbearably hot and smelled disgusting inside.

When they first arrived at the house, the men who had traveled in the van were happy that they had reached Houston and were about to start the good jobs they had been promised. But soon, as they realized that the armed guards were not there to protect them but to control them, they grew disgruntled. Two days after they arrived in Houston, five heavily armed Mexican men with tattoos like the ones Jorge had had on his arms arrived and gathered the men together. The apparent leader of the group told the men that they must pay the coyote who had arranged their transport an additional entrance fee to the United States. They would have to work it off by working in a factory. The coyote would take their room and board out of their wages until they completely paid off their debt. The captive men grew angry, looking for some way to vent their anger and frustration. The girls stayed together and out of sight as much as they could.

Pilar never stopped thinking about escape. One of the younger guards, who'd been recruited in the United States, liked to watch the three girls. Pilar took advantage of this to draw him into conversation: "Señor, I was wondering where we are. You seem to be an important man here. I would think you would know all about where we are in this big city?"

"This is East Houston," he said.

"Is this a nice part of town?"

He snorted. "No, this is a very poor area. Too many Spanish people crossing the river, coming to Houston, living on top of each other like ants in an anthill. There are some good people living around here, some have papers or are citizens, but it's still a dangerous part of the city."

Pilar assumed they could get help from other Mexicans living nearby if they could escape their guards. She had been watching and trying to determine the most promising time to get away from them. She decided their best opportunity would be during the afternoon. The guards always nodded off in the shade of oak trees in the front and back yards after lunch. She studied the locks on the doors. She knew a little about hardware from when she'd helped her father in the store. She thought the cheap locks on the doors of the old house would be easy to pick. Their captors primarily relied on the armed men outside and the growing atmosphere of hopelessness inside to keep their prisoners from escaping.

But there was still the chain-link fence around the house. How could they get through it? Pilar studied the fence from all of the windows of the house. The people who used to live in the house to the north had owned two large dogs. The guards used to keep a dog at the house where the prisoners were, but it had grown old and died and had not been replaced. Over time, the dogs had dug a hole under the fence where they'd passed from one side to the other. The dogs were gone, but the hole was still there. Pilar and Josefina were petite—small enough, she believed, to lie down and slip under the fence where the dogs had dug. Teresa was another matter, but Pilar didn't have any other ideas. Since they had been living mostly on dry tortillas and beans since they got on the truck out of Mexico, all of them had lost weight, even Teresa. Pilar had to hope Teresa had lost enough weight to squeeze under the fence.

Since she didn't know what was going to happen to them or when, Pilar felt pressure to act as soon as her plan was formulated. The only thing she still needed was something to pick the lock on the door with.

She thought of her silver barrette. But she had left it behind as a clue on the off chance someone was looking for her and found the place they had been confined. She asked Josefina and Teresa if they had anything thin and strong she could use to pick a lock. She searched the drawers in the kitchen without luck. Then she quietly went to each of the few female captives, asking them if they had a thin metal object on them. Just as she was about to give up, a woman handed her a safety pin she had used to hold up her bra.

"Perfect," Pilar said. "Tomorrow after lunch we will make our escape."

• • •

Pilar estimated that she could run from the back door and slide under the fence, making it to the house next door, in one minute or less. She had noticed that a Mexican family lived there. She would get them to telephone the American police, who would rescue them.

So, on the third day of their confinement, Pilar, Josefina, and Teresa crouched in the kitchen, peered out the window, and waited until both of the guards sitting under an oak tree in the backyard finished their lunch and leaned against the trunk of the tree to take a nap. Their guns lay on the grass beside them. Five long minutes after she saw the guards' shoulders and heads slump forward, Pilar inserted the safety pin into the lock on the back door and slowly jiggled it until she heard the click that meant it was unlocked. Another minute passed while she waited for her breath to be normal again, and then she slowly opened the door just wide enough to slip outside. She kept her eyes on the guards as Josefina and Teresa followed her.

When they were all outside, she whispered to the others, "Run to the yellow house to the left. Now!" All of them took off, Pilar in the lead. The noise of their feet stirring up the gravel on the driveway between the houses woke the guards, however. The men grabbed their guns and jumped to their feet.

Pilar slipped easily under the fence and reached the back door of the yellow bungalow. She pounded on the door.

"Help! Help us! We are being held captive. Call the police!"

A young boy's face appeared in the window. "Mama, Mama," he yelled in Spanish to someone inside the house. "Las señoritas!"

Pilar heard a man's voice inside yelling in Spanish, "Don't open the door, Tomás. Get away from the window. It's none of our business. Come here." The man sounded scared.

How can these people not help us?

Looking back, Pilar could see that one of the guards had caught up with Teresa, who had not quite made it through the fence. He dragged her to the ground with his gun drawn. Pilar pounded on the door harder. She begged, "Please, please help us."

"I am going to put a bullet through this one's head if you two aren't back inside the house in one minute," the guard yelled to Pilar and Teresa in a stone-cold voice.

Pilar knew that she could dash around the yellow house and perhaps get away herself. But the sight of Teresa, terrified, with a gun pointed at her head made her stop.

I can't sacrifice her life for mine, she thought. *This was my plan, and she is just a child.*

Pilar walked back to the house where they had been confined; she was frustrated and angry. She'd thought the family next door would help them get free. But they had turned her away, probably afraid to get involved with the gunmen next door or the police. Suddenly Pilar felt tired, more tired than she had ever felt in her life. She wanted to go to sleep and never wake up. Any other escape seemed impossible. As Pilar passed the guard who had yelled, he kicked her as hard as he could in the back of her legs, making her stumble. "If you try that stunt again, we will kill all three of you! Understand?"

She didn't want the guards to see her cry, but once Pilar was back in the house, tears of frustration and hopelessness came. Exhausted, she fell asleep thinking, *Maybe escape is impossible.*

CHAPTER 10

REUNION

Alejandro strode into Yolanda and José's house, tired from the drive from San Miguel de Allende. It was almost Christmas 2010. The delicious aroma of warm tamales greeted him. Concepción, almost four years old, was wearing her prettiest dress and sat on the living room floor, playing with a doll. When he lifted her up in his arms, she squealed with delight, as she always did when her father returned from work. Yolanda was like a mother to her during the days when Alejandro was gone, but she loved being with her father most of all.

Without Pilar's income, Alejandro and Concepción had at first been destitute. His own parents had still had younger children at home and had been too poor to help them. But Yolanda and José had insisted Alejandro and Concepción move in with them. Yolanda took solace in taking care of her granddaughter, who so strongly resembled Pilar.

During the first weeks following Pilar's disappearance, Alejandro had left Concepción with Yolanda and driven his old truck to Mexico City, where he'd cruised randomly through the busy streets, hoping to catch sight of Pilar.

At the end of a month, José and Yolanda had sat him down and told him that behavior had to stop. He had no money for gas or alcohol, and they were not going to provide it any longer. They told him that he had a daughter who needed him. Alejandro must stop feeling sorry for himself, get sober, and find a way to provide financially for his child. They would help him with her care, but he had to get other work.

Alejandro had then tried working in José's store, as well as various types of manual labor, but he was an artist and was unhappy doing work he did not consider creative. Eventually he resurrected an old idea.

In the fall of 2008, one year after Pilar disappeared, Alejandro borrowed money for art supplies and began creating paintings of local life and landscapes. When he had more than a dozen paintings that he thought were good, he took them to the markets in the tourist towns to the north, just as he had described to Pilar. Many tourists liked them immediately and bought them as souvenirs of their time in Mexico. Soon he was selling as many as he could create. After a year, during which his customers from the United States told friends how much they enjoyed his paintings, a prominent gallery owner in San Miguel de Allende went to see his work, realized his talent, and offered to carry his art.

By 2010, he was making enough money to rent a small studio in San Miguel, where he began painting portraits. His portraits of beautiful Concepción, in particular, were quite popular with tourists. Eventually, North American and wealthy Mexican families commissioned him to paint portraits of their children. His clients appreciated his handsome face and gentle demeanor, and they referred their friends to him. By December 2010, he was making a more than sufficient living for himself and his daughter, who continued to stay under the daily care of her grandparents. Concepción loved it when Yolanda would tell her stories about her mother, whom she didn't remember. When she asked why her mother wasn't there, Yolanda told her she'd had to go away for a while, even though she hadn't wanted to, but they hoped she would be able to come home one day.

"My apologies for being late for Diego's going-away party," Alejandro said to Yolanda, who had entered the room and was drying her hands on her apron.

"Don't worry, Alejandro," José told him, watching his granddaughter play from his favorite chair. "Diego isn't here yet. But I'm glad you are. Maybe now YoYo can drive you crazy with her preparations for the big party instead of me." He smiled at Yolanda, letting her know he was just teasing. Carlos was doing a good job running the store, and José preferred being part of the happy turmoil in the house.

"Something smells wonderful," Alejandro said. "What are you making?"

"All of Diego's favorite dishes, of course," Yolanda said proudly. "Once he gets to Houston, he will eat nothing but hamburgers and pizza. They say Americans have terrible eating habits—no one cooks anymore. I want my son to remember the good Mexican food he ate growing up. Maybe then he will come home often."

They heard a car door close. José went to the window. "It's our son," he said proudly.

Diego had become a son of whom his parents could be proud. He had achieved celebrity status in Mexico as a fútbol star in only two years' time. Next season he was going to play for a Major League Soccer team in the United States.

When Diego entered the house, Carlos and José each warmly hugged him. He had not been home after he'd moved to Mexico City. He'd avoided San José because everyone knew his part in Pilar's disappearance, and he felt ashamed. As Diego had become highly successful on the fútbol pitch, however, friends and neighbors seemed to have forgotten his part in Pilar's disappearance—although he never did. Señor Marco, their next-door neighbor, no longer sighed when he spoke Diego's name. Now he was quick to tell strangers that he had known Diego all of his life and never doubted the boy was destined for greatness.

After eating a wonderful dinner, José, Yolanda, Alejandro, and Diego moved to the living room. Carlos took Concepción to her room, where he would read to her and put her to bed.

"I have something to tell you," Diego said. "Alejandro, I promised you that I would not stop searching until I found Pilar and brought her back to you."

"I remember," Alejandro replied, sipping lemonade. He had stopped drinking alcohol after the family intervention.

"That is the main reason I moved to Mexico City. It was always my dream to play fútbol with a professional club. But I also wanted to be where I was more likely to be able to find out what happened to Pilar," Diego said. "I believe she answered that ad in the Mexico City newspaper for a secretarial job because it paid more money than she was making here. The ad was a fraud, aimed at luring girls to a phony employment agency. Someone kidnapped the girls, and a cartel smuggled them to the United States. Most likely, they took her, at least initially, to Houston. It is the largest hub for sex slavery in the United States."

Yolanda gave José a sorrowful look, and he put his arm around his wife.

Diego looked at Alejandro to gauge his reaction. Alejandro's hands were shaking, but his face showed no expression.

Diego continued, "At the end of this season, I received several offers from US clubs to play in their city. I accepted the offer from the Storm, the Houston fútbol club, even though they are a relatively new club, in order to continue my search. I believe if she was taken to the US, she would have at least passed through Houston. I have not given up on finding Pilar. Most girls would have fallen apart by now. But Pilar is strong, and I believe with all my heart that she has survived, and I will find her. It is my fault she got into this situation. I won't give up."

Yolanda hung on Diego's every word. When her son finished, she stifled a tear and asked, "Do you really believe that, Diego? I pray to the Virgin every day that she will come home and see her daughter, even though I know others think I am a deluded old woman." She looked at her husband.

"Now, YoYo," José said, "I want to see Pilar again just as much as you do. I love my daughter. But it has been three years, after all, and I don't want you to be disappointed."

To Diego's surprise, he saw his father wipe a tear that had fallen on his cheek. Diego had never seen his strong father cry before. He wasn't sure what to do.

Just then Carlos entered the room, relieving the tension. He walked to the sofa and sat down beside his father. They had grown close since Diego left and Carlos started taking over the operation of the store. "Diego," Carlos said, "I know you have never given up on finding our sister. I have faith in you. If anyone can find her, it is you."

Then Alejandro spoke. "Diego, I have gone over every possible thing that could have happened to Pilar since that day. I know people say I am living in denial and should accept that Pilar is dead and find another woman for my daughter's sake. I feel in my heart, though, that she is alive."

Alejandro stood up and walked to the window. He looked at the rising moon, which was full that night. "It would be like Pilar to try to solve our financial problems by herself," he continued. "I know you think you are to blame for her kidnapping. But I blame myself. I was not a reliable husband. I was selfish. I drank and argued with her about stupid things. I should have gotten off the couch and found a way to take care of my family. Pilar was always stronger than me."

Yolanda had tears in her eyes, and she got up to fetch a box of tissues from a table across the room. "We all carry some guilt, Diego," she said. "Just before she left, I told Pilar about all the people who were leaving San José to look for better-paying jobs in Monterrey and Mexico City. So I am also to blame for my careless gossip. When the Jiménez Factory closed down in 2007 and all the other factories and craftsmen started laying off people, things were desperate in San José. People make mistakes when they are under pressure. Only God knows why this happened, but I believe he always knows best, and this is all part of his plan."

"If God planned for evil people to kidnap Pilar, maybe he's to blame, Mama," Diego scoffed.

"Diego!" Yolanda scolded. "Don't blaspheme God. I brought you up better than that."

José shook his head at Diego as if to say, "Please don't provoke your mother."

Alejandro spoke up: "Diego, I appreciate you continuing to try to find Pilar. I can't do it myself, although there is nothing I would rather do. But I have to give Concepción a stable home and travel back and forth to San Miguel and Guanajuato to make a living."

"We all understand that," Diego said. He looked directly at his brother-in-law.

"I've wondered about how each of you will feel toward Pilar when I do find her. She may have been forced to do things some husbands would find unacceptable, Alejandro." Then he looked at his mother. "She may have been forced into a life that would be sinful in the eyes of your God."

"He is your God too, Diego. I wish you would remember that," Yolanda said, crossing herself.

"I don't care where she has been or what she has done; I love her and I want her back," Alejandro said. "I have never loved anyone else and never will. When you find her, please tell her that."

José rose and pulled Diego aside. He whispered so no one else could hear: "We all love Pilar and want her back, Diego. If you find that's not possible, at least we want to know what happened to her so Alejandro can go on with his life."

"I understand, Papa," Diego said. "But maybe I will have better luck finding her after I move to Houston."

CHAPTER 11

VICTOR

When John Chavez signed in to the desktop computer in his light-filled office on the twenty-fifth floor of One Shell Plaza in Houston, Texas, one morning in February 2011, he opened his inbox. The subject line of the first email contained a question:

RE: ARE YOU RELATED TO VICTOR CHAVEZ, WHO CAME FROM SAN JOSÉ, MEXICO?

The question took John Chavez by surprise. It was the only line in the email, sent to his work account. He didn't know what to make of it.

The short answer was yes. John's father was named Victor Chavez. He had passed away two years earlier from lung cancer. He'd never stopped smoking cigars, no matter how much John and his sister, Mary, had begged him to quit. John knew his father had come from Mexico in the 1960s, when he was a teenager. The border between Mexico and the US was pretty much open then, and he did not have papers, but he eventually became a US citizen during the Reagan amnesty program. Their mother, Angela, had had grandparents born in Mexico, but she'd been born in San Antonio, where her father had been a successful contractor. Neither Victor nor Angela had maintained ties with their Mexican heritage, preferring to assimilate in search of the American Dream.

Victor became highly successful in his adopted city and country. He had an entrepreneurial nature and a strong work ethic. Angela was a congenial, ambitious, intelligent woman. She had been well educated in all-girls private schools before she moved to Houston, and she was bilingual. During the 1970s, he and Angela opened a fresh fruit and produce stand in the Houston Heights, where many immigrants from Mexico lived. Over time, the produce stand became a boutique grocery store. One store grew into two and then three. By the time John was in middle school, the Chavez family also owned a dozen high-end specialty grocery stores in the best neighborhoods of southwest and west Houston. They moved to the upscale Tanglewood subdivision, where they lived in a comfortable ranch house on a large tree-shaded lot. English was the only language spoken in their home.

Victor and Angela enrolled John and then Mary, who was five years younger, in the Forest School, an elite private prep school. John and Mary led busy lives, full of sports, summer camps in the Texas hill country, and social events. They were never interested enough to ask their father about his heritage.

After graduating from Rice University, John attended the University of Texas Law School, finishing number one in his class. He then joined Hayden & Williams, the oldest and one of the most prestigious law firms in Texas, to begin his career as a corporate transaction lawyer.

From the beginning, John was considered a rising star at the firm, putting in countless billable hours. He acquired a mentor who saw that he was on all the right firm committees and belonged to the right clubs. He soon married Sara Beth Collins, the prettiest young woman working in the firm's attorney recruiting office. Sara Beth's family had "oil money" and lived in River Oaks. Three hundred people attended their wedding at St. John's Episcopal Church and the reception at the River Oaks Country Club. As soon as Sara Beth became pregnant, she retired to stay at home with their twins, Ashley and Andrew. They lived in a new house on Chevy Chase Drive, a wedding gift from Sara Beth's parents. She was an officer in the Junior League, president of the

Kappa Alpha Theta Alumni Association, and a charming hostess for clients and friends. Victor proudly told anyone who would listen that his son was living the American Dream.

John's younger sister, Mary, took a different direction with her life. She majored in sociology and English at Rice University, finishing with honors in less than four years. Over her father's objections, Mary spent one year with Teach for America in one of Houston's most challenging ghetto schools before earning her law degree with honors from Yale University. To the surprise of everyone, she turned down job offers from all the big Houston law firms and went to work with Harris County Legal Aid in 2009. She focused on helping foster children, homeless youth, and battered women.

John and his sister were close, often meeting for dinner at his home or at Mary's more modest one, a renovated hundred-year-old bungalow in the Woodland Heights neighborhood, close to downtown. Unlike back when her parents had opened their produce stand, the Heights was now a trendy transition area, full of young professionals.

John reread the strange email. He had never heard of San José, Mexico. The sender's name was Diego Gonzales. That meant nothing to him either. He hit DELETE and the message was gone.

• • •

John forgot about the odd message until he opened his computer two weeks later to find a new one:

> I MUST LOCATE VICTOR CHAVEZ, WHO LEFT SAN JOSÉ, MEXICO, FOR THE UNITED STATES IN 1966. IT IS IMPORTANT THAT I CONTACT HIM OR HIS FAMILY. IF YOU HAVE ANY INFORMATION, PLEASE CONTACT DIEGO GONZALES AT 832-666-2010 OR BY RETURN EMAIL AT YOUR

EARLIEST CONVENIENCE. PLEASE PARDON
THE INTRUSION.

"How weird," John said out loud.

"What's weird?" Elena, his secretary, asked. She was bringing him his morning coffee.

"I keep getting these emails from some guy named Diego Gonzales asking me if I am related to a Victor Chavez. I don't know if this is a scam or what," John told her, accepting his cup.

"Did you say Diego Gonzales?" Elena asked. "*The* Diego Gonzales? Let me see." She peered over his shoulder.

"I guess I'm out of the loop, Elena. Who in the hell is Diego Gonzales?"

Elena, who was young and single, rolled her eyes at her boss.

"He is a new player on the Storm soccer team. He was a rock star in Mexico, and the Storm signed him. He's tall, dark, hot, and single! Why is he emailing you? I've never heard you mention an interest in soccer."

"I don't know beans about soccer. But somebody went to the trouble of looking up my father's name. So, whatever this is, it's specifically targeted at me. I deleted the first message. Maybe I should do that again."

"Then again," Elena mused, "it could be from the real Diego Gonzales. He did just arrive here a few weeks ago. Is San José, Mexico, where your father came from?"

"I'm not sure. My father's name was Victor Chavez, and he probably came from Mexico about that time, but I have no idea from where. He would never talk about the old country—he insisted we were citizens of the United States and should be thankful for it."

"Well, I think you should at least show Diego Gonzales the courtesy of a reply. If it is really him, you should invite him here. After all, he is new to town and probably lonely," Elena said with a grin. "I would be happy to call him and make the arrangements. Wow!"

John's phone rang just then, and he didn't think about the email again until that night. He and Sara Beth had put the children to bed. His wife poured Rombauer Chardonnay into two of her Waterford white wine glasses, and they sat on the sun porch, as was their habit at the end of the day.

Sara Beth was telling him about the schedule for an upcoming charity gala she was chairing at River Oaks Country Club later in the spring. Half listening, John remembered the emails from Diego.

"Honey, the strangest thing happened. I received a couple of emails from a guy who Elena says is the new star of the Storm, asking if I am related to Victor Chavez."

"Your dad?"

"I don't know. I guess it could be. I can't decide whether to answer the guy or not."

"Well, if you know he's a reputable person, why not?" Sara Beth said. "Besides, if he's a big celebrity, maybe we can get him to do something for one of our charities."

"I guess I could meet him at the office for ten minutes and see what he wants. Elena is begging me to invite him in because he's 'hot.'"

"Maybe I should come too." Sara Beth smiled.

"What is it about you women and athletes?" John asked, smiling and ruffling her hair.

"Do you think you should invite Mary, since it concerns your family?"

"I'll give her a call and see if she's interested."

• • •

Diego appeared at the reception desk exactly on time. Elena could see that he was slim but muscular and handsome, just as she had expected. What surprised her was his serious air. He was not at all the flamboyant jock type she had expected. Instead he stood straight and tall a few feet away from the reception desk, where the pretty young receptionist kept trying to catch his eye. He had a black leather portfolio tucked under his arm.

Elena introduced herself as John Chavez's assistant, and Diego politely introduced himself with a warm smile. She escorted Diego upstairs to a small conference room, where John and Mary sat on the window side of a long mahogany table. Behind them, the Houston skyline stretched across the window. Two paintings of the West Texas landscape hung on opposite walls. John studied Diego with curiosity. He certainly had the build and height of a professional athlete, but his demeanor struck him as intense, although restrained. He was well mannered, thanking Elena before she left. He wore pressed Polo slacks and a navy blue sport coat over a white cotton shirt that was open at the neck. His shoes were Italian leather loafers. His only jewelry was an Omega watch. Diego nodded deferentially at John and Mary.

"Mr. Gonzales, welcome. I am John Chavez, and this is my sister, Mary. Won't you have a seat? Would you like something to drink?"

"No, thank you, señor. I will not take up too much of your time. I am not certain you are the people I have been looking for."

Diego noted that John had a slight build. He wore horn-rimmed glasses and a three-piece suit, and he sat very straight. He looked serious and older than his thirty-two years. Mary looked more relaxed and friendly, the pink in her cheeks set off by her tailored pale-pink silk blouse and pearls. Both of them had dark brown eyes and black hair. Mary's shiny, thick hair hung straight to her shoulders and was parted on the side. She was well groomed, with trimmed fingernails that were painted light pink. He thought she was very pretty.

"I was surprised when I received your emails, Señor Gonzales. Our father's name was Victor Chavez. He passed away two years ago. We know he came from Mexico, but he never told us anything about his family or history. Why are you looking for Victor Chavez?"

"Please, señor, call me Diego. I am sorry my English is not very good. I have been studying hard for the past year when I have time, but I am still a student."

"Your English is very good," Mary assured him. She thought he was a strikingly handsome man.

"To answer your question, the Victor Chavez for whom I am looking was the brother of Julio and Miguel Chavez, all of whom lived in my hometown of San José. Miguel was the youngest son. His oldest son, Alejandro, married my sister, Pilar."

Diego reached in his leather portfolio. He took out a small, faded snapshot. "This is a picture of Julio, Miguel, and Victor Chavez, taken the day of the Confirmation of Victor and the little girl in the picture in 1964. Victor is on the right, next to the girl."

John took the photo, and he and Mary studied it.

"You know, John. He looks a lot like you as a boy," Mary said. "He has the same cowlick and facial structure. Who is the pretty little girl, Diego?"

"Her name was Isabel Lourdes Torres Gomez," Diego said. "She's dead, sadly. She died only two years after this photo was taken."

"How? That's so young," Mary asked.

"It's a tragic story. Julio, the oldest brother, was dying of lung cancer in late 2009. He knew that I was searching for information about Victor's whereabouts. He summoned me and told me he could not go to God without confessing what he had done."

Diego cleared his throat before he went on. "Julio said he and Victor grew up next door to Isabel. Both brothers loved her. One night, when Julio was fourteen and Victor was twelve, Julio found Isabel and Victor in the courtyard of their home, kissing. He was jealous and lost his temper. He beat Victor until his brother was bruised and bleeding. Isabel watched, horrified. The next day, Julio was sorry and looked for Victor to apologize. But he couldn't find him. Victor and Isabel had run away.

"Two days later, a search party found Victor—dirty, crying, and crouched over the dead body of Isabel. They had tried to swim across a swollen river that was higher than usual, and she had drowned."

Mary let out a deep breath and looked at John. "That could explain why Dad was sometimes moody and never wanted to talk about Mexico," Mary said.

"Isabel's parents and the townspeople blamed Victor for Isabel's death. As soon as he was able, Victor packed a few belongings and left San José without telling anyone goodbye or contacting them again. That was in 1966. Julio told me this story on his deathbed in 2009. He confessed to being a coward in not telling anyone what caused Victor and Isabel to run away."

"How tragic for everyone!" Mary exclaimed. She was an instinctively empathetic person.

Looking directly at John, Diego said, "You are probably wondering why this stranger has been searching for Victor Chavez? I am here to ask your help."

"Help with what?" John asked.

"I am a foreigner in this country and do not know its ways—its legal system and its customs. I searched for your father hoping he would help me to find a girl I let down—my sister, Pilar. If your father is the Victor Chavez I seek, Pilar is the wife of your first cousin and my best friend as a boy, Alejandro Chavez."

Diego had finished talking, and John and Mary sat quietly, trying to take in and process this surprising new information about a possible family they hadn't known even existed before today.

John thought that Diego appeared to be a sincere, honest man. In his practice, he had seen all types of men and learned to be a pretty good judge of character. Yet John's immediate reaction was not positive. He had a full load of work at the firm and responsibilities at home. *Is this something with which I want to get involved? I'm not even sure our dad is the same Victor Chavez.*

Mary, on the other hand, was excited to learn that she might have a whole new family in Mexico. "Of course we will help you," Mary said after a few minutes. "Tell us what you know. You said someone took her; was she kidnapped or did she run away?"

"I believe she was kidnapped," Diego said. "It was my fault. I was selfish and left her in a vulnerable situation. In October of 2007, I drove her to Mexico City for a job interview. But instead of staying with her, I went to watch a professional soccer team practice. The interview was a trap, and she disappeared. I swore I would find her and bring her home, no matter how long it took."

"What did you do?" Mary asked.

"I was playing fútbol with a minor league club in León. The only way I could think of to get to Mexico City to be able to continue searching for her was to become a player with a professional club in the capital. San José is at least two hours away. It was too far to go back and forth, play fútbol, and help my papa in his store. I had always loved soccer more than anything and was good at it. I worked very hard until I was signed to be a striker for a Mexico City club."

"How long did that take?" Mary asked.

"Two seasons," Diego answered. "Then, during the two years I played with the Mexico City club, in between practice and matches, I searched. One night, I met an old man who told me he had seen girls taken from an office building in the neighborhood where Pilar disappeared. Gang members locked them in the back of a van and drove away. I believe the Sangre Negra cartel smuggled her across the border, probably to Texas. So I needed to get to the United States. When our club won the CONCAF championship last year, US teams, including Houston, sent me offers."

"Why did you focus on Houston?" Mary asked.

"Julio told me a mutual friend from San José visited Houston on business about fifteen years ago. He saw Victor's name on grocery stores. Curious, he went to see if it was the boy with whom he'd grown up. It was, although Victor was not interested in discussing old times.

It also just so happens Houston is the center of sex trafficking in the United States, so if Pilar was taken anywhere on this side of the Rio Grande, she probably has at least been through Houston."

"What? Surely not," John protested. "I've never seen any sex trafficking in Houston. We have a big Hispanic population, and I'm sure some of them are not legal, but they are good people. They work hard and are very family and church oriented. Of course, the newscasters talk about gang violence, but the gangs stay in their own neighborhoods and just kill each other."

"God, John, you live in such an inner-loop bubble," Mary murmured.

"I do not want to argue, señor," Diego said, "but in addition to the many good people from my country who live here, there are some bad people from Mexico and Central America. Gangs smuggle drugs and guns across the border, and the cartels have learned they can make a lot of money smuggling and selling girls. Houston has a reputation as a place where men can find any type of woman or child for sex. Some are willing prostitutes but many are victims, slaves. They are forced to sell their bodies, and the pimps keep the money. If they try to escape, they are beaten or killed or their families are murdered."

"Do you think that is what happened to your sister?" John asked, looking less comfortable.

"I am prepared to learn the worst. Nevertheless, if she is alive, I am determined to find and rescue Pilar from whatever situation she is in."

"I am a lawyer and a social worker, Diego," Mary said. "I work with a lot of young people who run away from home. They often become victims of pimps, international and American. I am sorry to learn a girl we are related to could be in the situation you describe."

"We don't know that we are related," John said.

"If the man Diego is searching for is our father," Mary responded, "then Pilar is our first cousin by marriage. Frankly, John, I am delighted to learn that we might have family."

"I would be grateful for any help you could give me," Diego said. "I don't know where to begin looking in this big city."

"Do you know anything that can get us started?" Mary asked.

"The old man said that Eduardo is the name of the pimp who put the girls into the van in Mexico City. He was a well-known pimp in the neighborhood. After the old man told me his story, I returned to the area from time to time. One night, I saw what I think was the same van and another abduction. I followed the van in my car to a heavily guarded house in the countryside. I didn't dare get any closer.

"A couple of weeks later, I went back to the house, and it looked deserted. I went in to look around and found a clue stuck in a wall between two stones in an out building, which seemed to have been used to hold and torture captives. This is the barrette Pilar had in her hair the day she disappeared." Diego pulled a tarnished silver barrette out of a pocket in his binder.

"How many years would that have been after she disappeared?" John asked, looking skeptical.

"Almost three years, señor. But when we were children, Pilar; our brother, Carlos; our friend Alejandro; and I would play a game where one person hides and the others search for them. The person hiding would place clues in between stones or under rocks so that the team-mate who was searching for the person hiding could find them before the other team found them. Pilar is very intelligent. She pushed the barrette into the wall so that it was not likely to be seen except by someone who was looking for such a clue."

"Did you find anything else?" Mary asked.

"No. Just then the local police pulled into the courtyard where I'd parked my car. They pointed their guns at me and told me to get out right away. They threatened to throw me in jail if I came back. I told them I was looking for my sister. One of them sneered, 'She's probably in Texas by now—or dead. Either way, you better forget about this place if you don't want to end up the same way.'"

"I would have been terrified!" Mary said.

"I was. And I realized there was nothing more I could do there in Mexico. I had to get to Texas. I thought if I could find your father, he might help me," Diego said.

I wonder if he would have helped? John thought. *He certainly didn't want anything to do with Mexico for as long as I knew him. Would he have softened if called upon to help another young girl?*

"Diego, I'll be honest," John said. "I am just a corporate lawyer with a large civil law firm. I don't know anything about criminal law. And obviously, I don't know anything about sex trafficking in Houston. I wouldn't know where to tell you to start—"

"Of course, we will help you," said Mary, cutting him off and smiling encouragingly at Diego. "But I must caution you that the Houston metropolitan area has about five million people. It is enormous. So is the state of Texas. It's a thousand miles from Beaumont to El Paso. Finding one girl who is probably being kept hidden will be like searching for a needle in a haystack."

CHAPTER 12

THE OTHER SIDE OF THE GALLERIA

Pilar let the hot water fall all over her head, feeling the soap suds wash away the filth that had accumulated in her long hair and on her body. It was the first opportunity to wash her entire body since the morning when she left San José. She had no idea how long ago that had been. Though the water cleaned her skin, it did nothing to remove the degradation and shame that she felt inside.

How foolish I was. I thought I could do anything—that I could save our family. I was just a stupid, naïve girl. I have ruined my life and caused everyone I love pain. I would give anything to hold my baby again and feel Alejandro's arms.

"Time's up! Get out of there before you use all the hot water," a man named Guillermo yelled at her, pulling back the shower curtain. He grabbed her arm, his thumb pressing hard against her soft flesh. Then he jerked her toward him so that her foot slipped in the wet tub and her knee jammed against the side of the tub. Pain shot through her body.

Josefina stood next to him in the bathroom, naked, shivering with fear and embarrassment, although all of them were long past innocence. Pilar thought that Josefina looked like a scared child. *That's because she is only a child, like Concepción. I must do a better job of protecting her than I have done for my own daughter,* Pilar told herself.

That morning, in early January 2008, Guillermo had come to the

stash house off Broadway, east of I-45, where the girls had been staying. The guards knew him. He ordered the girls to get in the backseat
of his dual-cab truck and said he was going to get them ready for work.
The motel room he took them to was small and shabby, with walls that
had once been painted light green but were now almost gray. There
was a broken table lamp on a small table, a dirty polyester floral bedspread, and a worn brown carpet on the floor.

"Put on the clothes that are on the bed," Guillermo barked at Pilar
as she walked out of the bathroom.

There was a bag on the bed. Pilar was dismayed at the stretchy satin
tank tops and short sequined skirts. The clothes were black and red
and unlike any garments she had ever seen. The tops were cut low in
front so that there could be no question as to what was inside.

"Where are the undergarments?" she meekly asked Guillermo, who
was still watching Josefina in the shower.

"You won't need them."

Shortly after Josefina exited the shower and she, Teresa, and Pilar
were dressed, three short, thin girls with black hair came to the room
carrying trays full of nail polish, files, and clippers. Pilar feared these
were new torture tools, but Guillermo told them to sit still while the
girls, who never looked directly at them, cleaned and polished their
finger and toe nails with red polish. The girls talked to each other
in a strange language Pilar had never heard before. While that was
happening, another girl dried Pilar's long hair with a hair dryer, cut
it off just below shoulder length, and used a curling iron to curl the
ends. Finally, one of the girls approached Pilar with a safety razor. Pilar
froze, not sure what would happen next, but the girl gave Pilar a timid
smile and pointed to her legs and armpits.

After they were done, Guillermo instructed Pilar, Teresa, and
Josefina to put on black shoes with thin high heels painted gold. Pilar
had never worn anything but sandals and low-heeled shoes. She found
it difficult to keep her balance and walk.

At 5 p.m., Pilar heard a series of knocks on the door. It was Eduardo. He was dressed in a pair of khaki slacks, a white Polo shirt, a brown leather belt with an oversized silver belt buckle, and brown Italian leather loafers. He flashed a smile and spread his arms to greet the girls, as if he were a young courtier coming to take them to a dance.

"Glad to see me, girls? I know it has not been a pleasant trip. That is regrettable but unavoidable. But now that we are reunited, we can get to work."

Eduardo smiled at Guillermo and said, "They look like movie stars. Maybe we should get you a job at Neiman Marcus." He winked at the girls.

Pilar shuddered at the sight of him. "Where are we going?" she asked. "I have a child who needs me. Please have pity and let us go home."

"I need you too, Pilar. I need you to make me lots of money," Eduardo said. "Besides, you girls are lucky! I captured you for Rosa Rodriguez, but I have a new client who will pay me more with less work. He owns a couple of classy men's clubs near the Galleria. Two big conferences are coming to town, and he needs extra girls in the back rooms. You'll work there for a while, entertaining a higher quality of customer than most girls see. It could be 'glamorous' if you look at it the right way. I can go back to Mexico and pick up three more girls off the street for Rosa for now.

"You just dance and smile and do whatever the customer tells you to do. Then you bring any money they give you to me. Any money, understand? Now let's go!"

"No!" Teresa said.

Everyone turned.

"I won't do your filthy work so you can make money off our backs!" Teresa sat on the floor with her arms and legs crossed and her mouth set in a grimace. "If I wanted to be a prostitute, I could have stayed home and done it. I don't care what you do to me or my damn family. They deserve to die."

"Guillermo," Eduardo said slowly, "take Teresa into the bathroom and persuade her that she will do what I tell her to do—but no marks on the face."

Guillermo strode across the room and picked up Teresa. He snatched the curling iron from where the girls had left it. She tried to scratch his face and bite his arm, but he was too big. He dragged her to the bathroom, slamming the door behind them. In a few minutes, they could hear Teresa's piercing screams.

Pilar held Josefina in her arms as the little girl sobbed. Pilar was terrified.

"Did you think that curling iron was just to make you look pretty?" Eduardo laughed. "It is also an excellent tool to make uncooperative girls behave. It will leave burns on her body but not anywhere obvious. She will heal, eventually."

Pilar felt light-headed. She had never imagined anyone could be so cruel to another human being. "Ay Diós!" she exclaimed.

"God has abandoned us," Josefina said.

"Shut up, you two," Eduardo said sharply. "There is no God. There is only Eduardo. Obey me and you might survive."

When Guillermo and Teresa emerged from the bathroom, Teresa's shirt had been torn. She had bright red burn marks on her stomach and lower back. She was writhing in pain.

"Ready to work now, Teresa?" Eduardo asked. Guillermo threw a new blouse at her.

As they prepared to leave the motel that evening, Eduardo said, "If you don't do what Guillermo tells you to do, he will beat and burn you, and our brother, Jesús, will kill your families in Mexico."

Pilar froze when she heard this. *Not only have I enslaved myself, but I have put Concepción, Alejandro, and my parents and brothers in mortal danger.* She wished this were a nightmare from which she could wake up.

Josefina was still holding on to her tight, and Teresa was moaning with pain from her burns.

• • •

Pilar sat in the backseat of a black Cadillac Escalade. The car followed the feeder road onto an entry ramp. She saw a sign that said they were traveling west on Interstate 10. In about ten minutes, to her left, she saw a cluster of the tallest buildings she had ever seen. They were close together and were beautiful. Glittering glass walls covered their sides, and some were topped with fanciful rooflines. Lights were coming on in some of the buildings. Crowded highways full of bright headlights circled. She felt very small. The car turned left off the highway onto a freeway marked 610 South. After they'd passed through a wooded area, another cluster of tall buildings appeared on the right. *How can a city have so many tall towers and cars?* Pilar wondered. *How will I ever find my way home if I do escape from Eduardo?* Josefina was holding her hand in a tight grip.

Guillermo exited the freeway. He turned right and drove on a six-lane street through what she guessed were stores because people were coming out of them carrying shopping bags. She sounded out the English letters of a large sign: "The Galleria." The people on the street looked like they were in a hurry but happy.

I want to scream for help! But these people don't see us.

The buildings grew smaller and more spread apart. Then Guillermo pulled into a parking lot behind a long white two-story building without any windows that looked like a walled castle in a children's book. The sign outside read "Jewel Box." Eduardo ushered them inside, where a large bald white man greeted him with a handshake. Eduardo spoke to the man in English. Pilar thought the man looked at the three girls as if he were inspecting a group of pots in the Mendoza Pottery Factory, deciding at the end of the day if they were good enough to be shipped off to a customer.

"They'll do," the man said. "Louise, get them ready."

A very thin middle-aged blonde white woman in a low-cut black sequined dress stood behind him, holding a cane in her hands. "Come with me," she ordered.

Louise led them to a small room with a CD player sitting on a table. She put on some salsa music and told them in Spanish to dance. When they stood numb, she ordered Josefina to dance, prodding her behind her knees with the cane. Josefina started to cry, but the woman yelled at her to stop acting like a baby. "Clients don't come here to see babies cry," she snickered. "They come here to feel the pleasure of being with a pleasant, compliant woman. You are a woman. If anyone asks you how old you are, say you are eighteen."

"I am only thirteen," Josefina sobbed. "I want my mama and papa. I want to go home."

The blonde woman smacked her across the back with the cane. "You were old enough to run away from home, now act like it. You are eighteen. Understand?" She whacked her again to make her point. "Now, how old are you?"

"Eighteen," Josefina sobbed.

"Good. Pull yourself together, and put on some of this mascara, blush, and lipstick. I am going to give each of you a room and bring clients to you. You must do whatever they tell you to do. But if they want intercourse, tell them it will cost extra, and make them wear a condom."

Horrified, Pilar put her arm around Josefina. She looked at Teresa, but the girl was tight-lipped and standing tall, although she still winced with pain from time to time.

"Condoms and price lists are on the tables in the rooms. Look like you are happy to be with them. When the time they paid for is up, a bell will ring in the room, and they should leave." The woman went on. "If they don't offer you a tip, ask for one. When they give it to you, put it in the slot at the top of the blue box on the table next to the couch. Someone will come by and collect the money at the end of the night. Comprende?"

Inside the building were no clocks, no windows. Louise put Pilar in a little room by herself with only a gold velvet-covered settee, a chair, and a small glass-and-chrome side table. A CD player, a box of condoms, and the box for tips sat on the table. She could hear music, a woman moaning, and male laughter coming from the next room. As she sat, Guillermo walked in and grabbed her, pulling at her neck.

"What is this?" he asked as he held out her silver crucifix.

"It was a gift from my parents. Please, please, don't take it," Pilar begged.

"Clients don't want to be reminded of religion when they are cheating on their wives with whores," Guillermo said, drawing his hand back quickly, breaking the chain. "Make no mistake, Pilar, you are a whore now, and you always will be a whore."

He threw the crucifix on the ground and walked out. As quickly as she could, Pilar rushed to the corner where her crucifix had fallen, snatched it up, and sat on the settee. She'd just hidden it beneath the pillow when the first client of the night came in.

After that, the night was a continuous stream of different men ordering her to do things for them. At first, Pilar thought they each looked different. But over time, they all began to look the same.

Because Pilar was in shock, she couldn't think of the words to communicate with the men—how to ask them for help or tell them what had happened to her. But none of them were interested in talking to her anyway. Most of them only wanted her to do things to them that Alejandro had never asked her to do. She knew the men thought they were having sex, but this was not the sex she knew and cherished. What was done in this place was impersonal, disgusting, and humiliating. But she was afraid not to comply.

When the night finally ended, Guillermo escorted the girls to the car. Pilar's eyes squinted at the early morning light. She was exhausted and thoroughly humiliated. She wanted to be detached from her body. After the long, horrible trip from Mexico City to the Jewel Box what was left of Pilar Chavez, wife of Alejandro Chavez, daughter of Yolanda and José Gonzales was dead.

• • •

Pilar awoke when Guillermo shook her.

"It's time to eat something and get ready for work," he said.

She had been too tired to notice where she'd fallen into bed last night, but now she realized she was back in the dingy motel room, sharing a bed with Josefina and Teresa. In the daylight, she could see that the windows were barred. During the night, she thought she had heard girls and customers in other rooms speaking Spanish, some English, even languages she had never heard before.

Every night for two years, Guillermo took Pilar, Josefina, and Teresa to the Jewel Box or another club that the same people owned. There were no calendars, clocks, or any way to keep track of time. But there had been Christmas decorations in the Jewel Box when they'd first gone there, and much later, the same decorations reappeared and then were taken down—making Pilar realize a year had passed.

In the small, windowless rooms in the back of these clubs, the men never stopped coming. There were old men and young men. Some were white, some were Hispanic, some were black or shades of brown. During sports seasons, athletes came to the clubs. Pilar tried to get the American men to talk so that she could learn more English and prepare for making her way home, should she escape, but most of the time she was too tired to try. Pilar and the other girls slept the majority of the days after their shifts. Sleep let them forget.

Despite Pilar's efforts to keep hope of escape alive in the younger girls, Teresa grew increasingly depressed. Sometimes she would cry uncontrollably, and this made her an unreliable worker. One day, Guillermo opened the bathroom door and discovered Teresa holding the shard from a glass she had broken on the floor against her wrists. He injected her with something that made her very calm. Before long, Teresa craved the injections. Pilar tried to talk Teresa into refusing. Another girl at the club told Pilar that Teresa was addicted to heroin. "She is beyond your help," the other girl said.

Maybe we are all beyond help, Pilar thought. After that, Pilar did not try to stop Teresa. She did not try to stop anything or anyone; she silently did what she was told to do. She was losing hope of ever getting home to her baby again. The basic human instinct to suffer to survive began to replace hope.

• • •

One night, a small Mexican man in a suit came into Pilar's room. He seemed somewhat uncomfortable, unlike most of her customers. He did not look her in the eyes at first. As if by rote, Pilar asked him if he wanted a dance, and he replied, "Sí, señorita, por favor," looking directly at her for the first time.

Pilar had stopped looking at the men as individuals; they were all just part of an unending flow of men. But something about his face and his accent made her look more closely at him. Slowly, she realized that she had once known this man, in her prior life, in Mexico. He was a buyer for a big company that purchased pottery from the Mendoza Pottery Factory. He visited the factory several times a year.

"Señor Trevino!" Pilar said. "I can't believe it is you! Gracias a Diós!"

The man looked unnerved. "I am sorry, señorita, how do you know my name? I didn't give my real name to anyone."

Rafael Trevino looked over the woman in front of him. She was made up and dressed like a high-class call girl and spoke the dialect of northern Mexico, but he never visited whores in Mexico. This was his first trip to Houston. How did she know who he was?

Sensing his confusion and discomfort, Pilar said, "You do not recognize me like this. I am Pilar Chavez. I worked in the office of the Mendoza factory in San José."

"Pilar Chavez? Pilar, what are you doing in this place dressed like this?"

"Oh, señor, evil people kidnapped me and are holding me captive," Pilar whispered. "Please help me get out of here." Pilar reached for his hand, but he pulled away before she could grab it.

Señor Trevino looked around nervously. "Pilar, there are guards all around this building and a high fence. I can't help you get out of here. These people would kill both of us."

"I don't care if they kill me. I am dead here anyway," Pilar said. "Please, please, señor, could you at least call the police when you leave and tell them there are girls being held captive here? Maybe they are honest. Maybe they will come rescue us and take the terrible people who are enslaving us to jail."

"I don't think the American police would take the word of a Mexican man and arrest rich American men, Pilar."

"You are my only chance, señor. I haven't seen anyone else who knows me or knows what happened to me since I was brought across the Rio Grande. I don't even know how long ago that was. But I know you must be here for a reason."

"I think it was just chance, Pilar."

Pilar tried to touch his hand again, but again he retreated. Defeated, she sank down onto the chair and was silent for a minute. "Señor, at least can you tell my husband, Alejandro Chavez, what happened to me? Where I am?"

"Pilar, I am so sorry for your misfortune. But understand my position. I have a good reputation to maintain. I have a wife and five children. If they found out I was in a place like this, my wife would kill me. No one can know I have been here."

The fact that this man, who had known her and her boss, who had always been friendly when she'd been a respectable woman, could so easily ignore the inhuman situation she was now in, refusing to help her in any way for the sake of his reputation, was difficult for her to accept. She'd thought she was beyond feeling anger, but now she felt deep, strong anger well up inside her.

Pilar rose and stood in front of him with her fists clenched. No longer caring if anyone outside the room heard her, Pilar said in a strong voice: "I have a child too, señor! I hope you go to your death knowing you could have helped a captive, abused woman get out of hell and back to her family, but you chose not to do so!"

"I'm sorry. I just can't risk it."

Pilar forced herself to calm down, knowing this man was perhaps her only hope of escape. "Well, could you send an anonymous note to my husband about where you saw me? You could send it to Señor Mendoza's address at the pottery factory. Please, señor."

Señor Trevino's demeanor had not softened. Any moral decision considered and definitively dismissed, he was now looking at Pilar with the original intent of his visit.

"I'm not promising, Pilar, but maybe I could do something like that. I will consider it."

"Please, please, señor," Pilar begged.

He said, "I always thought you were a beautiful woman. You have changed, but I am still feeling aroused. Maybe it would help me make up my mind if you let me get intimate with you."

Pilar was horrified and totally deflated, but she did what he asked. She had no choice.

As Señor Trevino put his hands on her body, entered her as if she were a stranger and not someone he'd known as a respectable woman, Pilar wondered if she could even hope that he would do the right thing.

Trying to escape from the situation, Pilar let her mind wander. Before Mexico City, she was considered a positive person who spread joy to those around her. But these long months of working at the Jewel

Box and sleeping beside Josefina and Teresa in the dingy motel had dimmed her faith in human kindness. The men who came to her every night, the people who sold her like a piece of meat, they had shown moral corruption worse than she could ever have imagined.

When Señor Trevino was satisfied, he quickly pulled up his pants and got ready to leave. Pilar swallowed any pride she had left and begged him again, "Please, señor, send a note to Señor Mendoza and tell him where I am. Ask him to tell my family what happened to me. I am so ashamed, but I want them to know I didn't leave them on purpose. I was just a foolish girl. I am so sorry."

"I said I will consider it, Pilar," Señor Trevino said, trying to make a quick exit. Then he stopped, fished in his pocket for money, and placed ten dollars in the tip jar. He hurried out the door, not seeing that Pilar's face had turned bright red with shame.

• • •

When the club was not very busy late at night, Pilar was able to sit in her room alone. She treasured these moments of quiet and privacy. If the rooms were unoccupied by customers, the cleaning crew, all of whom were Mexicans, were permitted to enter the girls' rooms to straighten up or vacuum the floor. The woman who came to clean Pilar's room was small and old. She never spoke.

Then one night Pilar heard the woman humming the Mother Mary lullaby. It was a slow, sweet song.

"I know that song," Pilar whispered. "My mother used to sing it to me when I was a child, and I sang it to my daughter."

The woman smiled when Pilar spoke. It was as if she had been waiting for this all along. "I sang it to my children too," the woman replied. "It was a long time ago, and they are all grown and gone now. But it still can bring the soul peace. Do you know what the words mean, señorita?"

"Hail Mary, mother to all little children. You love each of us. You will hear us in our troubles, and if we pray to you, you will answer our prayers."

"Sí," the woman replied.

"She hasn't heard me, señora," Pilar murmured.

"Have you prayed to her?"

"At first, when I was kidnapped and taken away from my husband and daughter, I prayed to her all the time to save me," Pilar sighed. "But here I am, so I guess she doesn't care about women like me."

"Of course she does, child," the woman whispered. She looked around. "The mother cares most about women who are forced to do immoral things by evil men. My name is Consuelo. Some people think I have an unfortunate life, cleaning up in a place like this. But I think it is God's plan that I can give words of comfort to girls who are victims of the Devil's followers."

Pilar thought of Señor Trevino and how she had been given a glimpse of salvation, only to be used by the man and casually tossed back into hell. "I don't think God or any person on this earth cares about me or can help me. No one even knows where I am. I have tried to escape but failed. But I have no one to blame but myself for my situation."

"Poor little one," Consuelo said. "Do you want me to pray with you for a minute? I will close the door."

Tears welled up in Pilar's eyes. The old woman was the first person to offer her a kind word, a sympathetic smile, in all the months since she left San José.

"Gracias," Pilar said. "You must be an angel. I will pray with you."

After that, Consuelo came to see Pilar whenever Pilar was alone. Mostly, they just talked and prayed, or Pilar would listen to the old woman sing while she worked. Pilar had managed to keep her silver crucifix. One night, Pilar handed it to the old woman and asked her to keep it. "I don't know how much longer I can hide this. If I ever escape from this life, you can give it back."

"Ay, little one, I look forward to that day," Consuelo said, taking the crucifix from Pilar.

• • •

One morning in the summer of 2008, Pilar, Josefina, and Teresa were asleep at the motel when Ivan, a swarthy East European man, appeared. The girls had seen him before with Guillermo.

"Here she is," Guillermo said, pointing to Teresa. "Take her."

The loudness of his voice caused all of the girls to wake up. Pilar and Josefina were horrified. Even though Teresa existed in a cocaine cloud, they had suffered through enough together to have formed a family of sorts. Josefina clung to Teresa as Ivan and Guillermo pulled her out of the girls' bed. Teresa didn't resist. She seemed for some time to have accepted her fate and didn't care what happened to her.

"Where are you taking her?" Josefina asked, crying, as Ivan led her outside.

He loaded Teresa into a rusty pickup truck idling in the parking lot.

"She is going to one of the Russians' places in the port," Guillermo growled after the door closed behind Teresa and Ivan. They heard the motor of his truck turn on. "She's too wasted for customers in the better clubs. They don't like druggies. Let this be a lesson to you not to refuse to do what I tell you to do. I can give you the needle, too."

"What's the port?" Pilar asked him.

"Port of Houston," Guillermo answered. "Tankers and cargo ships from every place in the world come in and go out all day, every day. It's one of the biggest ports in the world. Many brothels and hookers down there. Those sailors are out to sea for months. They go crazy wild for pussy when they get back on shore. They don't care if a woman is alive or dead. Not a great place to end up. But the way she's going, before long she won't care."

Pilar shuddered as Josefina clung to her.

"Just when you think things can't get any worse," Guillermo mused, "they do!" Then he laughed at what he considered his cleverness.

Is this what Eduardo will do to us someday? Pilar shuddered.

CHAPTER 13

LOS ARBOLES

I n March 2009, the owner of the Jewel Box told Eduardo he was going to have to cut the number of girls working there, including Pilar and Josefina. He explained that with the economy crashing, business was slow.

Eduardo told the girls, "You're moving today. Pack up your things."

Josefina looked around the dreary motel room and shrugged. She had nothing to pack.

Pilar had continued to hope that Señor Trevino would eventually let Señor Mendoza or Alejandro know what had happened to her. Now, even if he did tell someone where she was, she would be gone.

"Where are we going?" she asked Guillermo.

"The barrio, chicas," he grumbled.

Guillermo drove the Escalade south on I-45. He exited at Telephone Road and turned right.

Most of the shops and used car dealerships, piled one on top of another, had signs in Spanish. They could hear airplanes overhead. The air had a putrid chemical smell.

"It looks like Mexico!" Josefina exclaimed.

Pilar had a bad feeling. The men and boys standing around smoking on Telephone Road were covered in tattoos and rough looking. No one was smiling. Trash lay on the sidewalks. The buildings had windows that were boarded up or blacked out.

At 2 p.m., Guillermo stopped in front of a long two-story wooden building painted yellow. The name "Los Arboles" was painted on the side of it in red. A bright yellow food truck advertising tacos and cabrito was parked in front. He pulled around back into a parking lot. From there, Pilar saw that the establishment was quite extensive. There were two old wooden shotgun houses on the side and one to the rear. There were patches of grass, untrimmed bushes, and covered walkways between some of the buildings. A ten-foot wooden fence surrounded the entire area.

When they entered the building, they walked into a large, low-ceilinged room. There were Formica-topped tables and stainless steel 1950s kitchen chairs with shabby red vinyl seats. A long bar, a large jukebox, and a pool table and rack were the only other things in the room. The walls were plastered with posters of bullfighters and half-clad women. A man putting away Modelo and Don Julio bottles behind the bar looked up at them, appraising them. Pilar and Josefina looked down.

"Looking for Rosa?" he asked Guillermo. He pointed to a door opposite the stage. "You bringing the new meat?"

Pilar winced.

"Sí," Guillermo replied. "Rosa's expecting a delivery of girls from Eduardo."

The man showed Guillermo and the girls into an office in the back of the bar area. It was larger than it looked from the outside. There were two wooden desks, one behind the other, and a few wooden chairs in front of the bigger desk. Only one window looked out on the driveway, so it was dark even in the middle of the day. A middle-aged woman sat at the first desk, smoking a cigarette. Her hair was bottle-black with a white streak running from her forehead back on the side. She wore thick black eyeliner and mascara over her watery brown eyes. Her lips and nails were painted purplish red.

"Señora Rodriguez," Guillermo said. "These are the girls from Mexico that you ordered from Eduardo."

Rosa didn't look up from the paper she was reading. "They'll do. Where's your devil of a brother? You know I like seeing his pretty face."

"Sí, señora," Guillermo said, backing away to the door to leave. "He'll be here to collect his money on Monday as usual."

Rosa Rodriguez stood up, and Pilar saw that her spine was curved so that her body was slightly bent over. She was hideous. Pilar shivered.

"Esther," Rosa yelled in a voice raspy from years of smoking tobacco.

A short, stocky woman with a brown complexion shuffled into the room, wearing baggy jeans, athletic shoes, and a man's black long-sleeved shirt. At first, Pilar thought she was a man.

"Esther is my bottom bitch," Rosa said. "You do everything she says or my son, Tito, will beat you, or worse." She turned to the stocky woman. "Get this new meat upstairs. They work tonight."

Pilar and Josefina followed Esther back through the main bar area and then through a curtained doorway to the right of the bar, where they climbed a narrow, dark flight of stairs. She led them past a slight young Mexican man with his hair in a ponytail who was twisting the arm of a young girl with a tattoo of a tiger on her neck. The girl whimpered, "Sí, Angel," and he let her go.

"Eduardo's still your padrón—or your pimp," Esther said to them. "Angel has his own girls."

"This is yours," Esther said to Pilar. She had stopped at a small room at the end of a long hallway where ten rooms lined both sides of the hallway. Then Esther pointed to an identical room next door and said to Josefina, "That's yours."

Pilar's room was small, only a few feet longer than her body, with no windows and a bare floor. The walls were plywood, as if the room had been carved out of a bigger space, and empty except for a lumpy twin-bed mattress on a small pallet. A metal chair sat in the corner next to a small table that held some objects Pilar could not identify, along with a pitcher and a glass. A light bulb hung from wires strung across the room. Pilar choked from the stench in the air.

Esther barked out instructions in Spanish in a hoarse voice: "You will work here at night and sleep here during the day. You get clean sheets once a week. The customers choose their girls. Don't talk to them; just do what they tell you to do. If you don't, Tito will beat you."

Esther cleared her throat and continued, "We sell you in increments of time. We sell condoms to the customers. If they refuse, don't argue with them. You can buy them if you have any money, which you probably won't. Eduardo doesn't splurge on his girls." Pilar couldn't believe how Esther could give these awful instructions in such an unimpassioned voice. It was as if she were reading from a grocery list she had long ago memorized. Then she realized this woman had given these warnings to many girls many times before.

"Eduardo will be here to check on you from time to time," Esther finished. "Remember, Eduardo may own you, but you work for Rosa. I enforce her rules. Understand, chicas?"

Pilar wanted to scream and say "no!" but she remembered the injections that Guillermo had given Teresa when the girl had been unreliable—how those injections had gotten her sent to a worse place. So Pilar said nothing.

"Your customers will come in a few hours," Esther said, walking away.

Terrified, Josefina wobbled a little, so Pilar led the young girl to her pallet. She sat on the floor beside Josefina's bed, brushing her hand across Josefina's forehead.

"I don't know what I would do without you, Pilar," Josefina said, her young voice wavering. "I'm just a stupid child. No, I'm a stupid whore. Without you I probably would have ended up a druggie like Teresa."

"You are stronger than you think, míja," Pilar said, smoothing her hair. "I know this place is horrible, but they won't be watching us all the time." Pilar leaned in and whispered next to Josefina's ear, "We will find a way to escape." But looking around at their new prison, Pilar wasn't certain she believed this herself anymore.

• • •

Time began to pass for the girls in a way similar to when they'd worked at the Jewel Box. Pilar and Josefina slept during the day and worked all night. The customers were more demanding than the men who'd bought them in the Galleria clubs, and these men were often drunk and violent.

Rosa was not afraid of violence. In fact, she seemed to encourage it. She permitted her clients to beat the girls so long as they did not leave any marks on their faces. If a customer complained about a girl, Rosa had her oldest son, Tito, beat her.

After a few weeks, Pilar began to worry about Josefina. Josefina was a small girl to start, but she became even thinner and more dispirited during that first year at Los Arboles. Many of the girls who had been there a long time had a vacant look in their eyes. Their actions looked automatic, as if the human life had been sucked out of them. Sickness was common. Pilar heard girls talk about the pain they felt down below, even to the point it became difficult to walk. Pilar made every effort she could to keep herself and Josefina clean and healthy, although she had little control over that. After six months of the life, Josefina started scratching herself and complaining of a burning sensation. Pilar knew she had contracted a disease.

Sometimes Josefina couldn't satisfy a customer. Pilar could hear these men assault her through the thin plywood walls that separated them. If Pilar was alone, she would go next door and try to head off the beating or take it herself. Once, Esther caught her trying to sneak into Josefina's room in such a situation. She called Tito. He beat both girls while Esther watched.

Some of the men refused to wear a condom. The thought of getting pregnant or contracting a disease terrified the girls. They had seen pimps beat girls whose bellies had grown big in order to kill what was growing inside them. If that didn't work, Tito would take them to a backstreet "doctor" who would cut the baby out of them. Sometimes word circulated that Rosa had moved a girl to one of the notorious brothels she owned around the port. Pilar was terrified of being sent to the port, so she did what she was told to do.

Pilar sometimes thought of escape, but it was hard to figure out how she could do it. Men with guns prowled around the property day and night. And then there was Esther—the watchdog's room was at the head of the stairs, and a bartender or bouncer was always at the bottom.

Eduardo appeared at least once a week to check on his property. First, though, he would spend an hour or two in Rosa's office. Rosa made no secret of the fact that she was enamored of Eduardo's good looks and charm. She was too smart to fully trust him, however.

For his part, Eduardo coveted Rosa's business and money. He flattered and teased her, trying to figure out how he could get a cut of her business.

One morning in June 2010, there was such a commotion in the building that it woke everyone. The girls gathered around the stairway to the cantina, listening. Above the general chatter, they could hear Rosa's gravelly voice screaming as if in agony.

Esther came up the stairs. Knowing she had information that the girls wanted, she leered at them and walked into her room without saying anything.

"Damn the bitch!" one of the girls whispered.

It wasn't until that night that they found out from customers that Rosa's daughter, Alba, who'd kept the books and managed the cash at Los Arboles, had been murdered. Her husband had found her in a dance hall on Highway 3 in South Houston with another man. He'd shot both in the parking lot and taken off.

The next afternoon, Pilar was asleep, dreaming of her daughter, when Eduardo came into her room and shook her. "Get up, Pilar. We have to go."

"Where are we going?" she asked, her voice heavy with sleep. Pilar had not been out of Los Arboles since she arrived. Her first thought

when her mind cleared was that Eduardo was taking her to the port.
"No!" she said, trying to shake off his grip on her arm. "I don't want to
go to the port. I've done what you told me to do!"

Eduardo stopped and smiled to himself as he pushed her down the
hall. Several thoughts rushed through Pilar's mind. After over a year of
doing the same thing every day, any change was confusing, frightening.

"Where are you taking me? Where is Josefina? I can't leave her
here alone."

When they reached the stairway, Esther came out of her room.

"What's going on?" she asked, blocking his path.

"I'm taking my girl to a new place," he told her, pushing her aside.

Josefina opened her door and cried, "Pilar, where are you going?
Don't leave me!"

"Be strong, Josefina," Pilar called as Eduardo dragged her down the
stairs. "I will come back for you. I promise!"

Eduardo took Pilar out a back door and loaded her into the back of
the black Escalade.

"Please, Eduardo, don't take me to the port," Pilar cried.

"You are not going to the port yet, Pilar. You are going to Walmart,"
Eduardo said. "We're getting you some new clothes. You're getting a
promotion."

Pilar sat in the backseat, scared, listening to the conversation
between the brothers.

"What's going on?" Guillermo asked Eduardo.

"Today is our lucky day, brother," Eduardo said. "Rosa is in sudden
need of an office assistant and bookkeeper, and I have one right here
in this car."

"Pilar?" Guillermo asked.

"Exactly." Eduardo smiled. "Remember where I told you I found her?"

"Some shitty little town," Guillermo said.

"She was the office manager and bookkeeper in a pottery factory.

There's not much difference between keeping the books and handling the money, whether you're selling pots or selling girls."

"But that's Alba's job," Guillermo said.

"It was. Alba's husband found her with another guy at a cantina and shot both of them on the spot—dead! When I heard the sad news, I immediately thought about putting Pilar in as Rosa's assistant. If we play our cards right, we could steal some of it away from her with the information Pilar gets."

"That's pretty good thinking." Guillermo smiled. "But how are you going to get Rosa to agree to let one of your whores work for her?"

"When I went to express my condolences, Rosa was moaning about how she was going to handle the books and cash without Alba. I told her I knew a girl with office experience and that her boss owed me a favor, so I could probably get her here tomorrow. When we get done fixing up Pilar, Rosa will never recognize her. Pilar was quite a beauty when I found her. The last couple of years have taken their toll, but new clothes, soap and water, and some makeup can work wonders."

Guillermo turned off I-45, and after a few miles he exited the 610 Loop and turned into the parking lot for Walmart.

Three hours later, Pilar was sitting on a bed in a room with Eduardo and Guillermo. A Walmart bag stuffed with two conservative dresses, a black pencil skirt, two white cotton blouses, a pair of black flat pumps, a black purse, and a cheap string of pearls and pearl studs lay beside her. The men were watching a soccer game on the television. The Storm were playing Miami. The sight of a soccer pitch full of handsome young athletes made Pilar think of Diego. "I wonder where he is now?" she murmured.

"What?" Eduardo asked.

"My brother is a fútbol player," Pilar mumbled.

"That brainless brother who left you alone in Mexico City?" Eduardo asked, looking at Guillermo. "He's probably digging ditches back in the countryside." They both chuckled. When a commercial came on, Eduardo turned to Pilar.

"Put on one of the new outfits I bought you. But first, take a shower and wash your hair. Make it look nice, like when I first met you in San José."

"Why? What do you want of me now?" Pilar asked. She felt weary.

"I told you, you are getting a promotion. You are going to work for me in a different way. You are going to be a trusted office assistant for Rosa Rodriguez. Her daughter, Alba, did that work, but Alba died. Rosa needs someone to do bookkeeping, count the cash, and deal with vendors. It will be just like when I met you at that factory, only instead of pots, the product is chicas."

Pilar was astonished. In the shower, she savored the hot water falling over her body, washing away the filth on her skin. She tried to absorb what this "promotion" might mean. *I won't have to screw those filthy men. Maybe I can find a way to escape. No more Esther! But I don't trust Eduardo.*

Then she realized what her new job meant: *I will be helping them sell other women, even Josefina!*

Pilar dried her hair and put on the plain dress and shoes Eduardo had picked out, then she looked in the mirror. *My skin is pale from being inside all the time. My eyes are not bright. There are dark circles under them. I think I see a few grays in my lifeless hair. It is longer than it has ever been. I always had strong muscles in my arms. They are gone now.* She stepped into the room where the men were still watching the game. Eduardo looked at Pilar and seemed pleased, but then his brow furrowed.

"Bring me the scissors, Guillermo," he said. He carefully cut off Pilar's hair just above her shoulders. Then he took some of her hair in the front and cut a few strands to form bangs. He handed her some pink lipstick and a pair of low-resolution reader glasses. "There! You are a new woman!"

She looked in the mirror again. *Who am I now?*

Guillermo drove Eduardo and Pilar back to Los Arboles the next morning. On the way, Eduardo gave her instructions.

"You will be Rosa's bookkeeper, cash manager, and office assistant. You will make her like and trust you. Find ways to be useful and expand your duties. At night, you will walk to the rear of the building, and Guillermo will be waiting to bring you back to me. You will tell me everything you see and learn about her business. If she catches on to what you are doing, she will kill you. Never go upstairs again where the other girls can see you. Try to avoid Esther. Understand?"

"Sí," Pilar said. She realized that Eduardo was putting her in a position where he needed her cooperation, so she finally had some leverage over him. "But there is something I need you to do for me in return."

"What?" Eduardo roared. "You think you can make demands on me? Did you hear the whore, Guillermo?"

Guillermo looked terrified.

Pilar was shaking, but she continued. "Josefina has caught a disease. Esther will just tell her to suffer and not tell the customers. You can take her to a doctor. I will do everything you ask me. All I ask is that you take care of Josefina in return."

Pilar was terrified as she finished. She knew Eduardo could kill her and Josefina or beat them for what he would call her "impudence." She also knew he wanted the information she would glean from her new position, and she was betting he was willing to pay for it in this small way. After all, he made money selling Josefina, too. It was in his best interest to keep her working.

The rest of the car ride was silent as Eduardo considered Pilar's request.

When Guillermo pulled the car up to Los Arboles, Eduardo finally said, "I will take Josefina to a doctor, but don't ever try something like this again, Pilar, or I will kill you both. I can always get other girls."

• • •

When Eduardo presented Pilar to Rosa, Rosa insisted on interrogating her. "What is your name and where are you from?" She asked. Pilar feared Rosa would recognize her as one of her girls, but Rosa never went upstairs, leaving Esther to rule that domain. She had only seen Pilar the day Guillermo brought her and Josefina to Los Arboles, and she had barely glanced at them then.

"Do you have family here in the United States?"

"No, I have no family," Pilar said, although her mind shot back to sitting at her mama and papa's table with Diego and Carlos when they were all children. She quickly shut that thought down.

"How do you know Eduardo?" Rosa asked.

"He is a customer of the business where I work now. I don't know him very well. He said I would make more money here."

Rosa's voice was sharp and probing when she began questioning Pilar. She knew enough about Eduardo to be distrustful. "I assume Eduardo told you the skill this position requires. What is your experience?" Rosa said.

"I worked in an office in a factory in Mexico for two years. I did all the ordering of supplies and shipping of finished products, paid the salaries, and kept the books for the business," Pilar said. That much was true. Then she went on, "I came across the river a year ago after my mother died, hoping to find a better life."

"I am pleased, Eduardo," Rosa said finally. "Pilar, you work at the desk behind mine in my office. You can live in one of my houses here on the property."

"She has a place to live, Rosa," Eduardo interrupted. "I have offered Guillermo to drive her to and from work until she learns the bus routes."

"I can keep my eye on her here, Eduardo," Rosa told him. "Do you think I would let anyone who knows everything about my business wander around the streets of Houston? Even with an honest man like you or Guillermo? I'm not that stupid."

Turning to Pilar, she said, "Do not leave this room unless I tell you to do so. Don't talk to anyone. If you tell someone what goes on here, one of my boys will slit your throat."

Pilar shuddered. She believed her.

Rosa smiled and said, "I am grateful to you, Eduardo. You have done well. You can go now."

Pilar watched Eduardo leave, his face flushed. She felt pleased.

During the first few weeks, Pilar found it almost liberating to be in the small office, often by herself since Rosa was awake all night watching the cantina. The madam often took naps during the day. The office had a window looking out at a driveway. Although the high fence blocked any view, she could see daylight. She ached to visit Josefina and tell her she was still close by, but she knew that would be too dangerous for both of them.

The bookkeeping system was simple. Tito or one of the other muscle guys stood at the door and collected the clients' entrance fees. Men paid for drinks from the bar. Tito and the barkeepers turned their money in to Rosa before they left in the morning. If a customer wanted to go upstairs and purchase time with a girl, he paid Rosa's sister, the cashier, for the time, for condoms, and for anything else he wanted. A man with tattoos on both arms and a tiger on his neck peddled drugs in the cantina. He paid Rosa a small commission. Rosa took these cash receipts and gave them to Pilar in the morning. On Mondays, the pimps like Eduardo collected their share of their girls' earnings from Rosa.

Pilar learned that Rosa owned brothels and cantinas all over the Channelview area and Southeast Houston. The receipts, net of pimp proceeds, also were funneled through the Los Arboles office. Pilar was astonished at how much money the business generated, more than $100,000 a month in most months.

Pilar put 20 percent of the gross cash receipts, net of the commission paid to her by the drug peddler, in an envelope every week for a big Mexican man to pick up. When Pilar asked Rosa how she should enter this cash payment on the books, Rosa grumbled to herself. Then she said, "Just put it under 'El Diablo.'"

Twice a week, on Monday and Wednesday afternoons, Tito would drive Pilar to a neighborhood branch bank in a black Ford F-150 to make a deposit. These were always in cash. Tito told Pilar to go to the same cashier every time, a white woman who seemed to know Tito. Pilar thought the cashier looked nervous when they approached her window. He told her not to talk with any of the other cashiers. He was always right beside her.

At least once a week, Eduardo visited Rosa. He would banter and flirt with her for a few minutes and then leave. If Rosa was not in the office, he would go directly to Pilar's desk.

"Tell me what you have learned about Rosa's business," he would say.

"She only gives me the numbers. That's all I know. She makes a lot of money," Pilar would answer. But she knew he knew that.

As Pilar settled in, she improved on Alba's bookkeeping system. Pilar also discovered that Alba had been siphoning off money for herself. When she showed Rosa what her daughter had done, Rosa was livid.

"That bitch! I gave her everything she had and she cheated me? I hope she burns in hell with that no-good husband of hers," Rosa spat. "If I'd known about this, I would have shot her myself!"

After that, Rosa came to trust and value Pilar, who always did what she was told and did it more efficiently than her daughter had ever done. Esther eventually recognized Pilar and took delight in exposing her to Rosa as one of Eduardo's upstairs whores. She was disappointed, though, when Rosa only chuckled and murmured, "That Eduardo is a sly devil."

One afternoon, after consuming an unusually large amount of the good tequila and rapping on how all men were disgusting animals, she confided that she had poisoned her husband after she found him upstairs repeatedly with the chicas. When she finished this story, she stood up suddenly, pounded her fist on the table, and said, "I couldn't let him give me some disease he caught from one of those whores. I asked him to stop, but he didn't. I had to kill the bastard!"

Pilar wondered if she should be more afraid of Rosa or Eduardo.

CHAPTER 14

KING OF HEARTS

Diego was eager to prove his worth as a new member of the Storm for the 2011 season. He was the first man on the practice field in the morning, stretching and practicing. He often stayed late after everyone else left so that he could do an extra workout. He was passionate about the game. On the pitch he played hard, eager to win a spot in the starting lineup.

Two weeks after their meeting in John's office, Diego and Mary met at the Craftsman-style bungalow she owned in Woodland Heights. It had been built in the 1920s, but she had had it renovated like many of the period houses in the neighborhood. Now it was painted light gray with white trim, had a wide front porch with white columns and a hanging swing, and included a white picket fence all around the small yard. Mature oak trees towered over pink and red knockout rose beds. She greeted him at the door with a bottle of tequila and a bottle of wine. "Hola!" she said. "Pick your poison."

"You are a gracious hostess, Mary," Diego said. "I don't drink alcohol anymore. I need my mind to stay sharp. But please, you go ahead. I'll have a glass of water, please."

While Mary poured Diego some mineral water and herself a glass of white wine, Diego surveyed her home. It was furnished simply but tastefully in shades of gray and white with accents of red. Bookshelves lined the walls on either side of a real wood fireplace. They were full of books and small frames of primitive art. Mary had placed a plate of chocolate chip cookies on the dining room table. They smelled like they'd just come out of the oven. As Diego sniffed them, he remembered the wonderful smells in his mother's kitchen.

His gaze settled on a silver-framed picture on the mantel. It showed a man standing with his arm around a woman in front of an awning that said "Victor Chavez Fresh Produce" and a table laden with beautiful fruits and vegetables. Diego asked, "Is this your father and mother?"

"Yes," she said. "They were always working at their stores."

"The resemblance between your father and his older brother is strong. Julio was a bigger man, but the facial features are the same. Alejandro, Pilar's husband, looks like Miguel, the youngest of the three brothers. They have a slimmer build than Julio and Victor. I wish that you could know Alejandro. He is an amazing artist. He paints pictures of the Mexican landscape and colonial architecture. He has a following in the towns where Americans live north of San José. He still grieves the loss of Pilar. His landscapes have a certain melancholy about them that people find romantic. Art and his daughter are his world."

"I would like to meet him someday," Mary said. "Do you have a picture of him?"

"Sí," Diego said, opening the blue journal he always carried with him. "This is Alejandro and Pilar on their wedding day."

Mary studied the picture. Pilar was a beautiful bride, beaming with happiness. She looked young and innocent. Alejandro stood proud and handsome beside her.

"Does Alejandro know what you found out about Pilar?"

"Just before I left Mexico, I told him and my parents that I believe she was kidnapped by sex traffickers and probably taken to Houston and that I would continue to search for her until I found her. He still loves her and wants her to come home. He was depressed about losing his job when the factory he worked in closed. When he couldn't find another job, he started drinking a lot. I think Pilar was desperate when she applied for what she thought would be a good job in Mexico City. He blames himself for all that happened to her."

"How old is Pilar's daughter?"

"Concepción is almost five years old. She looks very much like her mother. Alejandro dotes on her and keeps her close to him. My mama and papa take care of her when he is working. We have always been a very close family."

"I'd like to meet them someday," Mary said. "John and I grew up without much family. I envied my friends who had lots of brothers and sisters and cousins. How wonderful and comforting that would be!"

"If you would like to meet the family, I promise you will, Mary," Diego said, smiling and holding her gaze.

"Okay, so let me tell you what I found out," Mary said. She realized she was very attracted to Diego, so she backed away from him and sat down on a club chair, hoping he would not notice. "There are two ways to find information about sex trafficking: law enforcement and nonprofit organizations. There is a task force made up of the Houston Police Department, the Harris County Sheriff's Office, the FBI, and some other agencies that is investigating the sex-trafficking industry in Harris County. I spoke with the police lieutenant in charge and learned that girls kidnapped from Mexico are only part of the picture. Traffickers smuggle in girls from all over the world. Asian girls work in the massage parlors around town, East European girls work in strip clubs, and most of the Hispanic girls work in cantinas and brothels in the barrios."

"What about white girls? Do American girls get caught up in this mess too?" Diego asked.

Mary sighed. "Half of the women who are trafficked are runaways—Americans who get trapped by pimps. White girls work mostly in hotels or men's clubs—but when business is booming and demand is high, sometimes attractive, fresh Hispanic girls work in the back rooms of the clubs."

Mary went on, "There are gentlemen's clubs all around the Galleria.

I was shocked to learn that girls are sold in clubs I pass every day on Westheimer and Richmond Avenue."

Diego realized his mission to find his sister, even if she was still in Houston, could be overwhelming. "Where should we start looking for Pilar?"

"There are hundreds of cantinas, brothels, and men's clubs all over Harris County. She could be in any of them," Mary said. "But I have a hunch. You said Pilar disappeared in late 2007. Back then, Houston was booming, and there were some big events and conventions in town. These would have created a high demand for sex."

"Pilar was young and beautiful," Diego said.

"The man I spoke with at one of the faith-based nonprofit organizations suggested we start looking in the high-end men's clubs and work our way down. He said four years is a long time for a girl to stay in one place, but someone may have seen her back then and remembered her."

"I will start right away," Diego said.

"Wait, Diego. There's more," Mary said. "The man told me it would be dangerous to be asking about a particular girl. The owners are on the lookout for undercover law enforcement or people who could disrupt their very profitable business. If anyone figures out what you are doing, they could beat you up or kill you. Some of the women in those places are willing prostitutes. A woman could turn you in to the owner if she thinks you are threatening her livelihood."

"If I am discreet, I don't see any harm in going in a club and looking around," Diego argued.

"We need to get you a guide," Mary said.

"I don't need a guide to a bar," Diego scoffed. "After all, I am a professional athlete."

Mary raised an eyebrow at that. "You need to go with someone who goes to these clubs on a regular basis, someone who is known and trusted by the owners or their thugs. Don't give up, Diego. Focus on your career. I'll keep working on a plan."

"Aye, Mary, you are logical, but I find waiting very frustrating." As he said this, Diego absently leaned forward and put his hand on Mary's. "But I will follow your lead for now."

Mary felt her body tingle at his touch.

• • •

The season opener was only a few weeks away. Diego didn't have time to wait for Mary to figure out a plan. He needed to act.

Diego had carefully observed his teammates. Paul Davies, a midfielder from the UK playing his third season in Houston, had caught his eye. Paul seemed to be the most flamboyant partier on the team. He was tall, blond, and single. He used his British accent to charm, and he was not shy about liking the ladies.

The day after his meeting with Mary, Diego approached Paul in the locker room. "Hola, Paul, can I talk to you?"

"Sure, what's up?" Paul replied.

"I heard you and Juan talking about going to some clubs tonight. I haven't had much fun since I've been in Houston. I've been busy getting settled," Diego said. "Would it be possible for me to come along?"

"Sure, Diego. I can always use another wingman," Paul said as he slapped him on the back. "Let's hit Sambuca and some of the other downtown spots and then head out to the Galleria for a nightcap." Then Paul called over to Juan, a midfielder from Argentina. "Can we use your new convertible for a night out?"

Juan was a relatively small but fast player. He admired Paul and hung around him most of the time. "Sure, amigo," Juan said.

Four hours later, Paul, Juan, and Diego left the bars around Market Square. Juan drove west on Memorial Drive to Loop 610 and exited at Westheimer, which ran through the middle of the Galleria shopping area. Neiman Marcus, Sak's Fifth Avenue, and the other stores were dark at that time of night. But the many men's clubs located west of the

Galleria were just getting started with the night's activities. Some of the clubs had walls that screened customers from the street, but others blatantly advertised that girls were available. Diego tried to memorize the names of the clubs as Juan slowly cruised the area: Heroes Club, Ricky's House of Treasures, King of Hearts, The Mile-High Club, and the Jewel Box, among others.

"This is where the action is, Diego," Paul said. "Juan, let's go to King of Hearts."

Juan pulled the car up to the valet. They went inside a large, dimly lit room. It was obvious from the way the doorman greeted Paul and Juan that they were regular customers. A hostess showed them to front-row seats at one of the bars. Cigar smoke permeated the air. A relentless disco beat surrounded them. Two big-breasted, topless girls in thongs were pole dancing on a stage in front of them, both white, one with blonde hair, the other brunette. Men along the bar stuffed money in their G-strings when the girls targeted them for attention.

Diego surveyed the room. Men in business suits or golf shirts and neat jeans sat at small tables. Attractive, well-groomed young women in scant outfits moved adroitly among the tables. Some took orders for drinks. Others flirted with the men, asking them if they would like to have a private lap dance.

Unsmiling, muscular males in black T-shirts with the club's logo stood silently around the walls and near the front door, keeping their eyes on the customers. Diego locked eyes with one of them for a minute, each man assessing the other. Diego forced a thin smile before he turned back around to watch the girls perform.

When he concluded that it was safe to resume surveying the layout of the club, Diego noticed a group of men gathered by a curtained doorway. The door opened, and an attractive middle-aged blonde woman in a black sequined dress led them inside.

"What's going on over there?" Diego asked Juan, nodding his head toward the door.

"That's the private lap dancing rooms," Juan replied. "You know, where a girl you choose gives you a private performance. Why? You see something you like? If not, they've got more in the back."

"Let's go see Marie," Paul said.

He tucked a bill into the G-string of the girl who had been flirting with him and led the way to the curtained door. The blonde woman welcomed Paul and Juan by name.

"This is our new friend from Mexico," Paul told her. "He needs to relax."

"You're a handsome one," Marie said to Diego, squeezing the muscle in his bicep. "What is your preference?"

"Do you have any beautiful ladies from my country?"

"Young?" she asked.

"At least eighteen," Diego answered. "I like experienced women. They are more exciting."

Marie took Diego by the hand and led him down a hall. He could hear low, slow music coming from behind curtained rooms. Occasionally he heard distinctly human sounds.

Marie drew back the curtains across one of the rooms. "This is Linda," she said. Then she was gone.

Linda was a young Mexican woman with long black hair. She sat on a gold velvet daybed in the middle of the room and wore a short white satin negligee. The contrast with her brown skin was striking. The faint smell of incense surrounded her. A soft Latin rhumba was coming from a Bose CD player on a bronze-and-glass side table. Diego realized he had foolishly hoped Pilar would be behind the curtain. Her face was burned into his mind all the time. The girl sensed his disappointment.

She looked nervous. "You don't like me?"

"No, it's not that," Diego said. "You are muy bonita. Please forgive me if I offended you, señorita."

Diego hesitated. "It's just that you resemble someone I know—my sister." He fumbled for the picture of himself and Pilar from his graduation day. "Look closely. Do you see the resemblance?"

Linda studied the picture. "No," she said. "But I can pretend I am your sister if you like." She gave him an impish look.

"That's not what I meant," he said. He wanted to leave but was afraid that would arouse suspicion. "Please, dance for me."

• • •

Later, while they were waiting for the valet to bring Juan's car around, Paul told Diego, "Honcho, the head of security, asked me how well I knew you."

"Why?"

"He said you spent a lot of time looking around the place—like you were checking it out. They're sensitive to undercover cops and those church types who don't have anything better to do than poke around in other people's business."

Diego made up a quick lie, hoping to calm any suspicion.

"Where I come from, Paul, you always want to know exactly where you are, who else is there, and where the exit is," Diego responded. "I didn't exactly have a privileged childhood in Mexico. I was trying to get my bearings."

"Well, you might want to be more discreet about your bearings in these places. Some of the security guys are paranoid and quick to overreact."

"I understand," Diego said. "Thanks for taking me."

"You're a strange dude, Diego. But you're a hell of a scorer, and that's good enough for me," Paul said. "Yeah, we'll do it again. I can see you need some taking care of, and you do help attract the ladies."

During March, Diego spent his evenings visiting the men's clubs. He went alone to a different club each night, using the same routine. None of the girls to whom he showed Pilar's picture recognized her. Some of them told him they had only been at that club a short time.

One Friday night, he decided to return to King of Hearts. Diego had a feeling he should give it one more try. Marie led him to a room where an attractive young Mexican woman was waiting. Diego had modified his routine to show the picture to the girl after she finished her dance. He thought she might be more willing to help him when he had his wallet open. The girl didn't recognize Pilar. Diego was on his way out the front door when Honcho grabbed him roughly by the arm, pushing him into a small room off the entrance to the club.

"Who are you?" the man asked, shoving him down onto a wooden chair.

"I'm just a guy enjoying a little feminine company at the end of a hard day," Diego answered, trying to appear calm.

"I knew you were trouble when I first saw you," the man said. "Who are you working for?"

"No one," Diego answered. "I'm just a player with the Storm. I am new to town." Diego was nervous. The guy was huge.

"Cut it out. I was watching you on the closed-circuit television. You showed Marisela a picture and asked her questions. You're looking for something," the man said, standing over Diego.

"I liked the girl. I was just showing her a picture from Mexico. She said she was homesick. I thought that might make her feel better."

"Bullshit!" Honcho yelled. "I'm going to get her. We'll see what she has to say."

As the man left, Diego heard him lock the door behind him.

Shit! Diego thought. *I've got to get out of here before he comes back.* Diego looked around for a way out. There was a high window in the room that he guessed opened above the valet station. Pulling the chair over to the window, he climbed up. The window was not locked. Diego lifted himself up, sliding the window open. It was a ten-foot drop to the driveway.

Potted Jerusalem palms lined the outside of the building. When the valets were busy with customers and had their backs to him, he crawled through, dove forward, and landed in one of the palms. *Whoosh!* Diego stifled a moan as the rough edges of the palms cut into his body.

A valet turned when he heard the noise. It was dark, though, and the man didn't see movement. Diego held his breath until the man turned around again, then he scrambled out of the palm and limped around the side of the building, feeling his way along the wall.

He heard Honcho run outside, cursing and asking the valets if they had seen a tall young Mexican guy leave the club. The valet who'd heard him fall in the palm plant said he thought someone was lurking around the building. Then Diego saw the beams of flashlights illuminate the palm plants and the driveway. A group of men gathered around the entrance. Honcho ordered them to spread out and search the area.

Diego was terrified. He made his way in the dark to the back of the King of Hearts, where he hid in a narrow, dark space between a set of dumpsters. About ten minutes later, two other security guards ran around to the back of the building, searching for him. They were only about ten feet away.

He held his breath.

Just as Diego couldn't hold his breath any longer, he recognized Honcho's voice. He summoned the two men back to the front of the club. Diego heard Honcho curse again, "Fuck! The bastard got away. Be ready for him if he comes back!"

Once the coast was clear, Diego made his way out from between the dumpsters onto a side street. His ankle throbbed, and he was bleeding. The palm plants had cut into him on his arms and shoulders where he'd tried to break his fall. He had parked several blocks away from the club and was now too disoriented to search for his car. He waited but didn't see a taxi anywhere.

Reluctantly, he pulled out his cell phone and dialed Mary's number. He didn't know who else to call.

"Hello?" he heard Mary's sleepy voice. Her clock showed it was 2 a.m.

"Mary, please, I need your help. I am a little hurt and not sure where I am. I don't have my car."

"Diego?" Mary asked, her voice more awake. "Where are you?"

"Near the Galleria," he winced. "I apologize, but could you possibly come get me?"

"You didn't go off on your own . . . ? Never mind. Tell me what buildings you can see, or a store. Do you know any of the streets?"

"I'm near Westheimer but on a parallel street. I think the Galleria is east of me. There is a Verizon Wireless store on the corner."

"Okay, I'll find the Verizon store. I'll be there in thirty minutes."

• • •

"What happened to you, Diego?" Mary asked. They were back in her living room. She had been too angry and he had been too embarrassed on the way home to discuss what had happened. Diego lay on the couch, although it was too short for his long body.

"I had an encounter with a palm plant," he grimaced. "The plant won."

Mary placed a bag of ice wrapped in a dish towel on Diego's shoulder and another one on his ankle. Neither looked broken, just severely bruised. She swabbed his cuts with alcohol and placed Band-Aids on them.

"These bruises are going to turn blue, and you will have swelling for a few days." She handed him four ibuprofen tablets and a glass of water. "Here, take these. What are you going to tell your manager and coach on Monday?"

"I'll tell them I made a pass at a tough female lawyer and she beat me up," he said.

Mary blushed. "If you go poking around men's clubs alone again, I will do that. You're a soccer player, not James Bond."

Diego didn't respond.

"Never mind. Did you learn anything?"

"I learned that these guys move their girls around regularly from place to place so that they don't get to know each other. None of the girls I talked to in five different clubs in the area recognized Pilar," Diego said, holding the bag of ice to his shoulder. "I also learned there isn't any place to question the girls privately, because some of the clubs have security cameras or listening devices in the rooms. Someone could always be watching. I'll have to find another way to get information."

"Correction: maybe now you will listen to me. You asked for my help because you said you didn't know Houston. Then you went off on your own and did exactly what I warned you was dangerous."

"You're right, Mary. I beg your forgiveness; from now on I will listen to you."

Mary turned away, realizing she was blushing again.

Diego's eyes were drooping, and he had slid down on the couch so that his head was resting on a throw pillow. One arm was dropped beside him. He was exhausted. "Stay here tonight, Diego. You can sleep where you are. I don't think you are capable of walking to the guest room. I'll feed you a hot breakfast in the morning, take you to get your car, and follow you to your apartment. Maybe I will lock you in. Tomorrow and Sunday you shouldn't do anything but lie in your bed and heal. On Monday you can go to practice, where you belong."

Diego did not answer. His eyes were closed, his body relaxed. Mary brought a comforter to cover him, took off his shoes, and placed a feather pillow behind his head.

She sat on the club chair and watched him sleep for a few minutes. She knew it was crazy since she had just met him, but it felt nice to have him in her house. Then she got up, locked the deadbolt on her front door, turned on the alarm system, and walked to her bedroom, taking the key to the front and back doors with her.

CHAPTER 15

PABLO'S SECRET

I n early April 2011, Diego received a telephone call from Pablo Trujillo Peña, one of his former teammates in Mexico City. Diego had been friendly with his teammates there but had not hung out and partied with them after practice or games. He had spent much of his free time searching for Pilar. When Pablo told him he was in Houston and asked if they could get together for drinks, Diego was mildly surprised. They agreed to meet at the bar in the Four Seasons Hotel downtown the next day.

The bar was a quiet, dark place frequented by lawyers, businessmen, and professional athletes. The small tables were far enough apart that normal conversations would not be overheard.

Pablo had been born in Mexico but had grown up in Houston, where his father's company had transferred him when Pablo was three years old. His Mexican parents had moved back to Mexico City when he was sixteen. His self-identity was more Texan than Mexican. When he walked into the Four Seasons Bar, Pablo was wearing lizard cowboy boots with his jeans and a big silver belt buckle.

They began their conversation with news about the old team. Then, after the waitress brought their drinks, Pablo cleared his throat and said, "Dude, I'm embarrassed to tell you this story. But since you've moved to Houston, I feel I need to do it. You know the picture of the girl taped to the inside of the door of your locker in Mexico City?"

Diego was surprised. He had not told any of his teammates or

coaches about his search for Pilar. He didn't want his coaches or managers to know he had anything else consuming his time besides playing
fútbol. "You have information about my sister?"

"Diego, I didn't realize she was your sister. I wish I had known,"
Pablo said after a pause. Then he took a drink.

"My sister is two years younger than me. Her name is Pilar. She is
married to my best friend growing up, Alejandro," Diego said.

After a minute of reorganizing his thoughts, Pablo continued.

"Ever since we moved back to Mexico City, I visit my old friends
and relatives in Houston during the off season. My friends like to
spend time in the men's clubs around the Galleria. They like the music
and the girls," Pablo said, "and I went with them when I was younger
and single. But I'm a married man now, and we have a little girl, Lisa.
She's one year old, and her mother and I adore her."

"Go on," Diego said.

"I think I met the girl in the picture in your locker—I mean your
sister—but I didn't know she was your sister at the time, I swear! The
girl I met looked just like the girl in the picture, although she was
wearing more makeup when I was with her. And she didn't look so
happy. It was a couple of years ago. I saw her a few times in a lap dance
room of a men's club. She struck me as sad but naturally beautiful. The
last time we went to the club, when I asked for her, they told me she
wasn't there anymore."

"When was that?" Diego asked, trying to suppress his anger that
Pablo had waited until now to tell him this.

"The last time I asked for her was in April of 2009—about two
years ago." Pablo folded and refolded his napkin. "That's all I know."

Diego's hands gripped the edge of the table. "You knew where Pilar
was, but you didn't tell me?"

"I wasn't sure it was her, and since she was in the States, there was
nothing you could do about it anyway. I didn't know she was more than
some girl you spent a night with and couldn't get out of your head. I

had no idea it was your sister. The girl was a prostitute, and I was afraid that if I sent you off on a wild goose chase, you could get hurt and not be able to play," Pablo protested. "But now that you are in Houston, I thought maybe you still wanted to find her. That's why I'm telling you this now. I'm sorry, Diego, I was young and stupid."

"Pilar is not a prostitute, Pablo. She was kidnapped in 2007 when we were together in Mexico City. Only we weren't together; I went off to watch a soccer practice and left her alone. She was a victim of a kidnapping. I have been searching for her ever since the day she disappeared. After looking for her in Mexico City, I found evidence she probably was smuggled into the United States and might be in Houston. That's why I chose to play with the Storm."

Diego's fists were clenched under the table. He was angry at Pablo for not telling him this sooner, but he needed to find out everything Pablo knew.

Besides, who am I to condemn a young man for the foolish decisions of youth?

"Bueno." Diego unclenched his fists. "What was the name of the club where you saw Pilar?"

"The Jewel Box," said Pablo. "It's a big place on Westheimer just west of the Galleria. Do you know it?"

"I have looked in many clubs, but I haven't been to that one so far," Diego said.

"Well, I've got to go meet my wife now, Diego," Pablo said. "It was good seeing you. I hear you are doing really well with your new team. And, Diego, I really hope you find your sister."

• • •

Although Pablo had told him the last time he'd seen Pilar at the Jewel Box was before April 2009 and it was now early 2011, Diego felt the need to go there right away—though he knew she probably was not still there. Perhaps someone remembered her or knew where she had been taken next.

He had the valet drive his car around to the front of the Four Seasons. He headed down Lamar and Allen Parkway toward the Galleria, but it was rush hour, and the traffic was heavy. Just as he approached the Union Pacific railway tracks on San Felipe, red lights started flashing, and the arms of the Union Pacific railroad crossing came down. He slammed his fist on the steering wheel of his BMW in frustration.

Just then, his cell phone rang. It was Mary.

"Hey, Diego," Mary asked in a cheery voice. "Where are you?"

"You won't believe this, Mary. I just got a tip from someone who saw Pilar here in Houston. Your instinct was right. She was working at a club called the Jewel Box. I'm headed there now."

"No, Diego!" Mary exploded.

Oh shit! Diego remembered. *I promised her I wouldn't go alone.*

"Don't do anything crazy," Mary went on. "That's good news, but let's not blow it. We need to think carefully about how to best use this information."

Mary's call and the slow movement of the hundred-car freight train in front of him made Diego stop long enough to think rationally. *Probably no one will talk to me about a girl, even if they remember her.*

"Okay, Mary. I guess you're right," Diego mumbled. "I will wait."

"You're close to the St. Regis Hotel just across the tracks," Mary said. "I'll meet you in the restaurant in thirty minutes. You'll wait for me, right?"

"Sí."

• • •

Half an hour later, Mary left her car with the valet and entered the lobby of the St. Regis. It was a stately traditional hotel set off by itself in an office park near the Galleria. An air of calm luxury permeated the entire building. She walked into the light-filled, glass-walled dining room, where only a few tables were occupied. It was early in the evening. Diego was sitting at a table for two, an espresso in front of him. Two young waitresses stood nearby, watching Diego. At Mary's approach, Diego rose and kissed her on both cheeks. The girls gave one another a disappointed look and walked away.

"Tell me what happened, Diego."

Diego told her the story of his meeting with Pablo and how he had learned that Pilar might have been at the Jewel Box two years earlier.

"Well, that's a stroke of luck," Mary said. "I wish he had told you about this sooner. But we are where we are. How should we use this information? You said there is a lot of turnover among the girls at the clubs so they don't get to know each other."

"That's my impression," Diego replied.

"Who is there year after year, besides the owners and the security guards? Who could we question that might have been at the Jewel Box two years ago?" Mary wondered.

Diego sipped his espresso while he thought about this. A waitress stopped by to ask if Mary would like to order something.

"Wait, I know!" Mary exclaimed. "The janitorial staff! They see who comes and goes but don't have a stake in the business. This being Houston, they all speak Spanish. One of them might talk to you if you explain you have come from Mexico looking for your sister. We just need to know when they get off work and find someone who recognizes Pilar's picture to tell us if she is still there—maybe even take her a message."

Mary was thinking as she talked, her voice growing more excited. Diego sat back and listened, impressed with her ability to analyze a problem and come up with a solution.

"But how do we find out when the staff leaves? Neither one of us can afford to sit up all night watching the club," Diego said.

"I'm thinking," Mary said. Then she spoke.

"Sometimes we hire investigators to do surveillance in difficult cases. I know a guy who works cheap and gets results—Steve Hernandez. He's creative. Steve is ex-military and spent fifteen years working undercover with the Harris County Sheriff's office. He grew up in the Rio Grande Valley and speaks Spanish fluently. After he retired, he opened a private detective firm, but he only takes cases that interest him. He's helped me with some pretty complicated cases."

"I trust your judgment, Mary," Diego said.

"Let me give him a call and see if he can help us."

"Okay, Mary, whatever it costs, I will cover it."

Two days later, Steve was sitting on the couch in Mary's cluttered office, a serious look on his face, when Diego arrived. Diego sized him up. He was average height and weight and bald on top with a longish fringe of gray hair. There was nothing about his face that you would remember from a casual meeting. He seemed like the perfect under-cover agent.

"I apologize for keeping you waiting, señor." Diego shook Steve's hand. "Practice ran late today."

"No problem," Steve said. "I'm a fan. Mary's been filling me in. I hate those fucking pimps who kidnap innocent young girls. They should all be locked up and gang butt-raped."

"I agree," Diego said. "I don't understand why they are not all in jail."

"There's too many of them for the police to catch, and the victims are too scared to testify against their pimps. Those bastards threaten them and their families or hook them on drugs. Besides, very few of those girls have someone who wants to help them. After a while, they figure they got no other future and no place else to go," Steve said. "What they are forced to do causes them to die from the inside out. Most of them are dead from one thing or another within ten years."

"Can you help us find Pilar, señor?"

"I'll help, son. It may take a little time, though, to do what Mary has suggested. First, I need to figure out when the staff gets off work.

Then I need to find one willing to talk. They might feel safer talking to a fellow Mexican. A lot of them aren't exactly legal, so they are very guarded. I'll let you know when I've got somebody."

"Gracias, señor. I am most grateful for your help."

• • •

In June, Steve contacted Mary.

"I've got a woman who is willing to talk," he said. "It took a while. The people who work in those places are scared to death. The club owners threaten the undocumented ones that they'll report them to INS if they tell anyone anything they see at work. Even if they are legally here, somebody in their family isn't. Or they are afraid of physical retaliation against themselves or their families."

"Why will this woman help us?" Mary asked.

"It's an old woman who cleans the floors and bathrooms and the back rooms. She said her heart aches for the young girls who are taken away from their families and forced to work there. She says if Pilar has someone who will take her out of that life, she will take the risk."

"What did she tell you, Steve?"

"She wants to talk to Diego. She wants to be sure he exists. She's legal, but she's taking a big chance even talking to a guy like me."

Mary was excited but a little nervous. She knew it was dangerous for this woman to come forward.

"Where and when should Diego meet her?" Mary asked.

"Do you know where the Taqueria Grande is, about one mile east of I-45 on Broadway? It's across I-45 from Hobby Airport. She said she'll meet us there on Sunday after early Mass. Diego and I should be there by 9:00 a.m."

"I'm coming too," Mary said.

"It's a pretty rough area of town, Mary. Are you sure you should go?"

"I'm not afraid. I have become so deeply invested in the search for this girl, who is probably my cousin, that I don't want to miss any part of it."

"Fine, then I'd better pick you up in my truck. I'll be at your house at 8:30," Steve replied and then hung up.

At 8:50 on Sunday morning, Steve, Diego, and Mary pulled up to the Taqueria Grande in Steve's old pickup truck. They parked in back and entered the restaurant by a side door. Steve surveyed the tables in the large, crowded room. Happy conversations between grandparents, parents, and small children took place at almost every table. Baskets of chips and salsa sat on the tables. Spanish-speaking waitresses bustled about among regular customers. They took orders and returned with steaming trays of breakfast tacos, migas, and sopapillas and honey. Delicious smells wafted in from the open kitchen. Piñatas hung here and there from the ceiling, adding to the festive atmosphere. Steve found the old woman sitting in a corner booth at the back of the res- taurant by herself.

"Buenas días, señora," Steve said, removing his straw cowboy hat. "This is Diego Gonzales, the young man I told you about who is search- ing for his sister, Pilar." The old woman, whose name was Consuelo, spoke only Spanish, and Steve addressed her in her language.

"Who is that?" Consuelo asked, looking uneasily at Mary.

"This is Maria Chavez. She is Pilar's cousin and my friend."

"Bueno." She nodded and smiled shyly at Diego and Mary.

Everyone sat, and a waitress appeared. Diego ordered café con leche for everyone and a basket of sopapillas and honey. Then he laid the pictures of Pilar and him at his graduation and Pilar and Alejandro on their wedding day on the table in front of her.

"Señora, please, these are picures of my sister, Pilar. Have you ever seen her?"

The woman stared at the pictures. She picked them up to examine them closely, as if she had trouble seeing. When she recognized the young woman she had talked with at the Jewel Box several years earlier, her face lit up with a smile. She looked at Diego. "Sí, señor. She is a very kind woman. She sometimes gave me money the men gave her before her padrón took it from her. She was sad. But she was strong. She told me she would get away somehow, someday. She has a husband and little girl in Mexico. She told me many times she wanted to see her daughter again."

Steve, Diego, and Mary sat silent, waiting, while Consuelo drank a little of her café. Then she continued, "She never gave up or used drugs or any of the things they tried to make her do. She kept a silver crucifix hidden; I don't know how. She gave it to me to keep for her until she was free. Sometimes I hold it and pray that Pilar will see her daughter again."

Consuelo reached into her purse and took out a tiny bundle of tissue paper. She unwrapped it and laid a small silver crucifix on the table.

Diego recognized Pilar's crucifix. *She is alive, and I am getting closer!* He asked Consuelo, "Do you know where she is now?"

"No, señor. When many people in Houston lost their jobs, the club was not so busy. Travelers stopped coming. Eduardo took Pilar and his other girl away."

"Who is Eduardo, señora?" Diego asked.

Consuelo spat on the floor. "Pig! Devil!" she hissed. "Eduardo Ayala kidnaps good girls in Mexico or even here. Then he and his devil brother, Guillermo, hold them captive and make them have sex with many men. He keeps all the money they are paid and drives around in a big black car. He told Pilar he would kill her husband and daughter and her parents if she did not do what he told her to do. Pilar said he knew where they lived, and she believed he would do it. She was afraid of him."

Diego's lips were tight, and the tendons in his arms were taut.

"Is there anything else you can tell us, señora?"

"I pray you find your sister, señor. She is a good girl. She has been forced to do the Devil's work. But she still prays to the Virgin to forgive her sins and let her see her family again."

"Thank you very much, señora," Diego said, hugging the woman to hide the tears in his eyes.

• • •

The drive in Steve's truck to Mary's house was silent and tense. About halfway there, Diego asked, "Steve, have you ever heard of this Eduardo Ayala?"

"Unfortunately, yes. He's a low-level Mexican crook who engages in sex trafficking, prostitution, and drug running. He has contacts with the Sangre Negra cartel and uses them now and then to do his dirty business. Sometimes, he does theirs. I'm told he can be charming and dangerously persuasive." He sighed. "The office has him on their radar, but they never can get enough evidence to bring him in. He goes back and forth across the border and hangs out in the East End barrio."

"What about his brother?"

"Guillermo? He's big, dumb, and mean. He supplies the muscle to back up Eduardo's activities. Eduardo likes to threaten people, and Guillermo scares them into doing what he tells them to do. Guillermo has probably killed a few people, but hard evidence and witnesses are never there. They're a very dangerous team. Of course, my information is a few years old."

"Can you talk to some of your old buddies and get an update on what they think Eduardo may be doing now?" Mary asked.

CHAPTER 16

TELEPHONE ROAD

Mary and Diego met late on a Saturday morning in June at La Madeleine Bakery in the River Oaks Shopping Center. The restaurant was full of joggers from Memorial Park and Buffalo Bayou Park, as well as young mothers out window-shopping and walking their babies on a beautiful day. Purple, pink, and white crape myrtles were budding out everywhere. It seemed that everyone wanted to be outside enjoying the sunshine. The pair sat at a table and shared croissants and cappuccinos while planning their next move in their search for Pilar.

"Okay," Mary said, "we know from talking to Consuelo that the name of the man keeping Pilar captive is Eduardo Ayala. Steve checked with his friends in the sheriff's office, and they told him that the word on the street is that Eduardo Ayala hangs out in the southeast part of town in the Telephone Road and Wayside area. Steve says the area is full of cantinas and brothels." She slathered fresh butter on a piece of croissant and offered it to Diego.

"Are you familiar with that neighborhood?" Diego asked, taking the croissant from her.

"I've never been there except to take Broadway directly to the airport," Mary replied, reaching across Diego's arm for the sugar. "It's not a part of town in which you want to wander around."

"Let's see what it looks like," Diego suggested as he took a bite of his croissant and waited to see what Mary would say. When Mary raised an eyebrow, he added, "We won't get out of the car. Promise."

When Mary didn't answer, he smiled, put his pastry on the plate they shared, and said, "Por favor, Maria? Please, Mary?" drawing out the syllables so the words took a long time, becoming a question.

Mary looked away so he couldn't see her smile. "If I don't go with you, you'll probably just go alone and get in trouble!" Mary scolded. She tried to keep her mouth in a straight line, but her smile kept creeping in. She took another bite to give her lips something to do. She was anxious herself to follow up on this new information.

An hour later, Mary and Diego were driving south on I-45 in Mary's Honda Accord. They'd agreed his BMW might attract unwanted attention. Mary exited at Telephone Road and turned right at the traffic light on the feeder road. Almost all the billboards and signs were in Spanish. There were panaderías serving fresh Mexican pastries, abogado offices advertising bail and legal services, taquerías, several used car lots, and an old banquet hall offering rooms for quinceañeras and weddings. A mild breeze from the southeast spread insidious pollution from the refineries and chemical plants along the nearby Houston Ship Channel.

"The air is like being back in Mexico City," Diego said.

Low-rent men's clubs, shabby cantinas, and run-down motels lined the street. The motels were built in the stone-bungalow style of the 1950s. Trees and overgrown shrubs formed partial screens. Some motels advertised rooms by the hour. Names like El Secreto, Bésame, Alibi Motel, and La Oficina suggested anonymity and more.

The road split, and Mary was unsure which way to go. When they reached the I-610 East Loop, Mary turned the car around, and they cruised back the way they had come. She caught her breath as she realized they could see the sparkling, architecturally modern skyline of downtown Houston ahead of them. It formed a backdrop to the run-down, seedy neighborhood. The sun was bright in a cloudless sky, making the tops of some of the beautiful steel-and-glass buildings glisten. The stately offices of Houston's downtown law firms, banks, and energy companies were within sight of this squalid, forgotten area, but few actually saw it.

"It's like there are two different cities on top of one another," she remarked.

The streets were empty, with few cars and no one on the sidewalks. "It's so quiet," Mary observed. "Where are all the people?"

"Sleeping, probably," Diego answered. "I bet things don't start happening around here until after dark. See how the windows are shuttered or blacked out to keep out the sun?"

Mary had not noticed this, but now that Diego pointed it out, she could see it was true. "Maybe we should come back at night. I can't tell which of these places are operational. There's no one on the street that we can talk to in order to get information about Eduardo."

"How's your Spanish, Mary?" Diego asked in a dry tone. Mary saw him eyeing her doubtfully. She realized she would stand out in her black Ann Taylor pencil skirt, white shirt, jacket, and pearls.

"For your information, Diego, I got As in Spanish in high school. And sometimes I try to converse with my sister-in-law's maid or the janitors who clean my office at night to practice," Mary said. Diego seemed to remain unimpressed, so she spat out, "Okay, I guess it's not so great."

"Sí." Diego let the word drag out. "You're not questioning anybody in this neighborhood. They would peg you immediately for the law and not say anything. Or maybe they'd think you were just crazy and tell you to get the hell out of this neighborhood pronto."

"Now look who's telling who to be cautious." She smiled. "There are so many potential places Pilar could be!"

Diego was silent for the next few minutes, thinking. Suddenly he said, "Stop here!" Park the car!"

Mary abruptly pulled to the right and parked.

"There!" Diego pointed at a large stone building with turret bell towers on either side. The words "Christ the Redeemer Roman Catholic Church" were carved in stone above the double wooden doors.

"In Mexico, the priest always knows what is going on in his parish," Diego said before dashing out of the car. He was on the sidewalk before Mary could unhook her seat belt.

An arrow on a small wooden sign indicated the church offices were at the rear. Mary and Diego followed a path to a heavy wooden door that had two large deadbolt locks on it. Diego knocked. After a minute, they heard someone inside shuffling to the door. An elderly man's voice asked, "Who is it?" in Spanish.

"Diego Gonzales y Maria Chavez. Queremos hablar con el padre," Diego said, answering that they wished to speak with the priest.

Dead bolts clicked open, and a thin white-haired priest, who looked to be in his seventies or eighties, opened the door. He had a welcoming smile, and his blue eyes were clear and bright. A yellowed, worn cassock hung off him loosely. Mary wondered if he had been a bigger man at one time or if the cassock was a hand-me-down from a larger priest. Diego was puzzled. He didn't look Hispanic.

"Por favor," the old man said as he gestured to them to enter and have a seat on some worn upholstered chairs, relics from the parish's more prosperous days. There were small statues of saints, a gilt crucifix, and pictures of the Holy Family and Pope John XXIII on the walls.

"What can I do for you?" he asked, switching to English. "We don't get many visitors from outside the parish these days. I am Padre Roberto, the rector. You have already introduced yourselves, but forgive me, my memory is not what it was. Have we met? What parish do you belong to?"

Diego ignored the last question, as he hadn't been to church since leaving his mother's house. He hadn't been on the best terms with God since Pilar's kidnapping.

"We haven't met, Padre. I am a newcomer to the city. I am from Mexico and arrived a few months ago to play soccer with the Storm," Diego said.

"Our parishioners are big fans." Padre Roberto smiled. "They can't always afford to buy tickets, but some of them follow the team more closely than their religion! After a winning game, it is the main topic of conversation during the entire week. I will pray your presence brings them more victories."

"I am a member at St. Anne's, Father," Mary said. "I'm an attorney with Harris County Legal Aid. I have done work for the diocese from time to time."

"I am sure God appreciates your good work. My parishioners are in desperate need of legal services of every type."

Mary winced. Harris County Legal Aid wouldn't accept many of his parishioners as clients. They could only serve citizens, and she guessed that many of the people in this neighborhood hadn't legally crossed the border. She hadn't thought about how the immigrant communities might need low-cost legal services too, although she knew that Catholic Charities and the International YMCA did some of that work.

"But you didn't come just to visit an old priest," Padre Roberto said. "What can we at Christ the Redeemer parish do for you?"

"I am looking for my sister, Padre. Her name is Pilar Chavez Gonzales. She was kidnapped in Mexico and trafficked to Houston. I have been searching for her for several years. Mary and her brother, John Chavez, are native Houstonians, but they are Pilar's husband's first cousins. I only recently found them. Mary is helping me search. I am very grateful to her," Diego said.

A smile appeared on Diego's face as he said the last sentence.

What a beautiful smile he has, Mary thought.

"We know the man who was keeping her captive as of two years ago," Diego went on, his smile disappearing as he got back to business.

"His name is Eduardo Ayala. The county sheriff's office constables think he has been doing business in the cantinas and brothels in this part of Houston."

Diego's shoulders dropped, and he sat back in the chair. "But there are so many places where Pilar could be, we don't know how to start looking. In my country, the priest knows what is going on in his parish. Pilar has always been a devout Catholic. Perhaps you have seen her at Mass?"

Padre Roberto's bright eyes became sad. "Unfortunately, you are not the first visitors who have knocked on my door seeking a lost daughter, sister, or even wife. The girls you are talking about are not permitted to go anywhere without their captors, certainly not to church. Once a girl escaped, and we found her huddled behind some pews in the sanctuary. We helped her get to a hospital and a rescue agency. The next Sunday, a gang drove past the church in a pickup truck when late Mass was letting out and sprayed the crowd with bullets. Fortunately, no one died, but many people were hurt."

Then defiance replaced the sadness in his eyes. "I would still help any girl who came to us. The people who run the cantinas and bordellos are an insult to God and a scourge to the good people who live in this neighborhood."

Just then, an older woman carrying fresh linens entered the room. The woman and priest exchanged greetings in Spanish. Then he told her that one of their guests only spoke English. "I beg your forgiveness," the woman said, "but I need to go to the San Jacinto Clinic for my volunteer shift, and I must vacuum in here before I leave. Would you mind, Padre, if you and your guests moved into the dining room?" she asked.

"Of course not, Señora Gutierrez. Come, my friends, I will show you some pictures from the days when Christ the Redeemer was a great, prosperous parish."

As they walked into the next room, Diego observed, "Padre, I must compliment you on your Spanish. You do not look like you are from south of the border, but your Spanish is flawless."

"I've been at this parish as long as I've been a priest. It was my first assignment, and I suspect it is God's plan that I stay here and do the best I can to provide hope and stability. When I arrived, we served people of European ancestry who worked at the refineries, chemical plants, or oil field service companies. Christ the Redeemer was a thriving parish with three priests living in the rectory and a convent full of nuns who taught at our parochial school. A growing number of Mexican immigrants settled here in the seventies and eighties after the government closed the open border with Mexico. Many of the newcomers had no money and no papers.

"Around that time white people who could afford it moved out to the suburbs. The neighborhood became overwhelmingly Hispanic. I loved the gentle Mexican people who joined the parish. Eventually, I learned Spanish. My own parents immigrated to the United States from Germany, but now Spanish is almost my first language.

"The immigrants couldn't get good paying jobs and didn't have the money to keep up the homes. This became a blighted area. That's when the cantinas and brothels took over. Now decent people dare not walk the streets after dark for fear of their lives."

"Don't the police patrol?" Mary asked.

"Yes. But Houston is a huge city, and their resources are thin. It's ironic. Men who work in the offices downtown slip down here at night to engage in sinful activities, while the working people in the neighborhood ride the bus downtown to clean their offices. The neighborhoods are only a few miles apart. Lord, forgive me. I get cynical sometimes." He made a hasty sign of the cross. "But you asked for my advice, not a history lesson. Forgive me."

Señora Gutierrez stuck her head in the door to tell Padre Roberto that she was leaving. "Don't forget to lock all the doors, Padre."

"Can you advise us how to find my sister if she is in this neighborhood?" Diego asked.

"I advise the two of you not to try to look for Pilar alone. God forbid, Mary could end up working at one of these places if these devils in the cantinas catch you snooping around. Diego, you could end up with a knife in your back. These padrónes are very protective of what they consider their property. They won't hesitate to kill to protect it."

"What about circulating flyers with her picture and a reward on it?" Diego asked.

"My son, if they know someone is looking for Pilar, they may kill her or ship her far away to another location in the city, even out of state." Padre Roberto looked weary. "Unfortunately, there are many other neighborhoods similar to Telephone Road where Pilar could be. The airports are surrounded by motels and houses used for prostitution and sex slavery."

Diego had been caught up in the old priest's story. But when he glanced at his watch, he realized he needed to be at practice soon. He squeezed Mary's arm lightly and got up from his chair.

"Padre, you have been generous with your time," Diego said. "We need to think about this and decide where to go from here."

"Please, can you leave a copy of your sister's picture with me? I would like to help you, and you can call upon me at any time. I might even see you at Mass if you don't have a parish in Houston yet?"

Diego was silent.

"Thank you for your time and for sharing so much information with us," Mary said. "My contact information is on this card."

"I will pray for you and your sister, my son. I wish every girl had someone who loved her as much as you obviously love your sister," the old priest said as he walked them to the door. Before he could open it, the door burst open, and a teenage boy ran into the room. "Padre, come quick! There was a shooting at El Secreto, and a dying man has asked for a priest!"

"Is this a normal occurrence, Padre?" Diego asked.

"Regrettably, yes," he answered, picking up his satchel where he kept supplies for the last rites from its resting place near the door.

CHAPTER 17

TANGLEWOOD

The 2011 Season of Major League Soccer was well underway, and Diego had to focus on winning games for the Storm. His extraordinary skill at passing and scoring quickly established him in the starting lineup. He was handsome and charismatic, which the sports media was quick to showcase. Soccer came in third in popularity behind football and baseball in Houston. But the Storm were winning games, and Houston soccer fans fell in love with the newest player.

One afternoon, in early July, Alonso "Pico" Melendez, an assistant coach, stopped Diego in the locker room before practice. "Hola, Diego. The public relations office called down here. They have an invitation for you." He handed Diego a small sealed envelope.

"What's this?" Diego asked.

"It's an invitation, amigo. A fan has invited you to a party."

"I do not go to parties," Diego said, pulling on his jersey.

"It's not just any fan. It's an invitation from Arturo Nuñez Escobar. He's a close friend of the head of the Spanish-language sports channel in town. He's noticed you, and that's good for you and the Storm. He's a very rich man in Mexico, and his family members have big houses here in the city."

"I am flattered, Pico, but I don't have the time."

Pico handed Diego his shoes.

"He also has a beautiful young daughter, Diego. Marisa is single and just graduated from university. She and her friends do a lot of charity work, so she gets her picture in the newspaper. Professional soccer is still relatively new in Houston. Our public relations people think it would help the team's popularity if some of our players were seen at the parties and big social occasions—at least that's what they tell me. According to them, Escobar's parties are exclusive. No one else with the Storm has ever gotten an invitation."

Diego looked annoyed. "I've got to get to practice, Pico. Can we talk about this another time?"

"You need to go. You don't have to stay all night. Just meet Señor Escobar and say hello to his daughter, mix a little with the crowd, and go home," Pico told him. "It might do you good to relax for a change. You are too intense. The season has a long way to go. I don't want you to burn out."

"Is this an order?" Diego asked, turning around on his way out to the pitch.

"Think of it as a firm suggestion."

• • •

That Saturday night Diego drove west on San Felipe and just past the Galleria area to the Tanglewood subdivision. He turned right onto Tanglewood Boulevard, a tree-lined road that ran for a mile diagonally through the neighborhood. He saw joggers, people walking their dogs, and people just strolling or sitting on benches, talking to their neighbors. Everyone was white and well dressed, even those wearing exercise clothes.

Most homes around him were sprawling one-story ranch houses set on large, beautifully landscaped lots. Here and there, developers had torn down houses built in the 1950s and replaced them with enormous two- and three-story mansions that took up the entire lot. Diego had never seen anything so grand. He remembered that this was where Mary had said she and John had grown up in one of the original houses.

When Diego arrived at Arturo Escobar's address, he noticed a truck with a private security service name on it, a black Cadillac Escalade SUV with dark windows, and three muscular Mexican men in jeans and black long-sleeve T-shirts standing in the driveway. He was familiar with that type in Mexico. But they seemed strangely out of place in this nice suburban neighborhood. After he'd parked, a valet took his keys and directed him through the front door of an elegant pink two-story Spanish-style stucco house with a green tile roof.

"Bienvenidos a mi casa," said a beautiful, petite young woman with long black hair parted in the middle and pulled back behind her ears. He was struck by her lovely brown eyes. She was wearing a short white eyelet sundress and gold jewelry that showed off her tan skin. "I am Marisa Escobar."

"Gracias, señorita. I am . . ."

"Diego," she finished, giving him a flirtatious smile. "I am a fan. My papa and I have seen you play. You are a great addition to the Storm."

"I am flattered, Marisa. I have heard good things about how your father supports the team," Diego said, smiling back. "I hope we can live up to his expectations this season."

"You've already lived up to mine," Marisa said. "Let me show you around."

She steered Diego through the house. It was the most beautiful home Diego had ever been in. They walked out onto a tropical, lavishly landscaped patio that overlooked an oval-shaped swimming pool and spa. A waterfall at the rear of the pool tumbled over rocks and large druzy quartz geodes, which sparkled under strategically placed lighting. A mariachi band dressed all in white played Mexican music, and four preteen girls danced together, giggling. On the patio tables, crystal bowls of cold boiled shrimp and crab claws sat on ice. Sizzling platters of beef and chicken fajitas and trays of bacon-wrapped quail were presented in beautiful traditional Mexican plates and bowls. The plates were square, painted in a distinctive Mexican style with a leafy green background and two blue fish painted in the middle.

Diego picked up an empty plate from the table and turned it over. "JMB Mexico" was written on the back. "Marisa, do you know where your parents bought this pottery?" Diego asked. "It is very authentic."

"No, my parents have always had it. They say it brings a little bit of home into our hectic lives in Houston. I think it comes from somewhere north of Mexico City, out in the country. Why? You don't look like someone who would be interested in interior décor." She squeezed his arm and smiled up at him.

"I am not," Diego said. "But I grew up in a little town north of Mexico City, San José, where traditional pottery was made by hand for centuries. It reminds me of my mother's table growing up."

"It must mean you were meant to be here then. I hope you feel at home in our home, too," Marisa said.

Across the pool, Diego noticed a hefty Mexican man with salt-and-pepper hair and mustache seated on a couch. There was an all-male crowd standing around him, talking among themselves, although it was obvious he was the reason they were gathered.

"Who are your guests, Marisa? And who is that gentleman in the center of things?" Diego asked, nodding toward the other group.

"Most of the people here are family, believe it or not. Many of my Mexican uncles, cousins, and other relatives have homes in Houston. The private schools here are excellent," Marisa replied. "People of means feel safer raising their children in the States than back in Mexico. You know, kidnappings, ransom demands, and all that. My father bought this house seven years ago, and my grandfather and uncle tore down old houses and built new homes on either side of us."

"So these people are all family?" Diego asked.

"No, silly," Marisa replied, laughing and touching his arm. "Houston is a very open, friendly city. The other guests are business associates of my father. Most of the white ones live in Houston. Some of the Mexicans are visiting from Mexico. The man you asked about is Papa. Come, I will introduce you."

She grabbed his hand and led him over. The man on the couch smiled as she approached. "Papa, let me introduce Señor Diego Gonzales," she said.

Diego bowed to the man. Señor Escobar took his hand and shook it warmly. "I am most pleased to make your acquaintance, Diego. We have watched you play and are greatly impressed with your skill. My daughter can't stop talking about you. I hope she is making you feel welcome."

"Papa, please," Marisa murmured.

"Of course, Marisa is a gracious hostess." Diego smiled.

"Well, enjoy yourself. Please have something to eat. An athlete needs nourishment. Marisa, make sure he tries some of the ceviche. Our chef makes the best ceviche north of the Rio Grande," Señor Escobar said. Then he turned to answer a question from another guest, and Diego knew the introduction was over.

Did he send me the invitation or did his daughter? Diego wondered. Then something caught his eye. There was a large, muscular Mexican man dressed like the men in the driveway who stood behind Señor Escobar. The man was watching everyone who approached. Diego thought he detected a bulge under his T-shirt just above his waist. *He's got a gun!*

As they began walking around again, Diego asked Marisa, "Why was that big man standing behind your father?"

"Papa likes to keep security guards around. He says people of means need a little security in a strange land. We had them when we lived in Mexico, too, though. I've gotten used to them. They may look scary at first, but they don't bite, and some of them are quite nice." Marisa smiled. "Come, let's get you some dinner."

After they had eaten, Diego told Marisa he was in training and needed to go home to bed.

"I hope I will see you again soon, Diego. Houston is a big city, and I would love to show you around. Here is my cell phone number and email address." Marisa leaned up and pulled Diego down to where she could kiss him on his cheek. "Will I hear from you soon?"

• • •

The following day Diego sought out Pico in his office after practice.

"How was the party, Diego? Did you have a good time?" Pico asked, leaning back in his chair.

"It was interesting. The house was impressive, and Marisa was muy amable. Even though she is a rich society girl, she made me feel comfortable." Diego remembered how she'd kissed his cheek and felt it grow hot where her lips had been.

"You should follow up on that one, Diego. She's a beauty and very rich."

"She is lovely. But I couldn't help but wonder, Pico, how did Señor Escobar make his money? There were security guards everywhere. That seemed strange to me, here in Houston."

Pico shrugged. "Nobody knows. Some people say he is an industrialist, others that he owns a shipping enterprise. Then I heard he was in the financial business. Some of his white neighbors don't like Mexicans living so close to them and are suspicious of the muscle men around the house. They say that there are tunnels running between the houses and drug money is behind all the wealth." He laughed. "Some Americans see rich Mexicans and immediately assume there is drug money. That's crazy! River Oaks, Memorial, and the Woodlands are all full of Mexicans who have made homes in Houston because it is safer. I wouldn't worry about it, Diego."

But Diego couldn't dismiss the image of the big man with the gun standing guard behind Marisa's father so casually. After all, he had become personally aware of the infiltration of the cartels in the United States. Wasn't he trying to find his sister who had been forced, possibly by a cartel, to live in the underworld of this beautiful city? He had no reason to think Marisa's father was engaged in illegal activities. But he had learned that not all that was beautiful on the surface was innocent underneath.

• • •

It wasn't long before Diego saw Marisa again. She was waiting for him near the locker room when he came off the field after the next home game. It had been a close, hard-fought game, but the Storm had won, with Diego scoring two goals.

"You were magnificent, Diego!" she greeted him. "I was hoping I could take you out to dinner to celebrate your victory . . . if you don't have other plans."

Diego started to make an excuse, but Marisa was so cute in her short white lace skirt and a Storm T-shirt visible under her black leather jacket, he found himself agreeing to meet her at the entrance to the stadium after he showered. Marisa had come to the game with her father, so they drove in Diego's car.

"Where are we going?" he asked.

"Tony's, near Greenway Plaza," Marisa told him. "It is small, but the restaurant stays open late, and many people think it is the best restaurant in Houston. They have a continental menu, and the food is excellent. I think you'll like it."

Diego didn't know what a continental menu was, and he was surprised at the elegance of the outside of the restaurant. He had not eaten at many restaurants where chandeliers hung from the ceiling and where the only job for the men in uniforms appeared to be opening the door for arriving diners.

When they entered the restaurant, the maître d' smiled and greeted

Marisa. "Would you like your usual table near the flower arrangement in the middle, Señorita Escobar?"

"Yes, Antonio. We are celebrating a victory, so would you please bring us a couple of glasses of Cristal?" She had her arm through Diego's, beaming at Antonio.

"Certainly," he replied. Then a hostess showed them to their table, and a waiter brought two beautiful crystal flutes of bubbling champagne.

Diego no longer drank alcohol. He took the glass, however, because he didn't know what else to do. He didn't drink it, but Marisa either didn't notice or just didn't bring it up. He could see that well-dressed white people at other tables were looking at them. That made him uncomfortable. But Marisa had a delightful, disarming personality, and it was pleasant to converse with a beautiful woman in his own language.

"I should tell you all my deep, dark secrets," Marisa said. "I am just a little younger than you, I think."

"I am sure you are," Diego replied, amused. "But my mother told me never to ask a lady her age."

"Well, I'll tell you anyway," Marisa said. "You are twenty-five or twenty-six, depending on which official source is correct. I am twenty-two. That's a good difference. Men always like to feel as though they are older and more superior. Right?"

"You mean women in our culture like to make men think they are superior." Diego laughed. "But we both know who usually rules the family."

"Cheers!" Marisa said, clicking her glass against Diego's. "I like your cultural acumen."

Diego could see why Marisa was a popular woman. She was beautiful, witty, and fun to be with. When she smiled, he forgot about the stressful thoughts he had had that day. When the waiter brought the menu, he didn't recognize most of the things on it. Intuitively sensing this, Marisa asked, "Do you mind if I order for us, Diego? I eat here all the time, and I know what is really good. What kind of food do you like?"

"I eat fairly healthy now," Diego replied.

Marisa ordered redfish for the two of them and green salads.

After Marisa ordered, Diego asked, "How long has your family been in Houston, Marisa?"

"We moved to Houston from Mexico when I was in high school. I attended an all-girls Catholic school here to finish. I just graduated from St. Thomas University. My major was art history. My parents insisted I live at home during college, but my best friend and I recently moved into a beautiful apartment in a high-rise building in the Galleria area on San Felipe. There is a doorman and security and all the things parents think their children need when they leave home. There is also shopping and good restaurants and spas and all the things all young women love to do."

"Very nice. I was told by an admirer at the stadium that your picture is in the paper a lot," Diego replied. "Why is that?"

Marisa laughed. "I volunteer for different museums in Houston." She took a sip of champagne and continued. "I'm also studying for the GRE. But that's just between you and me."

"What is that?" Diego asked. The waiter brought their food to the table, so Marisa didn't answer until he left them.

"It's the test you take to get into graduate school. I know everyone thinks I am a dumb party girl, but I want to be a museum director someday. I graduated with a 3.8 grade point average, and I speak excellent Spanish and English. I would like to curate Latin American art and then move on to be head of a museum."

Diego was surprised but tried not to show it. He cut into the redfish on his plate and listened as she went on. "I haven't been able to convince Papa that a girl can be smart and tough enough to operate a business. He's very old-fashioned when it comes to women. He has traditional male ideas about how men should protect and shelter their women and make their life comfortable and pleasant. He likes to say, 'Don't worry your pretty little head about things, Marisa. Men will always want to take care of you.'" Marisa frowned.

Diego nodded. "I hope you know that not all men think women are not as smart as men."

"That makes you even more attractive, Diego. If that's possible." She smiled.

Diego realized that he'd was actually been thinking of Mary when he'd made that comment.

"How about you?" Marisa asked. "Tell me all about yourself before you came to Houston."

"There's not a lot to tell," Diego said. "I grew up in a small town in Guanajuato province, with a brother and sister. My father owns a store and wanted me to take it over when he retired, as he did from his father. But I hated standing still behind a counter, making small talk with the customers and selling stuff all day. My brother, Carlos, is learning to take over now when our papa retires. Carlos is much better suited for that work. He loves it."

"And why did you decide to become a famous fútbol player?" Marisa asked.

The waiter topped off their water glasses and asked them if they were satisfied with their food. Diego thought it was the best meal he had ever had, but he just said, "Sí, gracias."

Then he answered Marisa's question. "All my life I wanted to be a professional fútbol player. I was not as good a student in school as my brother and sister, because I was always more interested in getting out to the fútbol pitch. I was naturally fast and good at the sport. When I was fourteen, coaches and agents were talking about me. Everyone thought I was special, destined to be playing at the professional level earlier than most players. When I got to the semi-professional level, I liked being a big fish in a little pond, as they say, and I didn't work hard anymore. My career stalled and almost died. A lot of people thought

I was lazy, but I wasn't lazy so much as I just didn't take life seriously."
Holding up the menu to hide his face, Diego said in a low voice, "And
then my sister was kidnapped, because I didn't take life seriously."

"How terrible, Diego. How did that happen?" Marisa asked, a sincerely concerned look on her face.

He cleared his throat, put the menu down, and continued. "Four
years ago, my sister, who was nineteen at the time and married, with
a nine-month-old baby, asked if she could go with me to Mexico
City when I ran errands for our papa. Stupidly, I left her alone for a
couple of hours in a bad neighborhood. I believe she was kidnapped,
smuggled across the border against her will, and forced into the commercial sex trade. My family and her husband, my best friend, were
devastated. Concepción, my niece, was left without a mother, all
because of my stupidity and selfishness. I swore to them then that
I would find her or find out what had happened to her. I have been
searching for her ever since."

"What did you do?" Marisa asked. She had put her fork and knife
down and was listening to Diego's story, rapt.

"The realization of what I had done made me grow up and finally
get serious. I worked hard at making it to the professional level. A
Mexico City team hired me, and when we won the championship last
year, I got offers from clubs all over the States. That's when I decided
to join the Storm."

"That's awful, Diego," Marisa said, reaching across the table to put
her hand on his. "But why Houston?"

"There were several reasons," Diego said, "but I think it was a good
choice. I have received information that the name of the padrón who
has been selling her is Eduardo Ayala and he hangs out in Southeast
Houston. She may be a captive in one of the cantinas there."

Just then the waiter appeared and asked if he could take away
their plates.

"I am so sorry, Marisa. You invite me for a beautiful dinner, and I tell you my sad story. I will not say any more. Now tell me more about what you enjoy doing."

• • •

The next day, the society column in the *Chronicle* reported under the "Seen in Houston" byline that "Socialite Marisa Escobar and Storm standout Diego Gonzales were spotted having an intimate late dinner at Tony's last night. As always, Marisa looked ravishing. Diego looked entranced."

Marisa continued to attend Storm games and often talked Diego into going out for something to eat afterward. He told her Tony's was too fancy for him, so they went to casual places. They followed his normal training diet of salads, fruit, vegetables, and lean meat, but occasionally they went to Hugo's or another good Mexican restaurant. Sometimes they ended the evening at Diego's apartment. Marisa was fun and made certain he knew she was available to him. She invited him to charity fund-raising galas and the ballet. Diego always declined, citing his need to get his sleep during the season. The thought of going to that type of event did not interest him; it terrified him.

Yet he enjoyed his time with Marisa. He was not sure why, but he never thought to mention his friendship with Marisa to Mary.

CHAPTER 18

SARA BETH

"Hey, sis," John said. He stood in the open door of her small, cluttered office at Legal Aid. It was August 2011. The floor was carpeted in industrial carpeting, and the venetian blinds on the windows belied the small budget of the office. There were some personal touches. Mary's degrees from Rice and Yale hung on the wall, and framed pictures of her and girlfriends at St. John's, Rice, and Yale, as well as a few pictures of John's twins, sat on the bookshelves. A small oriental rug that Mary had purchased on a trip to Turkey covered the floor under two Chippendale guest chairs she had brought from her parents' house after she and John sold it.

"This is a nice surprise," Mary said as she looked up from the pleading she was drafting. "What brings you down here in the middle of a Wednesday afternoon? The economy is picking up. Aren't you busy doing the big, sexy deals?"

John shrugged, walking in. "Yeah, the usual exciting stuff: company A buys out company B. There are hundreds of assets and liabilities to catalogue and transfer—thousands of agreements to draft that keep scores of eager young lawyers billing away into the early hours of the morning. It's thrilling. You don't know what you're missing."

"No thanks," Mary grimaced. "I'd rather help real people with real-life legal problems. But I appreciate someone's got to keep the wheels of commerce turning so oil keeps flowing through the pipelines and the Galleria stays crowded with shoppers."

"I'll ignore your sarcasm for now," he said, sitting down in one of the guest chairs. "I stopped by because there's something I want to talk to you about. I thought your office might be the best place."

Mary watched his eyes survey her degrees hanging on the wall. She knew he hadn't understand how she could throw away an Ivy League legal education by working at Legal Aid. He always told her that's where people in the bottom half of the class worked, which annoyed her.

Mary had graduated with honors at Yale Law and been a senior editor on the *Yale Law Review*, which was an automatic ticket to a Wall Street law firm. But she hadn't even interviewed with them. The proceeds from the sale of the family grocery stores was more than enough to make both children comfortable, but she believed life was about more than money. She loved her clients and found purpose in her work.

"Spill it," Mary said. "I've got to get these papers filed with the court before 5:00."

"I want to talk to you about Diego," John said.

"What about Diego?" She looked up. "I thought you liked him."

"I do. Diego is a good man and a hell of an athlete."

Mary's annoyance was growing. "But?"

"You seem to be spending a lot of time with him," John said.

"Is that a problem?"

"It's just that we think this idea of an illegal alien prostitute being a member of our family could be embarrassing if it got out." John took off his glasses and wiped them with a tissue from the box on Mary's desk, not looking at her.

Mary sat back in her chair and put down her pen. She squinted her eyes at her brother as if seeing a strange new person.

"Who are you, John Chavez, son of a Mexican immigrant who came across the border without an official invitation from the United States of America?"

Her brother shifted uncomfortably in his chair.

"Pilar Chavez is not a prostitute, John. Prostitutes sell their bodies willingly for money. Young women who are kidnapped, beaten, threatened, and forced to have sex with any man who pays their captors for the opportunity to assault them are not prostitutes."

Mary stared at him and continued, "The sex-trafficking business is unspeakably inhumane. We should have compassion for Pilar and women like her and try to help them—not condemn and shun them."

John got up out of his chair and walked across the room to her bookshelf, where Vernon's Revised Texas Statutes were displayed, before turning around and saying, "You are a lawyer, Mary. Under the law today, these women, Pilar included, are prostitutes. That's a fact, regardless of your feelings about how things should be."

"I'm also a woman and a human being who knows that sometimes the law, as written by men for the most part, is wrong," Mary said. "I admire Diego for trying to rescue his sister. I'm grateful to have the opportunity to help him."

John waited, eyes on the wall again, reading the degrees she knew he thought she'd tossed aside. "Are you sure it's your feelings for truth and justice and not your feelings for Diego motivating you?" John asked, looking at his sister, his own face still blank.

The blood rushed to Mary's face.

"I saw the way you looked at him," John said. "You may not even realize it. He's a handsome man, for sure. I'd even say he has charisma in a macho sort of way. But be careful, Mary. We don't know anything about him besides what he's told us—and even he is guessing about Pilar's situation. He can't know for sure she was kidnapped. He's going on circumstantial evidence. For all we know, Pilar is a willing participant. Can you objectively consider that? Put your lawyer hat on for a minute, Mary."

Mary's face was warm, but the heat of her anger flowed into her chest. "Of course, I have considered that. I just feel like he is right about what happened to her."

"There are those feelings again!" John quipped.

Mary stood up abruptly and walked toward the window in her office, weighing her words carefully now. "You started this conversation by saying 'we' are concerned. Who's 'we'?"

When John didn't reply, she turned to face him.

"Does 'we' include Sara Beth? Is she concerned that her society friends might find out she's distantly related by marriage to a sex slave? Would they snub her if they knew this dirty little secret?" Mary felt her anger color her words.

"Sara Beth has a right to be concerned about how this might be perceived." John's face finally showed some emotion: he was angry now too. "She's worked hard to secure a respected place for our family in the community."

"Oh, please," Mary said, exaggerating the words. "No one will ever know about Pilar unless Sara Beth tells them. Of course, that would require a little discretion on Sara Beth's part!"

"It's not just Sara Beth," John interrupted her.

Just then the intercom on Mary's desk rang. Mary pushed the button, and her secretary asked if she wanted to take a call from another lawyer she had been trying to reach all day.

"Tell him I'll call him back, Suzanne," Mary said sharply. Then she looked at John and asked, "Is there another 'we'?"

"Mary, you must realize there are important people in my firm who wouldn't look favorably upon this whole situation. I'll be up for partnership consideration in a year. My firm is conservative. I will be the first person of Hispanic heritage up for partner. It's important that my family have an impeccable reputation."

"Ah, the corporate 'we.'" Mary sighed.

"Besides, think of your position," John said. "What you do here is sanctioned and respected by the bar. But you are not supposed to be representing illegal immigrants. 'Illegal' means they are breaking the law. It's outside the scope of your charter."

"Pilar didn't exactly intend to immigrate to the United States, John. She was kidnapped and smuggled across the border against her will by criminals. Besides, I am not providing legal representation to Pilar or Diego. On my own personal time, I'm helping an upstanding young man who is in this country legally. He asked for our help finding and saving a sister for whose misfortune he feels responsible. Do you remember the story he told us about our father and Isabel, the young girl with whom he ran away? I think that part of Dad's occasional moodiness, his wanting to forget about his life in Mexico, and his drive to succeed in this country all rose out of that event. He probably felt responsible for her death all his life. I can't ease Dad's pain now, but maybe I can do that for Diego. Maybe that's why he appeared in our life."

"Or maybe cosmic redemptions don't exist! Maybe Dad had the right idea that we should not get involved in an unhappy heritage in the old country and just be glad we're living in the States!" John practically shouted at his sister.

Mary and John were both angry now—something entirely new to their relationship. Neither of them liked it. Finally, John asked in a calmer voice, "Do you deny that you have romantic feelings for Diego?"

"My romantic feelings, even if I have any, don't matter. Diego has two obsessions in his life—finding Pilar and winning soccer games. There isn't room for anything or anyone else. Those are the things that define him right now." Mary walked back to her desk and sat down again in her chair, ruffling some papers.

"Look, Mary," John sighed, taking her hands in his. "My selfish objectives aside, I don't want to see you get hurt. I think you are leaving yourself open to getting hurt emotionally by a man who you admit has overriding interests that consume him. They may make him incapable of receiving and giving love."

"Who said anything about love?" Mary retorted. She abruptly stood up again and went to the window to adjust the blinds, turning away from her brother so he couldn't see her frustrated expression.

"Aside from whatever feelings you have about Diego, I don't want you to put yourself in situations that are dangerous for you. I suspect you have been going into bad areas of town. You don't know what you're dealing with. These Mexican and Central American gangs are all over the news. They are ruthless killers. I don't want you to lose your life searching for someone it is unlikely Diego will find. Pilar disappeared more than four years ago. Odds are she is in a physical or psychological situation where she is beyond saving."

Mary started to say something, but John raised his hand.

"Don't say anything now, Mary. Just please think about what I have said. Somewhere in that big brain is a reason you can accept to stop this senseless and dangerous quest."

Mary's lips were tight and her shoulders back. She was trying to control her anger.

Then John's voice became almost plaintive: "Look, Mary, stop thinking about Diego and consider me. I love you, Mary. I need my sister to be here for me—to listen to my stupid problems, be the fun aunt to my children, and be my best friend. I don't know what I would do if anything happened to you."

Mary knew John was sincere. They had always been each other's best friends. She thought about what it would be like for her if she lost John, and softened.

"Okay, John. I hear you. And I'll consider your concerns." She hugged him a long time, trying to make sense of her own feelings about Diego. She was rational enough to know they were an unlikely pair, but she admired his devotion to his family—and the physical attraction was strong.

• • •

A week later, Mary dialed Sara Beth.

"Hey, Mary!" Sara Beth drawled. "You caught me on my way home from tennis at the club."

"Hey, Sara Beth. John and I have both been so busy lately, it's been a while since we've gotten together for dinner. Would Sunday night work for you all? I'm going to invite Diego, too. John told me you all have reservations about him, since he appeared out of nowhere. Dinner would give us a chance to get to know each other better and for John and you to ask Diego any questions you have." Mary knew it was a long shot, but she felt that Sara Beth was the key to John's acceptance of her helping Diego.

Sara Beth hesitated but said, "That would be delightful, Mary. What time would you like us to come?"

"Let's make it a casual family dinner with the kids around seven. I'll cook King Ranch casserole and make margaritas. What do you think?"

"Great. I'll bring dessert," Sara Beth replied.

That Sunday, Diego arrived at Mary's bungalow at 6:45, carrying a bouquet of red roses for the hostess.

"They're beautiful, Diego. Thank you," Mary said, taking the roses to put them in a vase. As she did so, their hands touched, and Mary felt herself blushing. She turned quickly to the kitchen, hoping he hadn't noticed.

"I have to admit, Mary, that I'm a little nervous about seeing John again and meeting his wife. I have learned that he is a very important lawyer in a prestigious law firm. I am only an uneducated boy from a little town in Mexico who is good at kicking balls around a field."

"Not to mention an international soccer star!" Mary laughed. "Don't worry about John. He's the nicest guy in the world. A little sheltered and narrow in his worldview maybe. He has spent his whole life in Texas—school, corporate law, and making money for his wife to spend."

"What is his wife like?"

"Mmmmm, that might be reason to be nervous," Mary replied.

"Why?" Diego looked concerned.

"Sara Beth is a good woman and a great mother. But she has led a certain life—best prep schools, best hill country summer camp, best sorority at UT, debutante, and on and on. She is like many of my good friends from school here." Mary sighed, placing the roses on the table. "She works hard, raising a lot of money for charitable causes in the city. Most of all she is a fierce protector of her husband and children's privileged place in Houston. You can't criticize her for wanting the best for them. But anyone who didn't grow up in Texas is suspect."

Diego smiled. "Like me?"

"Sí, mi amigo." Mary smiled. "If you want to charm anyone, it's Sara Beth."

"I see," Diego said. "Charm is not my strongest skill, but I'll do my best."

Just then the doorbell rang, but before Mary could get to the door, two blond toddlers threw it open, rushing in and hugging her around the legs.

"Aunt Mary!" they screamed. Then, "Where's your TV? Can you put the Disney Channel on?"

Mary laughed. "Only if you give me a kiss first," she said, kneeling to collect kisses from her twin three-year-old niece and nephew.

"Where do I put the dessert?" John asked, juggling a pecan pie and a carton of Blue Bell Homemade Vanilla ice cream as he walked in. "Hey, Diego. It's good to see you again."

Diego walked over and took the pie from John, freeing John's hand for a serious handshake.

Then Sara Beth made her entrance. Diego thought she was striking. She was relatively tall for a woman but wore four-inch-high Christian Louboutin heels with a pair of stylish dark blue tapered jeans. Her hair appeared naturally blonde and hung down past her shoulders.

She wore a white cashmere sweater over her Pilates-tuned trim body with a large silver necklace and substantial diamond stud earrings. Her engagement ring was an impressive knuckle-sized diamond, and she carried a red shopper bag on her arm that said "Prada." Her face was naturally beautiful, so she wore only pink lipstick and black mascara over her light green eyes. Her posture was straight, and she looked like someone who was accustomed to being admired and obeyed.

She gave Mary a light hug and an air kiss before turning to Diego.

Looking him over for just long enough not to be rude, she gave a tepid smile and said, "Hello, Diego. I'm John's better half. It's nice to finally get to meet you. I suppose we should have invited you over before this, but we've been terribly busy with family and social obligations. I'm sure you understand." She extended a limp French-manicured hand.

Diego took her hand in his, kissed it lightly, and looked directly into her eyes with his deep, dark brown ones. "It is an honor to make your acquaintance, Señora Chavez. Mary has told me many wonderful things about you."

"You can call me Sara Beth," she said, charmed despite herself.

Behind her, Mary smiled at Diego and gave him a thumbs-up.

Mary had set out placemats, silverware, and napkins on the antique oak dining room table that had been her mother's. Despite Sara Beth's initial objection, the children ate cheese pizza in front of the TV in the study, so the adults could talk freely.

Mary had already mixed the margaritas with a kicker of Cointreau. She poured a glass for Sara Beth, John, and herself. Then she gave Diego a glass of Perrier with lime. They stood in the kitchen and caught up on local gossip for a half hour while the casserole baked. When the buzzer on the oven signaled that dinner was ready, Mary asked everyone to have a seat wherever they wanted to sit. Chips, salsa, and guacamole were already on the table.

When everyone was seated and the casserole served, Mary started the conversation. "Diego has been telling me a lot about our heritage.

I've learned about the town Dad grew up in in Mexico and the people there. Is there anything you all would like to ask him?"

"Well, I was wondering about Victor's family," John said after a pause. "You said he had a brother. Did he have any other siblings? Who were their parents?"

"Victor had two brothers, Julio and Miguel, and three sisters. The girls married local boys from San José, most of whom worked in the pottery factories. They produced ten children among them.

"Miguel, the youngest, has four children, the oldest of which is Alejandro. Alejandro is married to Pilar. Miguel's other children are much younger. There are many relatives, most of them still living in San José," Diego explained. "A few moved to bigger cities after the pottery industry declined."

"That boggles my mind," John said. "Mary and I grew up in Houston without any relatives, except a few who live in San Antonio. Our parents were so busy working, we never saw much of them. I can't even imagine what it would be like to live among so many cousins in one little town."

"There are no secrets among families in San José," Diego said. "There are good and bad aspects to that. Before you ask a girl on a date, you must first ask your mother if she is a close relative."

Everybody chuckled.

"I think it sounds wonderful," Mary said. "I always envied the kids who came from big families. They seemed to have more confidence, maybe because they knew someone always had their back."

"I tried to always be there for you, Mary," John said.

"Of course you did. That's not what I meant. But children in large families have a whole network of support." Mary reached across the table and took John's hand. They smiled at each other—quarrel forgotten.

"But you were four years older than me. Once you went to college and law school, I was on my own," Mary said, rising to refill everyone's water glasses and to sneak a quick look at her niece and nephew, who had been quiet for a long time. Satisfied that they were still mesmer-ized by Mickey and Minnie, she returned to the table.

"What were Dad's parents like, Diego?" Mary asked, trying to change the subject.

"I didn't know them, but my mother told me they were wonderful people—always laughing and very loving toward their children. His father especially doted on Victor, who was exceptionally bright and personable. But everything changed after Victor disappeared. Victor's mother was distraught. She didn't believe he would do anything wrong. She suspected something terrible must have happened to cause him and Isabel to run away. Her instinct was correct, but Julio never told anyone what had happened."

"What were Victor's parents' names?" John asked.

"His mother's name was Maria Elena, and his father's name was Juan Pablo."

John held the fork he was using to eat his pecan pie in midair.

"Is something wrong?" Diego asked when everyone stopped eating.

"My name is Mary Ellen," Mary said. "And it seems Dad named his son after his own father; Juan Pablo means John Paul in English, of course."

"But Juan is a very common name in Mexico, isn't it?" Sara Beth asked, her tone harsh. "John is the most common name in English. That could just be a coincidence."

She still doesn't want to believe Pilar is related to them, Mary thought.

"Of course, señora," Diego replied after a few seconds of silence.

"You use John Paul Chavez professionally, John. Anyone could know that," Sara Beth said too quickly.

Mary and John both looked at her, embarrassed.

"Of course, señora," Diego replied. He kept his eyes on Sara Beth and John. "I wouldn't blame you if you were skeptical about the infor-mation I have given you. I am a stranger, after all."

"Diego, could you help me clear the table for dessert?" Mary asked.

When they reached the kitchen, Mary said, "Please don't be offended, Diego. Sara Beth is not a mean person. It just takes her a while to get accustomed to new things. Some people have a self-identity and a routine life in which they are most comfortable. But she'll come around."

When Mary and Diego returned with plates of pecan pie and ice cream, Sara Beth had regained her composure and complimented Mary on the dinner.

Diego thought quietly about where the conversation had ended and asked, "Mary and John, did your father keep anything personal from his childhood? Did he have anything that could connect him to San José?"

John and Mary looked at each other and thought for a few minutes. Then John said, "We found a jewelry box in the back of Dad's closet after he died. There was a small silver crucifix inside. It looked as if it had belonged to a girl. We assumed it had belonged to our mother, who'd died two years earlier than Dad, but she didn't wear a lot of jewelry, never religious jewelry, and it seemed odd that it was hidden away. It was a cheap box, and the silver was severely tarnished, as though it was old. I suppose it could have been from Mexico. I don't know what happened to it. Do you, Mary?"

"I know exactly where it is," Mary said, getting up from the table. "I kept it and put it with the rest of Mom's keepsakes. I'll get it."

No one spoke while Mary walked to her bedroom. A few minutes later she was back, holding a small, tattered paper box. She placed it in the middle of the table, and everyone stared at it, as if it were a bomb that might explode.

"Well, for God's sake, open it," Sara Beth said. She waved her arm over the box as if to mimic a sleight-of-hand trick. As she did so, the scent of Chanel N° 5 wafted through the air.

Mary lifted the top off the box. Inside was a small, almost black crucifix on a delicate silver chain. She picked it up and dangled it from her fingers.

"I have seen that type of crucifix before," Diego said. "In San José, parents give their daughters similar ones for their Confirmation when they accept the church and become a young woman. Pilar almost never took hers off."

"Another coincidence," Sara Beth whispered under her breath.

"Sara Beth!" John admonished her this time.

Annoyed at being admonished, Sara Beth got up and found her purse. She applied a thick coat of pink lipstick before returning to the table.

"Our parents inscribed Pilar's initials on the back of her crucifix," Diego said. "Mary, do you have any silver polish?"

"Sure," Mary said, getting up to go to the kitchen.

She returned with some Hagerty silver polish and a clean, soft tea towel. Slowly, she began to rub away years of tarnish. When the silver shone again, she turned the cross over. On the back were the initials ILTG.

"Isabel Lourdes Torres Gomez," Diego said. "That's the young girl who drowned in the river."

Sara Beth was silent, but her facial expression was sour. It was obvious that Sara Beth didn't want to be related to family in Mexico, especially not a woman she considered an illegal alien and prostitute. John and Mary were fair complexioned and attractive, had been educated in all the best schools, were completely assimilated, and had been left relatively well-off financially when their parents passed away and the children sold the grocery stores so they could focus on their law practices. Sara Beth had managed to ignore their Hispanic heritage up until now.

Sara Beth turned to Diego and smiled. "I read in the *Chronicle* that you've been dating Marisa Escobar. She's certainly a beautiful young woman, and I hear her father is very wealthy. How serious is it? Will we be going to a Mexican wedding soon? How delightful that would be!"

CHAPTER 19

PADRE ROBERTO

"Mary, can you call me today? I have something important to tell you." Padre Roberto's voice was full of excitement.

Mary had missed the call when it had come in because she'd been in court all morning. It wasn't like the old priest to get excited. She had been volunteering after work sometimes, helping his parishioners with legal issues, but she'd never heard him so animated. He often said, "I have seen everything in my worldly lifetime. Nothing surprises me now." She wondered what had gotten the man so riled up, so she called him back immediately.

"Mary, I have seen her," Padre Roberto said, not even saying hello when she answered her phone. "I have seen Pilar! I couldn't say for sure, but I am almost positive I saw her."

Mary's heart stopped. "Where did you see her, Padre?"

"At the bank. Señora Ramirez, who makes the deposit of the Sunday collections, went to visit her daughter in San Antonio for Labor Day week, so I went this afternoon instead. I thought the walk would do me good. At the counter, I noticed a young woman at the next window. There was a big Mexican man with her. He would look around and back at her. He seemed to be very familiar with the teller."

"But you got a good look at her face?" *Could it be?*

"Yes. When the woman finished making deposits, she turned toward me to go. We looked at each other. Mary, I have never seen such sad eyes in all my days in the priesthood. She was a beautiful woman, just like in Diego's picture, but older and pale. It was as if, for an instant, she recognized me as someone she used to know. But the big man called to her, and she quickly turned away and left with him. Mary, he called her 'Pilar.'"

This may be the break we need, Mary thought.

"Good work, Padre. I must call Diego. The Storm are playing out of town, but he will want to know. Thank you so much. This sighting is the most promising information yet. Not only is she alive, but she's still in Houston!"

"Let's hope so," Padre Roberto said.

"Did you see which way they went when they left the bank?" Mary asked.

"They got into a black pickup truck. A parishioner interrupted me, and I did not see which way they went."

· · ·

Diego was surprised when he saw Mary's number come up on the caller ID of his mobile phone. She had avoided his calls after Sara Beth ended the dinner party at Mary's house with her question about his relationship with Marisa Escobar. Diego had been so surprised that Sara Beth knew about his friendship with Marisa that he hadn't been able to respond that night. The dinner party had wrapped up soon after. Mary had said she would clean up the next day and hadn't asked him to stay when John and Sara Beth had left. Since then, when they did talk on the phone, she kept the conversation short.

Not seeing or talking with her, Diego realized how important Mary had become in his life. He missed her companionship, her intellect, and her wry sense of humor. He knew he would not be as far along in his search for Pilar without her. He thought she was an attractive woman, but he was aware of the difference in their educations and socioeconomic backgrounds, so he hadn't dared to think about her in romantic terms.

He had continued to spend time with Marisa after home games. She was beautiful and amusing. She reminded him of the good things in his culture and took his mind off the pressure of winning soccer games and searching for Pilar. She made him laugh—something he had not done much of during the past four years. He knew she wanted more out of the relationship, but he had too much else going on in his life. Sometimes, she fixed a simple meal of tacos and guacamole at his apartment and spent the night. Besides, he didn't like galas, polo games, and the ballet—the types of amusements she and her social friends did.

"Mary," Diego answered, "I am so glad to hear your voice."

Mary didn't speak for a moment, but then she said, "Diego, I have some good news. Padre Roberto was at the bank making a deposit this morning and thinks he saw Pilar! She's alive, Diego! And she's probably not far away."

Diego listened to Mary's report of Padre Roberto's encounter. Then he said, "I am in Miami, but I will be back in Houston at midnight. I have missed seeing you. Can we get together?"

"Okay," Mary said after a minute. "We need to figure out where this takes us."

• • •

At the same time, Marisa had been growing frustrated that her relationship with Diego was not getting more serious. She was determined not only to keep but to deepen his interest in her. She called him as soon as she thought he would be awake on the day after he returned to Houston from Miami.

"Diego," she greeted him with excitement in her voice. "I think I know something that may help you find your sister."

"What are you saying, Marisa. How could you?" Then Diego remembered that he had told Marisa about his search for Pilar the first night they had had dinner together in the fancy restaurant. He never discussed it after that.

"Well," Marisa said, "while you were out of town, I was thinking about how you'd told me you think she might be captive in a cantina. Occasionally I have heard my papa's security men mention that they were going to the cantinas after work. So, on the off chance that he knew the pimp who is keeping your sister, I struck up a conversation with Beto, one of the local men who grew up here in Houston. He is the most talkative anyway."

Diego held his breath.

"I asked Beto if he had ever heard of a man named Eduardo Ayala when he was visiting the clubs on the east side of town. I said that one of my friends had asked me about him. He seemed surprised and told me that I should stay away from friends who knew that bastard, Eduardo. He said that he was a dangerous man and I should forget I had even heard his name.

"I told Beto that my friend said Eduardo owed him money and he was trying to find him to get his money back. I asked Beto if he knew where Eduardo lived. I promised that I would just pass on the information. I wouldn't go anywhere near Eduardo."

"What did he say?" Diego asked, now extremely interested.

"He said he didn't know where he lived but that Eduardo hung around a club called Los Arboles on Telephone Road a lot. Poor Beto, he looked very uncomfortable and said my papa would probably not be happy he had told me that. I kind of felt sorry for him, but I would do anything to help you, Diego."

"Muchas gracias, Marisa, that is helpful," Diego said. "But I care about you, Marisa, and I don't want you to do anything that might get you in trouble with your papa or otherwise."

After they said goodbye and hung up, Marisa walked out on the veranda with a glass of white wine. She felt pleased with what she had done. Diego was very grateful. She wondered what would happen now.

Chapter 20

MARISA

Diego got another call from Marisa late that afternoon. This time, however, she sounded aggravated.

"Diego," she said, "Papa is sending me to Europe for several weeks on a shopping trip with my mother. We leave tonight, and I won't be able to see you before I go."

"I'm sorry, Marisa," Diego said. "Is this trip unexpected?"

"Yes, the timing of this exile to Europe makes me think my questioning Beto about Eduardo Ayala may be what caused it, for some reason. Beto told the head of Papa's security guard about our conversation, and he told Papa. This afternoon, Papa gave me a stern lecture about my not poking my nose into sordid things that good girls shouldn't know about. He means well. He is just old-fashioned and very protective of women."

"I understand, Marisa," Diego said.

"One thing I need to tell you, Diego. I know it was a mistake. Papa asked me who my friend was who was looking for Eduardo. I didn't know what to say. When he pressed me, I told him it was you. I hope that doesn't cause a problem. It was a stupid thing to do. I'll miss you, Diego. I hope to see you when I get home."

"Thank you, Marisa. We all do stupid things. I am a prime example of that. I didn't mean to cause you any trouble when I told you about my personal problems. I'm sorry if I did."

"Don't worry about it, Diego. I want to help you. You know I am crazy about you. I only hope you feel the same way about me."

Diego hesitated. Then he said, "Thank you for this information, Marisa."

As soon as he hung up with Marisa, Diego called Mary and asked if she could come to his apartment in Midtown that evening. He was anxious to tell her this latest information. Midtown was a recent redevelopment of the area between the office buildings in downtown Houston and the Museum District, which was home to the Houston Museum of Fine Arts, Contemporary Arts Museum, Glassell School of Art, and Rice University. New mid-rise high-end apartment complexes and restaurants were rapidly replacing old commercial buildings and run-down rooming houses and apartments. Young professionals chose to live there for its proximity to downtown, restaurants, the theater district, and the sports stadiums.

When Mary arrived, Diego was excited. "I know where Eduardo hangs out, Mary. There is a cantina named Los Arboles on Telephone Road. I called Padre Roberto and asked him if he is familiar with it. He said it is a notorious cantina and brothel where mostly Hispanic men can have sex with Hispanic girls. An old woman and her family own it. He said they are ruthless people. And didn't Padre Roberto see Pilar at a bank on Telephone Road? I bet she is somewhere in that area. I am getting closer!"

Mary listened but then said, "Diego, I can't help worrying. Maybe my brother is right. Maybe you are putting yourself in too much danger."

"I appreciate your concern, Mary, but I can't give up now. I don't want to endanger you. I seem to have a way of doing that to young women. If you want to stay out of this, I will completely understand."

Mary knew she wouldn't be able to deter Diego. He wouldn't stop until he found Pilar or got himself killed trying. She cared deeply about him. She admired his passion to find his sister and redeem himself. She loved talking, joking, and just being with him. She didn't want him to get hurt.

Mary asked Diego if she could have a Diet Coke. She used the time while he was in the kitchen to think. When he returned, she said, "I think we should call Steve. He speaks local Spanish and wouldn't attract attention in that place. If he's willing, he could go in and try to find Pilar, if she is there."

"As always, Mary, you come up with a good plan. I believe you are the smartest person I have ever met," Diego said.

I guess that's something, Mary thought.

After a pizza dinner, Diego walked Mary to her car, which was parked a block away from his apartment building. He noticed a big black SUV with darkened windows parked across the street. He thought he might have seen it before, but he quickly forgot about it, preoccupied with how they could find out if Pilar was at Los Arboles.

Leaving Midtown, Mary drove west on Allen Parkway and then north across I-10 and into the Heights. When she crossed White Oak Drive, Studewood Street narrowed to two lanes. She was aware of a high pair of headlights that seemed to be following her quite closely, but she dismissed it as one of Houston's many bad drivers. Suddenly, the driver of a dark pickup truck in front of her hit his brakes and stopped the truck completely. She barely avoided rear-ending it. In her rearview mirror, she watched with horror as a black SUV with darkened windows almost hit her from behind before it, too, abruptly stopped. Neither vehicle moved. The passenger-side door of the SUV opened and closed a few moments later, but she didn't see anyone. She realized that her little car was wedged between the two vehicles so that she couldn't move it. She was trapped. She became uneasy with the unusual situation and hit her horn once. There was no response.

When the truck didn't move and no one got out, she grew frightened. This situation was more than just bad driving—it was scary. She opened the glove compartment, reached in, and took out her Glock, releasing the safety. She firmly gripped it with her right hand, ready to use it if necessary. After several more minutes, cars stopped behind the SUV began to beep their horns. Suddenly the pickup truck burned rubber and drove off. When she made a sharp left turn into 6 ½ Street, the SUV kept going straight.

Unnerved, Mary took a roundabout way to her house on Bayland Street in Woodland Heights until she felt certain no one was following her. When she got home, she made sure all the dead bolts on her doors were locked and the gate to her driveway closed and locked. Then she placed her gun and cell phone on her bedside table. But she barely slept.

• • •

Steve agreed to help them. He told Mary that he had heard during his undercover days with the sheriff's office that Los Arboles was a seedy place where girls and drugs were for sale. He'd never been inside the place, though. He decided to go on a weekday night, under the theory there would be fewer customers and more available girls from which to spot Pilar. Diego insisted on going with him, although Steve tried to talk him out of it.

"You don't understand how bad these hombres are, Diego," Steve said. "Mary will kill me if anything happens to you."

"So I will just ride shotgun for you," Diego said. "I mean I will be the lookout. I won't go anywhere that isn't public."

Reluctantly, Steve agreed.

Driving past Los Arboles, they passed a yellow taco truck in front of the entrance. Steve parked his truck around the corner. The driver of the taco truck was talking on a cell phone when Steve and Diego passed by. Two heavy, muscular men stood outside the front door, inspecting the customers who approached. Steve tipped his straw cowboy hat to them. Diego nodded, keeping his head down.

"The entry fee is five dollars each," one of them barked.

Diego was familiar with bars and cantinas, but he was taken aback by the shabby roughness of Los Arboles. He half hoped he would not find Pilar living in such a place. But then again, if he could find her, he could take her to safety. So he took out the money for the cover charge for himself and Steve and paid the big man.

The customers inside the cantina were mostly Hispanic working-class men. Expressionless, scantily clad girls waited on tables. A juke-box blared Tejano music, and tobacco smoke filled the air. Every once in a while, the scent of marijuana overwhelmed the tobacco smoke. They sat at a table and ordered beers, which they drank slowly, keeping to themselves. After a half hour, Steve told Diego, "Stay here. If all hell breaks out or I don't come back in an hour and a half, get out quick. Here are the keys to the truck."

Then Steve got up and approached the bartender.

"I hear a guy can get some time with a chica here," he said.

"If he pays the price," the bartender answered.

"What's the price? I'm up from Brownsville. I've been working off-shore. I just got paid."

"Talk to the lady at the small table," the bartender said, pointing to a table to his right. Rosa's sister, Tina, was counting money.

When Steve approached, the woman said in an automatic voice, "It's fifteen for condoms, sixty-five for fifteen minutes, two hundred for an hour, and five hundred for girls under fourteen."

Steve gave her two hundred. Without getting up and with one hand, she pulled open a curtain covering a narrow stairway.

"What about your friend?" the woman asked, nodding at Diego, who was seated at a nearby table, close enough to hear.

"He's a newlywed," Steve said. "Still saving himself for his bride. He'll learn soon enough when the niños arrive and she keeps her legs closed tight."

The woman laughed.

Diego waited for Steve for what seemed like hours, but it was only forty-five minutes. He kept his Astros cap on and his face down, not wanting any Storm fans to recognize and draw attention to him. He finished his beer and ordered a second one the third time a waitress asked him if she couldn't bring him anything or do anything for him. He just smiled and gave her a tip that he thought would satisfy her need to push drinks and whatever else she was implying. It had been several years since he had drunk alcohol. He didn't want to drink too much and lose his focus in what he perceived was a dangerous situation.

Diego was relieved when Steve finally came through the curtain beside the bar an hour later. He motioned to Diego that they were leaving, and Diego quickly joined him. Once outside Los Arboles, Diego felt his shoulders unlock and his jaw loosen.

Inside Steve's truck, Diego plied him with questions. "What happened upstairs? Did you find Pilar? Tell me everything just like it happened."

"Hold on, pardner," Steve replied. "I'd like to get a few blocks away from this place."

Once back on I-45, Steve started talking.

"I walked up to the second floor where the madam's bottom girl met me. Her name is Esther. Nasty woman! I wanted to see all that's available, but no kids. I told her I needed a mature woman to satisfy me.

"Esther gathered the girls who weren't currently with customers. She ushered them into a small room where I could inspect them and choose one. I looked for a girl who fit Pilar's description. But I didn't see her. So I told Esther that a friend of mine had been here and he'd said he'd had a good time with a Mexican girl named Pilar, or Paula, or Patricia, or something like that. When she heard Pilar's name, one of the girls gasped and lifted her bowed head. Esther told me that Pilar wasn't there anymore. I didn't get the impression Esther liked Pilar."

Diego let out a groan. "Did she say where Pilar is now?"

"No, and I didn't want to arouse her suspicion, so I didn't ask. She wouldn't have told me anyway. I pointed to the girl who had reacted when I said Pilar's name and said I would take her. She led me to a tiny room. The odor from tobacco, weed, and sex was terrible. The room only had a tiny mattress and a chair in it. I sat down on the chair, and she immediately took off her dress. God! She was thin. She looked like a child. Then I told her to sit on the bed. I asked her why she'd reacted when I said the name Pilar; I asked if she knew her.

"She was clearly terrified of talking to me. Usually the girls are threatened with beatings if they talk to customers. So I reassured her that I would not do anything to harm her and asked her not to tell anyone what I said to her.

"She sat down on the bed and nodded as if to agree, but her shoulders were hunched and she looked uncomfortable.

"I asked her what her name was, and she said it was Josefina. I told her that was a pretty name. It was my little sister's name. She seemed to relax some when I talked to her slowly, like you talk to a child. Then I told her that Pilar's family had sent me to find her. I told her I wanted to help Pilar, and I would help her, too, if I could."

"What did she say?" Diego asked. "Does she know where Pilar went?"

"Hold on, son. I'm getting there," Steve said.

Just then, they were approaching the downtown cutoff that would take them to Midtown. "Your place, Diego?"

"Sí," Diego replied. "It's too late to go to Mary's. We will have to tell her about this tomorrow. But go on."

"I asked her to tell me what she knew about Pilar.

"After a few minutes of silence, in a voice so low I had to strain to hear her, she told me that Eduardo had kidnapped Pilar, herself, and a girl named Teresa in Mexico City. She told me he made them have sex with men all the time and takes all the money. She told me about working in the men's clubs. She said Teresa hadn't been able to take it, so Eduardo had had his brother torture her and hook her on drugs. Then he sold her.

"She said Eduardo had brought Pilar and her to Los Arboles. She thinks she will probably die there, but she doesn't care anymore. Pilar was her only friend. She always told Josefina that they would escape. Pilar took care of Josefina, kept her from taking drugs or giving up."

"That sounds like Pilar," Diego said. "She always took care of everyone."

"I asked her if Pilar had escaped. She shook her head no. She said Eduardo had come in a hurry one day and taken her away with him. Then she called Eduardo a bastard and spat.

"I asked her when he'd taken Pilar. She told me she didn't know what day it was but it was, a day or two after Alba, the madam's daughter, died. Pilar said she would come back for Josefina, but she has not. When Josefina asks Eduardo about Pilar, he says nothing. She is afraid that Pilar might never come back for her."

Diego's shoulders slumped.

"I asked her if she could remember anything about Eduardo taking Pilar away that might help me find her. Josefina said that Pilar asked Eduardo where he was taking her and Eduardo said: 'To get new clothes.' He said Pilar was getting a promotion. I asked her if there was anything else she could tell me. After a few minutes, she said that Pilar must have had something Eduardo wanted. Pilar knew Josefina had contracted a disease. Eduardo came back a few days later and took Josefina to a doctor. Eduardo cursed Pilar and said Josefina could thank Pilar for making him waste his time on her."

"That must mean Pilar is still alive!" Diego said.

"I stayed with Josefina a little while so no one would get suspicious. Then I made her promise that she would keep our conversation between us. When I got up to leave, she begged me to help her get out of there. She said she was so ashamed—that she knew everything that had happened to her was her own fault, but she couldn't take much more of that place and Esther and all the filthy men. She looked desperate. I've seen a lot of evil in my day, Diego, but being with that poor, helpless little girl made me feel like crying myself . . . or ramming my fist into the face of Eduardo Ayala and every one of those fucking bastards that would do what he has done to that little girl."

• • •

Steve, Mary, and Diego met at Mary's house the next night, where Steve told Mary what occurred the night before. Mary was not happy that Diego had gone with Steve to Los Arboles, but she had come to realize she couldn't control Diego. Diego was disappointed that they still didn't know where Pilar was, but Steve and Mary assured him they were making progress.

"Let's sit down at the table and make a timeline of where we are," Mary said, going to her office. Steve and Diego took seats at the dining room table and waited for her to come back. When she did, she brought her laptop and sat at the head of the table.

"Let's google Rosa's daughter's obituary. Josefina said her name was Alba. Let's try Alba Rodriguez, although she may have had a different last name." After about fifteen minutes, Mary said, "Here it is! She died in September 2010." Mary wrote the date, September 10, 2010, at the top of the legal pad. "At that point, Eduardo took Pilar away from the brothel and bought her new clothes. He must have had a different use for her where it was necessary she dress in street clothes. Last week, Padre Roberto saw Pilar doing business at a bank in the neighborhood. What did you say Pilar did before Eduardo kidnapped her, Diego?"

"She was the office assistant and bookkeeper for a pottery factory in San José. She did everything in the office," Diego said.

"Does she speak English?" Mary asked.

"Some. We studied basic English in school, and she had to deal with English-speaking customers at the pottery factory."

"If Eduardo took Pilar the day after the owner's daughter died, I wonder if there could be a connection. He said Pilar was getting a promotion. Do we know if the daughter worked in the family business?" Mary asked.

"Padre Roberto said one of his parishioners who supplies food to the cantina told him the owner had a daughter and a son who worked in the business. The daughter worked with her mother in the office, and the son supplied the muscle," Diego said.

"So, is it possible Pilar could have taken the daughter's place in helping the mother keep the books for the business? It's hard to imagine that after all the years she was enslaved, Pilar could maintain her ability to think clearly in an office situation," Mary said, shaking her head. "I've read that most girls lose all self-esteem and clear thought after even a short time."

"Pilar is the strongest woman I know, Mary. She gets that from our mother," Diego said, rising from his chair. "I can believe she would be able to separate the horrible life she is forced to live from the inner good, strong woman she has always been."

Steve said, "I was struck by Josefina's description of how Pilar tried to take care of her during their captivity. It sounded as though Pilar had become a mother figure to the young girl. She kept her hopes up that they would escape one day. In my experience, captive women will do anything for their children. Sometimes pimps make the women have a baby so they can use the child to force the mother to do what they want them to do. That could be the relationship that developed between Pilar and Josefina. Pilar could have found strength in taking care of Josefina."

"That makes sense," said Mary. "I need a glass of water." She rose and walked to the kitchen. "Does anyone else want anything?"

"I'll take a beer if you have one," Steve said.

"Water for me, por favor," Diego said.

When Mary returned, she continued her train of thought. "If Pilar is working for the owner at Los Arboles, she would have valuable information concerning her businesses. I bet the madam never lets her out of her sight. Rosa probably keeps her isolated on the property. But where? Josefina hasn't seen her, so she's not in the brothel."

Steve stood up, stretched, and said, "Well, unless you have access to the Third Army Infantry, Mary, I don't see any way to get in there and rescue those girls. There are armed guards all around the building, a lookout in the taco truck parked in front, and a ten-foot wooden fence along the back of the property. Damn, it's frustrating to know what goes on in there and not be able to just storm the doors and rescue those poor girls!"

Mary's doorbell rang suddenly, jolting everyone out of their thoughts.

"Are you expecting anyone, Mary?" Diego asked.

"No. It's kind of late for company."

Ever since the event on Studewood a week ago, when the two cars had blocked her car, Mary had been nervous about unusual sounds and noises. She hadn't told anyone what had happened, but now she wished she had. She hesitated, and Steve and Diego watched her reaction.

"Um, would you mind seeing who it is, Steve?" Mary asked and then mumbled, "There have been some weird things going on in the neighborhood lately."

"Sure, Mary. You seem scared. Should I have my gun drawn?" Steve asked.

"Whatever you think," Mary replied.

Steve had been joking, so he was surprised at her response.

Steve walked to the door and looked through the keyhole. There was a boy who looked to be about fourteen standing outside holding a pizza box.

"Anyone order a pizza?" Steve asked.

"No," Mary and Diego replied.

Steve took the handgun he always carried out of its pocket inside the leather vest he wore to conceal it. He held the gun low. Then he slowly opened the door.

The boy handed him the box. "No charge," he said and walked quickly to a big black SUV parked in front of the next house.

Mary watched the delivery from the front window with the plantation shutters half open. Then she said, "I may have seen that SUV before."

"Where?" Steve asked.

"You are shaking, Mary," Diego said, concerned.

Mary sat down in a club chair. "I didn't mention it before because I didn't know if it was important."

"Mention what?" Steve asked. "What happened?"

Mary sighed. "The night I was at your apartment, Diego, something weird happened on my way home. After I crossed White Oak, a pickup truck stopped suddenly in front of me. I braked in time to avoid hitting him. But then a big black SUV pulled up close behind me. I think it may have been following me. Neither car moved for a while. I was blocked in. Eventually, someone in a car behind the SUV honked his horn, and the pickup truck took off. I took a roundabout way home in case the SUV followed me, but I don't think it did. I thought it may have been teenagers pulling a prank, or it could have been something more sinister. I admit I was shaken by the incident. I have slept with my gun on my bedside table. But nothing has happened since."

"You should have told me about it at the time, Mary!" Steve scolded.

"I know. I just didn't know if it was a freak one-time incident or what. Maybe I was hoping that was what it was."

Everybody looked down at the box again. "Let me open it," Steve said. "You two stand back."

He sniffed, but the box smelled like a hot pizza, nothing else. He slipped on a pair of thin latex gloves he always kept in a vest pocket and slowly opened the lid. Inside, on top of a pizza, was Mary's rear license plate. She hadn't noticed it was missing. Someone had smeared blood all over it and punched holes in it.

Steve stepped back, his surprise and concern evident.

Mary felt sick. *Someone knows what we are doing. John warned me that what we are doing is dangerous. I just want to save a woman who has been kidnapped and forced into human slavery. Or is John right; am I just infatuated by an adventure with a handsome stranger?*

She looked up at Diego, who had stepped behind her after Steve opened the box to reveal its contents. She realized he was holding her. She looked up at him for reassurance. Instead, she saw intense concern on his face.

Have I put Mary at risk, as I did with Pilar? And maybe Marisa? Diego wondered. "I am so sorry to have involved you in my problem, Mary and Steve."

"No, it's all right. I want to help you, Diego," Mary said, although she realized her voice was a little weaker than normal.

"Part of the job," Steve said. "But shit!" He paced back and forth. "We've been careful. How did anyone find out about us?"

No one spoke for a minute. Then, moving away from Diego, picking up her legal pad and pencil, and trying to regather her composure, Mary took a seat at the dining room table. "Let's think about who knows what we are doing," she said.

Diego sat down at the table across from her. "John and Sara Beth know, of course."

"That's a nonstarter," Mary said. "They don't want any involvement with Pilar, and their lives are too busy to play games."

"There's Padre Roberto," Diego said. "It could have been someone else at his church."

"Unlikely," Mary said. "After the sex traffickers sprayed his congregation with bullets a few years ago, he knows to be careful."

"What about Consuelo, the old woman from the Jewel Box?" Diego asked.

"I don't think so," said Steve. "She seemed sincere in wanting to help Pilar, and we were careful about where we met her."

"What about your teammate Pablo from Mexico City—the one who told you about seeing Pilar at The Jewel Box?" Mary asked Diego. "Could he have told someone with ties to the gangs?"

"I don't think so," Diego replied. "I got the impression that getting married and having a daughter changed his view of women as disposable objects. He seemed sincerely contrite about not telling me he had seen Pilar earlier—especially when he found out she was my sister."

Everyone was silent for a few minutes. Then Diego rose and crossed his arms in front of him. "When Mary left my apartment in Midtown the other night, I noticed a black SUV parked across the street. The windows were tinted, but I thought I saw two men inside. The car looked familiar, but there are so many SUVs in Houston, I didn't think any more about it," Diego said.

Mary shivered. "It was probably the same SUV that blocked me in on Studewood. Whoever it was, they followed me, and someone must have gotten out and stolen my license plate while I was sitting there."

"Damn!" Diego swore, slamming his fist on the table. "I should have paid more attention to it. I know where I saw that SUV before!"

Mary and Steve looked at Diego, surprised, waiting for more. Diego walked over to the window and then turned to face them.

"I may have made a mistake," Diego said, looking away.

"Spill it, amigo," Steve said.

Looking at Mary, Diego said, "I was trying to untangle myself from a girl who was more interested in me than I was in her."

Mary couldn't help brightening inside when Diego said this.

"Marisa Escobar?" Mary asked. "Sara Beth mentioned a while ago that you and she had been an item."

"An item?" Diego asked.

"Never mind," Mary said. "Go on."

Diego walked back to the table and sat down again, looking at Mary. "She has been very kind to a fellow countryman. She makes me feel comfortable, and we have become friends. I told her that someone had kidnapped my sister in Mexico and I suspected they'd brought her to Houston. I might have mentioned Eduardo's name."

Diego was not looking at the others. He felt foolish. He had bared his soul to a woman he hardly knew—a woman whose father employed a private army in their home, who could be involved in illegal activities.

Diego remembered the man with the gun standing behind Arturo the night of the party and the extreme security surrounding his home. Marisa had told him that her father's decision to send her out of the country might have been motivated by the fact that he knew Diego was looking for Eduardo Ayala. Diego was embarrassed. He had let his friends down and possibly exposed them to a very dangerous situation.

"What?" Mary and Steve said together.

"Diego!" Steve exclaimed. "You didn't tell me you were seeing her! Her father, Arturo Escobar, has been a person of interest for the authorities for years. Only no one could ever get close enough to get any solid information. He keeps a close circle, and security surrounds his house."

"I know. I saw the SUV in his driveway. But I didn't put it together until now," Diego replied, feeling foolish.

"You've been to his house?" Steve asked, surprised.

"Only once. One of the coaches delivered an invitation for me to attend a party there. He said I should go because Escobar is a big team supporter. That's where I met Marisa. She's a fan too."

"I bet," Mary said.

"She came to all my home games, and sometimes we went to Beck's Prime or 100% Taquito or Hugo's afterward. I told her about Pilar the first time we went to dinner. I was nervous in such a fancy restaurant. It was just conversation with a girl who is a good listener. I wasn't thinking about her father." Diego got up and started pacing around the dining room. He knew he was not telling them the extent of his relationship with Marisa but reasoned that it was not serious—on his part at least. And he didn't want Mary to cut him off again. He had felt unhappy and anxious when she didn't return his calls after the dinner party.

"Was Marisa your source for Los Arboles?" Mary asked. She longed to find out if Diego's relationship with Marisa was romantic, as the *Chronicle* article and Sara Beth had suggested, or just companionship with someone with common interests.

"Yes. I didn't tell you my source was Marisa because you wouldn't return my calls or kept them very short after the night of the dinner party with John and Sara Beth."

Now Mary felt foolish. She hadn't given Diego a chance to deny her sister-in-law's implication that he and Marisa were in a romantic relationship. *This is why you are not supposed to get emotionally involved with a client*, she thought, although Diego was not technically a client, she reasoned.

Diego tried to justify himself. "Marisa asked one of her father's security guards if he knew where Eduardo lived or hung out—but I didn't tell her to do it. It was her idea. She said she was trying to help me."

"Where is Marisa now?" Steve asked.

"Her father sent her with her mother on a shopping trip to Europe after his guards told him that Marisa was asking about Eduardo Ayala."

Steve had gotten up and was pacing up and down while he listened to Diego and Mary's conversation.

"Damn, Diego! Arturo Escobar is bad news big-time. This changes everything. Amateur night is over," Steve said.

"I don't blame you if you don't want to help me anymore," Diego said. "I screwed this up. I guess I'm still the irresponsible mess I was when I abandoned Pilar."

Mary felt several emotions. She felt sorry for Diego. He had made a mistake, but it was an honest one. She also wanted to hug him right there, on finding out that he was not in a romantic relationship with Marisa. She realized that didn't affect how he felt about her, but at least he wasn't romantically committed to someone else.

"I'm not quitting," Steve said. "But you need bigger guns than Mary and me. Eduardo Ayala is a small-fry pimp in the Mexican–American underworld, with a dim-witted muscle of a brother. Arturo Escobar is a big fish, maybe even cartel. He's not going to risk exposure to protect Eduardo's hide. He must be involved in something bigger over there."

"Do you think Escobar could be involved in sex trafficking, Steve?" Mary asked.

"I know the sheriff's office thinks he is involved in drug smuggling from Mexico. Trafficking women for commercial sex could be an expansion business. Guys like him never lose an opportunity when they smell money. We need to get in touch with the Harris County–FBI sex-trafficking task force. Are you ready to tell your story to them, Diego?"

"I will do whatever it takes to find Pilar," Diego said. Then he took Mary's hand. "But I don't want to involve you anymore, Mary. I am very, very sorry I have put you in danger. I don't know what I would do if anything happened to you." He realized how important Mary had become to him—not just as an ally in searching for Pilar but also as a woman.

Mary started to protest, but Steve put up his hand. "Diego is right, Mary. We need to figure out a way to keep you safe. Can you move in with your brother and sister-in-law temporarily?"

"And admit they were right? No way. I've got my security system and my Glock." Mary was vehement. "Our dad made sure we knew how to use it."

She is such a brave woman! Diego thought. *Her passion and strength are a beautiful thing to behold.*

"I am going to contact my old buddies in the sheriff's office. It may take a while for this to feed up the bureaucratic chain to the Feds. In the meantime, Diego, watch your back and focus on winning games. Don't talk to Marisa again. Better this ends with a broken heart than a dead body. And don't go back to Telephone Road. If we're lucky, they will think you've learned your lesson and backed off. Can you do that?"

CHAPTER 21

JOHN

Mary sat next to her brother on her sofa at 5:30 p.m. on a Wednesday night in late September. It had been two weeks since Steve told Mary what Josefina had said about how Eduardo Ayala had brought her and Pilar to Los Arboles and what they were forced to do there. The following day, Steve had reported to his old friends in the sheriff's office about his visit to the cantina and bordello. The sheriff's office had been waiting for a long time for confirmation by a reliable source of sex-trafficking activities at the club. The FBI had the authority to authorize a raid, so the sheriff was eager to get the Feds to take action against Los Arboles as soon as possible.

Mary and Diego were just as anxious. So when she'd heard that the sheriff's office needed to get the FBI involved, Mary had decided to take action. She'd called John and invited him over for a glass of wine with Diego and "another friend." She hadn't been sure he would come, since he had made his position clear about not wanting to get involved in the matter of Pilar. She'd been delighted when he'd accepted her invitation.

She brought him a glass of cabernet and then placed herself next to him on the couch. Steve and Diego sat on either side in the club chairs, Steve holding a beer and Diego a glass of mineral water.

"I'm here, Mary. Now what is this all about?" John asked. "I told Sara Beth I would be home in time for dinner at 7:00."

John was sizing up Steve, whom he had just met. With his jeans, cowboy boots, scruffy beard, and denim shirt, Steve was probably someone John would think was an unlikely friend for his sister.

"This won't take long," Mary said. She cleared her throat. "You know that I have been helping Diego search for Pilar—"

"And I have expressed our reservations about that," John curtly interrupted.

"Hear me out," Mary said. "Steve has been working with us. He is a retired Harris County Sheriff's Office undercover detective, now private investigator. Steve has helped me before at the Legal Aid clinic, and I hired him to help us find Pilar. We believe Pilar is alive, and we know where she may be. That's the good news. But there is bad news too. Some pretty nasty characters are keeping her at a cantina in the barrio. Some of them have learned that we are looking for her and are not happy about it."

"Oh, God, Mary!" John nearly shouted. "This is exactly what I warned you about!" John got up from the couch and began to angrily pace back and forth in front of the coffee table, stopping in front of Diego. "This is your doing, Diego! Are you satisfied now that you have put my sister in a dangerous situation, too?"

Diego turned red and looked abashed but didn't respond. Mary stood up and said, "That's not fair, John. I offered to help Diego find Pilar, and I would do it again! Pilar is in an ungodly situation. There are hundreds of girls just like her in Houston, and I feel compelled to do what I can to curb this awful sex-trafficking business. Please, sit down now and hear me out."

John was angry. But he sat down again on the couch so that his back was to Diego.

Mary continued. "Steve talked to the sheriff's office and told them everything we know about Pilar, Josefina, Eduardo, and Los Arboles. Members of the joint task force that investigates human trafficking in Harris County have heard rumors about underage girls being sold in the cantina for years. They have received anonymous reports that the woman who runs the business, Rosa Rodriguez, sells minor girls for sex, sells drugs on the premises, and engages in other illegal activities. Nothing has happened, though, because there are many such cantinas in the barrio, and the information they had about this one was not sufficient to get a warrant for a raid."

"But we can change that," Steve broke in.

"And what is your part in this vigilante threesome?" John addressed Steve in an icy voice.

Mary answered. "Steve grew up in the Valley and speaks Spanish. He went inside the bordello and secretly talked to a girl named Josefina. Josefina told Steve that Eduardo Ayala had kidnapped and smuggled her, Pilar, and another girl to Houston and sold them to hundreds of men. About six months ago, right after the death of the madam's bookkeeper, Eduardo took Pilar out of the bordello and bought her new clothes. Pilar was a bookkeeper in her village in Mexico. I suspect Pilar is being forced to help Rosa in her business."

Diego finally spoke up. "If Mary is right, Pilar could know things that would allow the authorities to arrest Rosa and shut down Los Arboles. We could free all of the girls!"

"Oh my God, Mary! What have you gotten yourself into? Sex trafficking? You are not the FBI or the attorney general," John cried. "You are just a—"

"Just a what?" Mary asked.

"Never mind, I didn't mean anything by that. I am just worried about your safety," John said. Then he grudgingly asked, "What does all this have to do with me?"

"I'm getting to that," Mary continued. "Conspiracy to engage in sex trafficking and harboring illegal aliens are federal offenses. The FBI is the proper authority to order a raid on the cantina. The special agent in charge of human trafficking in the Houston office is your friend from law school, Michael Torres. That's where we want your help. These ess

padrónes, like Eduardo, move girls around all the time. From what we can tell, Pilar has been relatively stable in her location, but that could change tomorrow. We need an audience to impress upon the FBI that this is a matter that should be given utmost priority."

"You want me to contact Michael and ask the FBI to put staging a raid on this particular cantina at the top of their to-do list?"

"Exactly," Mary replied.

John didn't say anything for a few minutes. The others sat still, waiting for his response.

"Mary, Mary," John sighed, "your heart is bigger than your normally impressive brain. You are still working on suppositions and circumstantial evidence—we have no hard facts about our blood relationship with Pilar or that she is really being held captive where you think she is. Are you ready to stake your professional reputation, and mine for that matter, on hope and circumstantial evidence?" He sounded incredulous.

"Yes, John, I am. I believe we are family. Our dad gave us the same names as Victor's parents. We found Isabel's crucifix hidden in Papa's closet. You resemble the picture of Victor that Diego showed us. Papa was sometimes moody and sad about something in his past; most likely it was Isabel's death. Maybe we can redeem him by rescuing his nephew's wife." Mary's voice became more intense. "Besides, even if Pilar is not where we think she is, even if she is not related to us, this is now about more than just one girl. We are lawyers, John. A lawyer's role in society is to seek justice. How can we turn our backs when confronted with unspeakable, immoral crimes? I do have a big heart, but my brain and conscience are working just fine. In this case, criminals have violated dozens of state and federal laws and basic human rights. They need to be brought to justice."

The air was charged as John considered his sister's words. It was a tense, hard silence. Diego and Steve fidgeted uncomfortably. Mary never dropped her gaze from John.

Finally, John said, "Okay, counselor, you've made your point. I'll see what I can do about getting Michael Torres to give you a chance to make your case to him. Actually, I'd rather see the proper authorities take over this investigation than have you continue to do things that could get you killed."

"And Diego," John said in a terse voice while pointing his finger at him, "I'm holding you personally responsible for my sister's safety."

"I will protect Mary with my life," Diego said, straightening his shoulders and looking John in the eye.

John threw up his hands as if to say, "I give up." Instead, he said, "I'd better get home before my wife figures out you have drawn me into your plots."

"Not a word!" Mary whispered in his ear as she hugged him.

"Not a problem!" he replied.

CHAPTER 22

PILAR'S DILEMMA

Every night after she finished counting the previous day's receipts and entering them in a ledger, along with any other task Rosa gave her, Pilar was alone in a small bedroom in one of the old wooden bungalows in the Los Arboles compound. A single bed, a chipped blond 1950s dresser, and a nonmatching bedside table were the only furniture in the room. Pretty winged fairies danced around the faded shade of a pink lamp, the only source of light in the room. As she looked at the lamp, Pilar wondered if an innocent little girl had once lain in this bed and dreamed happy thoughts about her future.

The room's only small window faced the ten-foot wooden wall that encircled the Los Arboles compound. Iron bars across the window limited the light coming from outside. Houston was still hot and humid in late September, and there wasn't any air-conditioning in her little room. It was miserable.

At night, while lying in bed, she could hear the noise from the cantina, especially when the men were watching a fútbol game on television. The crowd would yell the names of the players who scored goals, like "Diego!" or "Jorge!"

How I loved sitting in the stands with Alejandro when Diego's fútbol club played, Pilar thought as the men in the cantina roared.

Concepción and Alejandro still appeared in her dreams, although they came less frequently now and their faces were less distinct. She dreamed of the three of them eating breakfast in their cozy kitchen. Concepción was pulling tortillas apart and throwing the pieces on the table. She thought that was hilarious and giggled.

She was having so much fun. How happy we once were! Or is that just a dream?

Sometimes the three of them bumped along the road leading north toward Guanajuato on a Sunday afternoon. They stopped for a lunch of tacos, fruit, and cheese. In these dreams, she rocked her baby to sleep in her arms while Alejandro sketched the landscape. She would tell him the picture was beautiful.

He kissed me and called me "my love."

Too often, images from the filthy cubicle where she'd toiled for the last year and a half would crowd out the beautiful dreams. The faceless, stinking, crude men who had raped and beat her thousands of times marched through her thoughts like a growing cancer. She had tried to blank out her mind while enduring the despicable things they did to her or forced her to do. Oblivion was the refuge she sought. But the horrible images slithered back into her mind no matter how hard she tried to fight them.

Many girls escape the horror of this life through drugs. Death comes quicker that way. Perhaps it is the only freedom a slave can know?

The guards outside her door didn't care how noisy they were at times. They would argue over sports or women. The door was thin, making it hard to sleep. Pilar was forced to lie awake, thinking thoughts she did not want to consider.

Pilar remembered that when she was at the men's clubs near the Galleria, she thought nothing could be worse.

I was wrong. At least the clients were clean and did not beat us. They had to wear condoms. Some of the men were lonely or troubled and only wanted to talk to someone who could never reveal their secrets. None of them realized how small their problems were in comparison to those of the girls in whom they confided.

Before she became confined to the office with Rosa and this room, Pilar clung to the hope that somehow she would find a way to escape. Even when she'd been abused in the tiny room upstairs next to Josefina, she'd thought they could maybe get away when Esther was not watching and the bartenders downstairs took a break. Now, constantly guarded and isolated at night, with Rosa's sharp eyes on her during the day, escape seemed impossible.

Sometimes, alone in the office they shared, before the cantina opened for customers, Rosa talked to Pilar for hours about her life, how she'd built her business, and her disappointment with her children. These conversations might give a stranger the impression that the two women were friends, but Pilar despised the old madam, and the wily woman was aware that Pilar knew enough to destroy her. She confided in Pilar because she was the only person around, and Rosa believed her secrets were safe since Pilar was her prisoner.

Years ago, when Pilar had been having her late-night conversations with Consuelo at the Jewel Box, she'd still prayed to the Virgin for help occasionally. After she experienced the living hell of Los Arboles, that changed.

God and the Virgin Mary have forgotten me, she had decided. *Or maybe the loving, all-seeing God of my childhood was just a fairy tale after all. A beneficent God would not let girls suffer this way. An almighty God would destroy people like Eduardo and Rosa.*

One afternoon, while Rosa was in the cantina working on inventory of the watered-down tequila they served the customers who were unlikely to notice, Pilar was sitting at her desk in the office they shared, thinking about Josefina, when Eduardo slinked into the room. Looking smug, he perched himself on the edge of Rosa's desk, facing Pilar. Until Eduardo had abruptly removed her from the bordello and sold her to Rosa, Pilar's maternal instinct to protect Josefina had been a sufficient reason to live: she couldn't do anything for herself or her daughter, but she could keep Josefina from despair and away from drugs or suicide.

She hadn't seen Josefina for many months now. She wondered if the child was still alive. During a few months in this place, a girl could be beaten to death, die of disease or bad abortion, or kill herself. Teresa could well be dead.

Pilar forced herself to speak civilly to Eduardo. "How is Josefina, Eduardo? Has she recovered from her disease?"

Eduardo ignored her question. "Do you have anything to tell me, Pilar?"

Pilar asked him, "Does Josefina know I am close by?" She hoped so, but Eduardo's silence made her fear the worst.

She hated Eduardo. He was more amoral, cruel, and brutal than she'd ever imagined a man could be. Rosa owned Pilar now, but Eduardo acted as if Pilar were still his property. He demanded that Pilar tell him the details of Rosa's businesses and how much money she was making. He claimed Pilar owed him for all the years he had "taken care of her." Hearing him say this, Pilar wanted to scream.

I will never tell that dog the truth. I am too valuable to Rosa for her to let him hurt me. At least I have some small power over him.

But guilt ate at Pilar. She was ashamed that she was helping Rosa to commit her crimes. *She is as despicable as Eduardo, and she is a woman!*

That made Pilar think of Alma, who had tricked her into being kidnapped. At the time, she couldn't understand how a woman could take part in the enslavement of other women. Alma had told her that after working as a whore, she'd had no other choice but to do what her enslaver demanded. She did what she had to do to survive.

Is that what has happened to me? Pilar wondered. *Am I no better than Alma?*

"How is Alma, Eduardo?" Pilar asked.

"No idea," Eduardo said casually, shrugging his shoulders and taking a pack of cigarettes out of his pocket. "I've been doing most of my business in the States in the past few years. I sold her to some guy in Mexico City. She's probably walking the streets, or dead, or maybe she's found another way to make herself useful to him. She was always smart and had more class than most whores."

Pilar shivered. *Alma was so beautiful.*

Feeling more anger at Eduardo than she usually dared to exhibit, Pilar asked, "And how is Teresa, Eduardo?"

Eduardo lit his cigarette and slowly breathed out tobacco smoke in Pilar's face. "I'm sure that one is dead," he said. "She was half-dead when I sold her. I didn't get shit for her. Damned drugged-out whore!"

Just then, Pilar saw Rosa headed for the office, shouting a loud command to Tito to sweep the cantina floor. Eduardo heard her and swiftly jumped down from her desk, turning to greet her with a smile. "I've been waiting impatiently to see your beautiful face, my dear Rosa," he said.

Rosa gave him a skeptical look and sat down at her desk. Both of them then talked, ignoring Pilar as if she were a piece of furniture.

Sometimes, lying in bed, Pilar heard news from the outside world when her guard listened to the radio. But the local Spanish-language stations they listened to didn't carry much in the way of real news. It was mainly advertisements for rodeos, dances, or Tejano concerts. To pass the time before she tried to sleep, she wrote on sheets of paper she stole from the office and hid in her room. Sometimes she wrote letters to Concepción about her happy childhood, even though she didn't think her daughter would ever see them. She wrote about Eduardo and what she knew about his business. Other times she wrote the stories Rosa told her: how she'd built her business and even whom she had killed to become the queen of the Houston bordellos. When she was finished writing, she would stuff the pages behind a loose floorboard and push her bed over it.

Eduardo had figured out that Rosa was generally out of the office on Thursday mornings, when she made Tito drive her to a Vietnamese nail salon on Broadway. At that time, Pilar would be alone in the office. One Thursday, he stormed into the office, startling her with his angry appearance. He had found out that certain information Pilar had given him about Rosa's business was fabricated. Pilar had tired of his constant verbal battery and made up a story one day just to get rid of him. To her horror, he threatened her with the only thing that she couldn't ignore.

"You gave me bad information, Pilar," Eduardo stormed. "You made a fool of me. You think now that Rosa regards you as indispensable, I can't touch you. But you are wrong. I know your weak spot."

"What are you talking about, Eduardo?" Pilar asked, not looking up from the work she was doing.

"I'm talking about your girlfriend—Josefina. I don't think you want anything bad to happen to her. What if Guillermo gave her a few heroin shots to get her hooked? It wouldn't take much. She's a scrawny little thing."

Pilar felt sick, but she didn't say anything.

"I get what I want sooner or later. So start telling me the truth or Josefina will be joining the junkies walking the streets at the port. Maybe I will sell her to the Turks. They like to have a few girls in the holds of their ships when they leave port."

Pilar was taken aback. She hadn't counted on this. But then again, she really didn't know if Josefina was still alive or Eduardo still owned her. After all, Eduardo had refused to answer that question every time Pilar had asked him.

She tried to seem calm when she asked, "How do I know Josefina is still alive? You haven't done anything to convince me of that, Eduardo."

"That scrawny bitch is right where you left her, Pilar. I may not be a trustworthy man in general, but you can trust me on that! I knew there was a reason I hadn't moved her onto the streets by now, but I didn't know exactly what it was. I know now. She's my leverage with you."

That night Pilar lay in her bed with the lights out, but she couldn't sleep. Her mind kept considering the terrible alternatives.

Rosa knows Eduardo tries to get information about her business from me.

But she feels comfortable knowing I hate Eduardo and do not help him. I am not sure if Josefina is still here or even alive. But I cannot take the chance on letting him do to Josefina any of the unspeakable things he threatens. But if Rosa finds out I am helping Eduardo, Rosa will have Tito kill me, and Eduardo will destroy Josefina anyway. I am in an impossible situation!

That night, she wrote in her journal: *This is the end. We are never going to get out of this alive.*

CHAPTER 23

RECONNAISSANCE

John was anxious to get Mary out of the private detective business and have the FBI take over the search for Pilar. He called his friend Michael at the FBI and asked him to meet with Mary so she could tell him what she had learned about sex trafficking at Los Arboles.

Michael considered sex trafficking a high-priority crime for his team. He had grown up in Houston and had a strong personal interest in ridding his hometown of the insidious activity. So he agreed to meet with Mary in his office the following Wednesday. Mary took Steve with her, too, so he could describe to the FBI what he had seen and heard at the cantina.

Mary had always been an exceptionally good, persuasive speaker. She was captain of the debate team in prep school and had continued to debate in college. Her moot court professor at Yale had tried to convince her that she would be a great trial lawyer. He'd said Mary could persuade anyone that black was actually white. She had no interest in arguing or litigation as a full-time activity, however, preferring to use her legal training to help the neediest clients with their legal problems. But in preparing to meet with the FBI, Mary marshaled her facts and her speaking talent, knowing that Pilar's life might depend on her being able to persuade Michael to take action against Los Arboles quickly.

Mary had met Michael Torres once when her brother and he were in law school. He was a tall, blond, attractive man who, even then,

struck her as a serious, straightforward person. So, after the prelimi-
nary greetings and introductions in Michael's government-issue office
in the northwest part of the city, she declined a seat or coffee, getting
right to the point. She told Michael how she, Diego, and Steve had
traced Diego's sister's trail from the Jewel Box to Telephone Road. She
told him how they'd identified her pimp as Eduardo Ayala, an international criminal, and about Arturo Escobar's threats to them when
he'd found out they were interested in Eduardo and Los Arboles. Then
she asked Steve to tell Michael about his visit to the cantina and the
bordello upstairs. When Steve recounted what Josefina had told him
about how Eduardo had kidnapped her, Teresa, and Pilar in Mexico
City, smuggled them across the border, and eventually brought them
to Los Arboles, Michael grew excited. He asked Steve some questions,
jotting down notes on a pad.

"My God, folks," Michael said. "We need to move on this right
away. Let me talk to the other members of the task force, Mary, and I
will get back to you in the next few days on how we will go forward."

As Mary was picking up her briefcase to leave, Michael said,
"You are a very persuasive young woman. The Justice Department
is always looking for good trial lawyers if you ever get burned out
on Legal Aid. I would be glad to put in a word for you. And if you
think you would like to use your investigative talents working for the
Bureau, give me a call."

"No thanks." Mary laughed. "I love my clients, and I love what I do.
They are not important people, but they deserve legal help too."

Two weeks after Mary and Steve met with Michael, there was a
planning meeting at the Legal Aid office with representatives of the
sheriff's office, the US Attorney, ICE, HPD, the investigative division
of the IRS, and the FBI. When Michael told the local heads of the
other agencies what Mary had found out, they were all interested.

The sheriff's office and HPD had been quietly watching Rosa's
growing business for a while. Escobar was already the subject of an

ongoing FBI investigation. Wealthy Mexicans owning homes in the best neighborhoods of Houston and the nearby Woodlands was not unusual. But as the Escobar family's enclave of heavily guarded, expensive homes in Tanglewood had expanded over the past five years, the amount of marijuana and cocaine on Houston's streets had also increased. Some midlevel distributors the police had arrested bore the full-arm sleeves of the Sangre Negra cartel. The FBI suspected that someone high up in the organization was living in Houston and directing distribution. The name "El Tigre" had begun to be heard on the streets. Michael Torres suspected Escobar might be El Tigre, but Escobar's circle, so far, had been impossible to infiltrate.

About six months earlier, the FBI had mounted a surveillance camera on a light pole across from Escobar's house. Most of the men coming and going were Hispanic and arrived in town cars from Intercontinental Airport. Some were white Americans, but they always wore hats and protected their identities from any potential surveillance. Diego was the first person they knew of who would talk to the FBI about what he had seen inside Escobar's house. Michael realized that if Mary was correct in her speculation that Pilar might know the financial aspects of Rosa's business and if Escobar was somehow involved, Pilar could have information that would bring down both the suspected drug lord and the madam. Michael had a high regard for John Chavez as a lawyer, and John had always told him his sister was the really bright one in the family. Consequently, he was inclined to give Mary's instincts full consideration.

The temperature on the late September afternoon when the meeting took place was in the high nineties and humid, which was typical for Houston. The conference room at Legal Aid was small. Cardboard file boxes were piled along the walls, making it seem claustrophobic. The overhead fluorescent light cast a harsh glare. It was stuffy, too, which motivated everyone to make this an efficient meeting. Mary thought it was a safe place, especially if Escobar's men were still following Diego.

He had been stopping by occasionally to make this visit seem ordinary. The others had entered through a back stairway.

Steve, Mary, and Diego sat on one side of the table and most of the government agents on the other.

Michael sat at the head of the table and opened the meeting. "We've all been briefed on the facts. We're here to establish a plan that will accomplish our goals."

"Which are?" Diego asked.

"We have dual objectives," Michael replied. "First, to take down Rosa Rodriguez. We believe Rosa is one of the biggest importers and sellers of trafficked Hispanic girls in Harris County. She also focuses on the youngest girls, some as young as ten years old. Sending her to jail will send a message to the other madams and pimps in the county that we are serious about sending all of them to prison."

Michael had brought a PowerPoint presentation on his laptop computer. He flashed a couple of pictures of Rosa, all taken from a distance, onto a screen.

"We've suspected for some time that Arturo Escobar is involved in drug smuggling through the Port of Houston and the Rio Grande Valley," Michael said. "He owns a relatively small commercial shipping line and a produce truck line that carries vegetables from Mexico up through the valley to Houston. Sangre Negra, a Mexican cartel that operates on both sides of the border, originated in the same part of Mexico in which Escobar grew up."

Michael flashed a picture of Arturo Escobar onto the screen. It had also been taken from a distance by the surveillance camera. It was difficult to make out his features. Then he showed a map of Mexico with the area where the cartel originated. "If we can get proof he is supplying drugs or girls to Rosa," he said, "it could help us get a warrant to search his home and business. Then we can take him down, too."

"And what about rescuing Pilar?" Diego asked.

"I'm getting to that," Michael said. "First, we need to establish that

Josefina and possibly Pilar are at Los Arboles. Victims of this business are moved around a lot or may disappear suddenly."

Diego seemed irritated and started to get up, but Mary put her hand on his arm. "Patience, Diego," she whispered. "The law doesn't move as swiftly as a soccer match." He sat back down.

"Mary," Michael said, "do you think you could convince the local priest who thinks he saw Pilar at the bank to help us? People tend to do their banking on the same day at roughly the same time."

"I think so. Padre Roberto said he would do anything to help us."

"Good. Steve, would you be willing to go back on active duty with the sheriff's office and resume your undercover work? I'd like you to return to Los Arboles and establish that Josefina is still there. If so, question her to find out if she has any more helpful information about Pilar or Eduardo. Your testimony on an affidavit will be key to obtaining a search warrant."

"Hell, yeah," Steve replied. "I took early retirement in the last year before my wife died of cancer so I could take care of her. It's been two years since she's passed on now. Frankly, this case has made me realize how much I miss putting away the bad guys. I don't think Escobar or Rosa's men know who I am."

"Good," Michael said. "When we looked into it, we found out that the bank where Rosa has her accounts filed a Suspicious Activity Report a few months ago about the deposits Rosa's daughter and Pilar have made. They suspect she may be structuring deposits so that the bank won't have to report them to the IRS. All the deposits were made with the same teller, a white woman who has financial problems due to a child's illness. The branch manager wanted to remove her from teller work, but I asked her to let the woman continue until we have firm evidence of a conspiracy. The IRS is looking into the bank records. When we talked to the manager, she said she'd first become suspicious because the amounts passing through the accounts far exceed what would be expected of a local cantina. If we find evidence of money laundering, we will ask the US Attorney to draw up a criminal complaint and application for arrest warrants for Rosa and the others associated and take them to the magistrate judge.

"As for Escobar, our people are reviewing every inch of video from the camera across the street from his house. We will do the same with any of the normal video feeds from surveillance cameras at the port, which might have caught comings and goings from his ships. His ships and trucks both carry agricultural produce and aren't large players, so they haven't been high priority. We will be looking for any known associate of Sangre Negra entering or leaving the house or ships. We will also be running facial recognition photos of Escobar's security detail against our database of known criminals."

"What can I do to help?" Diego asked Michael.

"Be patient and trust us for now. If we find your sister, she will need lots of help at that point.

"We all have our assignments," Michael concluded. "Let's go get 'em."

• • •

Mary called Padre Roberto that afternoon, as soon as everyone had left the conference room.

"Would you be willing to return to the bank where you saw Pilar and her bodyguard on the same day and at the same time, Padre?" Mary asked. "The FBI wants to verify that she is still on Telephone Road."

"Certainly," the priest agreed. He sounded excited at the prospect of being included.

"When did you say you saw her?" Mary asked.

"Why, it was midmorning on a Monday."

Mary was disappointed that they would have to wait five days until Monday. Anything could happen in five days. But she didn't see that they had a choice.

"Okay, Padre, I would like to be there too, if you don't mind. I think we should go separately so that we don't look like a posse. We shouldn't acknowledge one another, either. Is that okay with you?"

"Of course, Mary. This is like we are secret agents or something. It's very exciting."

On the following Monday, Padre Roberto was at the bank soon after it opened. He found a seat in a corner of the lobby, next to a broad Jerusalem palm, where he could see all the tellers but where he hoped customers coming into the bank would not notice him. He didn't want to be distracted by friendly parishioners. He didn't even look around to see if he could spot Mary. She had entered the bank when the security guard had unlocked the doors. She'd said she wanted to open an account and was sitting in a corner, pretending to be filling out the paperwork. The security guard was not used to having two people sitting in the lobby, but they didn't seem to be causing any trouble, so he ignored them. After all, one was a priest.

At five minutes past 10 a.m., Pilar entered the lobby, followed by the large Hispanic man. Padre Roberto and Mary each watched as they approached a white female teller, who nodded in recognition. "Buenos días, señora, señor," the teller greeted them in a serious voice. The bodyguard was carrying a black briefcase. He opened it, and the priest watched as Pilar took out several neatly tied bundles of cash, handing them to the teller with deposit slips.

"Nine thousand nine hundred dollars?" the teller asked, almost in a whisper. Mary could read her lips.

"Yes," Pilar answered.

While the teller counted the cash, Padre Roberto studied the woman he'd identified as Pilar. She was still beautiful, but she looked wearier than she had the first time he'd seen her. Mary was seeing Pilar for the first time; she saw a family resemblance to Diego.

As Pilar and her guard turned to leave, Padre Roberto tried to catch Pilar's eye and give her an encouraging smile, but Pilar looked away, and she and the big man left the bank. When she thought it was safe,

Mary walked outside and memorized the license plate of Tito's truck. It drove off in the direction of Los Arboles. She emailed the license plate number to Michael, knowing he would want to have it traced.

• • •

Steve and Diego made a return visit to Los Arboles the Thursday night following the meeting with the government agencies. Steve still wore jeans and work boots but switched out a denim work shirt for a camo T-shirt and an oil field services cap for his Stetson. Diego wore jeans, cowboy boots, and a black T-shirt. "Same drill as last time," he told Diego after they had sat at a table for a half hour. Then Steve paid Rosa's sister money for an hour with a chica, and Diego watched him disappear behind the curtain to the stairs.

This time Steve was gone practically the entire hour and a half. Diego was already nervous, but as one hour passed, he began to feel the adrenaline high, similar to what he felt at the end of a close game when his team was behind by one point. Three rough-looking men drinking beers at a table about ten feet away kept looking at Diego and then talking seriously among themselves. They stopped a waitress, pointed at Diego, and asked her a question. She shook her head and moved on.

Diego grew more nervous. He kept his head low and pretended he didn't notice them. Then the largest of the three walked slowly over to Diego while the other two watched with intense interest. The jukebox was blaring a trumpet-heavy Tejano song, and the noise among the customers had been getting steadily louder as the night wore on. Diego knew that if this man attacked him, the other customers would be more likely to join in than to defend him. He was used to getting injured on the soccer pitch, but this was different. He was frightened but girded himself for the fight.

"Hey!" the big man said to Diego.

Diego looked up at him, not smiling.

"Ain't you José Garza, the new second baseman for the Astros? I got money on it with my buddies over there," the man said, pointing to the other two men.

Diego felt his muscles loosen and the blood flow again in his arms and hands, which had been under the table, clenched.

Diego let out a sigh. "Sorry, amigo, I'm not him. You aren't the first person to make that mistake, though. I wish I had his athletic talent, his girls, and his bank account!"

The man laughed and slapped Diego on the back good-naturedly. Then he walked back to his friends, shrugging his shoulders.

Within ten minutes, Steve finally emerged from the curtained stairway and sat down at the table with Diego.

"I see you broke your vow of abstinence," Steve said, pointing at the empty beer bottle in front of Diego.

"Some events call for exceptions to the rule. Can we get the hell out of here now?" Diego asked.

"Sure, buddy," Steve said. "Stay cool. These cantinas have a way of getting to you, but don't let it show."

Once in the truck, Diego said, "The girl must have still been there; you were gone a long time."

"Yeah," Steve replied. "Josefina is there, but she's hanging on by her fingernails. We've got to get her out of there soon or there will be nothing to get out."

"So what happened?" Diego asked.

"I asked the old broad, Esther, for Josefina. But she was with another customer, so I had to wait. Esther tried to sell a different chica and then offered me 'fresh meat' if I wanted to pay more."

"What's fresh meat?" Diego asked

"Little girls under the age of fourteen. I declined, of course. Made me sick to think of it."

"That is disgusting," Diego said.

Just then, the light at Telephone and the feeder road to I-45 turned red. A car full of teenagers raced past them to the left, running the light. They were drinking and yelling as they crossed under the Interstate. "Crazy kids," Steve said. "They are going to kill themselves and somebody else, too."

When the light turned green, he made a left to get on I-45 North and continued his story. "I had to wait thirty minutes. I used the time to look around. Most of the customers are local working-class Hispanics. One guy told me there was a separate entrance to the bordello for 'rich' clients. That was where the youngest girls were available for purchase. There was a handwritten sign on the wall that contained the price list for time with the girls, condoms, et cetera. It was like I was in a butcher shop choosing cuts of meat. Finally, Esther returned, roughly pushing Josefina at me.

"The girl looked even thinner than when I'd seen her the first time. She was passive, as if she were totally defeated. Her shoulders were slumped, and she didn't look at me. When we were alone in her filthy little room, I told her to sit on the bed, and I sat on the chair across from her. When I lifted her chin to look at me, her eyes widened. 'Have you come to rescue me?' she asked, her voice trembling. 'I can't live like this anymore. Without Pilar, I am alone.'

"'Don't give up hope, Josefina,' I told her. 'Help is coming, but I need to ask you some questions.' I asked if she knew any more about what had happened to Pilar. She said that she'd heard Esther complaining to another girl. She'd cursed Pilar and said Pilar thought she was better than her, just because she was Rosa's favorite now. I asked if she thought Pilar could be somewhere else in the compound. 'Maybe,' she replied. She said that once when Eduardo had left her, he'd said he was going to see her girlfriend. She then said, 'Pilar is my only friend.' He'd also told her she was getting used up. She told me that if Eduardo sells her to the port, she'll kill herself.

"I told her to just hold on a little longer and I would get her out of there. I made her promise that she wouldn't mention me or our conversations to anyone. Then, Diego, she wrapped her thin little arms around me, clung tight, and whispered, 'Thank you, señor.' It was like when my own little girl was afraid of the dark and I tucked her in and told her she was safe. We will find Pilar, Diego, but we have to take care of Josefina, too."

"Of course, my friend," Diego said.

"She said she wouldn't tell anyone about me but that if I didn't come soon, she wouldn't be there. I'm not sure how much longer she can last."

CHAPTER 24

DAYLIGHT

E verything was in place. Based on an affidavit of the forensic agents' review of the bank records, and an affidavit signed by Steve as to what he'd seen and heard inside Los Arboles, the federal magistrate judge issued arrest warrants for Rosa, Tito, and others. They were to be charged with conspiracy to commit money laundering, conspiracy to harbor illegal aliens, and conspiracy to commit sex trafficking. Warrants were also issued for the arrest of Esther, Eduardo, and Guillermo on charges of conspiracy to commit sex trafficking and conspiracy to harbor illegal aliens.

It was 1 a.m. on Sunday morning, almost two weeks after the planning session at Legal Aid. Traffic was heavy as cars and pickup trucks cruised Telephone Road, their drivers looking at the many options for late-night sex. Customers packed all levels of Los Arboles. Tejano music from the jukebox blared over conversations about the Texans, the Storm, and the Astros. Cigarette smoke and low lights made everything seem secretive. The VIP room on the second floor, where big spenders raped the youngest girls, was full. Men filed upstairs from the cantina below for fifteen minutes or an hour of nonconsensual brutality.

Bouncers stood and talked at the entrances to the cantina. Tito was at the main entrance, where he collected the entry fee, unaware that FBI agents, sheriff's deputies, ICE agents, TABC agents, HPD officers, and other law enforcement were in the bushes across the street and behind the parking lot, watching and waiting for the signal to advance. Although it was against protocol, Michael allowed Mary, Steve, and Diego to be there but at a distance. They had to wait in the back of an HPD cruiser, blocks away from the action.

At precisely 1:15 a.m., Michael Torres gave the signal.

"All units move in!"

The lookout in the taco truck heard the first officers yell, "Search warrant! Come out of there now!" He quickly pushed a button that sounded an alarm inside the cantina and in the bordello upstairs. Flashing blue lights lit up the cantina and the rooms above. Confused customers ran to the doors, trying to escape. Police officers and deputies detained those who made it out.

Upstairs, as soon as the alarm went off, Esther screamed at the customers to leave while she gathered the girls. She pushed them to a hidden stairway leading to an enclosed walkway, which ended several houses away from the cantina.

Rosa yelled at Tito to grab Pilar from her room. Pilar knew too much. Tito barged into her room and yanked her roughly from her bed. He pulled her down the hallway to a hatch door that led to an elaborate system of underground tunnels and hidden surface passageways leading away from the cantina. Rosa's late husband had had the escape route built soon after they opened the place for business. It had not been maintained after his death, and Tito had never been inside it. He stumbled in the dark, cursing and pulling Pilar along behind him.

The hatch door and tunnels came as a surprise to the agents, officers, and deputies. Once discovered, however, HPD officers continued the chase with wide-beam flashlights lighting the way.

The tunnel into which Tito had pulled Pilar was narrow, and he was a big man, making travel more difficult. Because of the gumbo nature of Houston's soil, underground structures are usually not built unless well reinforced, which these were not. Tito dragged her along on her knees through the mud. Finally, the tunnel came to a dead end. Then he nervously turned and pointed his gun at Pilar.

Looking up, Pilar saw a rope hanging from a wooden panel over their heads.

"Tito, pull on the rope! I think that's a hatch or door above us," she shouted.

Tito pulled hard on the rope, and a plywood door fell open. He pulled down a rug, which covered the hatch inside the house. Dust flew with it. The room they climbed into was dark. Tito let go of Pilar and crept over to a window. He lifted the drawn shade, and they could see flashing lights on top of cars and hear the clamor of a confused, angry crowd. A woman screamed hysterically, and someone yelled, "Shut her up, will you!"

From the tunnel, Rosa cursed her son as she drew closer.

"Don't let them take the girl. I said to kill her," she yelled to Tito.

Pilar studied the door to the street. It had two keyless dead bolts. *If he turns away, I think I can get to the door and open it before he catches me.*

Tito was pacing around the room, as if preoccupied with finding a way to escape. He opened a door to another room and stepped into it, his back to Pilar. Just then, Rosa's hands appeared through the hatch.

"Lift me up!" she commanded.

Pilar lunged for the door and quickly dismantled the deadbolts. When the door opened, she burst out into the street. "Help me! Help me!" she screamed in English.

Two deputies stationed at the back of the property heard the screams and rushed toward her. Stepping hard on his mother's hand as he crossed the room, Tito barreled out behind Pilar, leveling his gun. He fired off one shot but missed. A deputy then shot him in the leg, bringing him to the ground. He writhed in pain.

Rosa had pulled herself up into the house. The door was wide open. Seeing what had just happened outside, she slammed the door shut, pulled a wooden table over the hatch door, and locked the dead bolts. "Damn the both of you!" she screamed.

It took several hours to sort through all the women and customers

who had been at Los Arboles that night. The police found Esther and
the chicas in another house. A bilingual agent explained to the girls
what was happening. Many of them cried tears of relief. The noise had
attracted a large crowd of neighbors, some of whom cheered the police;
others looked scared, keeping in the shadows.

FBI agents found Eduardo hiding in the stock room behind the
bar. Guillermo was rounded up with the other "muscle" guarding the
compound. The FBI arrested both of them.

Mary had called Padre Roberto from her cell phone when the officers moved in to alert him to the raid. He dressed quickly and hurried
down the street to see if he could be of assistance. His housekeeper
followed him, distributing what blankets and linens she could find in
the rectory to the frightened, half-naked girls.

HPD forced Rosa out of the house where she was holed up by
shooting out a window and throwing tear gas inside. As the FBI agents
led the scowling madam past the crowd, some of them spat at her.

As soon as Michael sent word that they could approach, Diego
darted out of the police cruiser. He made his way through the crowd,
searching faces for his sister. The scene was chaotic, and he had to
go through the crowd of rescued women twice before he found her.
When he recognized Pilar, covered with mud, exhausted, standing in
the muddied T-shirt she slept in, he ran toward her.

• • •

Pilar saw a man running at her. Frightened, she quickly backed away
from him and crouched down on the ground with her head between
her knees. "Stay away!" she begged.

"Pilar," he cried, "it's Diego."

"I don't understand," Pilar mumbled to no one. She knew she was
outside the cantina on the street. The girls from the bordello, as well
as men and women in uniforms, were milling around her. It was noisy

with people she did not know yelling and crying and even praying. Some of the uniformed women were trying to get her attention and talk to her. They seemed calm and concerned, but she was afraid to talk to them. Rosa would kill her if she talked to the police. *Were they police?* She looked around for Tito, but when she saw him, he was limping badly, his leg covered in blood. Two policemen were leading him away in handcuffs.

I don't know where I am. Who are all these people? Where is Rosa . . . Where is Eduardo?

The man who had been running toward her was holding her arms, trying to get her to stand up. She resisted. "The police have arrested Rosa and Eduardo, Pilar. You are safe now. They can't hurt you anymore."

Pilar heard the words but couldn't bring herself to believe them. After four years of being beaten and abused and told she was nothing by any man with whom she'd come in contact, all men signified danger to her. She buried her face deeper in her arms and said nothing.

"You don't recognize me, do you, Pilar? I'm Diego—your brother. I am so glad we found you," the man said. Pilar heard his words, but she couldn't look at him.

"I am your brother, Pilar," Diego repeated. "Do you remember Mami and Papi and Carlos? Do you remember Alejandro, your husband, and your beautiful daughter, Concepción? Can you remember the people who love you most of all? We have never stopped loving you. We have missed you terribly. I am so sorry, Pilar. I let you down."

Alejandro and Concepción are in my dreams, Pilar thought. *Am I dreaming now? I remember I had brothers. Was one of them Diego? Did I watch him play fútbol?*

"Diego?" Pilar whispered. She vaguely remembered playing with a carefree boy and tried to find him in this tall, serious grown man.

"I've been searching for you every day since you went away, Pilar," Diego said softly. "I was careless and selfish. I never should have left you alone in Mexico City."

Pilar began to shake all over and cry. She hadn't been able to cry in a long, long time. Girls who cried were brutally punished. Besides, she had become inured to sadness. Now this man was kneeling beside her, and as he carefully put his arms around her, stroking her hair, he said, "I am going to take you home, míja."

"I'm sorry, son," an FBI agent said, approaching them. "I have a warrant for her arrest on charges of conspiracy to commit money laundering."

Diego was confused. "No, my sister is one of the victims," he explained.

Pilar shook as he put handcuffs on her limp wrists and recited, "You have the right to remain silent . . ." She was submissive but looked at Diego, a question in her eyes.

"But we have rescued her. She's my sister. I'll take care of her," Diego protested.

"It's not that simple, Diego," he heard Mary say. He hadn't been aware she was standing beside him, her eyes filled with tears as she watched Diego and Pilar's reunion.

"This cannot be!" Diego exclaimed. "She is innocent. She is a victim!"

Taking his arm, Mary said, "We'll work through this," as the officer led Pilar away.

Pilar stopped, turned, and looked back at Diego. "Find Josefina," she pleaded.

The FBI agent took Pilar to a waiting bus. "Where are we going?" Pilar asked.

"The Federal Detention Center downtown."

Pilar was too exhausted to ask any more questions.

It was dark when they arrived at the detention center, but Pilar was overwhelmed by what she could see of the building itself. It was huge, taking up a whole city block at San Jacinto and Texas Avenues. Instead of normal windows, there were slits in the marble façade. Armed guards met them at the bus and escorted them inside. Pilar was booked in, fingerprinted, photographed, issued prison clothes, medically evaluated, and eventually escorted to a cell with other detainees. She looked around at the bars on the cell and at the other girls and women.

Have I gone from one prison to another?

CHAPTER 25

FAMILY

The Monday after the raid, Mary hired James Zamora, a highly respected lawyer with a history of success in criminal immigration cases, to represent Pilar. James had grown up in Houston and attended Houston public schools but had an Ivy League law degree. His family was of Basque descent, and he spoke fluent Spanish. He was attractive, with brown hair and eyes, well dressed, and poised. In describing him, Mary said the words "smooth," "polished," and "brilliant" came to mind.

James had been successful in his practice and didn't have time to take on a new client. But he thought Mary was an attractive, highly intelligent young woman and had dated her a few times when she'd first returned to Houston from law school. She'd ended it when her workload at the Legal Aid Clinic had begun to consume her. Besides, he was twelve years older than she was, which she considered too much of a difference. When Mary called, he saw this as an opportunity to renew the relationship, so he agreed to take Pilar's case.

Pilar was being held on the conspiracy to commit money laundering charge because she was a material witness. James immediately presented a writ of habeas corpus to the federal court, seeking release of Pilar on bail. The prosecution opposed bail on the grounds that Pilar was a citizen of Mexico and thus a flight risk. The judge concurred, and much to Diego's disappointment, Pilar remained in federal detention in the big prison on San Jacinto and Texas Street downtown.

Pilar couldn't understand why she was being jailed by the American authorities. The only explanation she could come up with was that she was a bad person and it was her destiny to be a prisoner of someone. She must deserve it for something she had done. The guilt and shame she had lived with for the past four years did not lessen. But at least she was not being beaten or forced to have sex with men, she ate regular meals, and she could clean her body.

The first day after she was locked up, she was escorted to a room where prisoners were allowed to meet with family members. The man who had said he was her brother was waiting for her there. The woman who had been with him last night was there also. Pilar sat in the chair that the guard indicated across from Diego, but she submissively kept her head down. *What do they want from me?* she thought.

Seeing her in the light, Diego was taken aback by her appearance. Her complexion was pale from four years without sunlight. Her beautiful face was gaunt, without a hint of a smile. She had always been thin and trim, but now she was skinny, like someone who was malnourished.

He spoke to her in a soft, slow voice in Spanish. "Míja, I am so happy we found you at last. It's Diego, your older brother. I used to tease you and play with you when we were growing up in San José. Do you remember?"

Pilar heard him and was processing his words, but she didn't say anything in response.

Diego tried again. "Mami and Papi and Alejandro and I have never given up on finding you and bringing you home. Do you remember Alejandro, your husband? Do you remember Concepción?"

Hearing her daughter's name, a name she'd said to herself almost every day of her captivity and which had helped keep her hope of escape alive, Pilar looked up at him.

"Do you know Concepción?" she asked. "Is my baby well?"

"Sí," Diego said, encouraged. "She is well with our family. We all love her, and we love you, Pilar. We have been so worried about you and have missed you very much."

"Concepción is safe and well." Pilar sighed. "Is Josefina well? I do not know where she is, and she does not know I am here." Pilar began to shake and seem agitated.

Diego looked at Mary, who also seemed surprised at Pilar's question. Mary lifted her shoulders as if to say, "I don't know."

"Sí," Diego said to Pilar. "We do not know where Josefina is at this minute, but she is safe."

Pilar silently considered his answer. Then, without looking at Mary, Pilar asked in Spanish, "Who is this woman?"

"This is Mary, or Maria, Pilar. She is the daughter of Alejandro's uncle Victor, who left San José before we were born. He came to the United States and had a son and a daughter here. They are your family too."

Pilar looked confused.

Just then a guard approached and took Pilar's arm. "Time is up for today, sir, ma'am. We like to keep these first visits short. Sometimes the women get very upset the first time they see family. You can come back tomorrow."

• • •

In the weeks that followed the raid, Rosa and Tito were indicted by a federal grand jury for conspiracy to engage in sex trafficking, conspiracy to harbor illegal aliens, and conspiracy to commit money laundering. They were held without bail. The list of crimes would grow over the next six months as federal agents conducted their investigation. Eduardo and Guillermo, who were also denied bail, were indicted for conspiracy to commit sex trafficking and conspiracy to harbor illegal aliens.

Diego and Mary felt relieved when they heard that the Ayala brothers were locked up.

James met with Pilar privately at the detention center as soon as he was engaged. At first, Pilar was reluctant to talk to any man, but gradually over the next two weeks of daily visits, James was able to make her feel somewhat comfortable with him and not fear him. Slowly, she related to him the story of her kidnapping, her travel to Houston, and her life working in the men's clubs and then in Los Arboles. When he told her that Rosa, Tito, Eduardo, and Guillermo were all in custody and couldn't hurt her or her family in Mexico, she eventually told him what she knew about their activities. She never failed to ask James if Concepción and Josefina were safe. He always assured her that they were.

James reported all this when he met with Mary and Diego in a historic building downtown two and a half weeks after his first meeting with Pilar. His office was in a well-furnished suite on the first floor, where he and his partner and three associates, two legal assistants, and office staff worked. James offered Diego and Mary chairs and something to drink. Mary sat down and said she would appreciate a cup of black coffee. Diego was angry Pilar was still in jail. He stood by the window, tall, muscles taut, silent.

James ignored Diego's attitude and explained Pilar's situation. "Unfortunately, Pilar is a small fish caught up in the bigger prosecution of Rosa Rodriguez and her cohorts. The FBI is leading the investigation into the federal charges. So a prosecuting attorney from the Department of Justice will be the prosecutor. They will probably assign the case to one of their more experienced guys. They see this as a big headline opportunity to show the public that they are tough on prosecuting sex trafficking."

"But what does my sister have to do with the madam's crimes?" Diego interrupted. "She was a victim!" Diego faced James now, his tone defiant.

"Please don't be offended, James," Mary said. "Diego has been searching for his sister in two countries for four years. He is a professional soccer player for the Storm—not a lawyer. All of this is understandably frustrating to him. I admire his devotion to family and his persistence."

James turned his attention to Mary. "Because Pilar kept the books and made the bank deposits, the Feds are threatening to indict her as a co-conspirator in the money laundering charge. The real interest of the authorities, though, is putting away Rosa, shutting down all her related businesses, and sending a message to the sex traffickers that their activities will not be tolerated. My instinct is that the Feds are giving us room to prove she will cooperate with them and that she has information they can use to put away their real targets."

"But she was forced to do what she did," Diego argued as he moved over to the empty guest chair and leaned down hard on it with his arms and hands.

"That doesn't matter. Best case, they will offer her a plea bargain or immunity if she agrees to testify against Rosa and the others. If she doesn't cooperate, or if what she knows isn't useful to the prosecution, she potentially could be charged as a co-conspirator and go to jail in this country for many years."

Diego's face paled. "But why can't they release her in the meantime? I will take care of her."

"Several reasons: First, she might disappear without telling what she knows. Second, it is for her safety. There may be people who would like her to be unable to testify—because she is dead."

Diego groaned.

"We don't know yet if and to what extent Arturo Escobar or Sangre Negra is involved in Rosa's operations. Believe me, your sister is in the safest place for her to be under the circumstances."

"So, even though we thought we'd rescued her, she is not safe?" Diego asked. He was incredulous, then began to worry.

"Unfortunately, yes. What you need to do is keep her calm while the Feds do their investigation. It may take a long time, and she is psychologically fragile. She only brightens when she asks me about her daughter. Why don't you show her lots of pictures of Concepción? Tell her stories about what she does and how she is doing well."

"I visit my sister every day that I am in town," Diego said. "Only now is she beginning to trust me and converse with me a little. But I will continue. She is more relaxed with Mary, probably because she is a woman." He looked at Mary and then said, "Probably because she is such a kind, wonderful person. Who could not love her?"

Mary was surprised at Diego's testament but happy. He had never expressed his feelings to her, really.

James seemed to pick up on the connection between Diego and Mary and frowned. He probably thought such an accomplished woman could not be romantically interested in a professional athlete. Then he said, "In the meantime, I will be trying to work the best possible plea deal for Pilar. Be patient. She's been through a terrible ordeal. Survivors often feel as though they are not the same person they were when they were taken. Guilt, shame, and self-loathing are all by-products of this kind of life. Give her time to recover and process. Love her and be supportive. She still has a difficult path ahead of her."

"How long will Pilar be in jail?" Diego asked as he ran his hand through his thick black hair in frustration.

"I don't know," James replied. "The FBI and Department of Justice are going to start questioning her in the next few days to determine what she knows. But be assured, I will be with her the whole time, looking out for her interests."

Mary put her hand on Diego's and said, "James is the best, Diego. He'll do all he can to get Pilar released as soon as possible."

Diego straightened, managed a grim smile, and offered his hand to James. "Thank you, señor. I am afraid I am not a very patient man, and I meant no offense. If Mary says you are the best, I have confidence in you. Remember, Pilar has a family who loves her and wants her back with them."

• • •

Diego and Mary visited Pilar as often as they could over the next two weeks. When Mary entered the room, Pilar's face brightened, and her shoulders, usually hunched over, relaxed. She became more comfortable with Diego and was recovering her memory of the time before she was kidnapped. But when Diego told Pilar that he wanted to take her home to Mexico and her family, she refused to consider it. She begged him for more pictures of Concepción, but she insisted she could not go home to her. She said she was not worthy of a good man like Alejandro. She said that he and Concepción were better off without her.

Diego worried about how he should break the good news of Pilar's rescue and the bad news of her imprisonment to Alejandro and his parents. He was also worried about how people in San José would receive her. Her immediate family wanted her to be home. Beyond that, he realized many people would shun her because of the life she had been forced to live. The abuelas would treat Pilar badly. But he had promised his parents and Alejandro that he would let them know if he found Pilar, so he decided he must tell them. To soften the blow, he also believed it would be best to do it in person.

Mary, John, Steve, and Diego sat around the table on Mary's back porch later that day. It was as much of a fall evening as Houston gets, and they were enjoying the respite from the summer's unending heat. Diego had brought pizzas from Star Pizza, and Mary had fixed a green salad.

After the raid on Los Arboles and the subsequent publicity about the hellish life the women had been forced to live there, John had come around to believing in Diego and accepting Pilar as family. John had a good heart; he'd told Mary he was ashamed that he had turned a blind eye to what horrors the sex traffickers were creating in his own hometown. He appreciated the good Mary, Diego, and Steve had accomplished not only for Pilar but also for the other victims. He'd also told her that he suspected even Sara Beth was a little embarrassed by her initial hostile attitude toward the whole situation. In any case, she didn't object now when she knew he was meeting with Diego and Mary about Pilar.

"I am going to San José to talk to Alejandro and my parents," Diego announced to the group.

"I assume you have told them you found Pilar," John said.

"No. I have not."

"Why not?" Mary asked, looking surprised.

"The news will come as a shock after all this time. I suspect my parents gave up a long time ago on my finding Pilar, although they never say it. Alejandro has continued to hope. He calls me from time to time when he is lonely and asks me if I think I will ever find her. I always say that I will. He still blames himself for making her go away. But I don't know how to explain that we rescued Pilar but she is in a jail. How do I tell them that we don't know if or when she will be free?"

Everyone was quiet for a while. Then John asked, "Would it help if Mary went with you to help explain the situation? She is a lawyer, after all." He winked at his sister. "Don't act so surprised. You've told us how happy it would make you to have a bigger family than just me. Besides, I'm curious myself about this family that we've suddenly discovered."

"Would you do that, Mary?" Diego asked, his face lighting up. "It would be wonderful. I would like my parents to meet you. They would love you, and Alejandro's family would be so happy to meet their niece."

"I don't know . . . ," Mary said.

"Please, Mary, it would mean so much to me. I would like to show you my home and introduce you to all of my family. Besides, I would miss you if I were away from you. I am not very good at expressing how I feel, but you must know that by now," Diego said, taking her hands and looking in her eyes.

"Give me a week to get things delegated at the office," Mary replied.

• • •

When Mary and Diego flew to Mexico City, she was overwhelmed by the massiveness of the city. Seeing her eyes widen when looking down at the never-ending urban landscape, Diego smiled and said, "Even though Houston is the fourth-largest city in the United States, it is only a quarter the size of Mexico City."

She was equally surprised at the openness of the countryside once they finally left the sprawling suburbs and drove north toward San José. She had spent several vacations in the beach resorts along both coasts of Mexico, but this was her first trip to the interior. She thought the countryside was beautiful.

When Diego parked the rental car in front of Yolanda and José's house, many people came spilling out the door. Neighbors, including Señor Marco, hurried to the car to greet them. Diego's accomplishments on the fútbol field now were a source of pride in the small town. He had been the first young man from San José to play on a Mexico City professional team, and now he was playing professional soccer in Houston, Texas. Young boys kicking soccer balls back and forth had been excitedly awaiting his arrival. When they saw him, they yelled his name: "Diego! Diego! Diego!"

Diego seemed embarrassed by the attention, but Mary laughed. "I didn't realize I was traveling with a local hero!"

"It's a far cry from the attitude toward me when I came home from Mexico City without Pilar," Diego murmured.

Yolanda and José stood in the doorway. José had his arm around Yolanda and was beaming like a proud parent.

Diego shook hands with some of the boys who hoped to soak up a bit of his talent. He had brought Christmas presents for the family, and he asked the boys to bring them in from the car. He came around the back of the car and opened Mary's door for her. Then he steered her through the crowd, keeping his arm around her. Yolanda grabbed him and hugged him as hard as she could. José enveloped both of them in his big arms.

"Mama, Papa," Diego said as he untangled himself, "may I present Maria Elena Chavez. Maria and her brother, Juan Pablo, are the children of Victor Chavez—Julio and Miguel Chavez's brother. They are Alejandro's first cousins."

"Truly?" Yolanda asked, astonished. "How did you find Victor's children? No one knows where Victor is."

"I searched for Victor when I arrived in the United States," Diego explained. "I knew I needed someone who knew the ways of that country to help me—" Diego stopped himself from mentioning Pilar yet. "Sadly, Victor died almost at the same time as his brother. But Julio knew I wanted to contact Victor. On his deathbed, Julio told me a story that he had been silent about for years. That information eventually led me to his children."

Diego saw Alejandro and Concepción standing inside the house behind his parents. Alejandro was holding Concepción's hand. Every time he saw the little girl, Diego was struck by the resemblance to Pilar when she was a child.

"Alejandro," Diego said, "this is your first cousin, Maria Elena. Maria, this is Alejandro and the beautiful Señorita Concepción Yolanda," Diego said, leaning down to give Concepción a kiss on the cheek.

"Maria, bienvenidos," said Alejandro, who spoke only Spanish, kissing her on both cheeks. "My family lost track of your father before I was born. It was a great mystery according to my grandmother, whose name was also Maria Elena. They will be excited and happy to find out he had children and that you have come home."

Mary held out her hand to Concepción, who reached out to shake it and then ran back to hide behind her father.

"And Pilar?" Alejandro said to Diego. "Have you found her? Do you know anything about my wife?"

Diego put his hand on his heart and said, "Please, we will talk about this soon, I promise." He glanced at Mary, who nodded.

Sensing the need to keep things welcoming for their new guest, Yolanda stepped forward and gave Mary a big hug. "Bienvenidos, Maria! I am so happy to learn about you and your brother. Is he with you?"

"No, he had to work, Señora Gonzales," Mary replied in Spanish. "He is a lawyer in Houston. But he sends his very best wishes to all of you."

"Por favor," Yolanda scolded. "Call us Yolanda, or YoYo, and José. We are practically family."

The neighbors who had been waiting outside streamed into the house. There was laughter and chatter such as Mary had never experienced. Yolanda had been cooking for days in anticipation of the visit, and so everyone was invited to sit down to eat and drink.

Mary's Spanish had improved, but it was still just conversational. She had to rely on Diego to translate more substantive discussions. She caught Diego looking at her, a question in his eyes. She smiled back at him. *This is what family feels like,* she thought.

Diego chose not to discuss Pilar that night, and no one pressed him for information. By the time family and friends left, everyone was tired and ready for sleep. He asked Alejandro to return alone the next day.

Alejandro appeared at the kitchen door early the next morning. When everyone was seated around the kitchen table, Diego said that he had something important to tell them.

"You know that I have been searching for Pilar ever since I left San José," he said. The room was quiet. "I found her, Alejandro. I should say 'we' found her. Without Maria's help, it would not have happened."

Yolanda made the sign of the cross and then raised her arms to heaven. "Gracias, Diós," she said. Then she got up and hugged Diego. "Gracias, Diego and Maria."

"Where is she?" Alejandro was shaken. "I had almost given up hope, Diego. How is she? Why didn't you bring her with you?"

"Let me explain, Alejandro." Diego cleared his throat and glanced at Mary for encouragement. "Pilar went to Mexico City to apply for what she thought was a good-paying secretarial job. It was a trap, however. Pilar and two other young girls were drugged and kidnapped. One of the cartels smuggled them across the border to Houston. They were kept as slaves and forced to sell their bodies."

Alejandro hung his head.

"Oh no!" Yolanda cried. José put his arm around his wife but nodded to Diego to continue.

"Their captors told them that if they didn't do what they ordered them to do, they would kill their families in Mexico. They knew who and where you and Concepción were, Alejandro. They also threatened to kill their mothers and fathers."

Hearing this, Yolanda gasped, and Alejandro buried his head in his hands.

"This last year, the madam who had come to own her forced Pilar to work as her bookkeeper. Pilar had to make illegal bank deposits. The American authorities raided the madam's business and arrested her, her son, and the men who had kidnapped Pilar—and they rescued all of the girls who had been forced to work there. Now, because of what she learned and did working as the madam's bookkeeper, there is a danger an American court could send her to prison for a long time."

"But you said she was forced to do it," Alejandro erupted.

"Maria and I have hired an American lawyer for her. Maria says he is the best. He will try to trade what she knows about the madam's business for her freedom."

Seeing the devastated faces of his family, he added, "He thinks there is a very good chance. These are bad people that the authorities are more interested in convicting. Pilar is not their main interest."

Diego waited a few minutes for his parents and Alejandro to take in all he had said. "Maria Elena is an American lawyer. Please, ask your questions. She will try to explain."

José and Alejandro asked Mary the same questions again and again. When everyone was exhausted from going over the facts, it was afternoon. "I must pick up Concepción," Alejandro said. "What do I tell my daughter about when she will see her mother?"

Mary spoke in a soft voice: "For now, I wouldn't tell anybody, including your daughter, anything. There is too much uncertainty. But rest assured that Diego and I are committed to doing all we can to free Pilar. She's my family too."

Alejandro kissed Mary on both cheeks and her hands. "Sí, you are. And I thank you and Diego with all my heart for finding my Pilar."

"Alejandro," Diego said, shifting uneasily in his chair, "Pilar says she cannot bring shame on you by returning to San José after all she has been forced to do."

"Diego, you know that Pilar is the love of my life. I blame myself and my selfishness for her going to Mexico City. I need her. It doesn't matter what she did. Can you tell her that?"

"Of course," Diego assured him. But Pilar had been firm, and he wasn't sure he could convince her.

Diego and Mary spent four days in San José before they had to return to Houston. Yolanda took to Mary's sweet personality immediately. Alejandro brought her to meet his parents and many relatives, who were delighted to know that Victor had had a good life in the United States. They warmly welcomed his daughter and made her feel at home.

Before they left, Mary told Yolanda, "I will never remember all the people I have met. But I will think of them forever with love."

"Remember, Maria Elena," Yolanda told her as Diego packed the car, "you always have a home with your family in San José."

To her son, she said, "You need to bring this beautiful young lady here often, Diego. I think that she is very good for you."

CHAPTER 26

THE PROSECUTION

"Tell me why we should offer your client a plea deal or immunity, James. Esther Diaz, Rosa's bottom girl, told us Pilar was Rosa's closest confidant. Rosa's son, Tito, told us Pilar kept the books. We know from the bank's records she made all deposits in amounts that she knew the bank wouldn't have to report to the IRS." Robert Grossman, one of the assistant US attorneys for the Southern District of Texas, leaned over the table in the interrogation room, glaring at Pilar while he barked at her lawyer. "She's not another dumb chica. She schemed her way out of the bordello to get close to Rosa."

Robert was the most senior attorney in the prosecutor's office and had a reputation for getting convictions at any cost. He was a large man who liked to wear dark three-piece suits and use his size and baritone voice to intimidate people. Pilar looked down at her hands. She was too broken and ashamed to meet his terrifying gaze. James had told her that unless they could strike a deal, she would be tried as a co-conspirator and potentially sent to prison in the US for many years.

"You don't want to do that, Robert," James said in a steady voice, as if he were speaking to a child who was acting in a rash manner. In contrast to Robert's dark clothes, James wore a light gray European-cut suit, crisp white cotton shirt, and light blue tie. "Señora Chavez was Rosa's victim, the same as those other poor girls. She was forced to work as a sex slave in the bordello for more than a year. Then Rosa forced her to sit in the same office with her, doing her dirty work on the financial end of the business. Every night the old woman locked my client up by herself in a guarded, shabby dark room. She had no choice or free will in anything that happened at Los Arboles." He squeezed Pilar's hand for encouragement under the table, but his face was expressionless. "It was just chance that she had the technical skills Rosa needed after her daughter died. Eduardo Ayala cleverly tried to use Señora Chavez as his pawn to steal Rosa's business. Pilar was in an untenable position—a helpless young woman caught between two mad dogs! Besides, she's a small fish. If you're smart, you can use what my client learned while working with Rosa to put the old lady away for good."

Robert ignored the veiled insult and began to ruffle some papers lying on the table as if he was looking for some data.

"We already have several girls who have agreed to testify against Rosa," Robert said, waving one of the papers at James and Pilar and rising to his full height.

"You think you have the girls now, but that won't last," James calmly replied. "Trafficking victims always say they will testify while they are in detention, but when they are released and their pimps threaten to harm them or their families, they will clam up or disappear. It's a long time between crime and trial, as you well know."

"The department is expediting this case because of its significance," Robert retorted.

Pilar tried to follow the mental game these two men were playing, but it was too confusing. All she knew for sure was that she was in a very dangerous position. She trembled.

"Rosa's son has agreed to cooperate," Robert said. "He'll tell the jury what I've told you."

"Tito, Esther, and others may take pleas and agree to testify, but it's obvious they're all dumber than dirt and would say anything to get a deal. Jurors are sure to doubt them," James scoffed.

"Why is a jury more likely to believe this girl?" Robert asked, giving Pilar a disparaging look.

Pilar jumped when the big, terrible man pointed his finger at her with disdain. She looked at James for help. James saw that she was shaken and trembling. He took off his suit jacket and wrapped it around Pilar's shoulders.

"Thank you, señor," Pilar whispered.

James got up from the table and stood eye to eye with Robert. "Aside from being a more sympathetic character than that bunch of sleaze you just listed, Señora Chavez has a good story to tell the jury. She was targeted and kidnapped by Eduardo Ayala, long considered a vicious criminal on both sides of the border. She had an unblemished character and a good job as an office manager and bookkeeper in a pottery factory in her hometown. She is from a close-knit family. Her brother, a professional athlete, has spent the last four years searching for her. She is not the usual runaway. Her English is good enough to be able to tell her story in a way that will make jurors see she is an intelligent, honest woman."

James and Robert were still standing and facing off like two dogs before a fight, but Pilar realized that both men were looking down at her now, evaluating her credibility. She hung her head, afraid that they would realize the shameful, unworthy woman she had become.

A female associate of Robert's who was sitting across the table from James was affected. She poured a glass of ice water from the pitcher on the table, got up, and walked around the table to Pilar. She set the glass down in front of her. Robert grimaced at his associate, who pretended not to notice while she returned to her seat.

Breaking the stalemate, James said, "Best of all, Robert, Señora Chavez has firsthand knowledge of the dirty details of the pimping, sex-trafficking, and money-laundering operations you need to prove in order to put Rosa Rodriguez and her family away for a long time. Let's face it, you don't have anything in writing that documents what went on at Los Arboles other than bank and telephone records. My client is willing to fully cooperate with the prosecution. In return, we want immunity from prosecution for her," James said. "She is a victim who deserves justice and mercy. Prosecuting this woman, who has suffered such undeserved brutality, would be a crime in itself." James raised his voice and brought his fist down on the table for emphasis of his point.

"So you argue," Robert said, acting unimpressed. He nodded to his associate to pick up his papers and then walked out of the room without the usual lawyerly pleasantries.

As soon as the door closed, Pilar let out a long sigh. She laid her head on the table in front of her. "That terrible man hates me. He knows I am shameful. He wants to lock me up, just like all the others. And he is angry with you for trying to help a girl like me."

"Don't give up, Pilar," James said. "The prosecution needs you. We just have to let Robert get over his own ego and convince him that you are more use to him on the witness stand than in prison."

Pilar thought, *So my fate is to go from one prison to another.*

Then she whispered, "I worry about Josefina, señor. Do you know where she is and what will happen to her?"

James sat down again at the table next to Pilar. He said, "ICE rounded up all the undocumented girls and took them to one of their INS detention centers. ICE will deport them back to Mexico unless they offer testimony against the defendants," James said.

"Poor Josefina. She will have nowhere to go. She always said her family would not want her now. She was only thirteen when she was brought here. What will she do to support herself other than sell her body again?"

"Diego asked me to represent her, but I told him I could not, because it would create a conflict of interest," James said. Then he smiled. "I arranged for a friend, a very good lawyer, to take her case."

Pilar felt relief. "Thank you, Señor Zamora. I am grateful."

James got up from his chair and started walking around the table. The room was small, without any windows. Every time he had to work in this room, he felt a little claustrophobic. "Pilar, I meant what I told

Robert about their evidence against Rosa not being as strong as it should be to put her away for good. Could you lead the Feds to any written records for Rosa's business? Right now, it's just a bunch of rats taking plea deals and scared women who may not testify against her. Even if you testify, it will be your word against hers. With nothing on paper to show what she was doing, who she was paying, and who was paying her, the Justice Department's case could fail to get the big payoff they want."

"What would help?" Pilar asked.

"Anything in writing," James said.

Pilar closed her eyes. She imagined herself back in the little room with the pink lamp and the dancing fairies. Then she thought she heard the guards outside her door and the sound of their radio, keeping her from sleep. Remembering those lonely nights made her feel sad. She didn't want to relive them, but then she spoke: "Every night after I started working for Rosa in the office, I was alone in my room with nothing to do," Pilar said. "Sometimes, to keep from going crazy, I would take paper from my office and write."

"About what?" James sounded intensely curious.

"Some of it was personal. Sometimes I wrote the stories Rosa told me, like how she'd built her business or how she'd hid property in the names of family members, all sorts of things. She liked to brag about ways she'd outsmarted men. She said all men were stupid and meant to be outwitted by clever women like herself.

"Once Rosa told me that she'd killed her husband with poison. She'd been angry because he'd been spending too much time visiting the girls upstairs. She said she was justified because he could have caught a disease from them and given it to her. She'd had him buried right away. She said he was fat, so she'd told everyone his heart stopped."

"Do you believe her?" James asked.

"Yes. She told Tito to kill me the night of the raid because I knew too much. He tried, but he missed, and a policeman shot him in his leg before he could shoot again."

"Did you write about anything else?" James asked, growing more excited with every revelation.

"I would write about Eduardo and Guillermo, how Eduardo sold us over and over and how he threatened to kill us and our families in Mexico. We saw Guillermo beat one girl almost to death to kill the baby inside her. He took one of Eduardo's other girls, who was pregnant, away for a couple of hours. She told us how the doctor had forced himself on her before he'd cut out the baby. Then Eduardo made her go right back to work."

Pilar, now speaking as if she were in a trance, told similar stories. James's face looked angry and hardened as he sat down beside her.

"Angel was another pimp who sold girls at Los Arboles. He was a friend of Eduardo. I think one of Angel's girls bled to death because they cut out her baby. We never saw her again after an old woman visited her room. There was blood all over the floor."

James carefully turned on the recorder on his phone so that he wouldn't miss anything she said.

"I hoped that one day after I was dead, someone would find what I'd written. Eduardo admitted many terrible things he'd done when he was drunk or in the mood to brag. He said he had been kidnapping girls for Rosa in Mexico for many years. He said he always got her the kinds of girls she wanted for her cantinas. He was angry that the cartel was now making Rosa use girls they'd brought to Houston, taking some of his profits."

"Where is the third girl whom Eduardo brought from Mexico with you and Josefina?" James asked.

"Eduardo told me that Teresa is probably dead now. He didn't care what happened to her if she couldn't make money for him. Guillermo tortured her and then hooked her on heroin. When she couldn't work, they sold her to a bad place."

James had been holding his breath. "Do you think what you wrote is still in your room?" he asked.

"Probably," Pilar said. "I hid the papers under a floorboard and then covered the board with my little bed. If Rosa had known about them, she would have been furious and had Tito kill me right away."

"Good. We've got to do everything we can to put all of those bastards away for good." Then James said, "You worked in the office. Robert told me the FBI did a thorough search but didn't find anything in the way of records in there. Do you know where there are any ledgers, receipts, anything that could tell us about her business dealings?"

"The records of Rosa's business aren't at Los Arboles."

"Do you know where they are?" James asked, surprised.

"Sí. When I needed old information, Rosa would give the key to Tito. He would drive me to a house farther down the street where she had file cabinets."

James seemed hardly able to contain himself. He got up and started pacing the room like a lion ready to pounce.

"Could you find that house again, Pilar?" he asked.

"Sí, it was a light green house with a child's swing hanging from a tree in the front yard. I don't think anyone lived there, though."

James asked another question. "Was Eduardo Ayala Rosa's business partner?"

"Only in that he kidnapped girls that Rosa needed to keep her brothels full. He wanted to be more than that, and Rosa liked to flirt with him, but she was too smart to trust him." Pilar thought for a minute and then said, "She did have someone to whom she paid twenty percent of the money from her businesses. She hated him and was afraid of him. She would curse him after his man picked up the money."

"Did she mention this partner's name?"

"She only called him 'El Diablo.' They spoke in Spanish on the telephone, but she left the office when she talked to him. His man's name was Chacho. He was a big Mexican with tattoos all over his arms. He was friends with Angel, the other pimp who brought girls to work upstairs."

Pilar laid her head down on the table again. "I am very tired, señor. Have I told you what you wanted to know?"

"Yes, everything you have told me is good, Pilar. It is very good." James smiled. "You should rest now and let me take care of this." James rang the buzzer for the guard to come and escort Pilar back to her cell.

• • •

Pilar was most comfortable and open when Mary was present, and Pilar had given James permission to share their confidential conversations with Mary. James appreciated Mary's sharp, analytical mind. He wanted her to help him analyze a defense for Pilar, so James named Mary as co-counsel to Pilar in order to preserve attorney-client privilege. Mary had been keeping her boss at Legal Aid informed of what she and Diego had been doing, and the woman agreed to let Mary take as much time as she needed to work with James. Mary had never practiced criminal law, but James assured her that was not why he wanted her on the team.

At 4 p.m. on Friday, Mary, James, and Pilar were waiting in the same room at the detention center where they had been earlier in the week. Pilar's attorneys sat on either side of her. Mary had never been in a detention setting. The somber nature of it made her nervous. Pilar reached out and held her hand, almost as if she were calming Mary. This was the first time James had seen Pilar take the initiative. He knew he had been right to include Mary in Pilar's representation.

At 4:20 p.m., another male assistant US attorney and two FBI agents who worked for Michael Torres finally followed Robert into the room. Robert was wearing his usual dark attire.

"What is so important that you needed to meet with me right away?" Robert barked at James, glaring at Pilar. "And who is this?" he asked, looking now at Mary.

"Mary Chavez is my co-counsel on this case," James said.

Robert stared at Mary. It was evident he was trying to place her. Then he smiled. "Aren't you a 'do-gooder' lawyer down at the Legal Aid Clinic?" he asked. Then he snorted dismissively.

Mary wanted to retort, *Yes, and I am also a Yale Law graduate and past editor-in-chief of the* Yale Law Review. But she held her tongue. A female mentor had once told her it was a tactical advantage to have your opponent underestimate you.

James looked directly at Robert when he spoke. "My client can lead you to hard evidence that can win your case, Robert."

"What evidence?" Robert asked. He glared at Pilar again, but Pilar did not look at him, as Mary had instructed.

"My client kept a journal of sorts in her prison cell at night. From what she tells me, entries in that journal reveal details of Rosa's holdings, which extend much farther than Telephone Road."

"The county deed records only show that one property," Robert said. "Why should we believe this girl?"

"Señora Chavez, if you please," Mary interjected.

Robert snorted again. His colleagues looked down so as not to show their expressions.

"Rosa put titles to properties she'd bought in family members' names. She ran cantinas and bordellos all over Southeast Houston. According to my client, the revenues were funneled through Los Arboles," James replied.

Robert leaned forward, interested but still skeptical.

"Rosa also told my client that she'd murdered her husband. She also instructed Tito to kill Señora Chavez on the night of the raid," James went on.

"Many of Rosa's men tried to keep women from escaping; I don't think that means anything special," Robert said, shrugging.

"Rosa realized my client knew too much. I've verified what happened with one of the deputies who witnessed the attempted murder," James said. "The officer who shot him."

"Murder and attempted murder are state crimes," Robert said under his breath, as if he were checking off a list.

Then James stood up, ready to deliver the coup de grace from a superior position.

"Señora Chavez says that there was an outside investor in Rosa's business who took twenty percent of the gross revenues. Who knows where that could lead? We assume someone other than Eduardo was selling drugs at Los Arboles and bringing in girls. Maybe there's another trophy here to put on your resume, Robert."

James couldn't help smiling at Pilar.

"You've got my attention," Robert said, looking at Pilar differently now, almost with curiosity about her as a person, or perhaps an asset that could be useful to him.

Mary saw Robert's look and felt disgusted. *So, Pilar is only a person if she can be used by men.*

"Where is this journal? And who is the investor?" Robert asked.

"Not until we get an agreement that would provide my client with full immunity from prosecution for all potential charges stemming out of the Los Arboles operation. In return, she will aid your investigation and fully cooperate in prosecuting Rosa, Tito, Esther, Eduardo, and Guillermo."

"We don't know that the journal is useful. Besides, it wouldn't be admissible in court," Robert countered.

Pilar's English was good enough to understand the gist of what the men were saying. Now she sank into her chair. Mary saw this and put her arm around her.

"The journal would be useful to the FBI for investigative purposes," James said. "Plus, Señora Chavez's testimony in court about admissions against interest that Rosa made to her while they were working in the same office would be devastating."

"Go on. If all this checks out, I may consider asking for leniency on sentencing."

"Not enough!"James insisted. He sat quiet for a minute, then turned to Mary. "What else do we have in our bag of treasures, counselor?"

Mary responded in an off-hand manner, "Oh, are you referring to the location of the file cabinet containing the records of Rosa's businesses going back several years?"

Robert was stunned. Agents, officers, and deputies had searched every inch of the Los Arboles compound, filming their walk-through for the local news stations. They'd found soiled linens, condoms, dirty teddy bears, a rosary, pictures of angels, and other personal items but no records except the cashier's notepad containing a listing of the men who had bought time with girls the night of the raid. That was helpful, but did not get them as far as they had hoped.

Robert got up from the table and motioned for the other members of the prosecution team to huddle with him in the hallway. They were gone for ten minutes, during which time Mary reminded James about what Josefina's lawyer had told him yesterday. When Robert and his team returned, Mary spoke before Robert could say anything:

"There is another victim who is willing to testify against Rosa and Eduardo. Señora Chavez believes she would be reliable. We think a jury would be sympathetic to what she has to say about what Eduardo and Rosa did to her, Pilar, and another girl, now presumably dead."

Robert stroked the five-o'clock shadow spread across his chin. "Who is that?"

"Josefina, one of the girls Eduardo trafficked from Mexico along with our client. ICE picked her up the night of the raid. Her attorney has assured us that she will testify that Eduardo trafficked them for Rosa and forced them to work in the bordello. She also witnessed Eduardo removing Señora Chavez by force in order to work as Rosa's bookkeeper."

At the mention of Josefina's name and realizing the prospect of seeing her again, Pilar brightened for the first time.

Robert and his associates moved to the back of the room and huddled together, speaking in whispers. Finally, Robert returned to the table.

"We can probably work something out for your client with a reduced sentence. As far as the other girl is concerned, we'll work with ICE and talk to her lawyer. Of course, I need to get this approved upstairs."

James grimaced. "I said immunity, Robert. That's a final offer or Señora Chavez will take her chances in court. I think a jury would be sympathetic to what this young woman was forced to endure."

Robert scowled, turned quickly, and left the room. The other lawyer and agents followed, leaving Pilar and her lawyers alone. Mary smiled encouragingly at Pilar and held her hand.

"Do you think he will do what you ask?" Pilar said quietly. For the first time in a long time, she sounded hopeful.

"He's positively salivating," James said. "Let's hope the information that you described is still where it was before the raid."

• • •

It was dark when Diego returned from practice. When he unlocked his apartment door, he was startled to find his apartment in shambles. His clothes were strewn everywhere, the sofa and chairs were flipped over, the coffee table broken. Papers were scattered on the floor. His TV screen was smashed.

Diego was shocked. He had not noticed anyone following him in recent weeks, so he'd thought Escobar had decided to leave him alone. But this was an unmistakable message that he and Mary were still in danger. He was more worried about what this meant for her than himself and tried to call her immediately to warn her not to go home alone. He got her voice mail, so he left her a message not to go home, to sleep somewhere else.

He put his cell phone back in the pocket of his jersey, pulled out the pocketknife he always carried, and started to go room by room, surveying the damage. All his soccer shoes had been slashed with a knife.

When he got to his bedroom, he saw a handwritten note on top of his pillow.

IF SHE TESTIFIES, SHE'S DEAD.

Diego sat down. The French doors to the balcony were ajar. Nothing was missing. *It wasn't thieves*, Diego thought. *They only came to leave a message.*

Mary picked up Diego's message on her phone and checked into the Houstonian Hotel, where she was a member. Then she called James to let him know what had happened.

The next day, Michael, James, Diego, and Mary met in the FBI offices. Michael had also invited Robert to the meeting. Diego told them about the destruction of his apartment and the note threatening Pilar.

"Who is so concerned about Pilar's testimony that they would threaten her life?" Michael murmured. Then he said, "Forensic accountants are going through the records from Rosa's file cabinet now. They've verified Pilar's claim that for the past five years, twenty percent of gross revenues were paid out in cash to a third party. Pilar made the payments to a man named Chacho, who was the courier for the person Rosa called 'El Diablo.'"

"Who is he?" Diego asked.

"It seems only Rosa knows El Diablo's identity," Michael said. "We've tried to get her to tell us who he is, but she's more afraid of El Diablo than she is of us. Claims she wants to keep her head. That makes me think we are dealing with a cartel."

Diego grimaced. He had concluded Marisa's father was a dangerous man. But he hadn't wanted to accept the conclusion that he might actually be part of a cartel. That raised the danger to a whole new level.

James said, "Steve, Mary, and Diego suspect the men who threatened Mary previously worked for Arturo Escobar. Escobar could be the partner."

"That makes sense," Michael said. "We've suspected him of being involved in drug trafficking. Maybe he supplied Rosa with women or drugs or both. Pilar said another one of the pimps, Angel, also paid Chacho money. Maybe Angel's girls were Escobar's property and Angel was their pimp. Rosa could have been paying protection money to Escobar. Or Escobar could have loaned Rosa money to expand her operations, and she was paying him back. There are lots of ways Rosa and Escobar could be entangled."

"Pilar made the payments to the courier, didn't she?" Mary asked.

"Yes," James said.

"She should be able to identify Chacho. If it's one of Arturo's regular men, that would be the link. If she could also identify Angel and testify he paid pimping money to Escobar's man, those two things could give you strong probable cause to get a warrant to search Escobar's home and businesses."

"I would love to take down Escobar," Michael said.

"How do we do that without subjecting Pilar to more danger?" Diego asked. He had been silent, listening up to that point.

"A while ago," Michael said, "when we first suspected Escobar could be part of Sangre Negra, we installed a pole camera across the street from his house. It also captures his security guards. They like to play basketball and kick soccer balls around in his driveway. If Pilar reviews pictures of the guards, maybe she can identify one of the men as Chacho."

Now Robert broke in. "Of course, if we come to an agreement with your client, she would have to testify in any trial of Escobar that the man she identified as Chacho was the man who picked up money every week from Rosa."

"If?" James asked. "Accept it, Robert, you need her."

Robert frowned but acknowledged, "We could tie in Escobar and Chacho, and possibly this Angel, as co-conspirators in Rosa's sex-trafficking operation and have one hell of a trial!"

Diego had been listening quietly, but Robert's statement made him furious. "That is out of the question! Pilar testifying against a madam and pimp in your country is one thing, but if she testified against anyone connected to the cartels, they would murder Alejandro, Concepción, and our parents."

"And you," Mary murmured. "We have to think of another solution."

"It's a terrible choice," James said. "Someone, probably Escobar, has already threatened to kill her if she testifies against Rosa. He realizes that Pilar can identify Chacho and maybe Angel and bring Escobar into this. If she doesn't testify as to what she knows, she could go to prison as a co-conspirator. And she might not be safe there. The only way to be sure Escobar can't reach her is for the Feds to take him down and lock him up for good."

"This can't be," Diego cried. "Is he right, Mary?"

Mary looked at Diego. "I'm afraid so, Diego."

Diego's arms dropped to his sides. He sat down, looking totally defeated.

• • •

Two days later, Pilar sat at a table with a young FBI agent, a forensic technician, Diego, and Mary. James was in court on another case. The technician had isolated and created pictures of each of the security guards. There were ten men in all and multiple shots of each.

The agent passed the photographs to Pilar. Diego saw that one shot included a young woman in a white dress talking to a big man. *Marisa!* Diego had refused to focus on what all this could mean for her. He did not believe she knew her father was engaged in illegal activities. And without her, Diego might not have found Pilar's location. *Ay, have I ruined the life of another innocent young woman?*

"Por favor, may I see that one?" Pilar asked the agent. She picked up the picture of Marisa with the head of her father's security force. She studied it carefully. "That's him," she whispered, shuddering. "That is Chacho."

Diego recognized him as the man standing behind Marisa's father on the terrace the night of their party.

"Are you sure?" the agent asked.

"Do you see the tattoo below his right ear? My husband is an artist, señor. I know how to look at pictures and observe details in what I see. It's a tattoo of el tigre. The men who raped us in Mexico before they brought us to the United States had the same tattoo." Pilar dropped the photo as if it were red hot.

"What about the girl?" the agent asked.

"I've never seen her," Pilar said. "She is very pretty."

"That's Marisa, Arturo's daughter," Diego spoke up. "She doesn't know anything about her father's illegal activities."

"How do you know?" the agent asked.

"She comes to all of the Storm home games, and we became friends. Before I knew what her father was, I confided to her that a man named Eduardo Ayala had kidnapped my sister from Mexico and taken her to Houston and that I was searching for her. She knew her father's security guards spent time in the cantinas. Without my knowing, she asked one of them if he knew Eduardo, and the guard told her that Eduardo hung out at Los Arboles. When her father found out about it, he immediately sent her out of the country. She called me before she left and told me where I could find Eduardo. Right after that call, they blocked Mary's car on Studewood and threatened her."

"I find it hard to believe she didn't know that her father was mixed up in illegal activities, especially with all that security around the house," the agent persisted.

"Please, señor," Diego said. "I am sure Marisa knows nothing. Do not bring her into this."

CHAPTER 27

THE RECKONING

The FBI worked quickly to close in on Arturo Escobar after Rosa's arrest. They wanted to link him somehow to Rosa's business in order to get a search warrant for his home and Houston office. The low-lying fruit was Angel.

It was easy to find Angel. He was an American citizen that HPD had arrested before for minor offenses, so they knew where he usually hung out. An FBI agent and HPD detective began shadowing him. After a week, they followed Angel to a produce truck—with an out-of-state license plate—that was full of drugs and two tied-up thirteen-year-old Mexican girls at a stash house in Channelview near the Port of Houston. As soon as the Federal Magistrate issued a warrant, they arrested Angel on charges of conspiracy to commit sex trafficking, harboring illegal aliens, and smuggling illegal drugs. They waited until Angel was alone so as not to tip off Escobar that they were closing in.

Once in custody, Robert met with Angel and his court-appointed lawyer while Michael and Mary watched from behind the dark window.

"Angel, do you have any idea of the severity of the crimes with which you have been charged?" Robert roared at him. Standing, he leaned forward against the interrogation table. "This isn't stealing hubcaps and a few months in jail. We have everything we need to send you away to federal prison for a long, long time."

Angel knew enough to have asked for a lawyer. He'd been assigned

David Cerillo, who had only recently been licensed. Angel sat loosely in his seat, a smirk on his face. David sat beside him. Angel was a slightly built young man with long, stringy black hair tied in a pony-tail. He had prominent tattoos on his body and wore jeans and a black leather jacket. David was a little overweight, dressed in what was prob-ably his only dark suit, and wore an out-of-style tie and brown shoes.

"Mr. Grossman," David said in a less-than-steady voice, "my client is a young man who has never been arrested for a felony charge before. I believe the prosecution should grant him leniency."

"Your client," Robert replied, leaning closer to David to make his point, "has a rap sheet with the local authorities that started when he first learned to walk. But he's big-time now. Angel pimps innocent young girls that gangs kidnap in Mexico. He picks them up at stash houses and forces them to let men rape and beat them for money in seedy cantinas and bordellos. We are preparing to try Rosa Rodriguez and her dirty gang. We'll lump Angel into the conspiracy trial with the others, since he pimped girls at Los Arboles. A witness saw him there paying money to a bag man for the cartel."

Angel's eyes widened. Hearing the word "cartel," David sat back as if reconsidering his position. He hadn't realized the seriousness of this case. But he couldn't help but cast a skeptical eye at his client, who looked like a scared teenager. "I'd like a minute to consult with my cli-ent, please," he said.

"Five minutes," Robert said, feeling confident he was dealing with an inexperienced defense lawyer. Then he turned off the microphone and left the room.

Out in the hallway, Robert joined Mary and Michael. "He'll talk," Robert said. "Just watch."

Reentering the room, Robert glared at Angel. Then he turned to David, who looked uncomfortable. He didn't say anything for several minutes.

"But I am a reasonable man," Robert said, "and I may be able to offer your client a deal if he pleads guilty and helps us find the people who were pulling his strings."

"What do you want?" David asked.

"We know he was paying at least part of the money the girls earned to a man named Chacho. We want Angel to tell us who Chacho worked for and where he took the money. We want to know anything Angel knows about the people who operated the stash house. We want to know if he picked up girls anywhere else and where he took them."

"And what are you offering in return?" David asked.

"Reduction in sentencing and placement outside a maximum-security prison. A scrawny little pimp like Angel would be somebody's bitch in no time if he wound up in max." Robert stood up. "I expect Angel will be ready to cooperate, or he'll be getting out of prison decades from now, at least what's left of him."

Angel's face reddened, and he leaned into his lawyer's ear, mumbling.

"My client will cooperate," David said.

"Okay, let's start with who owns the stash house where we spotted you picking up the drugs and girls?" Robert asked.

"Not sure, man. Word on the street is that Sangre Negra operates the house," Angel said.

"Who does Chacho work for? Where does he take the money?"

"I don't know, man. It's not like I'm important. I know that she-devil Rosa and I know Chacho, but nobody tells us padrónes who is getting the big money. Word is he drives the money to Laredo."

"Where else do you pick up girls?" Robert asked.

"There's another stash house off Wayside," Angel said. "And sometimes Chacho sends word to pick them up at the port."

Robert narrowed his eyes.

"What ship do you meet?"

"There's a couple. They come from Mexico carrying produce."

"Is that all?"

"And drugs . . . and girls sometimes."

Robert asked for something from the young attorney sitting beside him. He showed Angel a picture of a tiger. "Do the ships have this symbol on them?"

"Yeah, man," Angel nodded. "El tigre."

• • •

One week later, the joint task force procured a warrant and conducted a raid on the Wayside stash house, as well as one of Escobar's ships as soon as it arrived at the Port of Houston. They found cocaine and marijuana hidden in produce containers and three bound, terrified girls between the ages of ten and fourteen.

Simultaneously, another team advanced on Escobar's Tanglewood home. A guard at the Tanglewood house called Chacho on his mobile phone when he saw the first federal agents approach.

The family was not there when they arrived. Arturo, his wife, and his children were attending a family dinner at the home of a cousin in River Oaks. It was a welcome home celebration for Marisa and her mother, who had just returned from their long trip to Europe. When Chacho received the call and whispered to Arturo that the FBI was raiding the Tanglewood house, Escobar quickly gathered his wife and children and ordered Chacho to drive them to Hobby Airport, where he kept a private Lear jet. Staffed by Sangre Negra, it was always waiting with a pilot ready to take off.

Agents, deputies, and HPD officers had hid in surrounding hangars, assuming that Escobar would try to make his escape by air if they failed to pick him up at his home.

When Chacho arrived at the private plane area of Hobby Airport, the airplane's door was open and its engine running. Chacho parked, and Escobar and Chacho got out of the car.

The FBI agent in charge gave the order, and the authorities ran onto the tarmac, yelling, "FBI. Stop where you are! Arturo Escobar, Chacho Cardenes, we have warrants for your arrest!"

Escobar stopped and turned toward the agents, his hand reaching into his jacket. Chacho pulled out his semiautomatic. Three loud gunshots pierced the air. Suddenly, Escobar fell forward. The pilot had shot him in the back twice and once in the back of his head. Blood flowed onto the ground as his body hit the tarmac.

Escobar's wife and Marisa screamed, horrified. The pilot shot Chacho in the head, killing him instantly. Then he dropped his gun, closed the door of the plane, revved the jet engines, and taxied quickly down the runway, not waiting for clearance from the tower.

Agents and police ran after the plane, shooting at the engines, but it was too late. It was on its way to Mexico. Sangre Negra did not like those who knew too much to come into the hands of the US authorities. Escobar had been in charge of US operations. He'd been important to the cartel, but no one was irreplaceable. Their pilots had been under standing orders from El Tigre, who was now heading Sangre Negra, to kill Escobar and his lieutenants if they were ever about to be apprehended.

Escobar's body lay on the tarmac. His wife knelt over him, weeping. Marisa, confused and crying, tried to keep the younger children from seeing their dead father.

Marisa screamed.

CHAPTER 28

THE TRIAL

Pilar and Josefina sat huddled on a bench in an alcove between the courtrooms on the eighth floor of the federal courthouse in Houston in late October 2012. One of the odd square windows in the perfectly square marble building lit the brown and cream marble walls and floor. James, Mary, and Josefina's lawyer sat on either side of them, attempting to buffer them from the spectators, prosecutors, defense lawyers, and reporters who had gathered for the trial. Pilar thought everyone was looking at her—some with disdain, a few with implicit threats in their eyes, others out of simple curiosity. Josefina kept her head down. She would not testify that day but wanted to be there to support Pilar.

As James had predicted, for one reason or another, all the other victims who had promised to testify against Rosa had disappeared. It would be up to Josefina and Pilar to tell judge and jury what terrible things had happened to the girls imprisoned on the second floor of Los Arboles. The small courtroom would be packed. The government was anxious to showcase their prosecution of the biggest sex-trafficking case in Harris County history.

After what seemed like hours but was actually only twenty minutes, the doors of the courtroom swung open, and the spectators and reporters rushed in, trying to get seats close to the front. When all were seated, the bailiff announced Judge Paul Rhimes. The trial of *The United States of America v. Rosa Rodriguez, Eduardo Ayala Perez, and Guillermo Ayala Perez* commenced.

James had told Pilar that the prosecution and defense counsel would make opening statements. They needed to stay close, but it would be a while before she would be called to testify. Waiting was painful. Diego attempted to relieve some of the tension. But attempts at lighthearted conversation were awkward, and Pilar preferred to stay silent, concentrating on what she wanted to say. Robert's assistant attorneys and James had been coaching her on answering planned and potential questions simply and in good English. James had told her the defense would cross-examine her and try to make her look like she was not telling the truth. That, in particular, frightened her. She had never spoken in front of a crowd or strangers. She was afraid she would be too frightened to answer or would be tricked by Rosa's lawyer into saying something she did not mean. She was still not comfortable when confronted by men.

The hours dragged by, and her fear grew. When it finally grew too intense, she stood up and looked for the exit—she wanted to run out of the courthouse. She felt cold and panic all over. James seemed to know what she was feeling. He gently put his arms around her and carefully sat her back down. He held her hand.

Mary got Pilar a bottle of water. Josefina laid her hand on Pilar's other hand. Pilar looked in the younger girl's eyes and saw quiet resolve. Josefina's attitude surprised Pilar and also calmed her.

"Don't worry, Pilar," Josefina said. "We have gone through hell together, and we will survive this together too. When we are done, Rosa and the others will have their turn in the flames."

This sober assurance from Josefina broke the tension Pilar felt. She realized the frail child had become a strong young woman. Josefina was wearing a conservative blue sheath dress, her curly hair short and neatly combed; she bore little resemblance to the unkempt waif who had been rescued from Los Arboles.

Finally, just after 11 a.m., James told Pilar that it was time for her to testify and led her to the closed courtroom door.

All eyes were on Pilar's petite form as she walked down the short aisle of the courtroom, past the court reporters, through the bar, and to a spot in front of the judge. Mary had dressed Pilar in a navy-blue wool dress and jacket, clothes suitable for a young professional. Her only jewelry was a simple strand of white pearls, borrowed from Mary, and pearl stud earrings. Pilar's natural pink color had returned to her face, and her hair was once more full and shiny. Onlookers saw an attractive twenty-four-year-old woman who could have been anyone they knew—a friend, a daughter. The bailiff swore her in and told her to be seated.

As she slid into the big leather witness chair, Pilar looked up, directly into the defiant eyes of the woman who had kept her imprisoned and brutalized for two years. Pilar had feared she would be cowed by Rosa's glowering stare, just as she had been so many times in the office they'd shared.

To her relief, that did not happen. Rosa wore a pink suit for the trial and no makeup except red lipstick. She looked old and washed out. Looking at Rosa's sneering face, Pilar felt herself grow stronger, indignant. Pilar wanted badly to tell everyone what this evil woman had done to her and to so many other helpless girls. She wanted the American authorities to put Rosa where she could never again do those terrible things to other girls. She sat up straight and steeled herself to admit to these strangers her embarrassing personal horrors.

Pilar looked at Eduardo and Guillermo sitting at another table. Eduardo wore the same arrogant smirk she had come to know and hate during the four years she had been under his control. Guillermo looked less confident. He always did what his older brother told him to do, even now, refusing to enter a guilty plea and take a deal from the prosecution.

Robert had made a strategic decision to forego the usual introductory questions of the witness and plunge directly into her testimony, which he knew would be explosive.

"Have you always lived in the United States, Señora Chavez?"

"No, señor. I was born and lived in Mexico, in the town of San José.

"What did you do there?" James asked.

"I was happy there, living with my husband and our nine-month-old daughter, Concepción. I worked as assistant to the owner of a pottery factory in the office."

"How did you come to be here?"

Pilar looked across the courtroom at Diego and Mary for grounding, as James had instructed, while she answered. "In 2007, bad times came to the pottery industry where my husband was an artist, and he lost his job. We were starving. The man I now know as Eduardo Ayala came to the factory where I worked in the office, pretending to be a buyer from a Mexico City department store. He gave me an ad for a secretarial job in Mexico City. He said it was a good job and would pay more money. I didn't think about it at first, but when all our money was gone, I thought it could help my family survive."

"And did you go to Mexico City and get this good job, señora?"

"There was no job. When I went to the interview, a woman named Alma, who worked for Eduardo, drugged me and two other girls, Josefina and Teresa. When we woke, we were all tied up. Eduardo came and said he owned us and if we didn't do what he told us, he would kill our families. He knew where they were, so I was afraid for them."

"What did Eduardo do to you then?" Robert asked.

Pilar had been speaking in a soft voice. When she continued her story, her voice became stronger.

"He gave us to terrible men who raped us, beat us, and treated us like animals. We were in a stone building with no clocks or windows, so we didn't know where we were or for how long. Then they stuffed us together in a small place inside a big truck. It took us across the river to Texas. Then a guard, a white man, raped me over and over in a warehouse before he put us in a smaller truck with no air or water. There were so many Mexican men we could not sit down for the long trip to Houston. They took the men's pants from them and locked all of us in a little house that smelled awful. We escaped and I made it to another house, but no one would help us. The guards caught us and kicked me, threatening to kill us if we did it again."

Pilar stopped, choking, as if she was remembering the horrible, frustrating occurrences of that night. There was no sound in the courtroom.

"No one would help us, señor," Pilar repeated, as if remembering that night and how disappointed she was when they pleaded with the neighbors for help without success.

"Objection!" Eduardo's lawyer said. "Irrelevant."

"The witness will confine herself to answering direct questions," Judge Rhimes said.

"Did you see Eduardo Ayala again?" Robert asked.

"Eduardo's brother, Guillermo, came and drove us to a dirty motel room where Josefina, Teresa, and I had to share one bed. That night Eduardo came to the motel. He made us wear much makeup and dance and have sex with many, many men in the back rooms of men's clubs."

"How long were you in the back rooms of the men's clubs?"

"More than one year. There were no clocks or calendars, so we were never sure what time or day it was. The days and nights were all the same."

"Where did you go from there?" Robert asked.

"One day, Guillermo drove us to Los Arboles and turned us over to Rosa and Esther. He told Rosa we were the girls from Mexico she'd ordered from Eduardo. They locked us up in very small rooms that smelled like sex and drugs and other bad things and sold our bodies to as many as thirty men in one night. Sometimes the men beat us. Rosa let them do it so long as they didn't make marks on our face."

"Objection!" Rosa's lawyer said. "Hearsay."

Pilar felt stunned, but she remained composed as James had trained her.

"Do you want to rephrase, Mr. Grossman?" the judge asked.

"How do you know Rosa knew about the beatings, Señora Chavez?" Robert asked.

"Esther was the boss of the girls upstairs. She watched the beatings and everything else and then told Rosa. She said it was one of Rosa's rules. Men hit me all the time, but once I had a black eye. She told Tito he'd broken Rosa's rule and he should throw the man out."

"Did you get any money from the men, señora?"

"Eduardo and Rosa kept all the money the men paid to rape us. They said we owed them for our food and bed in return for them taking care of us. But they said they would kill us if we tried to escape. There were guards with guns everywhere and Esther watching us all the time. We couldn't escape."

"What were you expected to do at Los Arboles?" Robert asked.

"We were forced to have sex with the men every night, even when girls were sick or pregnant or had the sex disease. The men didn't have to wear condoms. They beat or cut the girls who became pregnant to kill the babies."

"Objection!" Rosa's lawyer said. "The witness isn't qualified to diagnose diseases or pregnancies."

Pilar looked at Rosa's lawyer. He glared back at her with a look of disgust, intended to intimidate her. She looked away.

"What makes you think the girls contracted venereal disease and were pregnant?" Robert asked.

"They would scream with pain and scratch themselves in their vagina area. I knew girls were pregnant because their bellies got very big and they would throw up a lot. I have a daughter, señor. I know what it's like to carry a child. Besides, these women asked me to feel the baby kicking sometimes. They still had to work until the baby got cut out."

Although Mary had heard Pilar tell about what she had experienced at Los Arboles, revelations like this still made her feel nauseated. She felt proud of Pilar being able to stay focused. She looked at Rosa. The woman's face was still, her eyes unreadable. Rosa's indifference caused a chill to run up Mary's spine.

"Did the other two girls Eduardo trafficked to Houston go to Los Arboles?" Robert asked.

"No. Guillermo injected Teresa with drugs while we were at the clubs. Then they sold her to a man who was going to take her to his place near the Port of Houston to sell her there."

"Do you know where Teresa is now, señora?"

"Once, I asked Eduardo where she is now, and he told me she is probably dead. He said she was half-dead when he sold her. She was a child—only fourteen or fifteen years old."

"Objection," Eduardo's lawyer interjected. "This is irrelevant information."

"Your Honor," Robert said, "this information shows the pressure the Ayala brothers put on the witness to do what they demanded, including work at Los Arboles."

"I'll allow it," Judge Rhimes said.

"How old were you when you went to Los Arboles, señora?"

"I was twenty-one, I think. I was one of the oldest girls. Eduardo said I looked younger. He told me to tell the men I was sixteen if they asked."

"How old were the other girls you saw there?"

"Most of the girls were younger than me, some as young as twelve. I think almost all of them were from Mexico or Central America. Everyone spoke Spanish. Only a few of us spoke English, too."

One of the jurors gasped when she heard how young some of the victims were. Spectators whispered among themselves. The judge told the juror not to show her emotions in court. Robert turned and looked directly at Rosa, who glared back at him.

"Did your situation ever change at Los Arboles, senora?"

"Yes."

"How did it change?"

"One day Eduardo pulled me out of my room and said I was going to work for him in a new way. He gave me new clothes and told me

I had to work for Rosa doing the kind of office work I'd done at the factory in San José."

"Why did he do that?"

"He said he wanted me to learn about Rosa's business so he could get some of it."

"Objection!" Eduardo's lawyer said.

"Overruled."

"And did you learn about her business?"

"Yes. But I never told him anything he could use."

"What were some of the things you learned while you shared an office with Rosa Rodriguez and kept her books?"

"Objection!" Rosa's lawyer said. "The witness is not an accountant. She is not qualified to testify about financial matters."

"Your Honor," Robert said, "Señora Chavez had business training in Mexico and worked as the office manager and controller for a pottery factory in her hometown for two years. She is qualified to testify about the financial transactions she witnessed firsthand working for Rosa Rodriguez."

"Overruled," Judge Rhimes said.

"I learned that she owned other properties. She sold girls like us in many places on the east side of Houston, especially around the port. All the money came through Los Arboles. She made me count it and make the bank deposits and payments to vendors and pimps. She made a lot of money. Some of it she shared with a partner, who is dead now. Besides money from selling girls, she made money from selling liquor, some of which was not good. She also got money from the drug dealers who sold drugs in the cantinas."

"Did you give the money directly to the partner?" Robert asked.

"No."

"Did you give it to someone else?"

"Yes, a man named Chacho."

"How much money?"

"I gave him twenty percent of all the money that came in once a week—about $25,000 in most months."

"Chacho was the head of security for Arturo Escobar, the deceased head of the Sangre Negra cartel in the United States," Robert triumphantly announced to the jury. "The details of these operations are contained in exhibits we have provided the court."

"Objection!" Rosa's lawyer yelled. "Escobar is not on trial here."

"Sustained. The jury will ignore Mr. Grossman's last statement about Arturo Escobar."

Robert didn't lose a beat. He asked Pilar, "What did Rosa Rodriguez tell you about her late husband's death, señora?"

"Objection! Irrelevant!" Rosa's lawyer shouted. Rosa shifted in her seat and looked scared for the first time.

"Judge, Rosa Rodriguez's admission directly to Señora Chavez about her husband bears directly on the ruthless manner in which she conducted the business and her callous disregard for human life. Besides, it is an admission against interest and thus is admissable."

"I'll allow it," Judge Rhimes said.

"Rosa told me she murdered her husband with poison. She said he'd been spending too much time upstairs with the girls. She knew many of them had the sex disease. She was afraid he would catch it from them and give it to her. She said that was why she'd had to kill him."

With few exceptions, the jury and onlookers had been silent, rapt during Pilar's testimony. But now there was an audible stir. Whispers of outrage could be heard from the onlookers, and the jurors glanced at one another and at Rosa, some showing unease.

"Order!" Judge Rhimes rapped his gavel, and the crowd quieted down.

Pilar looked at Rosa. She saw pure hatred in her eyes but no regret. Then Pilar looked at Diego, who was smiling.

• • •

Pilar's testimony had taken the rest of the first day. When the trial convened the following morning, Rosa's lawyer, a tall, broad-shouldered Hispanic man with a deep voice, stood and strode across the courtroom to cross-examine Pilar.

This was the part of the trial Pilar had dreaded the most.

"So, Miss Chavez, you admit that you were a prostitute for four years?"

"No, señor. I was not a prostitute, ever."

"So you admit you were a prostitute in different men's clubs before you chose to ply your trade at Los Arboles?"

"No, señor. Prostitutes sell their body willingly. I was forced to sell my body, without my consent, by Eduardo." Pilar tried to remember all that Mary had told her in preparation for this line of questioning.

"So you admit you went to work at Mrs. Rodriguez's cantina voluntarily?"

"No, señor. Eduardo and Guillermo forced me to go to Los Arboles, and Rosa and Esther and Tito wouldn't let me leave. There were men with guns everywhere."

"So are you blaming everyone else for your bad choices in life?" The defense lawyer leaned in menacingly at Pilar when he asked this question in a loud voice. This big man terrified Pilar, but she was resolved to not let him intimidate her out of testifying.

"Objection!" Robert said. "The defense lawyer is badgering the witness."

"Sustained," Judge Rhimes ruled. "Stick to the facts of the case, counselor."

Rosa's lawyer stepped back from Pilar. He looked Pilar over, as if appraising a sexy girl in a bar. Then he asked, "Isn't it true, Señora Chavez, that you were attracted to Eduardo Ayala when you met him in San José, and you really went to Mexico City in hopes of leaving an unemployed, alcoholic husband in a dying town and having a liaison with a handsome stranger?"

"No, señor," Pilar responded firmly. "I loved—I love my husband and never expected to see the man who came to the factory when I went to Mexico City. I answered an ad in a newspaper. I didn't know he'd put it there to lure girls. I was trying to save my family from starving by making more money until my husband could find work. I would never have left my home, my husband and child, and my parents and brothers, except that I was desperate."

"Hmmmph!" Rosa's lawyer sneered, as if he were listening to a melodrama he had heard many times. He tried another angle.

"Isn't it true that you schemed with Eduardo to become Rosa's helper so that you could get out of the brothel and help him steal Rosa's business?"

"No, señor. I was brought up never to hate anyone. But I hated Eduardo and I hated Rosa for what they did to us. They are both evil. I didn't want to help either of them, but Eduardo said they would kill my family in Mexico, or Josefina, if I refused."

"This Josefina—isn't it true you and she had a romantic, sexual relationship?"

"No, señor. I love Josefina like a daughter or a sister but never in that way."

"Objection," Robert said. "Hearsay, and counsel has no proof."

"Withdrawn.

"You went to the bank twice every week. If you were a prisoner as you claim, why didn't you ask someone there for help?"

"Tito was always right beside me with his gun. I believed the bank teller he always used was working with him. I didn't think she would help me, and if she told Tito I'd tried to escape, he would kill me."

"Why did you never try to escape if conditions were as you describe at Los Arboles? You claim to be a smart woman."

"I was locked up alone with a guard outside my door at night. I was always trying to think of a way for us to escape, but it was impossible. Just before we got rescued, I was ready to give up."

Rosa's lawyer boomed in a loud voice and leaned toward Pilar again. "Isn't it true that you have exaggerated the conditions at Los Arboles in order to obtain a favorable plea deal and avoid prosecution for your part in the alleged conspiracy to commit money laundering?"

"I have only told the truth about what happened at Los Arboles, señor. I could tell you many more terrible things I saw. Everything I did with Rosa's money, I was forced to do or die."

This hostile questioning from each of Rosa and Eduardo's defense lawyers went on for the rest of the day and all of the morning of the next day. By the time the judge ended the cross-examination, Pilar was exhausted, but she'd been determined and answered every question. When the judge finally told her she was excused, a wave of relief ran through her whole body. James and Mary were smiling at her as she walked toward them, and Diego hugged her and said, "I am so proud of you, little sister."

• • •

Josefina was the first witness following lunch on the third day of trial. Josefina was still learning English, so her lawyer tried to keep his questions simple and had an interpreter nearby if needed.

"Señorita Flores, have you always lived in the United States?" Robert began his questioning.

"No, señor," Josefina answered.

"How did you come to be here?"

"Eduardo, señor."

"How did Eduardo bring you to this country?"

"I lived with my family in a small town outside Mexico City. I wanted to be a movie star when I grew up. I was a good girl, religious, and a virgin. I met Eduardo in the store where I bought movie magazines. He said he placed actresses with movie and TV producers. He took pictures of me in the store. Later, he said an agent wanted to interview me for a new telenovela, but I had to go with him to Mexico City. I was only thirteen years old and stupid. My parents were good people. I was foolish to go with Eduardo. He promised we would be home before dinner. At my interview, a woman who pretended to be an agent, but who worked for Eduardo, drugged me. I woke up a prisoner with Pilar and Teresa. Eduardo paid some terrible men to take us across the river in a big truck. But first, they raped us many times until I wanted to die."

"Do your parents know what happened to you?" Robert asked.

"No, señor. I would be too ashamed. They surely think I am dead. If you send me back to Mexico, I don't know how to do anything except sell my body. I will kill myself before I do that again."

"Did Eduardo and Rosa force you to have sex with men without your consent at Los Arboles, señorita?"

"Yes, many men, every day—sometimes twenty or thirty men," Josefina answered.

"Did you contract a sexually transmitted disease?"

"Rosa and Eduardo ruined me. I caught a sex disease at Los Arboles, and it hurt so bad I could barely walk. Pilar made Eduardo take me to a doctor in exchange for her working for Rosa in the office. I would have died without Pilar taking care of me as much as she could."

"Have you been told by a medical practitioner that the disease had a lasting effect on your health, señorita?"

Josefina bit her lip. Then she looked at Rosa and added in a louder voice, "Because I had the venereal disease for a long time, a doctor at the refuge where I am staying told me I probably will never be able to have a baby. He said I could have died!"

"Objection!" Rosa's lawyer yelled over the mumbling of the spectators.

Robert questioned Josefina for the rest of the afternoon about what she had seen and heard in the bordello. The fourth day of the trial was taken up with defense lawyers trying to impeach Josefina's testimony. But Josefina remained strong and did not fold under pressure.

After that, Pilar and Rosa were finished with their testimony, but the trial continued for ten days. Esther, Tito, and the others charged had all pleaded guilty in return for a reduction in sentence and testified against Rosa. Eduardo had been holding out. But after Pilar and Josefina finished their testimonies, Eduardo's attorney convinced him to make a deal with the United States Attorney to plead guilty in exchange for the United States Attorney's recommendation that he be given a sentence of 180 months in prison, a $50,000 fine, and probation of five years after his release. Guillermo followed suit for a slightly shorter sentence.

The judge sent the case to the jury on the eleventh day of the trial. Six hours later, the jury returned a verdict against Rosa of guilty on all counts.

CHAPTER 29

REDEMPTION

Pilar was looking at the front-page headline in the *Houston Chronicle*:

NOTORIOUS MADAM SENTENCED TO LIFE
IN PRISON FOR HER ROLE IN OPERATING
HOUSTON CANTINA/BORDELLO

Even with all she had gone through and suffered, Pilar tried not to be vengeful. But she couldn't help smiling at the thought of Rosa locked up in prison with no chance of escape—as she had done to so many innocent young girls over the years.

"Maybe there is justice," Pilar said to Diego.

It was late November 2012, five years since her abduction in Mexico City. The weather was cool, and Mary had just planted a bed of pink and red cyclamen at the foot of the deck in her backyard. Trickling water from a stone fountain in the middle of the small grassy area had a relaxing effect on Pilar, Mary, Steve, Josefina, and James, who sat on the teak bench and chairs. "Damn!" Steve said as he looked over her shoulder at the paper. "The Feds have set a record for moving fast with this one."

"The Justice Department was hungry for a big win in the sex-trafficking business. It's a fast-growing cancer," James said. He smiled at Pilar and Josefina. "You should be proud of yourselves, ladies. Your testimony helped to seal her fate. You are an amazingly strong woman, Pilar. Not many women have your fortitude." James had come to sincerely admire—and become genuinely fond of—Pilar over the past year.

He glanced at Mary and Diego. They seemed more interested in holding hands than the news. He thought, *I really missed out on that one. But I'm glad she's happy.*

Everybody was in better spirits these days. After the assassination of Chacho and Arturo, Pilar no longer had to fear testifying against cartel members. James had gotten her full immunity from prosecution in return for her testimony against Rosa and the Ayala brothers. She'd been granted continuing presence status and allowed to live with Mary until the resolution of the trial, with the promise of a T visa later if she wanted it. Because Pilar was a victim of trafficking, a T visa would allow her to stay in the United States and apply later for a green card.

Pilar passed the paper to Josefina. She had been promised a T visa as well in return for her testimony. She had been living in a faith-based refuge that helped victims of sex trafficking. Counseling, medical attention, and English lessons were helping her recover from years of trauma.

James asked Pilar and Josefina, "Will you stay in the United States or go back to Mexico? Either way, I must tell you, there is the possibility someone will want to retaliate against you for testifying, although the chances are reduced since most of the Rodriguez and Ayala families are in jail, the Mexican authorities have picked up Jesús Ayala, and Sangre Negra did us the favor of getting rid of Escobar and Chacho. You can always go into the Federal Witness Protection program, but then you will be on your own. I will gladly help you on the legal end of whatever you decide, pro bono."

"There is nothing for me to go back to in Mexico," Josefina said. "I was thirteen when I left home. My parents probably think I am dead. I know my relatives believe 'Once a whore, always a whore.'"

When Steve looked at Josefina, he barely recognized the dirty, almost emaciated, frightened girl he'd found upstairs at Los Arboles. Josefina was eighteen years old now, a young woman. The care and good food she had received at the refuge had allowed her natural beauty to be revealed. Her curly brown hair was shiny, trimmed neatly above her shoulders. Her hazel eyes were bright again. He detected hopefulness in her young face. Since their first encounter, Steve had felt protective of Josefina, as if she had become a daughter to him.

"If James can work out your legal status, I think I can get you work with a nonprofit organization that provides counseling and rehabilitation to other young women like you, Josefina," Mary said.

"I would like that." Josefina spoke in English now. "I am still young. I am scared of fitting in in this new country where I am just learning the language, but I want to start a new life here. I promise I will work hard."

"That's wonderful, Josefina," Steve said.

Just then the door to the kitchen opened, and John walked out onto the deck. He had become a regular member of the Pilar support group now. Everyone exchanged greetings. John gave Pilar a hug, and Mary got up from her chair to let John sit next to Pilar.

"Go on with your conversation," John said. "I just came by to say hello and maybe get a glass of Mary's homemade lemonade and chocolate chip cookies."

"Coming up," Mary said, heading for the kitchen.

"What about you, Pilar?" James asked. "Diego tells me your family in Mexico is anxious to have you come home."

"But you can live with me and Mary here in Houston if you want to stay," Diego said.

Pilar looked at Mary and Diego at the end of the table. The diamond on Mary's left hand sparkled in the sunlight. They both wore the smiles of people in love.

I remember when Alejandro and I were that happy. We were so innocent.

We didn't know what cruel times were in store for us. Could we ever be happy again? Could I hold my daughter in my arms and not have my sins infect her?

"Pilar," Diego said, walking over and kneeling in front of her to take her hand in his, "Alejandro told me again last night that he wants you to come home. He doesn't care what you were forced to do. He feels responsible, as we all do, for what happened to you. He wants to be a family again."

Pilar hung her head and shook it.

Diego handed her a handwritten note. "This is from Mami."

Pilar read the letter:

> Pilar, you should not resist God's plan. I believe he chose you to do his work here on earth because of your inner virtue and strength. He intended you to bring down the Devil's disciples who committed crimes against many innocent girls. Come home to those who love you. Your earthly reward is to be reunited with your family and live in peace for the rest of your life.
>
> I love you,
> Mami.

"Mami has a simple way of looking at life," Pilar said, smiling for the first time.

"Well, you know how Mami sees the world. Who knows? Maybe she's right." Diego smiled back.

"I don't know whether I should blame God for letting Eduardo kidnap me or thank God for Diego rescuing me." Pilar sighed. Josefina gave her a knowing look. "Maybe someday, this will all make sense."

"Of course, Pilar," Mary said. "It hasn't been that long."

"I want so badly to hold my daughter and feel Alejandro's arms around me again." Pilar sighed. "But I can't face them or the people in San José. I would be ashamed. You know there are no secrets in San José. Concepción might be called 'daughter of a whore.' It is best they should forget me."

There was an embarrassed silence when no one knew what to say. Mary took the opportunity to ask if anyone wanted anything else to drink. Then she returned to the kitchen to fill orders and retrieve some chips, guacamole, and pico de gallo.

"Pilar," Josefina said, "selfishly, I would miss you. I would never have survived if you hadn't taken care of me. But if I could return to people who loved me and wanted me, I would run to them."

"Alejandro understands, Pilar," Diego said. "He has rented a house and studio in San Miguel de Allende. It is in an area where mostly Americans live. Many of the neighbors are his customers. He never told them or Concepción where you were. He only said you'd had to go away but would be returning. When you are ready to meet strangers and people get to know you, they will love you. No one needs to know what happened to you. You can start a new life."

Mary set the drinks and snacks down on the table and jumped in, "Diego enrolled Concepción in a private school in San Miguel. He says she is doing well there. The house has a guest room, and your parents can visit often. Carlos is running the store. Everyone understands you need time to recover. No one will push you to do anything until you are ready."

Mary went on. "Pilar, Diego and I visited San Miguel recently. I love it and want to get married in the cathedral. We want you to be there, and Josefina will be able to travel to and from Mexico to spend time with you when she gets her visa."

"Does that mean Sara Beth will get to go to a wedding in Mexico after all?" John asked, grinning at Diego and Mary.

"How delightful that will be!" Mary smiled back.

But Pilar's smile fled her face and her eyes were dark with memories. "I am unworthy of Alejandro now."

Diego felt his own eyes moisten. "Can you forgive me for my part in your kidnapping?"

Pilar looked at him in surprise. "Diego, I never blamed you, or Alejandro, or anyone but myself. It was my pride and my lack of faith in my husband that drove me to Mexico City. I thought God was punishing me for those sins, not sending me on Mami's holy mission." Pilar placed her hand over Diego's and spoke softly, "Sometimes I thought there must not be a God, that everything happens by chance or solely because of one's good or bad decisions. I still don't know. I am grateful to you for not giving up on me, for rescuing us from hell. I am thankful for what you and Mary and James did to send Rosa and the rest to jail. You are a hero, Diego, just as I thought when we were kids. And I couldn't be happier that you and Mary have found one another. Mary will be a sister to me."

Mary reached for a tissue. She couldn't hide the tears that this tender moment caused. Josefina beamed at Pilar.

Finally, with a thick voice, Steve tried to lessen the intensity of the emotions that Pilar's words brought out in all of them. "Well, shit! All's well that ends well, I always say."

Mary laughed.

"Pilar," Diego said, "Alejandro wants desperately to talk to you himself. Would you talk to him tonight?"

"I'm not ready yet," Pilar replied. "Tell him to call in a few days, if he even wants to at all."

Diego, Mary, and James exchanged conspiratorial looks.

James said, "You have done a great amount of good by cooperating and testifying against Rosa, Eduardo, and the others, Pilar. Michael is grateful, and he was able to get a tourist visa for Alejandro."

"Alejandro is in Houston?" Pilar gasped and put her right hand over her mouth. "That is impossible!" she cried.

"Steve is leaving to go pick him up in a few minutes. He will meet his flight at Intercontinental Airport in just over an hour," James said.

Pilar almost jumped out of her chair and looked at her brother with panic written all over her face. "I can't see him, Diego! I would be so ashamed to face him. And I look ugly now, old."

Part of her was thrilled at the thought of seeing Alejandro. But she was also terrified. It would take longer than a year for the shame now ingrained in her to subside. What could she possibly say to him? What would he see in her now that she had undergone so much mistreatment by other men? She could never again be the innocent, happy childhood sweetheart he had fallen in love with.

"Nothing could take away your beauty, míja. It comes from your heart," Diego said, putting his arms around her and resting her head on his chest. She was sobbing.

When Pilar had recovered at least some of her composure, Mary helped her change into a new white dress that Mary had secretly bought for the occasion. She brushed Pilar's hair and put some pink lipstick on her lips, which were trembling. During the time Pilar had been allowed to live with Mary after her release from detention, they had become extremely close—like sisters.

Diego moved some comfortable chairs into Mary's home office. When they heard Steve's truck park in front of the house, Diego led Pilar into the office.

"Can you stay with me, Diego?" Pilar asked.

"If you want me to," Diego replied, smoothing Pilar's hair.

They heard Mary open the front door. She hugged Alejandro and then introduced him to John, James, and Josefina. A few minutes passed, and then Pilar saw Alejandro in the doorway to the office, looking at her.

Alejandro's face lit up with a boyish, familiar smile. He stopped a few tentative steps away from her.

He looks older too, Pilar thought. *There are more gray hairs and a more serious look in his dark eyes. He is as handsome as I remembered, though.*

"My love," Alejandro said in Spanish, "I have waited too long to see you again. I have missed your beautiful face and your sweet nature.

Please, forgive me for letting you down." Tears came to his eyes. "Come home to me and our daughter. We need you, and I will never let anything bad happen to you again."

Pilar started sobbing, but she didn't move any closer. Through her tears, she managed to say, "Oh, Alejandro, I am not fit for a good man like you. So many men have used my body and done terrible things to it. How can I touch our innocent daughter? It is better you tell her I died but that I always loved her . . . and her father."

"Mary and Diego told me what you went through, Pilar, all of it. I have read the stories in the American papers about the place where you were kept prisoner. I don't care. It wasn't my sweet Pilar they abused. It was someone who doesn't exist anymore. She died when you became free to be yourself again, to raise your daughter, and to let me love you. We will be a family starting over in a new life. My paintings sell for good money. Just come home to me and Concepción, and we will work everything out together."

When Pilar didn't say anything, Alejandro continued: "I decided you would be my wife when I saw you wearing your white veil at First Holy Communion. I knew then we were meant to be together forever. I don't know why such a terrible thing happened to us, but I know our love is strong enough to overcome it. Your brother found you when almost no one thought he could. Please, show us you forgive us all by coming home."

Pilar's body relaxed somewhat, and she leaned toward him. "Tell me about Concepción."

As Alejandro pulled from his pockets some new pictures of Concepción in her school uniform, Diego let go of Pilar's hand and tiptoed out of the room.

• • •

Mary, Diego, John, Alejandro, and Pilar stood at the ticket counter at

George Bush Intercontinental Airport after checking bags for the flight to León, Mexico. Diego had wanted to avoid flying into Mexico City. Carlos would pick them up and drive them to San Miguel. Yolanda and José were already at the house in San Miguel with Concepción, who was very excited. Her father had told her by telephone that her mother was coming home with him for Christmas.

Steve had brought Josefina to see them off. As they said goodbye, Steve pulled a small box out of his shirt pocket and handed it to Pilar. She opened it and gasped. Her silver crucifix and chain were inside. "Where did you find this?" Pilar asked. "I thought it was lost forever. I didn't know where I'd lost it."

"I went back to the Jewel Box and found Consuelo. She said you'd told her if you ever got free of that life you would come back and claim it. She was happy to give it to me when I told her you were rescued and are going home to your husband and child. She thanked God and said it was proof her life had meaning."

Pilar had blocked out the memories of her time at the men's clubs as much as she could. Now she could see the tiny room with the velvet couch and the little old lady who had come late at night to clean it and talk and pray with her. Pilar began to cry, but she wasn't sure whether it was tears of gratitude or release or sadness about that time in her life. Seeing her distress, Alejandro wrapped his arms around her, as if to protect her from her own thoughts.

"I can't believe you retrieved the crucifix," Mary said. "You are an angel, Steve. I'm going to give you a big kiss for that." She kissed him on the cheek.

Steve blushed.

Then he said, "Good luck, Pilar. I am glad things worked out for you and Josefina. Your happy ending is the rare exception, I'm afraid."

"I can never thank you enough for what you have done," Pilar said, looking at Mary, Diego, and Steve. Pilar hugged Josefina one last time. "We will see each other again soon."

"Many kisses," Josefina replied. "May God protect you."

AUTHOR Q&A

1. How did you first get involved in the topic of sex trafficking?

About five years ago, I read an article about a Mexican woman who traveled from her village to Monterrey to apply for a secretarial job and woke up as a sex slave in a brothel in El Paso. Then I learned that Houston is the largest hub for sex trafficking in the country. Both of these things had a lasting effect on me. I couldn't imagine a more terrible life for a woman than to be imprisoned, raped, and beaten by many different men every day with no hope of escape other than death. I was appalled that the wonderful city I live in, and raised my children in, could be riddled with the cancer of sex trafficking. In discussing what I had become aware of with friends, I found that almost none of my friends knew anything about sex trafficking or its existence in Houston.

In 2013 I became board chair of a faith-based organization that provided low-cost and free legal services to immigrants. In that role, I visited a secret refuge for rescued teenage girls and learned how few resources were available for survivors of sex trafficking.

2. What kind of research went into producing *Searching for Pilar*?

I began by reading books written by trafficking survivors and people who worked for international agencies combating sex trafficking. *God in a Brothel,* by Daniel Walker, was particularly inspiring. I also read about the business of sex trafficking in Siddharth Kara's first book.

After I wrote the first draft, I conducted the same due diligence I pursued as a doctoral candidate and a securities lawyer. People I knew introduced me to prosecutors, FBI agents, police officers, and survivors, who told me their stories. I have friends who are federal judges, attorneys who clerked in the federal judicial system, and practicing attorneys. They advised on the parts of the book involving law enforcement and the judicial system. For the chapters that take place in Mexico, I visited Mexico City and San Miguel de Allende. The town of San José is fictional but inspired by the city of Maria Hidalgo. A former law partner who grew up in Mexico and a professor of comparative literature at the University of Houston who lives part time in Mexico City did cultural reviews of the chapters that take place in Mexico.

3. What are the main messages you wish for your novel to convey to readers?

* Sex slavery is a widespread chronic disease in the United States that is hidden in plain sight, not only in cities but in rural areas.

* Commercial sex is not "sex" in the sense of intimacy or expressing love between two people. It is pure violence and brutality exercised by the strong over the helpless.

* Everyone needs to be informed and proactive in helping to combat it. Loving in its broadest sense—realizing trafficked girls and women are human beings deserving of our help and compassion, not objects to be used and discarded—is one antidote.

* Sex trafficking would not be the immensely profitable, prolific business it is today if men did not buy sex from young girls and women. Law enforcement should focus on catching the buyers and sellers and rescuing the girls and women—recognizing that sex slaves are the victims of the crime of sex trafficking and providing them with physical and psychological healing rather than sending them to jail. The legal penalty for buying sex from trafficked girls and women of any age should

be harsh, publicized, and enough to make buyers not engage in this activity. Josefina was underage, but Pilar was not. That does not make her suffering, or the pain it caused her family, any less.

* Finally, for some reason, the courts have been much too lax in punishing sex traffickers and men who pimp sex-trafficked girls. Many times convictions are punished with probation rather than prison time. Our judges need to be much harsher in assessing punishment.

4. Do you believe your novel and ones like it can affect change to the sex-trafficking industry? How?

I started writing *Searching for Pilar* in 2015, before sex trafficking got the attention it has today. But many people are still either blind to the sex-trafficking industry or think it is something in which the girls and women cooperate. Most people do not appreciate the physical and psychological brutality that binds the victims to the traffickers. Academic statistical studies and survivor stories have been available for some time, but the average person is not going to buy them and read them for entertainment. But there is a large reading public for suspense, thriller, legal, and mystery novels.

My hope is that mainstream readers will pick up *Searching for Pilar* because it looks like a "good read" and, in the course of reading it, become more aware of the horror that forms the backdrop for Diego's search for Pilar.

5. In your novel, the justice system seems to be deeply flawed in how the law enforcement agents handle Pilar and the other victims' situations. Is this a common reaction to real-life victims? What does the law say about women rescued from this kind of life?

The federal sex-trafficking statute, The Trafficking Victims Protection Act of 2002, recognizes a trafficked person as a victim. Rosa and Eduardo's trial took place in 2012, and that was the law then in effect, although in 2015, Congress adopted the Justice for Victims of Trafficking Act, which carried forward and amplified that persons who are trafficked are victims with certain rights.

There is no federal law against prostitution, and rescued victims are not prosecuted as prostitutes as they would be if state law controlled. Sex-trafficking victims trafficked into the US illegally are deported to their country of origin unless they testify against their trafficker and become eligible for a T visa, which allows them to stay in the country and work. In that case, counseling, medical care, and other forms of assistance may be provided through nonprofit organizations.

In 2003, Texas and Washington were the first states to adopt an anti-human trafficking law. Section 20A of the Texas Penal Code has been amended several times to provide a comprehensive framework designed to enable the prosecution of all persons involved in a venture to traffic another for sex or labor purposes. Some states have passed laws exempting all trafficking victims from prosecution as prostitutes and are focusing on tougher enforcement and penalties for buyers. Hopefully, the Texas Legislature and our governor will do so in 2019.

6. What was the most shocking or unexpected story or fact you came across while researching for this novel?

I learned many things that shocked me. Among them—

* I learned that most girls and women in the commercial sex industry have been trafficked at some time, and the majority of victims are under eighteen, often well under fourteen.

* I learned that the internet and online publications like Backpage, as well as male customer chat rooms, make it easy

for any American man to buy girls and women in any place at any time—not only in big cities but in small towns all across the country.

* I was surprised how many men think it is okay to buy and rape young girls who they must know are underage.

* I was surprised how difficult it is for a survivor of sex trafficking to get rehabilitation and not have to fall back on selling her body again to survive.

* I was most surprised that half of the sex-trafficking victims in the US are everyday American girls and women who are falsely romanced or psychologically tricked into servitude as a sex slave, not girls and women brought into the country illegally like Pilar.

7. The sex-trafficking industries in Mexico City and Houston are known for being very active. Did you consider basing your story in any of the other regions that are active? What drew you to these two particular cities?

Early on in this project, I wrote a few chapters about two fictional sisters living in Belarus, an impoverished part of the former Soviet Union, kidnapped by Russian mobsters and trafficked to Atlantic City, New Jersey. They were forced to work in strip clubs and dingy motels. I planned to intertwine their story with Pilar's through internet trading among pimps, thus bringing attention to how globalization and the internet affect sex trafficking in modern society.

As a PhD candidate, I studied and visited the Soviet Union, and I grew up in Atlantic County, New Jersey, so I am familiar with both locations and the respective cultures. Ultimately, I decided my novel would be simpler and better if I limited it to one girl's story. Besides, it is common knowledge that Atlantic City has historically been a place where corruption and the commercial sex industry flourish. The volume of the commercial sex business in Houston is less well known but more typical of what is occurring all over our country today. For that reason, it is more shocking.

8. This is a pretty sensitive topic. Were any scenes particularly difficult for you to write? What were the easiest and why?

The most difficult chapter to write was "Captives." I read about everything that El Tigre, Jorge, and the other cartel men did to Pilar, Josefina, and Teresa somewhere or other. Putting it together and describing their experience was not a pleasant exercise. I felt angry. The old woman's situation and her hopelessness also depressed me. I worried about how my readers would react to such disgusting brutality. Friends who read the chapter both with and without the rape scenes said the rape scenes were hard to read but essential to understanding how horrible the experience would be for the girls.

"Daylight" came easily. It was as if I had been looking forward to Pilar's rescue for a long time, and the raid flowed under my fingers on the keyboard. "The Trial" was something I initially resisted writing because I practiced business/finance law and didn't have any trial experience, but my wonderful editor encouraged me to have Pilar confront the traffickers. Lawyer friends who had worked in federal courthouses corrected my worst mistakes about the rules of federal criminal procedure, and it turned out to be a highly satisfying experience. I felt Pilar's initial fear and reluctance about testifying in court and then her excitement about telling her story and seeing the people who had been so cruel to her squirm. The character I had the most difficulty developing was Diego. A male friend, whose son was a Major League Baseball player, helped me by describing the life and ego of a potential "star" male professional athlete. The rest of his life came together after that.

9. Do you have a favorite character? A least favorite?

Of course, I loved Pilar. She made a mistake in going to Mexico City alone, but her reasoning was understandable. I loved her intelligence and strength. She had strong moral tendencies and tried to protect Josefina and Teresa, who she realized were more vulnerable than she was. You may consider Pilar's actions foolish or tragic, but they were the catalyst that made most of the characters grow into better people in the end. I grew to admire Diego for the responsible manner in which he worked to correct his mistake.

I think Mary was my favorite character, though. She could have stayed home and lived off her inheritance or had a fluff law practice. Instead, she worked hard and used her legal skills to serve others less fortunate. Her thought process was impressively analytical. She saved the day at the end by marshaling all the resources available to her and saved Pilar from going to prison. My least favorite character was Sara Beth. She was selfish, judgmental, and parochial. I may have overemphasized her worst qualities, but my intent was for her to symbolize how easy it is for basically good people to be complacently comfortable, ignoring a terrible problem in society.

10. The geography of Houston plays a major part in telling this story. What kind of research did you do in finding out the routes and places these women are taken in the city?

All of the sites in the novel are closer to each other than one would think. For Houstonians, this story takes place "inside the Loop." I have lived within one mile of the Galleria for practically all of the years I have lived in Houston. I lived in Tanglewood for fourteen years, and my older daughter, a big firm lawyer, and her family live there now. My younger daughter, an environmental geologist, and her family live in the Heights in a century-old house that was the inspiration for Mary's house. I spent over thirty years working in downtown

Houston for a large law firm like the one where John is an associate. For several years I lived in the Clear Lake area of Houston and traveled through Southeast Houston on my way to work downtown every day. Occasionally, I would be on Old Galveston Highway, in the Channelview area around the Port of Houston, or Telephone Road for one reason or another. For a time I was chairperson of a nonprofit immigrant legal services organization headquartered at a community development corporation office in a heavily Hispanic neighborhood across I-45 from Hobby Airport, where gangs are prevalent and thousands of undocumented immigrants crowd together in the poorest living conditions. We ate at Mexican restaurants on Broadway like the one where Steve, Diego, and Mary met with Consuelo.

Once I started writing the book, I took a van tour with Children at Risk to view sites where sex trafficking takes place, including the men's clubs in the Galleria area and the abandoned Las Palmas II nightclub, the inspiration for Los Arboles. For Pilar's detention and trial scenes, I visited the Federal Detention Center, a massive building that takes up an entire city block, and the United States District Courthouse, where the trial takes place. As one of the largest, most diverse regions in the world, Harris County presents unlimited opportunities to find and describe both the best and worst aspects of humanity.

11. Did you struggle in telling such an emotional story? Did you have to make any preparations to get in the right mood or mindset to write from these perspectives?

The stories that I read written by survivors of sex trafficking were raw, frank, and shocking. Sometimes I had to stop reading, because what the men and madams did to these girls was too dreadful. How many times can you read about a fourteen-year-old child being beaten by predators who paid their traffickers for the "right" to do so without feeling sick? But it also motivated me to try to draw from and relate their common experience in a way that did not minimize the tragedy but that made it more likely others would read my book and learn what these girls lived through. My occasional discomfort was minor compared to what these girls suffered.

12. Do you think the fight against sex trafficking has had success over the years? Has the industry gotten worse? What do you think it will take to take down this intricate and dangerous business?

Because it is an underground industry, it is difficult to document the number of persons involved in sex trafficking at any time. Thus, it is hard to know whether or not efforts to date against sex trafficking have reduced the number of victims. I looked at the *Houston Chronicle* recently and searched for stories involving sex traffickers. I was distressed to find many stories about arrests of people operating sex-trafficking networks, including one FBI sting on a group led by a woman and her husband and sons operating a large-scale operation a few miles from the location of Los Arboles.

But awareness of sex trafficking has grown over the past ten years, especially in the past five. Nonprofit groups like Polaris, which operates the National Sex Trafficking Hotline; Tahirih Justice Center; New Friends; New Life in Dallas; and many others have brought attention to the issue and serve as resources for victims as the organizations lobby for changes in law.

I am proud to say that leadership of the city of Houston has taken an aggressive stance against all forms of human trafficking in recent years. The last two mayors of Houston have appointed an advisor on human trafficking who reports directly to the mayor. In preparing for and during the recent Super Bowl event, the mayor's office, HPD, FBI, and other agencies engaged in a coordinated campaign to raise community awareness and to cut down on the sex trafficking that, it is believed, surrounds major sporting events and conventions. In 2014, the city of Houston and ten of the largest men's clubs in the Galleria, like the fictional Jewel Box, entered into an agreement that the clubs would eliminate private rooms and allow cameras inside that could be viewed by police. There is some controversy over this settlement, however, and hundreds of other men's clubs are in operation throughout Harris County. The city now has a unique multifaceted "City of Houston Anti-Human Trafficking Strategic Plan," a copy of which is available at humantraffickinghouston.org, to cut down on human trafficking. City officials believe some of these tactics are working. Other cities are expressing interest in what Houston is doing, and some are following suit.

At the same time, the internet and technology have made it easier for sex traffickers to offer girls, women, and boys to prospective buyers. Under the guise of the First Amendment, internet journals like Backpage explicitly advertise trafficked girls and women to anyone in any place who is seeking anonymous sex. Chat rooms like The Erotic Review, exist where buyers can discuss and compare sex slaves they have purchased. There are billions of dollars being made in sex trafficking. Larger, more organized groups—like the fictionalized Sangre Negra cartel, Russian and East European mafia organizations, and Asian drug traffickers—continue to enter the business.

13. Who did you write this novel for?

I started the novel in 2015 because friends told me they didn't know anything about sex trafficking and didn't believe it existed in Houston. Houston is a great place to live. The city prides itself on being the most diverse region in the country. But rich and poor, illegal and legal, and different ethnic groups tend to cluster in particular neighborhoods. It is easy for well-to-do people to not know what sordid activities are going on in disadvantaged areas—and even in their own pleasant neighborhoods. I wrote *Searching for Pilar* for my neighbors and friends in Houston, as well as for people I will never meet in all parts of this country who are not aware that someone's daughter is being manipulated or captured, trafficked, and forced into sex slavery in their own town every day. But I also wrote it for those readers who simply enjoy a good suspense story that delves into the issues of different types of love, the importance of family, good and evil, greed and altruism, and whether or not there is a God who plays an active role in man's life.

14. How can readers learn more about the subject of human trafficking, including sex trafficking?

I am an author. I don't pretend to be the authority on sex trafficking, although I have learned a lot researching and writing this book. For anyone interested in knowing more about the different kinds of modern slavery in the world (sex slavery, labor trafficking, organ trafficking, and debt bondage) and the economic underpinnings that have made modern slavery the profitable and prolific business it has become, I suggest reading Siddharth Kara's *Modern Slavery: A Global Perspective* (Columbia University Press, 2017). He also wrote the screenplay for the movie *Trafficked*, which is an excellent film about three girls from different countries who were sex slaves in a ranch/brothel in South Texas.

A good source of information about the anti-sex trafficking movement in the United States today, particularly in Texas, is *The Sex Trafficking Marketplace: Addressing Demand through Legislation and Tactics*, published by Children at Risk, funded by the Texas Bar Foundation (of which I have been a fellow for many years), and available on Children at Risk's website, childrenatrisk.org.

READER'S GUIDE

1. Religion plays a big part in the lives of some of the characters. Discuss the theme of religion and how it impacts the characters in a good way or bad way.

2. Love is a recurring theme throughout *Searching for Pilar*—familial love, mother-daughter love, love for friends, and sexual love. Discuss the roles these different kinds of love play in the characters' lives.

3. Fear is a huge motivator in keeping the girls, the uninvolved workers around them, and even rescued girls from resisting the sex traffickers. Should you sympathize with the neighbors, the cleaning staff, and even those actively involved in the sex trafficking despite their lack of action in helping the girls? Or should they have been willing to risk their lives and their families' lives to do the right thing? Should rescued girls be forced to testify against their traffickers in court? What would you do if you were in that situation?

4. Does it come as a surprise that such reprehensible business is conducted in and around "good" neighborhoods in Houston? Discuss how this could be going on without people knowing or how it has affected your view of such "good" places.

5. Discuss the evolution of Pilar's characterization over the course of her story as she goes from naïve country girl to sex slave to

protector of the other girls to her eventual role as a bringer of "justice" to her traffickers. How did your feelings about her change over time?

6. Many characters take blame for what happened to Pilar, including Alejandro, Diego, Yolanda, and Pilar herself. Which characters in the book are to blame for what happened to Pilar?

7. Discuss the aftermath of sex trafficking on the lives of victims. Many of the survivors, including Pilar, felt that they could not go home for fear of being shunned by their families or because they felt tainted, shamed, and undeserving of love. How much of that could be a realistic reaction of the family, and what can be attributed to the psychological effects of their abuse? Is there a difference between domestic and international victims?

8. Who do you consider to be the biggest "bad guy" of the story and why? Could he/she have chosen a different life?

9. Should John and his wife have been more helpful? Could John have realistically done anything other than use his connections to spur the FBI to action at the end? Were any of their concerns about the impact the situation would have on their own lives valid?

10. Do you think Marisa had anything to do with her father's illegal business? Or was she completely innocent? Regardless, she had ulterior motives and tried to manipulate Diego. Are her actions excused because she was a girl in love, or does she deserve some blame for possibly endangering Diego and Mary when she spilled his secret mission?

11. Do you think the men who buy trafficked girls should be severely

punished with prison sentences, fines, or public embarrassment? Would such drastic actions reduce the demand for trafficked girls? If not, what would?

12. Could Diego have rescued Pilar if he had not found Mary? What motivated Mary in helping Diego and ultimately rescuing Pilar?

13. How much do poverty, greed, and economics explain or excuse sex trafficking? Is sex trafficking inevitable in modern society?

ABOUT THE AUTHOR

 PATRICIA HUNT HOLMES spent thirty years as a public finance attorney with the international law firm of Vinson & Elkins LLP. She was consistently listed in Best Lawyers in America, Texas Super Lawyers, and Top Lawyers in Houston and awarded the highest degree by her peers in Martindale Hubbell. She was a frequent speaker at national public finance and health-care conferences. Patricia has also served on the faculty of the University of Missouri—Columbia, the University of Tennessee, and the University of Texas Health Science Center at Houston. She has written and published in the fields of intellectual history and law.

Searching for Pilar is her first novel. The story involves Houstonians of all stations helping a young stranger from Mexico rescue his sister from the horrific life of a sex slave in Houston's glitzy Galleria area men's clubs and barrio cantinas. It is influenced by her career in law. It is also consistent with her experience as a member and board member of social service organizations in Houston that focus on helping women, including the United Way of the Texas Gulf Coast Women's Initiative, Dress for Success Houston, and the American Heart Association's Circle of Red. She was a founding member and first board chair of Houston Justice for Our Neighbors, which provides free and low-cost legal services to immigrants.

For the past five years, she has been taking writing workshops with Inprint, associated with the outstanding University of Houston Creative Writing Program. She began to write *Searching for Pilar* after learning that Houston is one of the biggest hubs for sex trafficking in the country.

Patricia grew up in Egg Harbor City, New Jersey, but has lived in Houston for forty-two years. She has two daughters, Hillary and Ashley, who have successful careers as an attorney and a geologist, and three adorable grandsons. She is an avid golfer and travels extensively.

Patricia holds a BA in English and history, an MA in history, and a Ph.D. in Russian and South Asian history with honors, all from the University of Missouri–Columbia. She received her JD from the University of Houston Law Center and was an editor on the *Houston Law Review*. In 2017, she was named to the Smithsonian Institution's Texas Host Committee.

Made in the USA
Middletown, DE
10 May 2019